The Monsieur Lecoq of the Sûreté Mysteries

Volume 2

The Monsieur Lecoq of the Sûreté Mysteries
Volume 2

File No. 113

and

A Disappearance

Émile Gaboriau

LEONAUR

The Monsieur Lecoq of the Sûreté Mysteries
Volume 2
File No. 113
and
A Disappearance
by Émile Gaboriau

FIRST EDITION

First published under the titles
File No. 113
and
A Disappearance

Leonaur is an imprint of Oakpast Ltd

ISBN: 978-1-78282-800-6 (hardcover)
ISBN: 978-1-78282-801-3 (softcover)

http://www.leonaur.com

Publisher's Notes

The views expressed in this book are not necessarily those of the publisher.

Contents

Chapter 1

In the Paris evening papers of Tuesday, February 28, 1866, under the head of *Local Items*, the following announcement appeared:

> A daring robbery, committed against one of our most eminent bankers, M. Andre Fauvel, caused great excitement this morning throughout the neighbourhood of Rue de Provence.
> The thieves, who were as skilful as they were bold, succeeded in making an entrance to the bank, in forcing the lock of a safe that has heretofore been considered impregnable, and in possessing themselves of the enormous sum of three hundred and fifty thousand *francs* in bank-notes.
> The police, immediately informed of the robbery, displayed their accustomed zeal, and their efforts have been crowned with success. Already, it is said, P. B., a clerk in the bank, has been arrested, and there is every reason to hope that his accomplices will be speedily overtaken by the hand of justice.

For four days this robbery was the town talk of Paris.

Then public attention was absorbed by later and equally interesting events: an acrobat broke his leg at the circus; an actress made her debut at a small theatre: and the *item* of the 28th was soon forgotten.

But for once the newspapers were—perhaps intentionally—wrong, or at least inaccurate in their information. The sum of three hundred and fifty thousand *francs* certainly had been stolen from M. Andre Fauvel's bank, but not in the manner described. A clerk had also been arrested on suspicion, but no decisive proof had been found against him. This robbery of unusual importance remained, if not inexplicable, at least unexplained.

The following are the facts as they were related with scrupulous exactitude in the official police report.

Chapter 2

The banking-house of M. Andre Fauvel, No. 87 Rue de Provence, is an important establishment, and, owing to its large force of clerks, presents very much the appearance of a government department.

On the ground-floor are the offices, with windows opening on the street, fortified by strong iron bars sufficiently large and close together to discourage all burglarious attempts.

A large glass door opens into a spacious vestibule where three or four office-boys are always in waiting.

On the right are the rooms to which the public is admitted, and from which a narrow passage leads to the principal cash-room.

The offices of the corresponding clerk, book-keeper, and general accounts are on the left.

At the farther end is a small court on which open seven or eight little wicket doors. These are kept closed, except on certain days when notes are due; and then they are indispensable.

M. Fauvel's private office is on the first floor over the offices, and leads into his elegant private apartments.

This private office communicates directly with the bank by means of a narrow staircase, which opens into the room occupied by the head cashier.

This room, which in the bank goes by the name of the "cash-office," is proof against all attacks, no matter how skilfully planned; indeed, it could almost withstand a regular siege, sheeted as it is like a monitor.

The doors, and the partition where the wicket door is cut, are covered with thick sheets of iron; and a heavy grating protects the fireplace.

Fastened in the wall by enormous iron clamps is a safe, a formidable and fantastic piece of furniture, calculated to fill with envy the poor devil who easily carries his fortune in a pocket-book.

This safe, which is considered the masterpiece of the firm of Becquet, is six feet in height and four and a half in width, made entirely of wrought iron, with triple sides, and divided into isolated compartments in case of fire.

The safe is opened by an odd little key, which is, however, the least important part of the mechanism. Five movable steel buttons, upon which are engraved all the letters of the alphabet, constitute the real power of this ingenious safe.

Before inserting the key into the lock, the letters on the buttons must be in the exact position in which they were placed when the safe was locked.

In M. Fauvel's bank, as everywhere, the safe was always closed with a word that was changed from time to time.

This word was known only to the head of the bank and the cashier, each of whom had also a key to the safe.

In a fortress like this, a person could deposit more diamonds than the Duke of Brunswick's, and sleep well assured of their safety.

But one danger seemed to threaten, that of forgetting the secret word which was the "Open sesame" of the safe.

On the morning of the 28th of February, the bank-clerks were all busy at their various desks, about half-past nine o'clock, when a middle-aged man of dark complexion and military air, clad in deep mourning, appeared in the office adjoining the "safe," and announced to the five or six employees present his desire to see the cashier.

He was told that the cashier had not yet come, and his attention was called to a placard in the entry, which stated that the "cash-room" was opened at ten o'clock.

This reply seemed to disconcert and annoy the newcomer.

"I expected," he said, in a tone of cool impertinence, "to find someone here ready to attend to my business. I explained the matter to M. Fauvel yesterday. I am Count Louis de Clameran, an iron-manufacturer at Oloron, and have come to draw three hundred thousand *francs* deposited in this bank by my late brother, whose heir I am. It is surprising that no direction was given about it."

Neither the title of the noble manufacturer, nor his explanations, appeared to have the slightest effect upon the clerks.

"The cashier has not yet arrived," they repeated, "and we can do nothing for you."

"Then conduct me to M. Fauvel."

There was a moment's hesitation; then a clerk named Cavaillon, who was writing near a window, said:

"The chief is always out at this hour."

"Then I will call again," replied M. de Clameran.

And he walked out, as he had entered, without saying "Good-morning," or even touching his hat.

"Not very polite, that customer," said little Cavaillon, "but he will soon be settled, for here comes Prosper."

Prosper Bertomy, head cashier of Fauvel's banking-house, was a tall, handsome man, of about thirty, with fair hair and large dark-blue eyes, fastidiously neat, and dressed in the height of fashion.

He would have been very prepossessing but for a cold, reserved

English-like manner, and a certain air of self-sufficiency which spoiled his naturally bright, open countenance.

"Ah, here you are!" cried Cavaillon, "someone has just been asking for you."

"Who? An iron-manufacturer, was it not?"

"Exactly."

"Well, he will come back again. Knowing that I would get here late this morning, I made all my arrangements yesterday."

Prosper had unlocked his office-door, and, as he finished speaking, entered, and closed it behind him.

"Good!" exclaimed one of the clerks, "there is a man who never lets anything disturb him. The chief has quarrelled with him twenty times for always coming too late, and his remonstrances have no more effect upon him than a breath of wind."

"And very right, too; he knows he can get anything he wants out of the chief."

"Besides, how could he come any sooner? a man who sits up all night, and leads a fast life, doesn't feel like going to work early in the morning. Did you notice how very pale he looked when he came in?"

"He must have been playing heavily again. Couturier says he lost fifteen thousand *francs* at a sitting last week."

"His work is none the worse done for all that," interrupted Cavaillon. "If you were in his place—"

He stopped short. The cash-room door suddenly opened, and the cashier appeared before them with tottering step, and a wild, haggard look on his ashy face.

"Robbed!" he gasped out: "I have been robbed!"

Prosper's horrified expression, his hollow voice and trembling limbs, betrayed such fearful suffering that the clerks jumped up from their desks, and ran toward him. He almost dropped into their arms; he was sick and faint, and fell into a chair.

His companions surrounded him, and begged him to explain himself.

"Robbed?" they said; "where, how, by whom?" Gradually, Prosper recovered himself.

"All the money I had in the safe," he said, "has been stolen."

"All?"

"Yes, all; three packages, each containing one hundred notes of a thousand *francs*, and one package of fifty thousand. The four packages were wrapped in a sheet of paper, and tied together."

With the rapidity of lightning, the news of the robbery spread throughout the banking-house, and the room was soon filled with curious listeners.

"Tell us, Prosper," said young Cavaillon, "did you find the safe broken open?"

"No; it is just as I left it."

"Well then, how, why—"

"Yesterday I put three hundred and fifty thousand *francs* in the safe; and this morning they are gone."

All were silent except one old clerk, who did not seem to share the general consternation.

"Don't distress yourself, M. Bertomy," he said: "perhaps the chief disposed of the money."

The unhappy cashier started up with a look of relief; he eagerly caught at the idea.

"Yes!" he exclaimed, "you are right: the chief must have taken it."

But, after thinking a few minutes, he said in a tone of deep discouragement:

"No, that is impossible. During the five years that I have had charge of the safe, M. Fauvel has never opened it except in my presence. Several times he has needed money, and has either waited until I came, or sent for me, rather than touch it in my absence."

"Well," said Cavaillon, "before despairing, let us ascertain."

But a messenger had already informed M. Fauvel of the disaster.

As Cavaillon was about to go in quest of him, he entered the room.

M. Andre Fauvel appeared to be a man of fifty, inclined to corpulency, of medium height, with iron-gray hair; and, like all hard workers, he had a slight stoop.

Never did he by a single action belie the kindly expression of his face.

He had a frank air, a lively, intelligent eye, and large, red lips.

Born in the neighbourhood of Aix, he betrayed, when animated, a slight Provencal accent that gave a peculiar flavour to his genial humour.

The news of the robbery had extremely agitated him, for his usually florid face was now quite pale.

"What is this I hear? what has happened?" he said to the clerks, who respectfully stood aside when he entered the room.

The sound of M. Fauvel's voice inspired the cashier with the factitious energy of a great crisis. The dreaded and decisive moment had come; he arose, and advanced toward his chief.

"*Monsieur*," he began, "having, as you know, a payment to make this morning, I yesterday drew from the Bank of France three hundred and fifty thousand *francs*."

"Why yesterday, *monsieur*?" interrupted the banker. "I think I have a hundred times ordered you to wait until the day of the payment."

"I know it, *monsieur*, and I did wrong to disobey you. But the evil is done. Yesterday evening I locked the money up: it has disappeared, and yet the safe has not been broken open."

"You must be mad!" exclaimed M. Fauvel: "you are dreaming!"

These few words destroyed all hope; but the very horror of the situation gave Prosper, not the coolness of a matured resolution, but that sort of stupid, stolid indifference which often results from unexpected catastrophes.

It was with apparent calmness that he replied:

"I am not mad; neither, unfortunately, am I dreaming: I am simply telling the truth."

This tranquillity at such a moment appeared to exasperate M. Fauvel. He seized Prosper by the arm, and shook him roughly.

"Speak!" he cried out. "Speak! who do you pretend to say opened the safe? Answer me!"

"I cannot say."

"No one but you and I knew the secret word. No one but you and myself had keys."

This was a formal accusation; at least, all the auditors present so understood it.

Yet Prosper's strange calmness never left him for an instant. He quietly released himself from M. Fauvel's grasp, and very slowly said:

"In other words, *monsieur*, I am the only person who could have taken this money."

"Unhappy wretch!"

Prosper drew himself to his full height, and, looking M. Fauvel full in the face, added:

"Or you!"

The banker made a threatening gesture; and there is no knowing what would have happened if they had not been interrupted by loud and angry voices at the entry-door.

A man insisted upon entering in spite of the protestations of the errand-boys, and succeeded in forcing his way in. It was M. de Clameran.

The clerks stood looking on, bewildered and motionless. The silence was profound, solemn.

It was easy to see that some terrible question, a question of life or death, was being weighed by all these men.

The iron-founder did not appear to observe anything unusual. He advanced, and without lifting his hat said, in the same impertinent tone:

"It is after ten o'clock, gentlemen."

No one answered; and M. de Clameran was about to continue, when, turning around, he for the first time saw the banker, and walking up to him said:

"Well, *monsieur*, I congratulate myself upon finding you in at last. I have been here once before this morning, and found the cash-room not opened, the cashier not arrived, and you absent."

"You are mistaken, *monsieur*, I was in my office."

"At any rate, I was told you were out; that gentleman over there assured me of the fact."

And the iron-founder pointed out Cavaillon.

"However, that is of little importance," he went on to say. "I return, and this time not only the cash-room is closed, but I am refused admittance to the banking-house, and find myself compelled to force my way in. Be so good as to tell me whether I can have my money."

M. Fauvel's flushed face turned pale with anger as he listened to this insolence; yet he controlled himself.

"I would be obliged to you *monsieur*, for a short delay."

"I thought you told me—"

"Yes, yesterday. But this morning, this very instant, I find I have been robbed of three hundred and fifty thousand *francs*."

M. de Clameran bowed ironically, and said:

"Shall I have to wait long?"

"Long enough for me to send to the bank."

Then turning his back on the iron-founder, M. Fauvel said to his cashier:

"Write and send as quickly as possible to the bank an order for three hundred thousand *francs*. Let the messenger take a carriage."

Prosper remained motionless.

"Do you hear me?" said the banker angrily.

The cashier trembled; he seemed as if trying to shake off a terrible nightmare.

"It is useless to send," he said in a measured tone; "we owe this gentleman three hundred thousand *francs*, and we have less than one hundred thousand in the bank."

M. de Clameran evidently expected this answer, for he muttered:

"Naturally."

Although he pronounced this word, his voice, his manner, his face clearly said:

"This comedy is well acted; but nevertheless it is a comedy, and I don't intend to be duped by it."

Alas! After Prosper's answer, and the iron-founder's coarsely expressed opinion, the clerks knew not what to think.

The fact was, that Paris had just been startled by several financial crashes. The thirst for speculation caused the oldest and most reliable houses to totter. Men of the most unimpeachable honour had to sacrifice their pride, and go from door to door imploring aid.

Credit, that rare bird of security and peace, rested with none, but stood with upraised wings, ready to fly off at the first rumour of suspicion.

Therefore this idea of a comedy arranged beforehand between the banker and his cashier might readily occur to the minds of people who, if not suspicious, were at least aware of all the expedients resorted to by speculators in order to gain time, which with them often meant salvation.

M. Fauvel had had too much experience not to instantly divine the impression produced by Prosper's answer; he read the most mortifying doubt on the faces around him.

"Oh! don't be alarmed, *monsieur*," said he to M. de Clameran, "this house has other resources. Be kind enough to await my return."

He left the room, went up the narrow steps leading to his study, and in a few minutes returned, holding in his hand a letter and a bundle of securities.

"Here, quick, Couturier!" he said to one of his clerks, "take my carriage, which is waiting at the door, and go with *monsieur* to M. de Rothschild's. Hand him this letter and these securities; in exchange, you will receive three hundred thousand *francs*, which you will hand to this gentleman."

The iron-founder was visibly disappointed; he seemed desirous of apologising for his impertinence.

"I assure you, *monsieur*, that I had no intention of giving offence. Our relations, for some years, have been such that I hope—"

"Enough, *monsieur*," interrupted the banker, "I desire no apologies.

In business, friendship counts for nothing. I owe you money: I am not ready to pay: you are pressing: you have a perfect right to demand what is your own. Follow my clerk: he will pay you your money."

Then he turned to his clerks who stood curiously gazing on, and said:

"As for you, gentlemen, be kind enough to resume your desks."

In an instant the room was cleared of everyone except the clerks who belonged there; and they sat at their desks with their noses almost touching the paper before them, as if too absorbed in their work to think of anything else.

Still excited by the events so rapidly succeeding each other, M. Andre Fauvel walked up and down the room with quick, nervous steps, occasionally uttering some low exclamation.

Prosper remained leaning against the door, with pale face and fixed eyes, looking as if he had lost the faculty of thinking.

Finally the banker, after a long silence, stopped short before Prosper; he had determined upon the line of conduct he would pursue.

"We must have an explanation," he said. "Let us go into your office."

The cashier mechanically obeyed without a word; and his chief followed him, taking the precaution to close the door after him.

The cash-room bore no evidences of a successful burglary. Everything was in perfect order; not even a paper was misplaced.

The safe was open, and on the top shelf lay several *rouleaus* of gold, overlooked or disdained by the thieves.

M. Fauvel, without troubling himself to examine anything, took a seat, and ordered his cashier to do the same. He had entirely recovered his equanimity, and his countenance wore its usual kind expression.

"Now that we are alone, Prosper," he said, "have you nothing to tell me?"

The cashier started, as if surprised at the question. "Nothing, *monsieur*, that I have not already told you."

"What, nothing? Do you persist in asserting a fable so absurd and ridiculous that no one can possibly believe it? It is folly! Confide in me: it is your only chance of salvation. I am your employer, it is true; but I am before and above all your friend, your best and truest friend. I cannot forget that in this very room, fifteen years ago, you were entrusted to me by your father; and ever since that day have I had cause to congratulate myself on possessing so faithful and efficient a clerk. Yes, it is fifteen years since you came to me. I was then just commencing the foundation of my fortune. You have seen it gradually grow, step by step, from almost nothing to its present height. As my wealth increased, I endeavoured to better your condition; you, who, although so young, are the oldest of my clerks. At each inventory of my fortune, I increased your salary."

Never had Prosper heard him express himself in so feeling and paternal a manner. Prosper was silent with astonishment.

"Answer," pursued M. Fauvel: "have I not always been like a father to you? From the first day, my house has been open to you; you were treated as a member of my family; Madeleine and my sons looked upon you as a brother. But you grew weary of this peaceful life. One day, a year ago, you suddenly began to shun us; and since then—"

The memories of the past thus evoked by the banker seemed too much for the unhappy cashier; he buried his face in his hands, and wept bitterly.

"A man can confide everything to his father without fear of being harshly judged," resumed M. Fauvel. "A father not only pardons, he forgets. Do I not know the terrible temptations that beset a young man in a city like Paris? There are some inordinate desires before which the firmest principles must give way, and which so pervert our moral sense as to render us incapable of judging between right and wrong. Speak, Prosper, Speak!"

"What do you wish me to say?"

"The truth. When an honourable man yields, in an hour of weakness, to temptation, his first step toward atonement is confession. Say to me, Yes, I have been tempted, dazzled: the sight of these piles of gold turned my brain. I am young: I have passions."

"I?" murmured Prosper. "I?"

"Poor boy," said the banker, sadly; "do you think I am ignorant of the life you have been leading since you left my roof a year ago? Can you not understand that all your fellow-clerks are jealous of you? that they do not forgive you for earning twelve thousand *francs* a year? Never have you committed a piece of folly without my being immediately informed of it by an anonymous letter. I could tell the exact number of nights you have spent at the gaming-table, and the amount of money you have squandered. Oh, envy has good eyes and a quick ear! I have great contempt for these cowardly denunciations, but was forced not only to heed them, but to make inquiries myself. It is only right that I should know what sort of a life is led by the man to whom I entrust my fortune and my honour."

Prosper seemed about to protest against this last speech.

"Yes, my honour," insisted M. Fauvel, in a voice that a sense of humiliation rendered still more vibrating: "yes, my credit might have been compromised today by this M. de Clameran. Do you know how much I shall lose by paying him this money? And suppose I had not had the securities which I have sacrificed? you did not know I possessed them."

The banker paused, as if hoping for a confession, which, however, did not come.

"Come, Prosper, have courage, be frank. I will go upstairs. You will look again in the safe: I am sure that in your agitation you did not search thoroughly. This evening I will return; and I am confident that, during the day, you will have found, if not the three hundred and fifty thousand *francs*, at least the greater portion of it; and tomorrow neither you nor I will remember anything about this false alarm."

M. Fauvel had risen, and was about to leave the room, when Prosper arose, and seized him by the arm.

"Your generosity is useless, *monsieur*," he said, bitterly; "having taken nothing, I can restore nothing. I have searched carefully; the bank-notes have been stolen."

"But by whom, poor fool? By whom?"

"By all that is sacred, I swear that it was not by me."

The banker's face turned crimson. "Miserable wretch!" cried he, "do you mean to say that I took the money?"

Prosper bowed his head, and did not answer.

"Ah! it is thus, then," said M. Fauvel, unable to contain himself any longer. "And you dare—. Then, between you and me, M. Prosper Bertomy, justice shall decide. God is my witness that I have done all I could to save you. You will have yourself to thank for what follows. I have sent for the commissary of police: he must be waiting in my study. Shall I call him down?"

Prosper, with the fearful resignation of a man who abandons himself, replied, in a stifled voice:

"Do as you will."

The banker was near the door, which he opened, and, after giving the cashier a last searching look, said to an office-boy:

"Anselme, ask the commissary of police to step down."

Chapter 3

If there is one man in the world whom no event can move or surprise, who is always on his guard against deceptive appearances, and is capable of admitting everything and explaining everything, it certainly is a Parisian commissary of police.

While the judge, from his lofty place, applies the code to the facts submitted to him, the commissary of police observes and watches all the odious circumstances that the law cannot reach. He is perforce the confidant of disgraceful details, domestic crimes, and tolerated vices.

If, when he entered upon his office, he had any illusions, before the end of a year they were all dissipated.

If he does not absolutely despise the human race, it is because often, side by side with abominations indulged in with impunity, he discovers sublime generosities which remain unrewarded.

He sees impudent scoundrels filching public respect; and he consoles himself by thinking of the modest, obscure heroes whom he has also encountered.

So often have his previsions been deceived, that he has reached a state of complete scepticism. He believes in nothing, neither in evil nor in absolute good; not more in virtue than in vice.

His experience has forced him to come to the sad conclusion that not men, but events, are worth considering.

The commissary sent for by M. Fauvel soon made his appearance.

It was with a calm air, if not one of perfect indifference, that he entered the office.

He was followed by a short man dressed in a full suit of black, which was slightly relieved by a crumpled collar.

The banker, scarcely bowing to him, said:

"Doubtless, *monsieur*, you have been apprised of the painful circumstance which compels me to have recourse to your assistance?"

"It is about a robbery, I believe."

"Yes; an infamous and mysterious robbery committed in this office, from the safe you see open there, of which my cashier" (he pointed to Prosper) "alone possesses the key and the word."

This declaration seemed to arouse the unfortunate cashier from his dull stupor.

"Excuse me, *monsieur*," he said to the commissary in a low tone. "My chief also has the word and the key."

"Of course, that is understood."

The commissary at once drew his own conclusions.

Evidently these two men accused each other.

From their own statements, one or the other was guilty.

One was the head of an important bank: the other was a simple cashier.

One was the chief: the other was the clerk.

But the commissary of police was too well skilled in concealing his impressions to betray his thoughts by any outward sign. Not a muscle of his face moved.

But he became more grave, and alternately watched the cashier and M. Fauvel, as if trying to draw some profitable conclusion from their behaviour.

Prosper was very pale and dejected. He had dropped into a seat, and his arms hung inert on either side of the chair.

The banker, on the contrary, remained standing with flashing eyes and crimson face, expressing himself with extraordinary violence.

"And the importance of the theft is immense," continued M. Fauvel; "they have taken a fortune, three hundred and fifty thousand *francs*. This robbery might have had the most disastrous consequences. In times like these, the want of this sum might compromise the credit of the wealthiest banking-house in Paris."

"I believe so, if notes fall due."

"Well, *monsieur*, I had this very day a heavy payment to make."

"Ah, really!"

There was no mistaking the commissary's tone; a suspicion, the first, had evidently entered his mind.

The banker understood it; he started, and said, quickly:

"I met the demand, but at the cost of a disagreeable sacrifice. I ought to add further that, if my orders had been obeyed, the three hundred and fifty thousand *francs* would not have been in."

"How is that?"

"I never desire to have large sums of money in my house overnight. My cashier had positive orders to wait always until the last moment before drawing money from the Bank of France. I above all forbade him to leave money in the safe over-night."

"You hear this?" said the commissary to Prosper.

"Yes, *monsieur*," replied the cashier, "M. Fauvel's statement is quite correct."

After this explanation, the suspicions of the commissary, instead of being strengthened, were dissipated.

"Well," he said, "a robbery has been perpetrated, but by whom? Did the robber enter from without?"

The banker hesitated a moment.

"I think not," he said at last.

"And I am certain he did not," said Prosper.

The commissary expected and was prepared for those answers; but it did not suit his purpose to follow them up immediately.

"However," said he, "we must make ourselves sure of it." Turning toward his companion:

"M. Fanferlot," he said, "go and see if you cannot discover some traces that may have escaped the attention of these gentlemen."

M. Fanferlot, nicknamed the Squirrel, was indebted to his prodigious agility for this title, of which he was not a little proud. Slim and insignificant in appearance he might, in spite of his iron muscles, be taken for a bailiff's under clerk, as he walked along buttoned up to the chin in his thin black overcoat. He had one of those faces that impress us disagreeably—an odiously turned-up nose, thin lips, and little, restless black eyes.

Fanferlot, who had been on the police force for five years, burned to distinguish himself, to make for himself a name. He was ambitious. Alas! he was unsuccessful, lacking opportunity—or genius.

Already, before the commissary spoke to him, he had ferreted everywhere; studied the doors, sounded the partitions, examined the wicket, and stirred up the ashes in the fireplace.

"I cannot imagine," said he, "how a stranger could have effected an entrance here."

He walked around the office.

"Is this door closed at night?" he inquired.

"It is always locked."

"And who keeps the key?"

"The office-boy, to whom I always give it in charge before leaving the bank," said Prosper.

"This boy," said M. Fauvel, "sleeps in the outer room on a sofa-bedstead, which he unfolds at night, and folds up in the morning."

"Is he here now?" inquired the commissary.

"Yes, *monsieur*," answered the banker.

He opened the door and called:

"Anselme!"

This boy was the favourite servant of M. Fauvel, and had lived with him for ten years. He knew that he would not be suspected; but the idea of being connected in any way with a robbery is terrible, and he entered the room trembling like a leaf.

"Did you sleep in the next room last night?" asked the commissary.

"Yes, *monsieur*, as usual."

"At what hour did you go to bed?"

"About half-past ten; I had spent the evening at a cafe near by, with *monsieur's* valet."

"Did you hear no noise during the night?"

"Not a sound; and still I sleep so lightly, that, if *monsieur* comes down to the cash-room when I am asleep, I am instantly awakened by the sound of his footsteps."

"Monsieur Fauvel often comes to the cash-room at night, does he?"

"No, *monsieur*; very seldom."

"Did he come last night?"

"No, *monsieur*, I am very certain he did not; for I was kept awake nearly all night by the strong coffee I had drunk with the valet."

"That will do; you can retire," said the commissary.

When Anselme had left the room, Fanferlot resumed his search. He opened the door of the private staircase.

"Where do these stairs lead to?" he asked.

"To my private office," replied M. Fauvel.

"Is not that the room whither I was conducted when I first came?" inquired the commissary.

"The same."

"I would like to see it," said Fanferlot, "and examine the entrances to it."

"Nothing is more easy," said M. Fauvel, eagerly; "follow me, gentlemen, and you come too, Prosper."

M. Fauvel's private office consisted of two rooms; the waiting-room, sumptuously furnished and beautifully decorated, and the study where he transacted business. The furniture in this room was composed of a large office-desk, several leather-covered chairs, and, on either side of the fireplace, a secretary and a book-shelf.

These two rooms had only three doors; one opened on the private stairway, another into the banker's bedroom, and the third into the main vestibule. It was through this last door that the banker's clients and visitors were admitted.

M. Fanferlot examined the study at a glance. He seemed puzzled, like a man who had flattered himself with the hope of discovering some indication, and had found nothing.

"Let us see the adjoining room," he said.

He passed into the waiting-room, followed by the banker and the commissary of police.

Prosper remained alone in the study.

Despite the disordered state of his mind, he could not but perceive that his situation was momentarily becoming more serious.

He had demanded and accepted the contest with his chief; the struggle had commenced; and now it no longer depended upon his own will to arrest the consequences of his action.

They were about to engage in a bitter conflict, utilizing all weapons, until one of the two should succumb, the loss of honour being the cost of defeat.

In the eyes of justice, who would be the innocent man?

Alas! the unfortunate cashier saw only too clearly that the chances were terribly unequal, and was overwhelmed with the sense of his own inferiority.

Never had he thought that his chief would carry out his threats; for, in a contest of this nature, M. Fauvel would have as much to risk as his cashier, and more to lose.

He was sitting near the fireplace, absorbed in the most gloomy forebodings, when the banker's chamber-door suddenly opened, and a beautiful girl appeared on the threshold.

She was tall and slender; a loose morning gown, confined at the waist by a simple black ribbon, betrayed to advantage the graceful elegance of her figure. Her black eyes were large and soft; her complexion had the creamy pallor of a white camellia; and her beautiful dark hair, carelessly held together by a tortoise-shell comb, fell in a profusion of soft curls upon her exquisite neck. She was Madeleine, M. Fauvel's niece, of whom he had spoken not long before.

Seeing Prosper in the study, where probably she expected to find her uncle alone, she could not refrain from an exclamation of surprise.

"Ah!"

Prosper started up as if he had received an electric shock. His eyes, a moment before so dull and heavy, now sparkled with joy as if he had caught a glimpse of a messenger of hope.

"Madeleine," he gasped, "Madeleine!"

The young girl was blushing crimson. She seemed about to hastily retreat, and stepped back; but, Prosper having advanced toward her, she was overcome by a sentiment stronger than her will, and extended her hand, which he seized and pressed with much agitation.

They stood thus face to face, but with averted looks, as if they dared not let their eyes meet for fear of betraying their feelings; having much to say, and not knowing how to begin, they stood silent.

Finally Madeleine murmured, in a scarcely audible voice:

"You, Prosper—you!"

These words broke the spell. The cashier dropped the white hand which he held, and answered bitterly:

"Yes, this is Prosper, the companion of your childhood, suspected, accused of the most disgraceful theft; Prosper, whom your uncle has just delivered up to justice, and who, before the day is over, will be arrested, and thrown into prison."

Madeleine, with a terrified gesture, cried in a tone of anguish:

"Good heavens! Prosper, what are you saying?"

"What, *mademoiselle*! do you not know what has happened? Have not your aunt and cousins told you?"

"They have told me nothing. I have scarcely seen my cousins this morning; and my aunt is so ill that I felt uneasy, and came to tell uncle. But for Heaven's sake speak: tell me the cause of your distress."

Prosper hesitated. Perhaps it occurred to him to open his heart to Madeleine, of revealing to her his most secret thoughts. A remembrance of the past chilled his confidence. He sadly shook his head, and replied:

"Thanks, *mademoiselle*, for this proof of interest, the last, doubtless, that I shall ever receive from you; but allow me, by being silent, to spare you distress, and myself the mortification of blushing before you."

Madeleine interrupted him imperiously:

"I insist upon knowing."

"Alas, *mademoiselle*!" answered Prosper, "you will only too soon learn my misfortune and disgrace; then, yes, then you will applaud yourself for what you have done."

She became more urgent; instead of commanding, she entreated; but Prosper was inflexible.

"Your uncle is in the adjoining room, *mademoiselle*, with the commissary of police and a detective. They will soon return. I entreat you to retire that they may not find you here."

As he spoke he gently pushed her through the door, and closed it upon her.

It was time, for the next moment the commissary and Monsieur Fauvel entered. They had visited the main entrance and waiting-room, and had heard nothing of what had passed in the study.

But Fanferlot had heard for them.

This excellent bloodhound had not lost sight of the cashier. He said to himself, "Now that my young gentleman believes himself to be alone, his face will betray him. I shall detect a smile or a wink that will enlighten me."

Leaving M. Fauvel and the commissary to pursue their investigations, he posted himself to watch. He saw the door open, and Madeleine appear upon the threshold; he lost not a single word or gesture of the rapid scene which had passed.

It mattered little that every word of this scene was an enigma. M. Fanferlot was skilful enough to complete the sentences he did not understand.

As yet he only had a suspicion; but a mere suspicion is better than nothing; it is a point to start from. So prompt was he in building a plan upon the slightest incident that he thought he saw in the past of these people, who were utter strangers to him, glimpses of a domestic drama.

If the commissary of police is a sceptic, the detective has faith; he believes in evil.

"I understand the case now," said he to himself. "This man loves the young lady, who is really very pretty; and, as he is quite handsome, I suppose his love is reciprocated. This love-affair vexes the banker, who, not knowing how to get rid of the importunate lover by fair means, has to resort to foul, and plans this imaginary robbery, which is very ingenious."

Thus to M. Fanferlot's mind, the banker had simply robbed himself, and the innocent cashier was the victim of an odious machination.

But this conviction was, at present, of little service to Prosper.

Fanferlot, the ambitious, who had determined to obtain renown in his profession, decided to keep his conjectures to himself.

"I will let the others go their way, and I'll go mine," he said. "When, by dint of close watching and patient investigation I shall have collected proof sufficient to insure certain conviction, I will unmask the scoundrel."

He was radiant. He had at last found the crime, so long looked for, which would make him celebrated. Nothing was wanting, neither the odious circumstances, nor the mystery, nor even the romantic and sentimental element represented by Prosper and Madeleine.

Success seemed difficult, almost impossible; but Fanferlot, the Squirrel, had great confidence in his own genius for investigation.

Meanwhile, the search upstairs completed, M. Fauvel and the commissary returned to the room where Prosper was waiting for them.

The commissary, who had seemed so calm when he first came, now looked grave and perplexed. The moment for taking a decisive part had come, yet it was evident that he hesitated.

"You see, gentlemen," he began, "our search has only confirmed our first suspicion."

M. Fauvel and Prosper bowed assentingly.

"And what do you think, M. Fanferlot?" continued the commissary.

Fanferlot did not answer.

Occupied in studying the safe-lock, he manifested signs of a lively surprise. Evidently he had just made an important discovery.

M. Fauvel, Prosper, and the commissary rose, and surrounded him.

"Have you discovered any trace?" said the banker, eagerly.

Fanferlot turned around with a vexed air. He reproached himself for not having concealed his impressions.

"Oh!" said he, carelessly, "I have discovered nothing of importance."

"But we should like to know," said Prosper.

"I have merely convinced myself that this safe has been recently opened or shut, I know not which, with great violence and haste."

"Why so?" asked the commissary, becoming attentive.

"Look, *monsieur*, at this scratch near the lock."

The commissary stooped down, and carefully examined the safe; he saw a light scratch several inches long that had removed the outer coat of varnish.

"I see the scratch," said he, "but what does that prove?"

"Oh, nothing at all!" said Fanferlot. "I just now told you it was of no importance."

Fanferlot said this, but it was not his real opinion.

This scratch, undeniably fresh, had for him a signification that escaped the others. He said to himself, "This confirms my suspicions. If the cashier had stolen millions, there was no occasion for his being in a hurry; whereas the banker, creeping down in the dead of night with cat-like footsteps, for fear of awakening the boy in the ante-room, in order to rifle his own money-safe, had every reason to tremble, to hurry, to hastily withdraw the key, which, slipping along the lock, scratched off the varnish."

Resolved to unravel by himself the tangled thread of this mystery, the detective determined to keep his conjectures to himself; for the same reason he was silent as to the interview which he had overheard between Madeleine and Prosper.

He hastened to withdraw attention from the scratch upon the lock.

"To conclude," he said, addressing the commissary, "I am convinced that no one outside of the bank could have obtained access to this room. The safe, moreover, is intact. No suspicious pressure has been used on the movable buttons. I can assert that the lock has not been tampered with by burglar's tools or false keys. Those who opened the safe knew the word, and possessed the key."

This formal affirmation of a man whom he knew to be skilful ended the hesitation of the commissary.

"That being the case," he replied, "I must request a few moments' conversation with M. Fauvel."

"I am at your service," said the banker.

Prosper foresaw the result of this conversation. He quietly placed his hat on the table, to show that he had no intention of attempting to escape, and passed into the adjoining room.

Fanferlot also went out, but not before the commissary had made him a sign, and received one in return.

This sign signified, "You are responsible for this man."

The detective needed no admonition to make him keep a strict watch. His suspicions were too vague, his desire for success was too ardent, for him to lose sight of Prosper an instant.

Closely following the cashier, he seated himself in a dark corner of the room, and, pretending to be sleepy, he fixed himself in a comfortable position for taking a nap, gaped until his jaw-bone seemed about to be dislocated, then closed his eyes, and kept perfectly quiet.

Prosper took a seat at the desk of an absent clerk. The others were burning to know the result of the investigation; their eyes shone with curiosity, but they dared not ask a question.

Unable to refrain himself any longer, little Cavaillon, Prosper's defender, ventured to say:

"Well, who stole the money?"

Prosper shrugged his shoulders.

"Nobody knows," he replied.

Was this conscious innocence or hardened recklessness? The clerks observed with bewildered surprise that Prosper had resumed his usual manner, that sort of icy haughtiness that kept people at a distance, and made him so unpopular in the bank.

Save the death-like pallor of his face, and the dark circles around his swollen eyes, he bore no traces of the pitiable agitation he had exhibited a short time before.

Never would a stranger entering the room have supposed that this young man idly lounging in a chair, and toying with a pencil, was resting under an accusation of robbery, and was about to be arrested.

He soon stopped playing with the pencil, and drew toward him a sheet of paper upon which he hastily wrote a few lines.

"Ah, ha!" thought Fanferlot the Squirrel, whose hearing and sight were wonderfully good in spite of his profound sleep, "eh! eh! he makes his little confidential communication on paper, I see; now we will discover something positive."

His note written, Prosper folded it carefully into the smallest possible size, and after furtively glancing toward the detective, who remained motionless in his corner, threw it across the desk to little Cavaillon with this one word:

"Gypsy!"

All this was so quickly and skilfully done that Fanferlot was confounded, and began to feel a little uneasy.

"The devil take him!" said he to himself; "for a suffering innocent this young dandy has more pluck and nerve than many of my oldest customers. This, however, shows the result of education!"

Yes: innocent or guilty, Prosper must have been endowed with great self-control and power of dissimulation to affect this presence of mind at a time when his honour, his future happiness, all that he held dear in life, were at stake. And he was only thirty years old.

Either from natural deference, or from the hope of gaining some ray of light by a private conversation, the commissary determined to speak to the banker before acting decisively.

"There is not a shadow of doubt, *monsieur*," he said, as soon as they were alone, "this young man has robbed you. It would be a gross neglect of duty if I did not secure his person. The law will decide whether he shall be released, or sent to prison."

The declaration seemed to distress the banker.

He sank into a chair, and murmured:

"Poor Prosper!"

Seeing the astonished look of his listener, he added:

"Until today, *monsieur*, I have always had the most implicit faith in his honesty, and would have unhesitatingly confided my fortune to his keeping. Almost on my knees have I besought and implored him to confess that in a moment of desperation he had taken the money, promising him pardon and forgetfulness; but I could not move him. I have loved him; and even now, in spite of the trouble and humiliation that he is bringing upon me, I cannot bring myself to feel harshly toward him."

The commissary looked as if he did not understand.

"What do you mean by humiliation, *monsieur*?"

"What!" said M. Fauvel, excitedly; "is not justice the same for all? Because I am the head of a bank, and he only a clerk, does it follow that my word is more to be relied upon than his? Why could I not have robbed myself? Such things have been done. They will ask me for facts; and I shall be compelled to expose the exact situation of my house, explain my affairs, disclose the secret and method of my operations."

"It is true, *monsieur*, that you will be called upon for some explanation; but your well-known integrity—"

"Alas! He was honest, too. His integrity has never been doubted. Who would have been suspected this morning if I had not been able to instantly produce a hundred thousand crowns? Who would be suspected if I could not prove that my assets exceed my liabilities by more than three millions?"

To a strictly honourable man, the thought, the possibility of suspicion tarnishing his fair name, is cruel suffering. The banker suffered, and the commissary of police saw it, and felt for him.

"Be calm, *monsieur*," said he; "before the end of a week justice will have collected sufficient proof to establish the guilt of this unfortunate man, whom we may now recall."

Prosper entered with Fanferlot, whom they had much trouble to awaken, and with the most stolid indifference listened to the announcement of his arrest.

In response, he calmly said:

"I swear that I am innocent."

M. Fauvel, much more disturbed and excited than his cashier, made a last attempt.

"It is not too late yet, poor boy," he said: "for Heaven's sake reflect—"

Prosper did not appear to hear him. He drew from his pocket a small key, which he laid on the table, and said:

"Here is the key of your safe, *monsieur*. I hope for my sake that you will some day be convinced of my innocence; and I hope for your sake that the conviction will not come too late."

Then, as everyone was silent, he resumed:

"Before leaving I hand over to you the books, papers, and accounts necessary for my successor. I must at the same time inform you that, without speaking of the stolen three hundred and fifty thousand *francs*, I leave a deficit in cash."

"A deficit!" This ominous word from the lips of a cashier fell like a bombshell upon the ears of Prosper's hearers.

His declaration was interpreted in divers ways.

"A deficit!" thought the commissary: "how, after this, can his guilt be doubted? Before stealing this whole contents of the safe, he has kept his hand in by occasional small thefts."

"A deficit!" said the detective to himself, "now, no doubt, the very innocence of this poor devil gives his conduct an appearance of great depravity; were he guilty, he would have replaced the first money by a portion of the second."

The grave importance of Prosper's statement was considerably diminished by the explanation he proceeded to make.

"There is a deficit of three thousand five hundred *francs* on my cash account, which has been disposed of in the following manner: two thousand taken by myself in advance on my salary; fifteen hundred advanced to several of my fellow-clerks. This is the last day of the month; tomorrow the salaries will be paid, consequently—"

The commissary interrupted him:

"Were you authorized to draw money whenever you wished to advance the clerks' pay?"

"No; but I knew that M. Fauvel would not have refused me permission to oblige my friends in the bank. What I did is done everywhere; I have simply followed my predecessor's example."

The banker made a sign of assent.

"As regards that spent by myself," continued the cashier, "I had a sort of right to it, all of my savings being deposited in this bank; about fifteen thousand *francs*."

"That is true," said M. Fauvel; "M. Bertomy has at least that amount on deposit."

This last question settled, the commissary's errand was over, and his report might now be made. He announced his intention of leaving, and ordered to cashier to prepare to follow him.

Usually, this moment when stern reality stares us in the face, when our individuality is lost and we feel that we are being deprived of our liberty, this moment is terrible.

At this fatal command, "Follow me," which brings before our eyes the yawning prison gates, the most hardened sinner feels his courage fail, and abjectly begs for mercy.

But Prosper lost none of that studied phlegm which the commissary of police secretly pronounced consummate impudence.

Slowly, with as much careless ease as if going to breakfast with a friend, he smoothed his hair, drew on his overcoat and gloves, and said, politely:

"I am ready to accompany you, *monsieur*."

The commissary folded up his pocket-book, and bowed to M. Fauvel, saying to Prosper:

"Come!"

They left the room, and with a distressed face, and eyes filled with tears that he could not restrain, the banker stood watching their retreating forms.

"Good Heaven!" he exclaimed: "gladly would I give twice that sum to regain my old confidence in poor Prosper, and be able to keep him with me!"

The quick-eared Fanferlot overheard these words, and prompted to suspicion, and ever disposed to impute to others the deep astuteness peculiar to himself, was convinced they had been uttered for his benefit.

He had remained behind the others under pretext of looking for an imaginary umbrella, and, as he reluctantly departed, said he would call in again to see if it had been found.

It was Fanferlot's task to escort Prosper to prison; but, as they were about starting, he asked the commissary to leave him at liberty to pursue another course, a request which his superior granted.

Fanferlot had resolved to obtain possession of Prosper's note, which he knew to be in Cavaillon's pocket.

To obtain this written proof, which must be an important one, appeared the easiest thing in the world. He had simply to arrest Cavaillon, frighten him, demand the letter, and, if necessary, take it by force.

But to what would this disturbance lead? To nothing unless it were an incomplete and doubtful result.

Fanferlot was convinced that the note was intended, not for the young clerk, but for a third person.

If exasperated, Cavaillon might refuse to divulge who this person was, who after all might not bear the name "Gypsy" given by the cashier. And, even if he did answer his questions, would he not lie?

After a mature reflection, Fanferlot decided that it would be superfluous to ask for a secret when it could be surprised. To quietly follow

Cavaillon, and keep close watch on him until he caught him in the very act of handing over the letter, was but play for the detective.

This method of proceeding, moreover, was much more in keeping with the character of Fanferlot, who, being naturally soft and stealthy, deemed it due to his profession to avoid all disturbance or anything resembling evidence.

Fanferlot's plan was settled when he reached the vestibule.

He began talking with an office-boy, and, after a few apparently idle questions, had discovered that the Fauvel bank had no outlet on the Rue de la Victoire, and that consequently all the clerks were obliged to pass in and out through the main entrance on the Rue de Provence.

From this moment the task he had undertaken no longer presented a shadow of difficulty. He rapidly crossed the street, and took up his position under a gateway.

His post of observation was admirably chosen; not only could he see everyone who entered and came out of the bank, but also commanded a view of all the windows, and by standing on tiptoe could look through the grating, and see Cavaillon bending over his desk.

Fanferlot waited a long time, but did not wax impatient, for he had often had to remain on watch entire days and nights at a time, with much less important objects in view than the present one. Besides, his mind was busily occupied in estimating the value of his discoveries, weighing his chances, and, like Perrette with her pot of milk, building the foundation of his fortune upon present success.

Finally, about one o'clock, he saw Cavaillon rise from his desk, change his coat, and take down his hat.

"Very good!" he exclaimed, "my man is coming out; I must keep my eyes open."

The next moment Cavaillon appeared at the door of the bank; but before stepping on the pavement he looked up and down the street in an undecided manner.

"Can he suspect anything?" thought Fanferlot.

No, the young clerk suspected nothing; only having a commission to execute, and fearing his absence would be observed, he was debating with himself which would be the shortest road for him to take.

He soon decided, entered the Faubourg Montmartre, and walked up the Rue Notre Dame de Lorette so rapidly, utterly regardless of the grumbling passers-by whom he elbowed out of his way, that Fanferlot found it difficult to keep him in sight.

Reaching the Rue Chaptal, Cavaillon suddenly stopped, and entered the house numbered 39.

He had scarcely taken three steps in the narrow corridor when he felt a touch on his shoulder, and turning abruptly, found himself face to face with Fanferlot.

He recognised him at once, and turning very pale he shrank back, and looked around for means of escape.

But the detective, anticipating the attempt, barred the passage-way. Cavaillon saw that he was fairly caught.

"What do you want with me?" he asked in a voice tremulous with fright.

Fanferlot was distinguished among his confreres for his exquisite suavity and unequalled urbanity. Even with his prisoners he was the perfection of courtesy, and never was known to handcuff a man without first obsequiously apologising for being compelled to do so.

"You will be kind enough, my dear *monsieur*," he said, "to excuse the great liberty I take; but I really am under the necessity of asking you for a little information."

"Information! From me, *monsieur*?"

"From you, my dear *monsieur*; from M. Eugene Cavaillon."

"But I do not know you."

"Ah, yes; you remember seeing me this morning. It is only about a trifling matter, and you will overwhelm me with obligations if you will do me the honour to accept my arm, and step outside for a moment."

What could Cavaillon do? He took Fanferlot's arm, and went out with him.

The Rue Chaptal is not one of those noisy thoroughfares where foot-passengers are in perpetual danger of being run over by numberless vehicles dashing to and fro; there were but two or three shops, and from the corner of Rue Fontaine occupied by an apothecary, to the entrance of the Rue Leonie, extended a high, gloomy wall, broken here and there by a small window which lighted the carpenters' shops behind.

It was one of those streets where you could talk at your ease, without having to step from the sidewalk every moment. So Fanferlot and Cavaillon were in no danger of being disturbed by passers-by.

"What I wished to say is, my dear *monsieur*," began the detective, "that M. Prosper Bertomy threw you a note this morning."

Cavaillon vaguely foresaw that he was to be questioned about this note, and instantly put himself on his guard.

"You are mistaken," he said, blushing to his ears.

"Excuse me, *monsieur*, for presuming to contradict you, but I am quite certain of what I say."

"I assure you that Prosper never gave me anything."

"Pray, *monsieur*, do not persist in a denial; you will compel me to prove that four clerks saw him throw you a note written in pencil and closely folded."

Cavaillon saw the folly of further contradicting a man so well informed; so he changed his tactics, and said:

"It is true Prosper gave me a note this morning; but it was intended for me alone, and after reading it I tore it up, and threw the pieces in the fire."

This might be the truth. Fanferlot feared so; but how could he assure himself of the fact? He remembered that the most palpable tricks often succeed the best, and trusting to his star, he said at hazard:

"Permit me to observe that this statement is not correct; the note was entrusted to you to give to Gypsy."

A despairing gesture from Cavaillon apprised the detective that he was not mistaken; he breathed again.

"I swear to you, *monsieur*," began the young man.

"Do not swear, *monsieur*," interrupted Fanferlot; "all the oaths in the world would be useless. You not only preserved the note, but you came to this house for the purpose of giving it to Gypsy, and it is in your pocket now."

"No, *monsieur*, no!"

Fanferlot paid no attention to this denial, but continued in his gentlest tone:

"And I am sure you will be kind enough to give it to me; believe me, nothing but the most absolute necessity—"

"Never!" exclaimed Cavaillon; and, believing the moment favourable, he suddenly attempted to jerk his arm from under Fanferlot's, and escape.

But his efforts were vain; the detective's strength was equal to his suavity.

"Don't hurt yourself, young man," he said, "but take my advice, and quietly give up the letter."

"I have not got it."

"Very well; see, you reduce me to painful extremities. If you persist in being so obstinate, I shall call two policemen, who will take you by each arm, and escort you to the commissary of police; and, once there, I shall be under the painful necessity of searching your pockets, whether you will or not."

Cavaillon was devoted to Prosper, and willing to make any sacrifice in his behalf; but he clearly saw that it was worse than useless to struggle any longer, as he would have no time to destroy the note. To deliver it under force was no betrayal; but he cursed his powerlessness, and almost wept with rage.

"I am in your power," he said, and then suddenly drew from his pocket-book the unlucky note, and gave it to the detective.

Fanferlot trembled with pleasure as he unfolded the paper; yet, faithful to his habits of fastidious politeness, before reading it, he bowed to Cavaillon, and said:

"You will permit me, will you not, *monsieur*?" Then he read as follows:

> Dear Nina—
> If you love me, follow my instructions instantly, without a moment's hesitation, without asking any questions. On the receipt of this note, take everything you have in the house, absolutely everything, and establish yourself in furnished rooms at the other end of Paris. Do not appear in public, but conceal yourself as much as possible. My life may depend on your obedience. I am accused of an immense robbery, and am about to be arrested. Take with you five hundred *francs* which you will find in the secretary.
> Leave your address with Cavaillon, who will explain what I have not time to tell. Be hopeful, whatever happens. Goodbye.
> Prosper

Had Cavaillon been less bewildered, he would have seen blank disappointment depicted on the detective's face after the perusal of the note.

Fanferlot had cherished the hope that he was about to possess a very important document, which would clearly prove the guilt or innocence of Prosper; whereas he had only seized a love-letter written by a man who was evidently more anxious about the welfare of the woman he loved than about his own.

Vainly did he puzzle over the letter, hoping to discover some hidden meaning; twist the words as he would, they proved nothing for or against the writer.

The two words "absolutely everything" were underscored, it is true; but they could be interpreted in so many ways.

The detective, however, determined not to drop the matter here.

"This Madame Nina Gypsy is doubtless a friend of M. Prosper Bertomy?"

"She is his particular friend."

"Ah, I understand; and she lives here at No. 39?"

"You know it well enough, as you saw me go in there."

"I suspected it to be the house, *monsieur*; now tell me whether the apartments she occupies are rented in her name."

"No. Prosper rents them."

"Exactly; and on which floor, if you please?"

"On the first."

During this colloquy, Fanferlot had folded up the note, and slipped it into his pocket.

"A thousand thanks, *monsieur*, for the information; and, in return, I will relieve you of the trouble of executing your commission."

"*Monsieur*!"

"Yes: with your permission, I will myself take this note to Madame Nina Gypsy."

Cavaillon began to remonstrate; but Fanferlot cut him short by saying:

"I will also venture to give you a piece of advice. Return quietly to your business, and have nothing more to do with this affair."

"But Prosper is a good friend of mine, and has saved me from ruin more than once."

"Only the more reason for your keeping quiet. You cannot be of the slightest assistance to him, and I can tell you that you may be of great injury. As you are known to be his devoted friend, of course your absence at this time will be remarked upon. Any steps that you take in this matter will receive the worst interpretation."

"Prosper is innocent, I am sure."

Fanferlot was of the same opinion, but he had no idea of betraying his private thoughts; and yet for the success of his investigations it was necessary to impress the importance of prudence and discretion upon the young man. He would have told him to keep silent concerning what had passed between them, but he dared not.

"What you say may be true," he said. "I hope it is, for the sake of M. Bertomy, and on your own account too; for, if he is guilty, you will certainly be very much annoyed, and perhaps suspected of complicity, as you are well known to be intimate with him."

Cavaillon was overcome.

"Now you had best take my advice, *monsieur*, and return to your business, and—. Good-morning, *monsieur*."

The poor fellow obeyed. Slowly and with swelling heart he returned to the Rue Notre Dame de Lorette. He asked himself how he could serve Prosper, warn Madame Gypsy, and, above all, have his revenge upon this odious detective, who had just made him suffer cruel humiliation.

He had no sooner turned the corner of the street, than Fanferlot entered No. 39, gave his name to the porter as Prosper Bertomy, went upstairs, and knocked at the first door he came to.

It was opened by a youthful footman, dressed in the most fanciful livery.

"Is Madame Gypsy at home?"

The groom hesitated; seeing this, Fanferlot showed his note, and said:

"M. Prosper told me to hand this note to *madame*, and wait for an answer."

"Walk in, and I will let *madame* know you are here."

The name of Prosper produced its effect. Fanferlot was ushered into a little room furnished in blue and gold silk damask. Heavy curtains darkened the windows, and hung in front of the doors. The floor was covered with a blue velvet carpet.

"Our cashier was certainly well lodged," murmured the detective.

But he had no time to purse his inventory. One of the door-curtains was pushed aside, and Madame Nina Gypsy stood before him.

Madame Gypsy was quite young, small, and graceful, with a brown or rather gold-coloured quadroon complexion, with the hands and feet of a child.

Long curling silk lashes softened the piercing brilliancy of her large black eyes; her lips were full, and her teeth were very white.

She had not yet made her toilet, but wore a velvet dressing-wrapper, which did not conceal the lace ruffles beneath. But she had already been under the hands of a hairdresser.

Her hair was curled and frizzed high on her forehead, and confined by narrow bands of red velvet; her back hair was rolled in an immense coil, and held by a beautiful gold comb.

She was ravishing. Her beauty was so startling that the dazzled detective was speechless with admiration.

"Well," he said to himself, as he remembered the noble, severe beauty of Madeleine, whom he had seen a few hours previous, "our young gentleman certainly has good taste—very good taste—two perfect beauties!"

While he thus reflected, perfectly bewildered, and wondering how he could begin the conversation, Madame Gypsy eyed him with the most disdainful surprise; she was waiting for this shabby little man in a threadbare coat and greasy hat to explain his presence in her dainty parlour.

She had many creditors, and was recalling them, and wondering which one had dared send this man to wipe his dusty boots on her velvet carpets.

After scrutinizing him from head to foot with undisguised contempt, she said, haughtily:

"What do you want?"

Anyone but Fanferlot would have been offended at her insolent manner; but he only noticed it to gain some notion of the young woman's disposition.

"She is bad-tempered," he thought, "and is uneducated."

While he was speculating upon her merits, Madame Nina impatiently tapped her little foot, and waited for an answer; finally she said:

"Why don't you speak? What do you want here?"

"I am charged, my dear *madame*," he answered in his softest tone, "by M. Bertomy, to give you this note."

"From Prosper! You know him, then?"

"I have that honour, *madame*; indeed, I may be so bold as to claim him as a friend."

"*Monsieur*! *You* a friend of Prosper!" exclaimed Madame Gypsy in a scornful tone, as if her pride were wounded.

Fanferlot did not condescend to notice this offensive exclamation. He was ambitious, and contempt failed to irritate him.

"I said a friend of his, *madame*, and there are few people who would have the courage to claim friendship for him now."

Madame Gypsy was struck by the words and manner of Fanferlot.

"I never could guess riddles," she said, tartly: "will you be kind enough to explain what you mean?"

The detective slowly drew Prosper's note from his pocket, and, with a bow, presented it to Madame Gypsy.

"Read, *madame*," he said.

She certainly anticipated no misfortune; although her sight was excellent, she stopped to fasten a tiny gold eyeglass on her nose, then carelessly opened the note.

At a glance she read its contents.

She turned very red, then very pale; she trembled as if with a nervous chill; her limbs seemed to give way, and she tottered so that Fanferlot, thinking she was about to fall, extended his arms to catch her.

Useless precaution! Madame Gypsy was one of those women whose inert listlessness conceals indomitable energy; fragile-looking creatures whose powers of endurance and resistance are unlimited; cat-like in their soft grace and delicacy, especially cat-like in their nerves and muscles of steel.

The dizziness caused by the shock she had received quickly passed off. She tottered, but did not fall, and stood up looking stronger than ever; seizing the wrist of the detective, she held it as if her delicate little hand were a vice, and cried out:

"Explain yourself! what does all this mean? Do you know anything about the contents of this note?"

Although Fanferlot betrayed courage in daily contending with the most dangerous rascals, he was positively terrified by Madame Gypsy.

"Alas!" he murmured.

"Prosper is to be arrested, accused of being a thief?"

"Yes, *madame*, he is accused of taking three hundred and fifty thousand *francs* from the bank-safe."

"It is false, infamous, absurd!" she cried. She had dropped Fanferlot's hand; and her fury, like that of a spoiled child, found vent in violent actions. She tore her web-like handkerchief, and the magnificent lace on her gown, to shreds.

"Prosper steal!" she cried; "what a stupid idea! Why should he steal? Is he not rich?"

"M. Bertomy is not rich, *madame*; he has nothing but his salary."

The answer seemed to confound Madame Gypsy.

"But," she insisted, "I have always seen him have plenty of money; not rich—then—"

She dared not finish; but her eye met Fanferlot's, and they understood each other.

Madame Nina's look meant:

"He committed this robbery in order to gratify my extravagant whims."

Fanferlot's glance answered:

"Very likely, *madame*."

A few minutes' reflection convinced Nina that her first impression was the correct one. Doubt fled after hovering for an instant over her agitated mind.

"No!" she cried, "I regret to say that Prosper would never have stolen one cent for me. One can understand a man robbing a bank to obtain means of bestowing pleasure and luxury upon the woman he loves; but Prosper does not love me, he never has loved me."

"Oh, fair lady!" protested the gallant and insinuating Fanferlot, "you surely cannot mean what you say."

Her beautiful eyes filled with tears, as she sadly shook her head, and said:

"I mean exactly what I say. It is only too true. He is ready to gratify my every wish, you may say; what does that prove? Nothing. I am too well convinced that he does not love me. I know what love is. Once I was beloved by an affectionate, true-hearted man; and my own sufferings of the last year make me know how miserable I must have made him by my cold return. Alas! we must suffer ourselves before we can feel for others. No, I am nothing to Prosper; he would not care if—"

"But then, *madame*, why—"

"Ah, yes," interrupted Nina, "why? you will be very wise if you can answer me. For a year have I vainly sought an answer to this question, so sad to me. I, a woman, cannot answer it; and I defy you to do so. You cannot discover the thoughts of a man so thoroughly master of himself that never is a single thought passing in his mind to be detected upon his countenance. I have watched him as only a woman can watch the man upon whom her fate depends, but it has always been in vain. He is kind and indulgent; but he does not betray himself, never will he commit himself. Ignorant people call him weak, yielding: I tell you that fair-haired man is a rod of iron painted like a reed!"

Carried away by the violence of her feelings, Madame Nina betrayed her inmost thoughts. She was without distrust, never suspecting that the stranger listening to her was other than a friend of Prosper.

As for Fanferlot, he congratulated himself upon his success. No one but a woman could have drawn him so excellent a portrait; in a moment of excitement she had given him the most valuable information; he now knew the nature of the man with whom he had to deal, which in an investigation like that he was pursuing is the principal point.

"You know that M. Bertomy gambles," he ventured to say, "and gambling is apt to lead a man—"

Madame Gypsy shrugged her shoulders, and interrupted him:

"Yes, he plays," she said, "but he is not a gambler. I have seen him lose and gain large sums without betraying the slightest agitation. He plays as he drinks, as he sups, as he falls in love—without passion, without enthusiasm, without pleasure. Sometimes he frightens me; he seems to drag about a body without a soul. Ah, I am not happy! Never have I been able to overcome his indifference, and indifference so great, so reckless, that I often think it must be despair; nothing will convince me that he has not some terrible secret, some great misfortune weighing upon his mind, and making life a burden."

"Then he has never spoken to you of his past?"

"Why should he tell me? Did you not hear me? I tell you he does not love me!"

Madame Nina was overcome by thoughts of the past, and tears silently coursed down her cheeks.

But her despair was only momentary. She started up, and, her eyes sparkling with generous resolution, she cried out:

"But I love him, and I will save him! I will see his chief, the miserable wretch who dares to accuse him. I will haunt the judges, and I will prove that he is innocent. Come, *monsieur*, let us start, and I promise you that before sunset he shall be free, or I shall be in prison with him."

Madame Gypsy's project was certainly laudable, and prompted by the noblest sentiments; but unfortunately it was impracticable.

Moreover, it would be going counter to the plans of the detective.

Although he had resolved to reserve to himself all the difficulties as well as the benefits of this inquiry, Fanferlot saw clearly that he could not conceal the existence of Madame Nina from the judge of instruction. She would necessarily be brought into the case, and sought for. But he did not wish her to take any steps of her own accord. He proposed to have her appear when and how he judged proper, so that he might gain for himself the merit of having discovered her.

His first step was to endeavour to calm the young woman's excitement. He thought it easy to prove to her that the least interference in favour of Prosper would be a piece of folly.

"What will you gain by acting thus, my dear *madame*?" he asked. "Nothing. I can assure you that you have not the least chance of success. Remember that you will seriously compromise yourself. Who knows if you will not be suspected as M. Bertomy's accomplice?"

But this alarming perspective, which had frightened Cavaillon into foolishly giving up a letter which he might so easily have retained, only stimulated Gypsy's enthusiasm. Man calculates, while woman follows the inspirations of her heart. Our most devoted friend, if a man, hesitates and draws back: if a woman, rushes undauntedly forward, regardless of the danger.

"What matters the risk?" she exclaimed. "I don't believe any danger exists; but, if it does, so much the better: it will be all the more to my credit. I am sure Prosper is innocent; but, if he should be guilty, I wish to share the punishment which awaits him."

Madame Gypsy's persistence was becoming alarming. She hastily drew around her a cashmere shawl, and, putting on her hat, declared that she was ready to walk from one end of Paris to the other, in search of the judge.

"Come, *monsieur*," she said with feverish impatience. "Are you not coming with me?"

Fanferlot was perplexed. Happily he always had several strings to his bow.

Personal considerations having no hold upon this impulsive nature, he resolved to appeal to her interest in Prosper.

"I am at your command, fair lady," he said; "let us go if you desire it; only permit me, while there is yet time, to say that we are very probably going to do great injury to M. Bertomy."

"In what way, if you please?"

"Because we are taking a step that he expressly forbade in his letter; we are surprising him—giving him no warning."

Nina scornfully tossed her head, and replied:

"There are some people who must be saved without warning, and against their will. I know Prosper: he is just the man to let himself be murdered without a struggle, without speaking a word—to give himself up through sheer recklessness and despair."

"Excuse me, *madame*," interrupted the detective: "M. Bertomy has by no means the appearance of a man who has given up in despair. On the contrary, I think he has already laid his plan of defence. By showing yourself, when he advised you to remain in concealment, you will be very likely to make vain his most careful precautions."

Madame Gypsy was silently weighing the value of Fanferlot's objections. Finally she said: "I cannot remain here inactive, without attempting to contribute in some way to his safety. Can you not understand that this floor burns my feet?"

Evidently, if she was not absolutely convinced, her resolution was shaken. Fanferlot saw that he was gaining ground, and this certainty, making him more at ease, gave weight to his eloquence.

"You have it in your power, *madame*," he said, "to render a great service to the man you love."

"In what way, *monsieur*, in what way?"

"Obey him, my child," said Fanferlot, in a paternal manner.

Madame Gypsy evidently expected very different advice.

"Obey," she murmured, "obey!"

"It is your duty," said Fanferlot with grave dignity, "it is your sacred duty."

She still hesitated; and he took from the table Prosper's note, which she had laid there, then continued:

"What! M. Bertomy at the most trying moment, when he is about to be arrested, stops to point out your line of conduct; and you would render vain this wise precaution! What does he say to you? Let us read over this note, which is like the testament of his liberty. He says, 'If you love me, I entreat you, obey.' And you hesitate to obey. Then you do not love him. Can you not understand, unhappy child, that M. Bertomy has his reasons, terrible, imperious reasons, for your remaining in obscurity for the present?"

Fanferlot understood these reasons the moment he put his foot in the sumptuous apartment of the Rue Chaptal; and, if he did not expose them now, it was because he kept them as a good general keeps his reserve, for the purpose of deciding the victory.

Madame Gypsy was intelligent enough to divine these reasons.

"Reasons for my hiding! Prosper wishes, then, to keep everyone in ignorance of our intimacy."

She remained thoughtful for a moment; then a ray of light seemed to cross her mind, and she cried:

"Oh, I understand now! Fool that I was for not seeing it before! My presence here, where I have been for a year, would be an overwhelming charge against him. An inventory of my possessions would be taken—of my dresses, my laces, my jewels—and my luxury would be brought against him as a crime. He would be asked to tell where he obtained so much money to lavish all these elegancies on me."

The detective bowed, and said:

"That is true, *madame*."

"Then I must fly, *monsieur*, at once. Who knows that the police are not already warned, and may appear at any moment?"

"Oh," said Fanferlot with easy assurance, "you have plenty of time;

the police are not so very prompt."

"No matter!"

And, leaving the detective alone in the parlour, Madame Nina hastily ran into her bedroom, and calling her maid, her cook, and her little footman, ordered them to empty her bureau and chests of their contents, and assisted them to stuff her best clothing and jewels into her trunks.

Suddenly she rushed back to Fanferlot and said:

"Everything will be ready to start in a few minutes, but where am I to go?"

"Did not M. Bertomy say, my dear lady, to the other end of Paris? To a hotel, or furnished apartments."

"But I don't know where to find any."

Fanferlot seemed to be reflecting; but he had great difficulty in concealing his delight at a sudden idea that flashed upon him; his little black eyes fairly danced with joy.

"I know of a hotel," he said at last, "but it might not suit you. It is not elegantly furnished like this room."

"Would I be comfortable there?"

"Upon my recommendation you would be treated like a queen, and, above all, concealed."

"Where is it?"

"On the other side of the river, Quai Saint Michel, the Archangel, kept by Madame Alexandre."

Madame Nina was never long making up her mind.

"Here are pen and paper; write your recommendation."

He rapidly wrote, and handed her the letter.

"With these three lines, *madame*, you can make Madame Alexandre do anything you wish."

"Very good. Now, how am I to let Cavaillon know my address? It was he who should have brought me Prosper's letter."

"He was unable to come, *madame*," interrupted the detective, "but I will give him your address."

Madame Gypsy was about to send for a carriage, but Fanferlot said he was in a hurry, and would send her one. He seemed to be in luck that day; for a cab was passing the door, and he hailed it.

"Wait here," he said to the driver, after telling him that he was a detective, "for a little brunette who is coming down with some trunks. If she tells you to drive her to Quai Saint Michel, crack your whip; if she gives you any other address, get down from your seat, and arrange your harness. I will keep in sight."

He stepped across the street, and stood in the door of a wine-store. He had not long to wait. In a few minutes the loud cracking of a whip apprised him that Madame Nina had started for the Archangel.

"Aha," said he, gaily, "I told *her*, at any rate."

Chapter 4

At the same hour that Madame Nina Gypsy was seeking refuge at the Archangel, so highly recommended by Fanferlot the Squirrel, Prosper Bertomy was being entered on the jailer's book at the police office.

Since the moment when he had resumed his habitual composure, he had not faltered.

Vainly did the people around him watch for a suspicious expression, or any sign of giving way under the danger of his situation.

His face was like marble.

One would have supposed him insensible to the horrors of his condition, had not his heavy breathing, and the beads of perspiration standing on his brow, betrayed the intense agony he was suffering.

At the police office, where he had to wait two hours while the commissary went to receive orders from higher authorities, he entered into conversation with the two bailiffs who had charge of him.

At twelve o'clock he said he was hungry, and sent to a restaurant near by for his breakfast, which he ate with a good appetite; he also drank nearly a bottle of wine.

While he was thus occupied, several clerks from the prefecture, who have to transact business daily with the commissary of police, curiously watched him. They all formed the same opinion, and admiringly said to each other:

"Well, he is made of strong material, he is!"

"Yes, my dandy looks too lamb-like to be left to his own devices. He ought to have a strong escort."

When he was told that a coach was waiting for him at the door, he at once got up; but, before going out, he requested permission to light a cigar, which was granted.

A flower-girl stood just by the door, with her stand filled with all varieties of flowers. He stopped and bought a bunch of violets. The girl, seeing that he was arrested, said, by way of thanks:

"Good luck to you, my poor gentleman!"

He appeared touched by this mark of interest, and replied:

"Thanks, my good woman, but 'tis a long time since I have had any."

It was magnificent weather, a bright spring morning. As the coach went along Rue Montmartre, Prosper kept his head out of the window, at the same time smilingly complaining at being imprisoned on such a lovely day, when everything outside was so sunny and pleasant.

"It is singular," he said, "I never felt so great a desire to take a walk."

One of the bailiffs, a large, jovial, red-faced man, received this remark with a hearty burst of laughter, and said:

"I understand."

To the court clerk, while he was going through the formalities of the commitment, Prosper replied with haughty brevity to the indispensable questions asked him.

But when he was ordered to empty his pockets on the table, and they began to search him, his eyes flashed with indignation, and a single tear dropped upon his flushed cheek. In an instant he had recovered his stony calmness, and stood up motionless, with his arms raised in the air so that the rough creatures about him could more conveniently ransack him from head to foot, to assure themselves that he had no suspicious object hid under his clothes.

The search would have, perhaps, been carried to the most ignominious lengths, but for the intervention of a middle-aged man of rather distinguished appearance, who wore a white cravat and gold spectacles, and was sitting quite at home by the fire.

He started with surprise, and seemed much agitated, when he saw Prosper brought in by the bailiffs; he stepped forward, and seemed about to speak to him, then suddenly changed his mind, and sat down again.

In spite of his own troubles, Prosper could not help seeing that this man kept his eyes fastened upon him. Did he know him? Vainly did he try to recollect having met him before.

This man, treated with all the deference due to a chief, was no less a personage than M. Lecoq, a celebrated member of the detective corps.

When the men who were searching Prosper were about to take off his boots, saying that a knife might be concealed in them. M. Lecoq waved them aside with an air of authority, and said:

"You have done enough."

He was obeyed. All the formalities being ended, the unfortunate cashier was taken to a narrow cell; the heavily barred door was swung to and locked upon him; he breathed freely; at last he was alone.

Yes, he believed himself to be alone. He was ignorant that a prison is made of glass, that the accused is like a miserable insect under the microscope of an entomologist. He knew not that the walls have stretched ears and watchful eyes.

He was so sure of being alone that he at once gave vent to his suppressed feelings, and, dropping his mask of impassibility, burst into a flood of tears. His long-restrained anger now flashed out like a smouldering fire.

In a paroxysm of rage he uttered imprecations and curses. He dashed himself against the prison-walls like a wild beast in a cage.

Prosper Bertomy was not the man he appeared to be.

This haughty, correct gentleman had ardent passions and a fiery temperament.

One day, when he was about twenty-four years of age, he had become suddenly fired by ambition. While all of his desires were repressed, imprisoned in his low estate, like an athlete in a strait-jacket, seeing around him all these rich people with whom money assumed the place of the wand in the fairy-tale, he envied their lot.

He studied the beginnings of these financial princes, and found that at the starting-point they possessed far less than himself.

How, then, had they succeeded? By force of energy, industry, and assurance.

He determined to imitate and excel them.

From this day, with a force of will much less rare than we think, he imposed silence upon his instincts. He reformed not his morals, but his manners; and so strictly did he conform to the rules of decorum, that he was regarded as a model of propriety by those who knew him, and had faith in his character; and his capabilities and ambition inspired the prophecy that he would be successful in attaining eminence and wealth.

And the end of all was this: imprisoned for robbery; that is, ruined!

For he did not attempt to deceive himself. He knew that, guilty or innocent, a man once suspected is as ineffaceably branded as the shoulder of a galley-slave.

Therefore what was the use of struggling? What benefit was a triumph which could not wash out the stain?

When the jailer brought him his supper, he found him lying on his pallet, with his face buried in the pillow, weeping bitterly.

Ah, he was not hungry now! Now that he was alone, he fed upon his own bitter thoughts. He sank from a state of frenzy into one of stupefying despair, and vainly did he endeavour to clear his confused mind, and account for the dark cloud gathering about him; no loophole for escape did he discover.

The night was long and terrible, and for the first time he had nothing to count the hours by, as they slowly dragged on, but the measured tread of the patrol who came to relieve the sentinels. He was wretched.

At dawn he dropped into a sleep, a heavy, oppressive sleep, which was more wearisome than refreshing; from which he was startled by the rough voice of the jailer.

"Come, *monsieur*," he said, "it is time for you to appear before the judge of instruction."

He jumped up at once, and, without stopping to repair his disordered toilet, said:

"Come on, quick!"

The constable remarked, as they walked along:

"You are very fortunate in having your case brought before an honest man."

He was right.

Endowed with remarkable penetration, firm, unbiased, equally free from false pity and excessive severity, M. Patrigent possessed in an eminent degree all the qualities necessary for the delicate and difficult office of judge of instruction.

Perhaps he was wanting in the feverish activity which is sometimes necessary for coming to a quick and just decision; but he possessed unwearying patience, which nothing could discourage. He would cheerfully devote years to the examination of a case; he was even now engaged on a case of Belgian bank-notes, of which he did not collect all the threads, and solve the mystery, until after four years' investigation.

Thus it was always to his office that they brought the endless lawsuits, half-finished inquests, and tangled cases.

This was the man before whom they were taking Prosper; and they were taking him by a difficult road.

He was escorted along a corridor, through a room full of policemen, down a narrow flight of steps, across a kind of cellar, and then up a steep staircase which seemed to have no terminus.

Finally he reached a long narrow galley, upon which opened many doors, bearing different numbers.

The custodian of the unhappy cashier stopped before one of these doors, and said:

"Here we are; here your fate will be decided."

At this remark, uttered in a tone of deep commiseration, Prosper could not refrain from shuddering.

It was only too true, that on the other side of this door was a man upon whose decision his freedom depended.

Summoning all his courage, he turned the door-knob, and was about to enter when the constable stopped him.

"Don't be in such haste," he said; "you must sit down here, and wait till your turn comes; then you will be called."

The wretched man obeyed, and his keeper took a seat beside him.

Nothing is more terrible and lugubrious than this gallery of the judges of instruction.

Stretching the whole length of the wall is a wooden bench blackened by constant use. This bench has for the last ten years been daily occupied by all the murderers, thieves, and suspicious characters of the Department of the Seine.

Sooner or later, fatally, as filth rushes to a sewer, does crime reach this gallery, this dreadful gallery with one door opening on the galleys, the other on the scaffold. This place was vulgarly and pithily denominated by a certain magistrate as the great public wash-house of all the dirty linen in Paris.

When Prosper reached the gallery it was full of people. The bench was almost entirely occupied. Beside him, so close as to touch his shoulder, sat a man with a sinister countenance, dressed in rags.

Before each door, which belonged to a judge of instruction, stood groups of witnesses talking in an undertone.

Policemen were constantly coming and going with prisoners. Sometimes, above the noise of their heavy boots, tramping along the flagstones, could be heard a woman's stifled sobs, and looking around you would see some poor mother or wife with her face buried in her handkerchief, weeping bitterly.

At short intervals a door would open and shut, and a bailiff call out a name or number.

This stifling atmosphere, and the sight of so much misery, made the cashier ill and faint; he was feeling as if another five minutes' stay among these wretched creatures would make him deathly sick, when a little old man dressed in black, wearing the insignia of his office, a steel chain, cried out:

"Prosper Bertomy!"

The unhappy man arose, and, without knowing how, found himself in the office of the judge of instruction.

For a moment he was blinded. He had come out of a dark room; and the one in which he now found himself had a window directly opposite the door, so that a flood of light fell suddenly upon him.

This office, like all those on the gallery, was of a very ordinary appearance, small and dingy.

The wall was covered with cheap dark green paper, and on the floor was a hideous brown carpet, very much worn.

Opposite the door was a large desk, filled with bundles of law-papers, behind which was seated the judge, facing those who entered, so that his face remained in the shade, while that of the prisoner or witness whom he questioned was in a glare of light.

At the right, before a little table, sat a clerk writing, the indispensable auxiliary of the judge.

But Prosper observed none of these details: his whole attention was concentrated upon the arbiter of his fate, and as he closely examined his face he was convinced that the jailer was right in calling him an honourable man.

M. Patrigent's homely face, with its irregular outline and short red whiskers, lit up by a pair of bright, intelligent eyes, and a kindly expression, was calculated to impress one favourably at first sight.

"Take a seat," he said to Prosper.

This little attention was gratefully welcomed by the prisoner, for he had expected to be treated with harsh contempt. He looked upon it as a good sign, and his mind felt a slight relief.

M. Patrigent turned toward the clerk, and said:

"We will begin now, Sigault; pay attention."

"What is your name?" he then asked, looking at Prosper.

"Auguste Prosper Bertomy."

"How old are you?"

"I shall be thirty the 5th of next May."

"What is your profession?"

"I am—that is, I was—cashier in M. Andre Fauvel's bank."

The judge stopped to consult a little memorandum lying on his desk. Prosper, who followed attentively his every movement, began to be hopeful, saying to himself that never would a man so unprejudiced have the cruelty to send him to prison again.

After finding what he looked for, M. Patrigent resumed the examination.

"Where do you live?"

"At No. 39, Rue Chaptal, for the last four years. Before that time I lived at No. 7, Boulevard des Batignolles."

"Where were you born?"

"At Beaucaire in the Department of the Gard."

"Are your parents living?"

"My mother died two years ago; my father is still living."

"Does he live in Paris?"

"No, *monsieur*: he lives at Beaucaire with my sister, who married one of the engineers of the Southern Canal."

It was in broken tones that Prosper answered these last questions. There are moments in the life of a man when home memories encourage and console him; there are also moments when he would be thankful to be without a single tie, and bitterly regrets that he is not alone in the world.

M. Patrigent observed the prisoner's emotion, when he spoke of his parents.

"What is your father's calling?" he continued.

"He was formerly superintendent of the bridges and canals; then he was employed on the Southern Canal, with my brother-in-law; now he has retired from business."

There was a moment's silence. The judge had turned his chair around, so that, although his head was apparently averted, he had a good view of the workings of Prosper's face.

"Well," he said, abruptly, "you are accused of having robbed M. Fauvel of three hundred and fifty thousand *francs*."

During the last twenty-four hours the wretched young man had had time to familiarize himself with the terrible idea of this accusation; and yet, uttered as it was in this formal, brief tone, it seemed to strike him with a horror which rendered him incapable of opening his lips.

"What have you to answer?" asked the judge.

"That I am innocent, *monsieur*; I swear that I am innocent!"

"I hope you are," said M. Patrigent, "and you may count upon me to assist you to the extent of my ability in proving your innocence. You must have defence, some facts to state; have you not?"

"Ah, *monsieur*, what can I say, when I cannot understand this dreadful business myself? I can only refer you to my past life."

The judge interrupted him:

"Let us be specific; the robbery was committed under circumstances that prevent suspicion from falling upon anyone but M. Fauvel and yourself. Do you suspect anyone else?"

"No, *monsieur*."

"You declare yourself to be innocent, therefore the guilty party must be M. Fauvel."

Prosper remained silent.

"Have you," persisted the judge, "any cause for believing that M. Fauvel robbed himself?"

The prisoner preserved a rigid silence.

"I see, *monsieur*," said the judge, "that you need time for reflection. Listen to the reading of your examination, and after signing it you will return to prison."

The unhappy man was overcome. The last ray of hope was gone. He heard nothing of what Sigault read, and he signed the paper without looking at it.

He tottered as he left the judge's office, so that the keeper was forced to support him.

"I fear your case looks dark, *monsieur*," said the man, "but don't be disheartened; keep up your courage."

Courage! Prosper had not a spark of it when he returned to his cell; but his heart was filled with anger and resentment.

He had determined that he would defend himself before the judge, that he would prove his innocence; and he had not had time to do so. He reproached himself bitterly for having trusted to the judge's benevolent face.

"What a farce," he angrily exclaimed, "to call that an examination!"

It was not really an examination, but a mere formality.

In summoning Prosper, M. Patrigent obeyed Article 93 of the Criminal Code, which says, "Every suspected person under arrest must be examined within twenty-four hours."

But it is not in twenty-four hours, especially in a case like this, with no evidence or material proof, that a judge can collect the materials for an examination.

To triumph over the obstinate defence of a prisoner who shuts himself up in absolute denial as if in a fortress, valid proofs are needed. These weapons M. Patrigent was busily preparing. If Prosper had remained a little longer in the gallery, he would have seen the same bailiff who had called him come out to the judge's office, and cry out:

"Number three."

The witness, who was awaiting his turn, and answered the call for number three, was M. Fauvel.

The banker was no longer the same man. Yesterday he was kind and affable in his manner: now, as he entered the judge's room, he seemed irritated. Reflection, which usually brings calmness and a desire to pardon, brought him anger and a thirst for vengeance.

The inevitable questions which commence every examination had scarcely been addressed to him before his impetuous temper gained the mastery, and he burst forth in invectives against Prosper.

M. Patrigent was obliged to impose silence upon him, reminding him of what was due to himself, no matter what wrongs he had suffered at the hands of his clerk.

Although he had very slightly examined Prosper, the judge was now scrupulously attentive and particular in having every question answered. Prosper's examination had been a mere formality, the stating and proving a fact. Now it related to collecting the attendant circumstances and the most trifling particulars, so as to group them together, and reach a just conclusion.

"Let us proceed in order," said the judge, "and pray confine yourself to answering my questions. Did you ever suspect your cashier of being dishonest?"

"Certainly not. Yet there were reasons which should have made me hesitate to trust him with my funds."

"What reasons?"

"M. Bertomy played cards. I have known of his spending whole nights at the gaming table, and losing immense sums of money. He was intimate with an unprincipled set. Once he was mixed up with one of my clients, M. de Clameran, in a scandalous gambling affair which took place at the house of some disreputable woman, and wound up by being tried before the police court."

For some minutes the banker continued to revile Prosper.

"You must confess, *monsieur*," interrupted the judge, "that you were very imprudent, if not culpable, to have entrusted your safe to such a man."

"Ah, *monsieur*, Prosper was not always thus. Until the past year he was a model of goodness. He lived in my house as one of my family; he spent all of his evenings with us, and was the bosom friend of my eldest son Lucien. One day, he suddenly left us, and never came to the house again. Yet I had every reason to believe him attached to my niece Madeleine."

M. Patrigent had a peculiar manner of contracting his brows when he thought he had discovered some new proof. He now did this, and said:

"Might not this admiration for the young lady have been the cause of M. Bertomy's estrangement?"

"How so?" said the banker with surprise. "I was willing to bestow Madeleine upon him, and, to be frank, was astonished that he did not ask for her hand. My niece would be a good match for any man, and he should have considered himself fortunate to obtain her. She is beautiful, and her dowry will be half a million."

"Then you can see no motive for your cashier's conduct?"

"It is impossible for me to account for it. I have, however, always supposed that Prosper was led astray by a young man whom he met at my house about this time, M. Raoul de Lagors."

"Ah! and who is this young man?"

"A relative of my wife; a very attractive, intelligent young man, somewhat wild, but rich enough to pay for his follies."

The judge wrote the name Lagors at the bottom of an already long list on his memorandum.

"Now," he said, "we are coming to the point. You are sure that the theft was not committed by anyone in your house?"

"Quite sure, *monsieur*."

"You always kept your key?"

"I generally carried it about on my person; and, whenever I left it at home, I put it in the secretary drawer in my chamber."

"Where was it the evening of the robbery?"

"In my secretary."

"But then—"

"Excuse me for interrupting you," said M. Fauvel, "and to permit me to tell you that, to a safe like mine, the key is of no importance. In the first place, one is obliged to know the word upon which the five movable buttons turn. With the word one can open it without the key; but without the word—"

"And you never told this word to anyone?"

"To no one, *monsieur*, and sometimes I would have been puzzled to know myself with what word the safe had been closed. Prosper would change it when he chose, and, if he had not informed me of the change, would have to come and open it for me."

"Had you forgotten it on the day of the theft?"

"No: the word had been changed the day before; and its peculiarity struck me."

"What was it?"

"Gypsy, g, y, p, s, y," said the banker, spelling the name.

M. Patrigent wrote down this name.

"One more question, *monsieur*: were you at home the evening before the robbery?"

"No; I dined and spent the evening with a friend; when I returned home, about one o'clock, my wife had retired, and I went to bed immediately."

"And you were ignorant of the amount of money in the safe?"

"Absolutely. In conformity with my positive orders, I could only suppose that a small sum had been left there overnight; I stated this fact to the commissary in M. Bertomy's presence, and he acknowledged it to be the case."

"Perfectly correct, *monsieur*: the commissary's report proves it." M. Patrigent was for a time silent. To him everything depended upon this one fact, that the banker was unaware of the three hundred and fifty thousand *francs* being in the safe, and Prosper had disobeyed orders by placing them there over-night; hence the conclusion was very easily drawn.

Seeing that his examination was over, the banker thought that he would relieve his mind of what was weighing upon it.

"I believe myself above suspicion, *monsieur*," he began, "and yet I can never rest easy until Bertomy's guilt has been clearly proved. Calumny prefers attacking a successful man: I may be calumniated: three hundred and fifty thousand *francs* is a fortune capable of tempting even a rich man. I would be obliged if you would have the condition of my banking-house examined. This examination will prove that I could have no interest in robbing my own safe. The prosperous condition of my affairs—"

"That is sufficient, *monsieur*."

M. Patrigent was well informed of the high standing of the banker, and knew almost as much of his affairs as did M. Fauvel himself.

He asked him to sign his testimony, and then escorted him to the door of his office, a rare favour on his part.

When M. Fauvel had left the room, Sigault indulged in a remark.

"This seems to be a very cloudy case," he said; "if the cashier is shrewd and firm, it will be difficult to convict him."

"Perhaps it will," said the judge, "but let us hear the other witnesses before deciding."

The person who answered to the call for number four was Lucien, M. Fauvel's eldest son.

He was a tall, handsome young man of twenty-two. To the judge's questions he replied that he was very fond of Prosper, was once very intimate with him, and had always regarded him as a strictly honourable man, incapable of doing anything unbecoming a gentleman.

He declared that he could not imagine what fatal circumstances could have induced Prosper to commit a theft. He knew he played cards, but not to the extent that was reported. He had never known him to indulge in expenses beyond his means.

In regard to his cousin Madeleine, he replied:

"I always thought that Prosper was in love with Madeleine, and, until yesterday, I was certain he would marry her, knowing that my father would not oppose their marriage. I have always attributed the discontinuance of Prosper's visits to a quarrel with my cousin, but supposed they would end by becoming reconciled."

This information, more than that of M. Fauvel, threw light upon Prosper's past life, but did not apparently reveal any evidence which could be used in the present state of affairs.

Lucien signed his deposition, and withdrew.

Cavaillon's turn for examination came next. The poor fellow was in a pitiable state of mind when he appeared before the judge.

Having, as a great secret, confided to a friend his adventure with the detective, and being jeered at for his cowardice in giving up the note, he felt great remorse, and passed the night in reproaching himself for having ruined Prosper.

He endeavoured to repair, as well as he could, what he called his treason.

He did not exactly accuse M. Fauvel, but he courageously declared that he was the cashier's friend, and that he was as sure of his innocence as he was of his own.

Unfortunately, besides his having no proofs to strengthen his assertions, these were deprived of any value by his violent professions of friendship for the accused.

After Cavaillon, six or eight clerks of the Fauvel bank successively defiled in the judge's office; but their depositions were nearly all insignificant.

One of them, however, stated a fact which the judge carefully noted. He said he knew that Prosper had speculated on the Bourse through the medium of M. Raoul de Lagors, and had gained immense sums.

Five o'clock struck before the list of witnesses summoned for the day was exhausted. But the task of M. Patrigent was not yet finished. He rang for his bailiff, who instantly appeared, and said to him:

"Go at once, and bring Fanferlot here."

It was some time before the detective answered the summons. Having met a colleague on the gallery, he thought it his duty to treat him to a drink; and the bailiff had found it necessary to bring him from the little inn at the corner.

"How is it that you keep people waiting?" said the judge, when he entered bowing and scraping. Fanferlot bowed more profoundly still.

Despite his smiling face, he was very uneasy. To prosecute the Bertomy case alone, it required a double play that might be discovered at any moment; to manage at once the cause of justice and his own ambition, he ran great risks, the least of which was the losing of his place.

"I have a great deal to do," he said, to excuse himself, "and have not wasted any time."

And he began to give a detailed account of his movements. He was embarrassed, for he spoke with all sorts of restrictions, picking out what was to be said, and avoiding what was to be left unsaid. Thus he gave the history of Cavaillon's letter, which he handed to the judge; but he did not breathe a word of Madeleine. On the other hand, he gave biographical details, very minute indeed, of Prosper and Madame Gypsy, which he had collected from various quarters during the day.

As he progressed the conviction of M. Patrigent was strengthened.

"This young man is evidently guilty," he said. Fanferlot did not reply; his opinion was different, but he was delighted that the judge was on the wrong track, thinking that his own glory would thereby be the greater when he discovered the real culprit. True, this grand discovery was as far off as it had ever been; but Fanferlot was hopeful.

After hearing all he had to tell, the judge dismissed Fanferlot, telling him to return the next day.

"Above all," he said, as Fanferlot left the room, "do not lose sight of the girl Gypsy; she must know where the money is, and can put us on the track."

Fanferlot smiled cunningly.

"You may rest easy about that, *monsieur*; the lady is in good hands."

Left to himself, although the evening was far advanced, M. Patrigent continued to busy himself with the case, and to arrange that the rest of the depositions should be made.

This case had actually taken possession of his mind; it was, at the same time, puzzling and attractive. It seemed to be surrounded by a cloud of mystery, and he determined to penetrate and dispel it.

The next morning he was in his office much earlier than usual. On this day he examined Madame Gypsy, recalled Cavaillon, and sent again for M. Fauvel. For several days he displayed the same activity.

Of all the witnesses summoned, only two failed to appear.

One was the office-boy sent by Prosper to bring the money from the city bank; he was ill from a fall.

The other was M. Raoul de Lagors.

But their absence did not prevent the file of papers relating to Prosper's case from daily increasing; and on the ensuing Monday, five days after the robbery, M. Patrigent thought he held in his hands enough moral proof to crush the accused.

Chapter 5

While his whole past was the object of the most minute investigations, Prosper was in prison, in a secret cell.

The two first days had not appeared very long.

He had requested, and been granted, some sheets of paper, numbered, which he was obliged to account for; and he wrote, with a sort of rage, plans of defence and a narrative of justification.

The third day he began to be uneasy at not seeing anyone except the condemned prisoners who were employed to serve those confined in secret cells, and the jailer who brought him his food.

"Am I not to be examined again?" he would ask.

"Your turn is coming," the jailer invariably answered.

Time passed; and the wretched man, tortured by the sufferings of solitary confinement which quickly breaks the spirit, sank into the depths of despair.

"Am I to stay here forever?" he moaned.

No, he was not forgotten; for on Monday morning, at one o'clock, an hour when the jailer never came, he heard the heavy bolt of his cell pushed back.

He ran toward the door.

But the sight of a gray-headed man standing on the sill rooted him to the spot.

"Father," he gasped, "father!"

"Your father, yes!"

Prosper's astonishment at seeing his father was instantly succeeded by a feeling of great joy.

A father is one friend upon whom we can always rely. In the hour of need, when all else fails, we remember this man upon whose knees we sat when children, and who soothed our sorrows; and although he can in no way assist us, his presence alone comforts and strengthens.

Without reflecting, Prosper, impelled by tender feeling, was about to throw himself on his father's bosom.

M. Bertomy harshly repulsed him.

"Do not approach me!" he exclaimed.

He then advanced into the cell, and closed the door. The father and son were alone together, Prosper heartbroken, crushed; M. Bertomy angry, almost threatening.

Cast off by this last friend, by his father, the miserable young man seemed to be stupefied with pain and disappointment.

"You too!" he bitterly cried. "You, you believe me guilty? Oh, father!"

"Spare yourself this shameful comedy," interrupted M. Bertomy: "I know all."

"But I am innocent, father; I swear it by the sacred memory of my mother."

"Unhappy wretch," cried M. Bertomy, "do not blaspheme!"

He seemed overcome by tender thoughts of the past, and in a weak, broken voice, he added:

"Your mother is dead, Prosper, and little did I think that the day would come when I could thank God for having taken her from me. Your crime would have killed her, would have broken her heart!"

After a painful silence, Prosper said:

"You overwhelm me, father, and at the moment when I need all my courage; when I am the victim of an odious plot."

"Victim!" cried M. Bertomy, "victim! Dare you utter your insinuations against the honourable man who has taken care of you, loaded you with benefits, and had insured you a brilliant future! It is enough for you to have robbed him; do not calumniate him."

"For pity's sake, father, let me speak!"

"I suppose you would deny your benefactor's kindness. Yet you were at one time so sure of his affection, that you wrote me to hold myself in readiness to come to Paris and ask M. Fauvel for the hand of his niece. Was that a lie too?"

"No," said Prosper in a choked voice, "no."

"That was a year ago; you then loved Mademoiselle Madeleine; at least you wrote to me that you—"

"Father, I love her now, more than ever; I have never ceased to love her."

M. Bertomy made a gesture of contemptuous pity.

"Indeed!" he cried, "and the thought of the pure, innocent girl whom you loved did not prevent your entering upon a path of sin. You loved her: how dared you, then, without blushing, approach her presence after associating with the shameless creatures with whom you were so intimate?"

"For Heaven's sake, let me explain by what fatality Madeleine—"

"Enough, *monsieur*, enough. I told you that I know everything. I saw M. Fauvel yesterday; this morning I saw the judge, and 'tis to his kindness that I am indebted for this interview. Do you know what mortification I suffered before being allowed to see you? I was searched and made to empty all of my pockets, on suspicion of bringing you arms!"

Prosper ceased to justify himself, but in a helpless, hopeless way, dropped down upon a seat.

"I have seen your apartments, and at once recognised the proofs of your crime. I saw silk curtains hanging before every window and door, and the walls covered with pictures. In my father's house the walls were whitewashed; and there was but one arm-chair in the whole house, and that was my mother's. Our luxury was our honesty. You are the first member of our family who has possessed Aubusson carpets; though, to be sure, you are the first thief of our blood."

At this last insult Prosper's face flushed crimson, but he remained silent and immovable.

"But luxury is necessary now," continued M. Bertomy, becoming more excited and angry as he went on, "luxury must be had at any price. You must have the insolent opulence and display of an upstart, without being an upstart. You must support worthless women who wear satin slippers lined with swan's-down, like those I saw in your rooms, and keep servants in livery—and you steal! And bankers no longer trust their safe-keys with anybody; and every day honest families are disgraced by the discovery of some new piece of villainy."

M. Bertomy suddenly stopped. He saw that his son was not in a condition to hear any more reproaches.

"But I will say no more," he said. "I came here not to reproach, but to, if possible, save the honour of our name, to prevent it from being published in the papers bearing the names of thieves and murderers. Stand up and listen to me!"

At the imperious tone of his father, Prosper arose. So many successive blows had reduced him to a state of torpor.

"First of all," began M. Bertomy, "how much have you remaining of the stolen three hundred and fifty thousand *francs*?"

"Once more, father," replied the unfortunate man in a tone of hopeless resignation, "once more I swear I am innocent."

"So I supposed you would say. Then our family will have to repair the injury you have done M. Fauvel."

"What do you mean?"

"The day he heard of your crime, your brother-in-law brought me your sister's dowry, seventy thousand *francs*. I succeeded in collecting a hundred and forty thousand *francs* more. This makes two hundred and ten thousand *francs* which I have brought with me to give to M. Fauvel."

This threat aroused Prosper from his torpor.

"You shall do nothing of the kind!" he cried with unrestrained indignation.

"I will do so before the sun goes down this day. M. Fauvel will grant me time to pay the rest. My pension is fifteen hundred *francs*. I can live upon five hundred, and am strong enough to go to work again; and your brother-in-law—"

M. Bertomy stopped short, frightened at the expression of his son's face. His features were contracted with such furious rage that he was scarcely recognisable, and his eyes glared like a maniac's.

"You dare not disgrace me thus!" he cried; "you have no right to do it. You are free to disbelieve me yourself, but you have no right for taking a step that would be a confession of guilt, and ruin me forever. Who and what convinces you of my guilt? When cold justice hesitates, you, my father, hesitate not, but, more pitiless than the law, condemn me unheard!"

"I only do my duty."

"Which means that I stand on the edge of a precipice, and you push me over. Do you call that your duty? What! between strangers who accuse me, and myself who swear that I am innocent, you do not hesitate? Why? Is it because I am your son? Our honour is at stake, it is true; but that is only the more reason why you should sustain me, and assist me to defend myself."

Prosper's earnest, truthful manner was enough to unsettle the firmest convictions, and make doubt penetrate the most stubborn mind.

"Yet," said M. Bertomy in a hesitating tone, "everything seems to accuse you."

"Ah, father, you do not know that I was suddenly banished from Madeleine's presence; that I was compelled to avoid her. I became desperate, and tried to forget my sorrow in dissipation. I sought oblivion, and found shame and disgust. Oh, Madeleine, Madeleine!"

He was overcome with emotion; but in a few minutes he started up with renewed violence in his voice and manner.

"Everything is against me!" he exclaimed, "but no matter. I will justify myself or perish in the attempt. Human justice is liable to error; although innocent, I may be convicted: so be it. I will undergo my penalty; but people are not kept galley-slaves forever."

"What do you mean?"

"I mean, father, that I am now another man. My life, henceforth, has an object, vengeance! I am the victim of a vile plot. As long as I have a drop of blood in my veins, I will seek its author. And I will certainly find him; and then bitterly shall he expiate all of my cruel suffering. The blow came from the house of Fauvel, and I will live to prove it."

"Take care: your anger makes you say things that you will repent hereafter."

"Yes, I see, you are going to descant upon the probity of M. Andre Fauvel. You will tell me that all the virtues have taken refuge in the bosom of this patriarchal family. What do you know about it? Would this be the first instance in which the most shameful secrets are concealed beneath the fairest appearances? Why did Madeleine suddenly forbid me to think of her? Why has she exiled me, when she suffers as much from our separation as I myself, when she still loves me? For she does love me. I am sure of it. I have proofs of it."

The jailer came to say that the time allotted to M. Bertomy had expired, and that he must leave the cell.

A thousand conflicting emotions seemed to rend the old man's heart.

Suppose Prosper were telling the truth: how great would be his remorse, if he had added to his already great weight of sorrow and trouble! And who could prove that he was not sincere?

The voice of this son, of whom he had always been so proud, had aroused all his paternal affection, so violently repressed. Ah, were he guilty, and guilty of a worse crime, still he was his son, his only son!

His countenance lost its severity, and his eyes filled with tears.

He had resolved to leave, as he had entered, stern and angry: he had not the cruel courage. His heart was breaking. He opened his arms, and pressed Prosper to his heart.

"Oh, my son!" he murmured. "God grant you have spoken the truth!"

Prosper was triumphant: he had almost convinced his father of his innocence. But he had not time to rejoice over this victory.

The cell-door again opened, and the jailer's gruff voice once more called out:

"It is time for you to appear before the court."

He instantly obeyed the order.

But his step was no longer unsteady, as a few days previous: a complete change had taken place within him. He walked with a firm step, head erect, and the fire of resolution in his eye.

He knew the way now, and he walked a little ahead of the constable who escorted him.

As he was passing through the room full of policemen, he met the man with gold spectacles, who had watched him so intently the day he was searched.

"Courage, M. Prosper Bertomy," he said: "if you are innocent, there are those who will help you."

Prosper started with surprise, and was about to reply, when the man disappeared.

"Who is that gentleman?" he asked of the policeman.

"Is it possible that you don't know him?" replied the policeman with surprise. "Why, it is M. Lecoq, of the police service."

"You say his name is Lecoq?"

"You might as well say '*monsieur*,'" said the offended policeman; "it would not burn your mouth. M. Lecoq is a man who knows everything that he wants to know, without its ever being told to him. If you had had him, instead of that smooth-tongued imbecile Fanferlot, your case would have been settled long ago. Nobody is allowed to waste time when he has command. But he seems to be a friend of yours."

"I never saw him until the first day I came here."

"You can't swear to that, because no one can boast of knowing the real face of M. Lecoq. It is one thing today, and another tomorrow; sometimes he is a dark man, sometimes a fair one, sometimes quite young, and then an octogenarian: why, not seldom he even deceives me. I begin to talk to a stranger, *paf*! the first thing I know, it is M. Lecoq! Anybody on the face of the earth might be he. If I were told that you were he, I should say, 'It is very likely.' Ah! he can convert himself into any shape and form he chooses. He is a wonderful man!"

The constable would have continued forever his praises of M. Lecoq, had not the sight of the judge's door put an end to them.

This time, Prosper was not kept waiting on the wooden bench: the judge, on the contrary, was waiting for him.

M. Patrigent, who was a profound observer of human nature, had contrived the interview between M. Bertomy and his son.

He was sure that between the father, a man of such stubborn honour, and the son, accused of theft, an affecting scene would take place, and this scene would completely unman Prosper, and make him confess.

He determined to send for him as soon as the interview was over, while all his nerves were vibrating with terrible emotions: he would tell the truth, to relieve his troubled, despairing mind.

His surprise was great to see the cashier's bearing; resolute without obstinacy, firm and assured without defiance.

"Well," he said, "have you reflected?"

"Not being guilty, *monsieur*, I had nothing to reflect upon."

"Ah, I see the prison has not been a good counsellor; you forget that sincerity and repentance are the first things necessary to obtain the indulgence of the law."

"I crave no indulgence, *monsieur*."

M. Patrigent looked vexed, and said:

"What would you say if I told you what had become of the three hundred and fifty thousand *francs*?"

Prosper shook his head sadly.

"If it were known, *monsieur*, I would not be here, but at liberty."

This device had often been used by the judge, and generally succeeded; but, with a man so thoroughly master of himself, there was small chance of success. It had been used at a venture, and failed.

"Then you persist in accusing M. Fauvel?"

"Him, or someone else."

"Excuse me: no one else, since he alone knew the word. Had he any interest in robbing himself?"

"I can think of none."

"Well, now I will tell you what interest you had in robbing him."

M. Patrigent spoke as a man who was convinced of the facts he was about to state; but his assurance was all assumed.

He had relied upon crushing, at a blow, a despairing wretched man, and was nonplussed by seeing him appear as determined upon resistance.

"Will you be good enough to tell me," he said, in a vexed tone, "how much you have spent during the last year?"

Prosper did not find it necessary to stop to reflect and calculate.

"Yes, *monsieur*," he answered, unhesitatingly: "circumstances made it necessary for me to preserve the greatest order in my wild career; I spent about fifty thousand *francs*."

"Where did you obtain them?"

"In the first place, twelve thousand *francs* were left to me by my mother. I received from M. Fauvel fourteen thousand *francs*, as my salary, and share of the profits. By speculating in stocks, I gained eight thousand *francs*. The rest I borrowed, and intend repaying out of the fifteen thousand *francs* which I have deposited in M. Fauvel's bank."

The account was clear, exact, and could be easily proved; it must be a true one.

"Who lent you the money?"

"M. Raoul de Lagors."

This witness had left Paris the day of the robbery, and could not be found; so, for the time being, M. Patrigent was compelled to rely upon Prosper's word.

"Well," he said, "I will not press this point; but tell me why, in spite of the formal order of M. Fauvel, you drew the money from the Bank of France the night before, instead of waiting till the morning of the payment?"

"Because M. de Clameran had informed me that it would be agreeable, necessary even, for him to have his money early in the morning. He will testify to that fact, if you summon him; and I knew that I should reach my office late."

"Then M. de Clameran is a friend of yours?"

"By no means. I have always felt repelled by him; but he is the intimate friend of M. Lagors."

While Sigault was writing down these answers, M. Patrigent was racking his brain to imagine what could have occurred between M. Bertomy and his son, to cause this transformation in Prosper.

"One more thing," said the judge: "how did you spend the evening, the night before the crime?"

"When I left my office, at five o'clock, I took the St.-Germain train, and went to Vesinet, M. de Lagors's country seat, to carry him fifteen hundred *francs* which he had asked for; and, finding him not at home, I left it with his servant."

"Did he tell you that M. de Lagors was going away?"

"No, *monsieur*. I did not know that he had left Paris."

"Where did you go when you left Vesinet?"

"I returned to Paris, and dined at a restaurant with a friend."

"And then?"

Prosper hesitated.

"You are silent," said M. Patrigent; "then I shall tell you how you employed your time. You returned to your rooms in the Rue Chaptal, dressed yourself, and attended a *soiree* given by one of those women who style themselves dramatic *artistes*, and who are a disgrace to the stage; who receive a hundred crowns a year, and yet keep their carriages, at Mademoiselle Wilson's."

"You are right, *monsieur*."

"There is heavy playing at Wilson's?"

"Sometimes."

"You are in the habit of visiting places of this sort. Were you not connected in some way with a scandalous adventure which took place at the house of a woman named Crescenzi?"

"I was summoned to testify, having witnessed a theft."

"Gambling generally leads to stealing. And did you not play *baccarat* at Wilson's, and lose eighteen hundred *francs*?"

"Excuse me, *monsieur*, only eleven hundred."

"Very well. In the morning you paid a note of a thousand *francs*."

"Yes, *monsieur*."

"Moreover, there remained in your desk five hundred *francs*, and you had four hundred in your purse when you were arrested. So that altogether, in twenty-four hours, four thousand five hundred *francs*—"

Prosper was not discountenanced, but stupefied.

Not being aware of the powerful means of investigation possessed by the law, he wondered how in so short a time the judge could have obtained such accurate information.

"Your statement is correct, *monsieur*," he said finally.

"Where did all this money come from? The evening before you had so little that you were obliged to defer the payment of a small bill."

"The day to which you allude, I sold through an agent some bonds I had, about three thousand *francs*; besides, I took from the safe two thousand *francs* in advance on my salary."

The prisoner had given clear answers to all the questions put to him, and M. Patrigent thought he would attack him on a new point.

"You say you have no wish to conceal any of your actions; then why did you write this note to one of your companions?" Here he held up the mysterious note.

This time the blow struck. Prosper's eyes dropped before the inquiring look of the judge.

"I thought," he stammered, "I wished—"

"You wished to screen this woman?"

"Yes, *monsieur*; I did. I knew that a man in my condition, accused of a robbery, has every fault, every weakness he has ever indulged in, charged against him as a great crime."

"Which means that you knew that the presence of a woman at your house would tell very much against you, and that justice would not excuse this scandalous defiance of public morality. A man who respects himself so little as to associate with a worthless woman, does not elevate her to his standard, but he descends to her base level."

"*Monsieur*!"

"I suppose you know who the woman is, whom you permit to bear the honest name borne by your mother?"

"Madame Gypsy was a governess when I first knew her. She was born at Oporto, and came to France with a Portuguese family."

"Her name is not Gypsy; she has never been a governess, and she is not a Portuguese."

Prosper began to protest against this statement; but M. Patrigent shrugged his shoulders, and began looking over a large file of papers on his desk.

"Ah, here it is," he said, "listen: Palmyre Chocareille, born at Paris in 1840, daughter of James Chocareille, undertaker's assistant, and of Caroline Piedlent, his wife."

Prosper looked vexed and impatient; he did not know that the judge was reading him this report to convince him that nothing can escape the police.

"Palmyre Chocareille," he continued, "at twelve years of age was apprenticed to a shoemaker, and remained with him until she was sixteen. Traces of her for one year are lost. At the age of seventeen she is hired as a servant by a grocer on the Rue St. Denis, named Dombas, and remains there three months. She lives out during this same year, 1857, at eight different places. In 1858 she entered the store of a fan-merchant in Choiseul Alley."

As he read, the judge watched Prosper's face to observe the effect of these revelations.

"Toward the close of 1858 she was employed as a servant by Madame Munes, and accompanied her to Lisbon. How long she remained in Lisbon, and what she did while she remained there, is not reported. But in 1861 she returned to Paris, and was sentenced to three months' imprisonment for assault and battery. Ah, she returned from Portugal with the name of Nina Gypsy."

"But I assure you, *monsieur*," Prosper began.

"Yes, I understand; this history is less romantic, doubtless, than the one related to you; but then it has the merit of being true. We lose sight of Palmyre Chocareille, called Gypsy, upon her release from prison, but we meet her again six months later, having made the acquaintance of a travelling agent named Caldas, who became infatuated with her beauty, and furnished her a house near the Bastille. She assumed his name for some time, then she deserted him to devote herself to you. Did you ever hear of this Caldas?"

"Never, *monsieur*."

"This foolish man so deeply loved this creature that her desertion drove him almost insane from grief. He was a very resolute man, and publicly swore that he would kill his rival if he ever found him. The current report afterward was, that he committed suicide. He certainly sold the furniture of the House occupied by Chocareille, and suddenly disappeared. All the efforts made to discover him proved fruitless."

The judge stopped a moment as if to give Prosper time for reflection, and then slowly said:

"And this is the woman whom you made your companion, the woman for whom you robbed the bank!"

Once more M. Patrigent was on the wrong track, owing to Fanferlot's incomplete information.

He had hoped that Prosper would betray himself by uttering some passionate retort when thus wounded to the quick; but he remained impassible. Of all the judge said to him his mind dwelt upon only one word—Caldas, the name of the poor travelling agent who had killed himself. "At any rate," insisted M. Patrigent, "you will confess that this girl has caused your ruin."

"I cannot confess that, *monsieur*, for it is not true."

"Yet she is the occasion of your extravagance. Listen." The judge here drew a bill from the file of papers. "During December you paid her dressmaker, Van Klopen, for two walking dresses, nine hundred *francs*; one evening dress, seven hundred *francs*; one *domino*, trimmed with lace, four hundred *francs*."

"I spent this money cheerfully, but nevertheless I was not especially attached to her."

M. Patrigent shrugged his shoulders.

"You cannot deny the evidence," said he. "I suppose you will also say that it was not for this girl's sake you ceased spending your evenings at M. Fauvel's?"

"I swear that she was not the cause of my ceasing to visit M. Fauvel's family."

"Then why did you cease, suddenly, your attentions to a young lady whom you confidently expected to marry, and whose hand you had written to your father to demand for you?"

"I had reasons which I cannot reveal," answered Prosper with emotion.

The judge breathed freely; at last he had discovered a vulnerable point in the prisoner's armour.

"Did Mademoiselle Madeleine banish you?"

Prosper was silent, and seemed agitated.

"Speak," said M. Patrigent; "I must tell you that this circumstance is one of the most important in your case."

"Whatever the cost may be, on this subject I am compelled to keep silence."

"Beware of what you do; justice will not be satisfied with scruples of conscience."

M. Patrigent waited for an answer. None came.

"You persist in your obstinacy, do you? Well, we will go on to the next question. You have, during the last year, spent fifty thousand *francs*. Your resources are at an end, and your credit is exhausted; to continue your mode of life was impossible. What did you intend to do?"

"I had no settled plan. I thought it might last as long as it would, and then I—"

"And then you would draw from the safe!"

"Ah, *monsieur*, if I were guilty, I should not be here! I should never have been such a fool as to return to the bank; I should have fled."

M. Patrigent could not restrain a smile of satisfaction, and exclaimed:

"Exactly the argument I expected you to use. You showed your shrewdness precisely by staying to face the storm, instead of flying the country. Several recent suits have taught dishonest cashiers that flight abroad is dangerous. Railways travel fast, but telegrams travel faster. A French thief can be arrested in London within forty-eight hours after his description has been telegraphed. Even America is no longer a refuge. You remained prudently and wisely, saying to yourself, 'I will manage to avoid suspicion; and, even if I am found out, I shall be free again after three or five years' seclusion, with a large fortune to enjoy.' Many people would sacrifice five years of their lives for three hundred and fifty thousand *francs*."

"But *monsieur*, had I calculated in the manner you describe, I should not have been content with three hundred and fifty thousand *francs*; I should have waited for an opportunity to steal half a million. I often have that sum in charge."

"Oh! it is not always convenient to wait."

Prosper was buried in deep thought for some minutes.

"*Monsieur*," he finally said, "there is one detail I forgot to mention before, and it may be of importance."

"Explain, if you please."

"The office messenger whom I sent to the Bank of France for the money must have seen me tie up the bundle, and put it away in the safe. At any rate, he knows that I left the bank before he did."

"Very well; the man shall be examined. Now you can return to your cell; and once more I advise you to consider the consequences of your persistent denial."

M. Patrigent thus abruptly dismissed Prosper because he wished to immediately act upon this last piece of information.

"Sigault," said he as soon as Prosper had left the room, "is not this Antonin the man who was excused from testifying because he sent a doctor's certificate declaring him too ill to appear?"

"It is, *monsieur*."

"Where doe he live?"

"Fanferlot says he was so ill that he was taken to the hospital—the Dubois Hospital."

"Very well. I am going to examine him today, this very hour. Take your pen and paper, and send for a carriage."

It was some distance from the Palais de Justice to the Dubois Hospital; but the cabman, urged by the promise of a large fee, made his sorry jades fly as if they were blooded horses.

Would Antonin be able to answer any questions?

The physician in charge of the hospital said that, although the man suffered horribly from a broken knee, his mind was perfectly clear.

"That being the case, *monsieur*," said the judge, "I wish to examine him, and desire that no one be admitted while he makes his deposition."

"Oh! you will not be intruded upon, *monsieur*; his room contains four beds, but they are just now unoccupied."

When Antonin saw the judge enter, followed by a little wizened man in black, with a portfolio under his arm, he at once knew what he had come for.

"Ah," he said, "*monsieur* comes to see me about M. Bertomy's case?"

"Precisely."

M. Patrigent remained standing by the sick-bed while Sigault arranged his papers on a little table.

In answer to the usual questions, the messenger swore that he was named Antonin Poche, was forty years old, born at Cadaujac (Gironde), and was unmarried.

"Now," said the judge, "are you well enough to clearly answer any questions I may put?"

"Certainly, *monsieur*."

"Did you, on the 27th of February, go to the Bank of France for the three hundred and fifty thousand *francs* that were stolen?"

"Yes, *monsieur*."

"At what hour did you return with the money?"

"It must have been five o'clock when I got back."

"Do you remember what M. Bertomy did when you handed him the notes? Now, do not be in a hurry; think before you answer."

"Let me see: first he counted the notes, and made them into four packages; then he put them in the safe; and then—it seems to me—and then he locked the safe; and, yes, I am not mistaken, he went out!"

He uttered these last words so quickly, that, forgetting his knee, he half started up, but, with a cry of pain, sank back in bed.

"Are you sure of what you say?" asked the judge.

M. Patrigent's solemn tone seemed to frighten Antonin.

"Sure?" he replied with marked hesitation, "I would bet my head on it, yet I am not sure!"

It was impossible for him to be more decided in his answers. He had been frightened. He already imagined himself in difficulty, and for a trifle would have retracted everything.

But the effect was already produced; and when they retired M. Patrigent said to Sigault:

"This is a very important piece of evidence."

Chapter 6

The Archangel Hotel, Madame Gypsy's asylum, was the most elegant building on the Quai St. Michel.

A person who pays her fortnight's board in advance is treated with consideration at this hotel.

Madame Alexandre, who had been a handsome woman, was now stout, laced till she could scarcely breathe, always over-dressed, and fond of wearing a number of flashy gold chains around her fat neck.

She had bright eyes and white teeth; but, alas, a red nose. Of all her weaknesses, and Heaven knows she had indulged in every variety, only one remained; she loved a good dinner, washed down with plenty of good wine.

She also loved her husband; and, about the time M. Patrigent was leaving the hospital, she began to be worried that her "little man" had not returned to dinner. She was about to sit down without him, when the hotel-boy cried out:

"Here is *monsieur*."

And Fanferlot appeared in person.

Three years before, Fanferlot had kept a little office of secret intelligence; Madame Alexandre was a trader without a license in perfumery and toilet articles, and, finding it necessary to watch some of her suspicious customers, engaged Fanferlot's services; this was the origin of their acquaintance.

If they went through the marriage ceremony for the good of the mayoralty and the church, it was because they imagined it would, like a baptism, wash out the sins of the past.

Upon this momentous day, Fanferlot gave up his secret intelligence office, and entered the police, where he had already been occasionally employed, and Madame Alexandre retired from trade.

Uniting their savings, they hired and furnished the "Archangel," which they were now carrying on prosperously well, esteemed by their neighbours, who were ignorant of Fanferlot's connection with the police force.

"Why, how late you are, my little man!" she exclaimed, as she dropped her knife and fork, and rushed forward to embrace him.

He received her caresses with an air of abstraction.

"My back is broken," he said. "I have been the whole day playing billiards with Evariste, M. Fauvel's valet, and allowed him to win as often as he wished, a man who does not know what 'the pool' is! I became acquainted with him yesterday, and now I am his best friend. If I wish to enter M. Fauvel's service in Antonin's place, I can rely upon M. Evariste's good word."

"What, you be an office messenger? you?"

"Of course I would. How else am I to get an opportunity of studying my characters, if I am not on the spot to watch them all the time?"

"Then the valet gave you no news?"

"He gave me none that I could make use of, and yet I turned him inside out, like a glove. This banker is a remarkable man; you don't often meet with one of his sort nowadays. Evariste says he has not a single vice, not even a little defect by which his valet could gain ten *sous*. He neither smokes, drinks, nor plays; in fact, he is a saint. He is worth millions, and lives as respectably and quietly as a grocer. He is devoted to his wife, adores his children, is lavishly hospitable, and seldom goes into society."

"Then his wife is young?"

"She must be about fifty."

Madame Alexandre reflected a minute, then asked:

"Did you inquire about the other members of the family?"

"Certainly. The younger son is in the army. The elder son, Lucien, lives with his parents, and is as proper as a young lady; so good, indeed, that he is stupid."

"And what about the niece?"

"Evariste could tell me nothing about her."

Madame Alexandre shrugged her fat shoulders.

"If you have discovered nothing, it is because there is nothing to be discovered. Still, do you know what I would do, if I were you?"

"Tell me."

"I would consult with M. Lecoq."

Fanferlot jumped up as if he had been shot. "Now, that's pretty advice! Do you want me to lose my place? M. Lecoq does not suspect that I have anything to do with the case, except to obey his orders."

"Nobody told you to let him know you were investigating it on your own account. You can consult him with an air of indifference, as if you were not at all interested; and, after you have got his opinion, you can take advantage of it."

The detective weighed his wife's words, and then said:

"Perhaps you are right; yet M. Lecoq is so devilishly shrewd, that he might see through me."

"Shrewd!" echoed Madame Alexandre, "shrewd! All of you at the police office say that so often, that he has gained his reputation by it: you are just as sharp as he is."

"Well, we will see. I will think the matter over; but, in the meantime, what does the girl say?"

The "girl" was Madame Nina Gypsy.

In taking up her abode at the Archangel, the poor girl thought she was following good advice; and, as Fanferlot had never appeared in her presence since, she was still under the impression that she had obeyed a friend of Prosper's. When she received her summons from M. Patrigent, she admired the wonderful skill of the police in discovering her hiding-place; for she had established herself at the hotel under a false, or rather her true name, Palmyre Chocareille.

Artfully questioned by her inquisitive landlady, she had, without any mistrust, confided her history to her.

Thus Fanferlot was able to impress the judge with the idea of his being a skilful detective, when he pretended to have discovered all this information from a variety of sources.

"She is still upstairs," answered Madame Alexandre. "She suspects nothing; but to keep her in her present ignorance becomes daily more difficult. I don't know what the judge told her, but she came home quite beside herself with anger. She wanted to go and make a fuss at M. Fauvel's; then she wrote a letter which she told Jean to post for her; but I kept it to show you."

"What!" interrupted Fanferlot, "you have a letter, and did not tell me before? Perhaps it contains the clew to the mystery. Give it to me, quick."

Obeying her husband, Madame Alexandre opened a little cupboard, and took out a letter which she handed to him.

"Here, take it," she said, "and be satisfied."

Considering that she used to be a chambermaid, Palmyre Chocareille, since become Madame Gypsy, wrote a good letter.

It bore the following address, written in a free, flowing hand:

For M. L. De Clameran,
Forge-Master, Hotel du Louvre.
To be handed to M. Raoul de Lagors.
(In great haste.)

"Oh, ho!" said Fanferlot, accompanying his exclamation with a little whistle, as was his habit when he thought he had made a grand discovery. "Oh, ho!"

"Do you intend to open it?" questioned Madame Alexandre.

"A little bit," said Fanferlot, as he dexterously opened the envelope.

Madame Alexandre leaned over her husband's shoulder, and they both read the following letter:

> Monsieur Raoul—
>
> Prosper is in prison, accused of a robbery which he never committed. I wrote to you three days ago.

"What!" interrupted Fanferlot, "this silly girl wrote, and I never saw the letter?"

"But, little man, she must have posted it herself, the day she went to the Palais de Justice."

"Very likely," said Fanferlot propitiated. He continued reading:

> I wrote to you three days ago, and have no reply. Who will help Prosper if his best friends desert him? If you don't answer this letter, I shall consider myself released from a certain promise, and without scruple will tell Prosper of the conversation I overheard between you and M. de Clameran. But I can count on you, can I not? I shall expect you at the Archangel day after tomorrow, between twelve and four.
>
> Nina Gypsy

The letter read, Fanferlot at once proceeded to copy it.

"Well!" said Madame Alexandre, "what do you think?"

Fanferlot was delicately resealing the letter when the door of the hotel office was abruptly opened, and the boy twice whispered, "*Pst! Pst!*"

Fanferlot rapidly disappeared into a dark closet. He had barely time to close the door before Madame Gypsy entered the room.

The poor girl was sadly changed. She was pale and hollow-cheeked, and her eyes were red with weeping.

On seeing her, Madame Alexandre could not conceal her surprise.

"Why, my child, you are not going out?"

"I am obliged to do so, *madame*; and I come to ask you to tell anyone that may call during my absence to wait until I return."

"But where in the world are you going at this hour, sick as you are?"

For a moment Madame Gypsy hesitated.

"Oh," she said, "you are so kind that I am tempted to confide in you; read this note which a messenger just now brought to me."

"What!" cried Madame Alexandre perfectly aghast: "a messenger enter my house, and go up to your room!"

"Is there anything surprising in that?"

"Oh, oh, no! nothing surprising."

And in a tone loud enough to be heard in the closet she read the note:

> A friend of Prosper who can neither receive you, nor present himself at your house, is very anxious to speak to you. Be in the stage-office opposite the Saint Jacques tower, tonight at nine precisely, and the writer will approach, and tell you what he has to say.
>
> I have appointed this public place for the rendezvous so as to relieve your mind of all fear.

"And you are going to this rendezvous?"

"Certainly, *madame*."

"But it is imprudent, foolish; it is a snare to entrap you."

"It makes no difference," interrupted Gypsy. "I am so unfortunate already that I have nothing more to dread. Any change would be a relief."

And, without waiting to hear any more, she went out. The door had scarcely closed upon Madame Gypsy, before Fanferlot bounced out of the closet.

The mild detective was white with rage, and swore violently.

"What is the meaning of this?" he cried. "Am I to stand by and have people walking over the Archangel, as if it were a public street?"

Madame Alexandre stood trembling, and dared not speak.

"Was ever such impudence heard of before!" he continued. "A messenger comes into my house, and goes upstairs without being seen by anybody! I will look into this. And the idea of you, Madame Alexandre, you, a sensible woman, being idiotic enough to persuade that little viper not to keep the appointment!"

"But, my dear—"

"Had you not sense enough to know that I would follow her, and discover what she is attempting to conceal? Come, make haste, and help me, so that she won't recognise me."

In a few minutes Fanferlot was completely disguised by a thick beard, a wig, and one of those long linen blouses worn by dishonest workmen, who go about seeking labour, and, at the same time, hoping they may not find any.

"Have you your handcuffs?" asked the solicitous Madame Alexandre.

"Yes, yes: make haste and put that letter to M. de Clameran in the post-office, and—and keep good watch."

And without waiting for his wife's reply, who cried out, "Good luck!" Fanferlot darted into the street.

Madame Gypsy had ten minutes' start of him; but he ran up the street he knew she must have taken, and overtook her near the Change Bridge.

She was walking with the uncertain gait of a person who, impatient to be at a rendezvous, has started too soon, and is obliged to occupy the intervening time; she would walk very rapidly, then retrace her footsteps, and proceed slowly.

On Chatelet Place she strolled up and down several times, read the theatre-bills, and finally took a seat on a bench. One minute before a quarter of nine, she entered the stage-office, and sat down.

A moment after, Fanferlot entered; but, as he feared that Madame Gypsy might recognise him in spite of his heavy beard, he took a seat at the opposite end of the room, in a dark corner.

"Singular place for a conversation," he thought, as he watched the young woman. "Who in the world could have made this appointment in a stage-office? Judging from her evident curiosity and uneasiness, I could swear she has not the faintest idea for whom she is waiting."

Meanwhile, the office was gradually filling with people. Every minute a man would shriek out the destination of an omnibus which had just arrived, and the bewildered passengers would rush in to get tickets, and inquire when the omnibus would leave.

As each newcomer entered, Gypsy would tremble, and Fanferlot would say, "This is he!"

Finally, as the Hotel-de-Ville clock was striking nine, a man entered, and, without going to the ticket-window, walked directly up to Gypsy, bowed, and took a seat beside her.

He was a medium-sized man, rather stout, with a crimson face, and fiery-red whiskers. His dress was that of a well-to-do merchant, and there was nothing in his manner or appearance to excite attention.

Fanferlot watched him eagerly.

"Well, my friend," he said to himself, "in future I shall recognise you, no matter where we meet; and this very evening I will find out who you are."

Despite his intent listening, he could not hear a word spoken by the stranger or Gypsy. All he could do was to judge by their pantomime and countenances, what the subject of their conversation might be.

When the stout man bowed and spoke to her, the girl looked so surprised that it was evident she had never seen him before. When he sat down by her, and said a few words, she jumped up with a frightened look, as if seeking to escape. A single word and look made her resume her seat. Then, as the stout man went on talking, Gypsy's attitude betrayed great apprehension. She positively refused to do something; then suddenly she seemed to consent, when he stated a good reason for her so doing. At one moment she appeared ready to weep, and the next her pretty face was illumined by a bright smile. Finally, she shook hands with him, as if she was confirming a promise.

"What can all that mean?" said Fanferlot to himself, as he sat in his dark corner, biting his nails. "What an idiot I am to have stationed myself so far off!"

He was thinking how he could manage to approach nearer without arousing their suspicions, when the fat man arose, offered his arm to Madame Gypsy, who accepted it without hesitation, and together they walked toward the door.

They were so engrossed with each other, that Fanferlot thought he could, without risk, follow them; and it was well he did; for the crowd was dense outside, and he would soon have lost them.

Reaching the door, he saw the stout man and Gypsy cross the pavement, approach a hackney-coach, and enter it.

"Very good," muttered Fanferlot, "I've got them now. There is no use of hurrying any more."

While the coachman was gathering up his reins, Fanferlot prepared his legs; and, when the coach started, he followed in a brisk trot, determined upon following it to the end of the earth.

The cab went up the Boulevard Sebastopol. It went pretty fast; but it was not for nothing that Fanferlot had won the name of "Squirrel." With his elbows glued to his sides, and holding his breath, he ran on.

By the time he had reached the Boulevard St. Denis, he began to get breathless, and stiff from a pain in his side. The cabman abruptly turned into the Rue Faubourg St. Martin.

But Fanferlot, who, at eight years of age, had been familiar with every street in Paris, was not to be baffled: he was a man of resources. He seized the springs of the coach, raised himself up by the strength of his wrists, and hung on behind, with his legs resting on the axle-tree of the back wheels. He was not quite comfortable, but then, he no longer ran the risk of being distanced.

"Now," he chuckled, behind his false beard, "you may drive as fast as you please, M. Cabby."

The man whipped up his horses, and drove furiously along the hilly street of the Faubourg St. Martin.

Finally the cab stopped in front of a wine-store, and the driver jumped down from his seat, and went in.

The detective also left his uncomfortable post, and crouching in a doorway, waited for Gypsy and her companion to get out, with the intention of following closely upon their heels.

Five minutes passed, and still there were no signs of them.

"What can they be doing all this time?" grumbled the detective.

With great precautions, he approached the cab, and peeped in.

Oh, cruel deception! it was empty!

Fanferlot felt as if someone had thrown a bucket of ice-water over him; he remained rooted to the spot with his mouth stretched, the picture of blank bewilderment.

He soon recovered his wits sufficiently to burst forth in a volley of oaths, loud enough to rattle all the window-panes in the neighbourhood.

"Tricked!" he said, "fooled! Ah! but won't I make them pay for this!"

In a moment his quick mind had run over the gamut of possibilities, probable and improbable.

"Evidently," he muttered, "this fellow and Gypsy entered one door, and got out of the other; the trick is simple enough. If they resorted to it, 'tis because they feared being watched. If they feared being watched, they have uneasy consciences: therefore—"

He suddenly interrupted his monologue as the idea struck him that he had better attempt to find out something from the driver.

Unfortunately, the driver was in a very surly mood, and not only refused to answer, but shook his whip in so threatening a manner that Fanferlot deemed it prudent to beat a retreat.

"Oh, Lord," he muttered, "perhaps he and the driver are one and the same!"

But what could he do now, at this time of night? He could not imagine. He walked dejectedly back to the quay, and it was half-past eleven when he reached his own door.

"Has the little fool returned?" he inquired of Madame Alexandre, the instant she opened the door for him.

"No; but here are two large bundles which have come for her."

Fanferlot hastily opened the bundles.

They contained three calico dresses, some coarse shoes, and some linen caps.

"Well," said the detective in a vexed tone, "now she is going to disguise herself. Upon my word, I am getting puzzled! What can she be up to?"

When Fanferlot was sulkily walking down the Faubourg St. Martin, he had fully made up his mind that he would not tell his wife of his discomfiture.

But once at home, confronted with a new fact of a nature to negative all his conjectures, his vanity disappeared. He confessed everything—his hopes so nearly realised, his strange mischance, and his suspicions.

They talked the matter over, and finally decided that they would not go to bed until Madame Gypsy, from whom Madame Alexandre was determined to obtain an explanation of what had happened, returned. At one o'clock the worthy couple were about giving over all hope of her re-appearance, when they heard the bell ring.

Fanferlot instantly slipped into the closet, and Madame Alexandre remained in the office to received Gypsy.

"Here you are at last, my dear child!" she cried. "Oh, I have been so uneasy, so afraid lest some misfortune had happened!"

"Thanks for your kind interest, *madame*. Has a bundle been sent here for me?"

Poor Gypsy's appearance had strikingly changed; she was very sad, but not as before dejected. To her melancholy of the last few days, had succeeded a firm and generous resolution, which was betrayed in her sparkling eyes and resolute step.

"Yes, two bundles came for you; here they are. I suppose you saw M. Bertomy's friend?"

"Yes, *madame*; and his advice has so changed my plans, that, I regret to say, I must leave you tomorrow."

"Going away tomorrow! then something must have happened."

"Oh! nothing that would interest you, *madame*."

After lighting her candle at the gas-burner, Madame Gypsy said "Goodnight" in a very significant way, and left the room.

"And what do you think of that, Madame Alexandre?" questioned Fanferlot, emerging from his hiding-place.

"It is incredible! This girl writes to M. de Clameran to meet her here, and then does not wait for him."

"She evidently mistrusts us; she knows who I am."

"Then this friend of the cashier must have told her."

"Nobody knows who told her. I shall end by believing that I am among a gang of thieves. They think I am on their track, and are trying to escape me. I should not be at all surprised if this little rogue has the money herself, and intends to run off with it tomorrow."

"That is not my opinion; but listen to me: you had better take my advice, and consult M. Lecoq."

Fanferlot meditated awhile, then exclaimed.

"Very well; I will see him, just for your satisfaction; because I know that, if I have discovered nothing, neither has he. But, if he undertakes to be domineering, it won't do; for, if he shows his insolence to me, *I* will make him know his place!"

Notwithstanding this brave speech, the detective passed an uneasy night, and at six o'clock the next morning he was up—it was necessary to rise very early if he wished to catch M. Lecoq at home—and, refreshed by a cup of strong coffee, he directed his steps toward the dwelling of the celebrated detective.

Fanferlot the Squirrel certainly was not afraid of his patron, as he called him; for he started out with his nose in the air, and his hat cocked on one side.

But by the time he reached the Rue Montmartre, where M. Lecoq lived, his courage had vanished; he pulled his hat over his eyes, and hung his head, as if looking for relief among the paving-stones. He slowly ascended the steps, pausing several times, and looking around as if he would like to fly.

Finally he reached the third floor, and stood before a door decorated with the arms of the famous detective—a cock, the symbol of vigilance—and his heart failed him so that he had scarcely the courage to ring the bell.

The door was opened by Janouille, M. Lecoq's old servant, who had very much the manner and appearance of a grenadier. She was as faithful to her master as a watch-dog, and always stood ready to attack anyone who did not treat him with the august respect which she considered his due.

"Well, M. Fanferlot," she said, "you come in time for once in your life. Your patron wants to see you."

Upon this announcement, Fanferlot was seized with a violent desire to retreat. By what chance could Lecoq want anything of him?

While he thus hesitated, Janouille seized him by the arm, and pulled him in, saying:

"Do you want to take root there? Come along, your patron is

waiting for you."

In the middle of a large room curiously furnished, half library and half green-room, was seated at a desk the same person with gold spectacles, who had said to Prosper at the police-office, "Have courage."

This was M. Lecoq in his official character.

Upon Fanferlot's entrance, as he advanced respectfully, bowing till his backbone was a perfect curve, M. Lecoq laid down his pen, and said, looking sharply at him:

"Ah, here you are, young man. Well, it seems that you haven't made much progress in the Bertomy case."

"Why," murmured Fanferlot, "you know—"

"I know that you have muddled everything until you can't see your way out; so that you are ready to give up."

"But, M. Lecoq, it was not I—"

M. Lecoq arose, and walked up and down the room: suddenly he confronted Fanferlot, and said, in a tone of scornful irony:

"What would you think, Master Squirrel, of a man who abuses the confidence of those who employ him, who reveals just enough to lead the prosecution on the wrong scent, who sacrifices to his own foolish vanity the cause of justice and the liberty of an unfortunate man?"

Fanferlot started back with a frightened look.

"I should say," he stammered, "I should say—"

"You would say this man ought to be punished, and dismissed from his employment; and you are right. The less a profession is honoured, the more honourable should those be who belong to it. And yet you have been false to yours. Ah! Master Fanferlot, we are ambitious, and we try to make the police force serve our own views! We let Justice stray her way, and we go ours. One must be a more cunning bloodhound than you are, my friend, to be able to hunt without a huntsman. You are too self-reliant by half."

"But, patron, I swear—"

"Silence! Do you pretend to say that you did your duty, and told all to the judge of instruction? Whilst others were informing against the cashier, you undertook to inform against the banker. You watched his movements: you became intimate with his valet."

Was M. Lecoq really angry, or pretending to be? Fanferlot, who knew him well, was puzzled to know whether all this indignation was real.

"If you were only skilful," he continued, "but no: you wish to be master, and you are not fit to be a journeyman."

"You are right, patron," said Fanferlot, piteously, for he saw that it was useless for him to deny anything. "But how could I go about an affair like this, where there was not even a trace or sign to start from?"

M. Lecoq shrugged his shoulders.

"You are an ass! Why, don't you know that on the very day you were sent for with the commissary to verify the robbery, you held—I do not say certainly, but very probably held—in your great stupid hands the means of knowing which key had been used when the money was stolen?"

"How! What!"

"You want to know, do you? I will tell you. Do you remember the scratch you discovered on the safe-door? You were so struck by it, that you exclaimed directly you saw it. You carefully examined it, and were convinced that it was a fresh scratch, only a few hours old. You thought, and rightly too, that this scratch was made at the time of the theft. Now, with what was it made? Evidently with a key. That being the case, you should have asked for the keys both of the banker and the cashier. One of them would have had some particles of the hard green paint sticking to it."

Fanferlot listened with open mouth to this explanation. At the last words, he violently slapped his forehead with his hand, and cried out:

"Imbecile! Imbecile!"

"You have rightly named yourself," said M. Lecoq. "Imbecile! This proof stares you right in the face, and you don't see it! This scratch is the sole and only clew to work the case upon, and you must go and lose the traces of it. If I find the guilty party, it will be by means of this scratch; and I am determined that I will find him."

At a distance the Squirrel very bravely abused and defied M. Lecoq; but, in his presence, he yielded to the influence which this extraordinary man exercised upon all who approached him.

This exact information, these minute details of all his secret movements, and even thoughts, so upset his mind that he could not think where and how M. Lecoq had obtained them. Finally he said, humbly:

"You must have been looking up this case, patron?"

"Probably I have; but I am not infallible, and may have overlooked some important evidence. Take a seat, and tell me all you know."

M. Lecoq was not the man to be hoodwinked, so Fanferlot told the exact truth, a rare thing for him to do. However as he reached the end of his statement, a feeling of mortified vanity prevented his telling how he had been fooled by Gypsy and the stout man.

Unfortunately for poor Fanferlot, M. Lecoq was always fully informed on every subject in which he interested himself.

"It seems to me, Master Squirrel, that you have forgotten something. How far did you follow the empty coach?"

Fanferlot blushed, and hung his head like a guilty school-boy.

"Oh, patron!" he cried, "and you know about that too! How could you have—"

But a sudden idea flashed across his brain: he stopped short, bounded off his chair, and cried:

"Oh! I know now: you were the large gentleman with red whiskers."

His surprise gave so singular an expression to his face that M. Lecoq could not restrain a smile.

"Then it was you," continued the bewildered detective; "you were the large gentleman at whom I stared, so as to impress his appearance upon my mind, and I never recognised you! Patron, you would make a superb actor, if you would go on the stage; but I was disguised, too—very well disguised."

"Very poorly disguised; it is only just to you that I should let you know what a failure it was, Fanferlot. Do you think that a heavy beard and a blouse are a sufficient transformation? The eye is the thing to be changed—the eye! The art lies in being able to change the eye. That is the secret."

This theory of disguise explained why the lynx-eyed Lecoq never appeared at the police-office without his gold spectacles.

"Then, patron," said Fanferlot, clinging to his idea, "you have been more successful than Madame Alexandre; you have made the little girl confess? You know why she leaves the Archangel, why she does not wait for M. de Clameran, and why she bought calico dresses?"

"She is following my advice."

"That being the case," said the detective dejectedly, "there is nothing left for me to do, but to acknowledge myself an ass."

"No, Squirrel," said M. Lecoq, kindly, "you are not an ass. You merely did wrong in undertaking a task beyond your capacity. Have you progressed one step since you started this affair? No. That shows that, although you are incomparable as a lieutenant, you do not possess the qualities of a general. I am going to present you with an aphorism; remember it, and let it be your guide in the future: *A man can shine in the second rank, who would be totally eclipsed in the first.*"

Never had Fanferlot seen his patron so talkative and good-natured.

Finding his deceit discovered, he had expected to be overwhelmed with a storm of anger; whereas he had escaped with a little shower that had cooled his brain. Lecoq's anger disappeared like one of those heavy clouds which threaten in the horizon for a moment, and then are suddenly swept away by a gust of wind.

But this unexpected affability made Fanferlot feel uneasy. He was afraid that something might be concealed beneath it.

"Do you know who the thief is, patron?"

"I know no more than you do, Fanferlot; and you seem to have made up your mind, whereas I am still undecided. You declare the cashier to be innocent, and the banker guilty. I don't know whether you are right or wrong. I started after you, and have only reached the preliminaries of my search. I am certain of but one thing, and that is, that a scratch was on the safe-door. That scratch is my starting-point."

As he spoke, M. Lecoq took from his desk and unrolled an immense sheet of drawing-paper.

On this paper was photographed the door of M. Fauvel's safe. The impression of every detail was perfect. There were the five movable buttons with the engraved letters, and the narrow, projecting brass lock: The scratch was indicated with great exactness.

"Now," said M. Lecoq, "here is our scratch. It runs from top to bottom, starting from the hole of the lock, diagonally, and, observe, from left to right; that is to say, it terminates on the side next to the private staircase leading to the banker's apartments. Although very deep at the keyhole, it ends off in a scarcely perceptible mark."

"Yes, patron, I see all that."

"Naturally you thought that this scratch was made by the person who took the money. Let us see if you were right. I have here a little iron box, painted with green varnish like M. Fauvel's safe; here it is. Take a key, and try to scratch it."

"The deuce take it!" he said after several attempts, "this paint is awfully hard to move!"

"Very hard, my friend, and yet that on the safe is still harder and thicker. So you see the scratch you discovered could not have been made by the trembling hand of a thief letting the key slip."

"*Sapristi*!" exclaimed Fanferlot, stupefied: "I never should have thought of that. It certainly required great force to make the deep scratch on the safe."

"Yes, but how was that force employed? I have been racking my brain for three days, and only yesterday did I come to a conclusion.

Let us examine together, and see if our conjectures present enough chances of probability to establish a starting-point."

M. Lecoq abandoned the photograph, and, walking to the door communicating with his bedroom, took the key from the lock, and, holding it in his hand, said:

"Come here, Fanferlot, and stand by my side: there; very well. Now suppose that I want to open this door, and you don't want me to open it; when you see me about to insert the key, what would be your first impulse?"

"To put my hands on your arm, and draw it toward me so as to prevent your introducing the key."

"Precisely so. Now let us try it; go on." Fanferlot obeyed; and the key held by M. Lecoq, pulled aside from the lock, slipped along the door, and traced upon it a diagonal scratch, from top to bottom, the exact reproduction of the one in the photograph.

"Oh, oh, oh!" exclaimed Fanferlot in three different tones of admiration, as he stood gazing in a reverie at the door.

"Do you begin to understand now?" asked M. Lecoq.

"Understand, patron? Why, a child could understand it now. Ah, what a man you are! I see the scene as if I had been present. Two persons were present at the robbery; one wished to take the money, the other wished to prevent its being taken. That is clear, that is certain."

Accustomed to triumphs of this sort, M. Lecoq was much amused at Fanferlot's enthusiasm.

"There you go off, half-primed again," he said, good-humouredly: "you regard as sure proof a circumstance which may be accidental, and at the most only probable."

"No, patron, no! a man like you could not be mistaken: doubt no longer exists."

"That being the case, what deductions would you draw from our discovery?"

"In the first place, it proves that I am correct in thinking the cashier innocent."

"How so?"

"Because, at perfect liberty to open the safe whenever he wished to do so, it is not likely that he would have brought a witness when he intended to commit the theft."

"Well reasoned, Fanferlot. But on this supposition the banker would be equally innocent: reflect a little."

Fanferlot reflected, and all of his animation vanished.

"You are right," he said in a despairing tone. "What can be done now?"

"Look for the third rogue, or rather the real rogue, the one who opened the safe, and stole the notes, and who is still at large, while others are suspected."

"Impossible, patron—impossible! Don't you know that M. Fauvel and his cashier had keys, and they only? And they always kept these keys in their pockets."

"On the evening of the robbery the banker left his key in the secretary."

"Yes; but the key alone was not sufficient to open the safe; the word also must be known."

M. Lecoq shrugged his shoulders impatiently.

"What was the word?" he asked.

"Gypsy."

"Which is the name of the cashier's *grisette*. Now keep your eyes open. The day you find a man sufficiently intimate with Prosper to be aware of all the circumstances connected with this name, and at the same time on a footing with the Fauvel family which would give him the privilege of entering M. Fauvel's chamber, then, and not until then, will you discover the guilty party. On that day the problem will be solved."

Self-sufficient and vain, like all famous men, M. Lecoq had never had a pupil, and never wished to have one. He worked alone, because he hated assistants, wishing to share neither the pleasures of success nor the pain of defeat.

Thus Fanferlot, who knew his patron's character, was surprised to hear him giving advice, who heretofore had only given orders.

He was so puzzled, that in spite of his pre-occupation he could not help betraying his surprise.

"Patron," he ventured to say, "you seem to take a great interest in this affair, you have so deeply studied it."

M. Lecoq started nervously, and replied, frowning:

"You are too curious, Master Squirrel; be careful that you do not go too far. Do you understand?"

Fanferlot began to apologise.

"That will do," interrupted M. Lecoq. "If I choose to lend you a helping hand, it is because it suits my fancy to do so. It pleases me to be the head, and let you be the hand. Unassisted, with your pre-conceived ideas, you never would have found the culprit; if we two together don't find him, my name is not Lecoq."

"We shall certainly succeed if you interest yourself in the case."

"Yes, I am interested in it, and during the last four days I have discovered many important facts. But listen to me. I have reasons for not appearing in this affair. No matter what happens, I forbid your mentioning my name. If we succeed, all the success must be attributed to you. And, above all, don't try to find out what I choose to keep from you. Be satisfied with what explanations I give you. Now, be careful."

These conditions seemed quite to suit Fanferlot.

"I will obey your instructions, and be discreet."

"I shall rely upon you. Now, to begin, you must carry this photograph to the judge of instruction. I know M. Patrigent is much perplexed about this case. Explain to him, as if it were your own discovery, what I have just shown you; repeat for his benefit the scene we have acted, and I am convinced that this evidence will determine him to release the cashier. Prosper must be at liberty before I can commence my operations."

"Of course, patron, but must I let him know that I suspect anyone besides the banker or cashier?"

"Certainly. Justice must not be kept in ignorance of your intention of following up this affair. M. Patrigent will tell you to watch Prosper; you will reply that you will not lose sight of him. I myself will answer for his being in safe-keeping."

"Suppose he asks me about Gypsy?"

M. Lecoq hesitated for a moment.

"Tell him," he finally said, "that you persuaded her, in the interest of Prosper, to live in a house where she can watch someone whom you suspect."

Fanferlot was joyously picking up his hat to go, when M. Lecoq checked him by waving his hand, and said:

"I have not finished. Do you know how to drive a carriage and manage horses?"

"Why, patron, can you ask this of a man who used to be a rider in the Bouthor Circus?"

"Very well. As soon as the judge dismisses you, return home immediately, make yourself a wig and the complete dress of a valet; and, having dressed yourself, take this letter to the Agency on Delorme Street."

"But, patron—"

"There must be no but, my friend; the agent will send you to M. de Clameran, who is looking for a valet, his man having left him yesterday."

"Excuse me if I venture to suggest that you are making a mistake. This de Clameran is not the cashier's friend."

"Why do you always interrupt me?" said M. Lecoq imperiously. "Do what I tell you, and don't disturb your mind about the rest. De Clameran is not a friend of Prosper's, I know; but he is the friend and protector of Raoul de Lagors. Why so? Whence the intimacy of these two men of such different ages? That is what I must find out. I must also find out who this forge-master is who lives in Paris, and never goes to attend to his furnaces. A jolly fellow, who takes it into his head to live at the Hotel du Louvre, in the midst of a tumultuous, ever-changing crowd, is a fellow difficult to watch. Through you I will have an eye upon him. He has a carriage, you are to drive it; and you will soon be able to give me an account of his manner of life, and of the sort of people with whom he associates."

"You shall be obeyed, patron."

"Another thing. M. de Clameran is irritable and suspicious. You will be presented to him under the name of Joseph Dubois. He will demand your certificate of good character. Here are three, which state that you have lived with the Marquis de Sairmeuse and the Count de Commarin, and that you have just left the Baron de Wortschen, who went to Germany the other day. Now keep your eyes open; be careful of your dress and manners. Be polite, but not excessively so. And, above all things, don't be obsequious; it might arouse suspicion."

"I understand, patron. Where shall I report to you?"

"I will call on you every day. Until I tell you differently, don't step foot in this house; you might be followed. If anything important should happen, send a note to your wife, and she will inform me. Go, and be prudent."

The door closed on Fanferlot as M. Lecoq passed into his bedroom.

In the twinkling of an eye he had divested himself of the appearance of a police officer. He took off his stiff cravat and gold spectacles, and removed the close wig from his thick black hair. The official Lecoq had disappeared, leaving in his place the genuine Lecoq whom nobody knew—a handsome young man, with a bold, determined manner, and brilliant, piercing eyes.

But he only remained himself for an instant. Seated before a dressing-table covered with more cosmetics, paints, perfumes, false hair, and other unmentionable shams, than are to be found on the toilet-tables of our modern *belles*, he began to undo the work of nature, and make himself a new face.

He worked slowly, handling his brushes with great care. But in an hour he had accomplished one of his daily masterpieces. When he had finished, he was no longer Lecoq: he was the large gentleman with red whiskers, whom Fanferlot had failed to recognise.

"Well," he said, casting a last look in the mirror, "I have forgotten nothing: I have left nothing to chance. All my plans are fixed; and I shall make some progress today, provided the Squirrel does not waste time."

But Fanferlot was too happy to waste a minute. He did not run, he flew, toward the Palais de Justice. At last he was now able to convince someone that he, Fanferlot, was a man of wonderful perspicacity.

As to acknowledging that he was about to obtain a triumph with the ideas of another man, he never thought of it. It is generally in perfect good faith that the jackdaw struts in the peacock's feathers.

His hopes were not deceived. If the judge was not absolutely and fully convinced, he admired the ingenuity and shrewdness of the whole proceeding, and complimented the proud jackdaw upon his brilliancy.

"This decides me," he said, as he dismissed Fanferlot. "I will make out a favourable report today; and it is highly probable that the accused will be released tomorrow."

He began at once to write out one of these terrible decisions of "Not proven," which restores liberty, but not honour, to the accused man; which says that he is not guilty, but does not say he is innocent.

> Whereas there do not exist sufficient charges against the accused, Prosper Bertomy, in pursuance of Article 128 of the Criminal Code, we hereby declare that we find no grounds for prosecution against the aforesaid prisoner at this present time; and we order that he shall be released from the prison where he is confined, and set at liberty by the jailer, etc.

"Well," he said to the clerk, "here is another one of those crimes which justice cannot clear up. The mystery remains to be solved. This is another file to be stowed away among the archives of the record-office."

And with his own hand he wrote on the cover of the bundle of papers relating to Prosper's case, its number of rotation: *File No. 113*.

Chapter 7

Prosper had been languishing in his cell for nine days, when one

Thursday morning the jailer came to apprise him of the magistrate's decision. He was conducted before the officer who had searched him when he was arrested; and the contents of his pocket, his watch, penknife, and several little pieces of jewellery, were restored to him; then he was told to sign a large sheet of paper, which he did.

He was next led across a dark passage, and almost pushed through a door, which was abruptly shut upon him.

He found himself on the quay: he was alone; he was free.

Free! Justice had confessed her inability to convict him of the crime of which he was accused.

Free! He could walk about, he could breathe the pure air; but every door would be closed against him.

Only acquittal after due trial would restore him to his former position among men.

A decision of "Not proven" had left him covered with suspicion.

The torments inflicted by public opinion are more fearful than those suffered in a prison cell.

At the moment of his restoration to liberty, Prosper so cruelly suffered from the horror of his situation, that he could not repress a cry of rage and despair.

"I am innocent! God knows I am innocent!" he cried out. But of what use was his anger?

Two strangers, who were passing, stopped to look at him, and said, pityingly, "He is crazy."

The Seine was at his feet. A thought of suicide crossed his mind.

"No," he said, "no! I have not even the right to kill myself. No: I will not die until I have vindicated my innocence!"

Often, day and night, had Prosper repeated these words, as he walked his cell. With a heart filled with a bitter, determined thirst for vengeance, which gives a man the force and patience to destroy or wear out all obstacles in his way, he would say, "Oh! why am I not at liberty? I am helpless, caged up; but let me once be free!"

Now he was free; and, for the first time, he saw the difficulties of the task before him. For each crime, justice requires a criminal: he could not establish his own innocence without producing the guilty man; how find the thief so as to hand him over to the law?

Discouraged, but not despondent, he turned in the direction of his apartments. He was beset by a thousand anxieties. What had taken place during the nine days that he had been cut off from all intercourse with his friends? No news of them had reached him. He had heard no more of what was going on in the outside world, than if his secret cell had been a grave.

He slowly walked along the streets, with his eyes cast down dreading to meet some familiar face. He, who had always been so haughty, would now be pointed at with the finger of scorn. He would be greeted with cold looks and averted faces. Men would refuse to shake hands with him. He would be shunned by honest people, who have no patience with a thief.

Still, if he could count on only one true friend! Yes: he was sure of one. But what friend would believe him when his father, who should have been the last to suspect him, had refused to believe him?

In the midst of his sufferings, when he felt almost overwhelmed by the sense of his wretched, lonely condition, he thought of Gypsy.

He had never loved the poor girl: indeed, at times he almost hated her; but now he felt a longing to see her. He wished to be with her, because he knew that she loved him, and that nothing would make her believe him guilty; because he knew that a woman remains true and firm in her faith, and is always faithful in the hour of adversity, although she sometimes fails in prosperity.

On entering the Rue Chaptal, Prosper saw his own door, but hesitated to enter it.

He suffered from the timidity which an honest man always feels when he knows he is viewed with suspicion.

He dreaded meeting anyone whom he knew; yet he could not remain in the street. He entered.

When the porter saw him, he uttered an exclamation of glad surprise, and said:

"Ah, here you are at last, *monsieur.* I told everyone you would come out as white as snow; and, when I read in the papers that you were arrested for robbery, I said, 'My third-floor lodger a thief! Never would I believe such a thing, never!'"

The congratulations of this ignorant man were sincere, and offered from pure kindness of heart; but they impressed Prosper painfully, and he cut them short by abruptly asking:

"Madame of course has left: can you tell me where she has gone?"

"Dear me, no, *monsieur.* The day of your arrest, she sent for a hack, got into it with her trunks, and disappeared; and no one has seen or heard of her since."

This was another blow to the unhappy cashier.

"And where are my servants?"

"Gone, *monsieur*; your father paid and discharged them."

"I suppose you have my keys?"

"No, *monsieur*; when your father left here this morning at eight o'clock, he told me that a friend of his would take charge of your rooms until you should return. Of course you know who he is—a stout gentleman with red whiskers."

Prosper was stupefied. What could be the meaning of one of his father's friends being in his rooms? He did not, however, betray any surprise, but quietly said: "Yes: I know who it is."

He quickly ran up the stairs, and knocked at his door.

It was opened by his father's friend.

He had been accurately described by the porter. A fat man, with a red face, sensual lips, brilliant eyes, and of rather coarse manners, stood bowing to Prosper, who had never seen him before.

"Delighted to make your acquaintance, *monsieur*," said he to Prosper.

He seemed to be perfectly at home. On the table lay a book, which he had taken from the bookcase; and he appeared ready to do the honours of the house.

"I must say, *monsieur*," began Prosper.

"That you are surprised to find me here? So I suppose. Your father intended introducing me to you; but he was compelled to return to Beaucaire this morning; and let me add that he departed thoroughly convinced, as I myself am, that you never took a cent from M. Fauvel."

At this unexpected good news, Prosper's face lit up with pleasure.

"Here is a letter from your father, which I hope will serve as an introduction between us."

Prosper opened the letter; and as he read his eyes grew brighter, and a slight colour returned to his pale face.

When he had finished, he held out his hand to the large gentleman, and said:

"My father, *monsieur*, tells me you are his best friend; he advises me to have absolute confidence in you, and follow your counsel."

"Exactly. This morning your father said to me, 'Verduret'—that is my name—'Verduret, my son is in great trouble, he must be helped out.' I replied, 'I am ready,' and here I am to help you. Now the ice is broken, is it not? Then let us go to work at once. What do you intend to do?"

This question revived Prosper's slumbering rage. His eyes flashed.

"What do I intend to do?" he said, angrily: "what should I do but seek the villain who has ruined me?"

"So I supposed; but have you any hopes of success?"

"None; yet I shall succeed, because, when a man devotes his whole life to the accomplishment of an object, he is certain to achieve it."

"Well said, M. Prosper; and, to be frank, I fully expected that this would be your purpose. I have therefore already begun to think and act for you. I have a plan. In the first place, you will sell this furniture, and disappear from the neighbourhood."

"Disappear!" cried Prosper, indignantly, "disappear! Why, *monsieur*? Do you not see that such a step would be a confession of guilt, would authorize the world to say that I am hiding so as to enjoy undisturbed the stolen fortune?"

"Well, what then?" said the man with the red whiskers; "did you not say just now the sacrifice of your life is made? The skilful swimmer thrown into the river by malefactors is careful not to rise to the surface immediately: on the contrary, he plunges beneath, and remains there as long as his breath holds out. He comes up again at a great distance, and lands out of sight; then, when he is supposed to be dead, lost forever to the sight of man, he rises up and has his vengeance. You have an enemy? Some petty imprudence will betray him. But, while he sees you standing by on the watch, he will be on his guard."

It was with a sort of amazed submission that Prosper listened to this man, who, though a friend of his father, was an utter stranger to himself.

He submitted unconsciously to the ascendency of a nature so much more energetic and forcible than his own. In his helpless condition he was grateful for friendly assistance, and said:

"I will follow your advice, *monsieur*."

"I was sure you would, my dear friend. Let us reflect upon the course you should pursue. And remember that you will need every cent of the proceeds of the sale. Have you any ready money? no, but you must have some. Knowing that you would need it at once, I brought an upholsterer here; and he will give twelve thousand *francs* for everything excepting the pictures."

The cashier could not refrain from shrugging his shoulders, which M. Verduret observed.

"Well," said he, "it is rather hard, I admit, but it is a necessity. Now listen: you are the invalid, and I am the doctor charged to cure you; if I cut to the quick, you will have to endure it. It is the only way to save you."

"Cut away then, *monsieur*," answered Prosper.

"Well, we will hurry, for time passes. You have a friend, M. de Lagors?"

"Raoul? Yes, *monsieur*, he is an intimate friend."

"Now tell me, who is this fellow?"

The term "fellow" seemed to offend Prosper.

"M. de Lagors, *monsieur*," he said, haughtily, "is M. Fauvel's nephew; he is a wealthy young man, handsome, intelligent, cultivated, and the best friend I have."

"Hum!" said M. Verduret, "I shall be delighted to make the acquaintance of one adorned by so many charming qualities. I must let you know that I wrote him a note in your name asking him to come here, and he sent word that he would be here directly."

"What! do you suppose—"

"Oh, I suppose nothing! Only I must see this young man. Also, I have arranged and will submit to you a little plan of conversation—"

A ring at the front door interrupted M. Verduret.

"*Sacrebleu*! *adieu* to my plan; here he is! Where can I hide so as to hear and see?"

"There, in my bedroom; leave the door open and the curtain down."

A second ring was heard.

"Now remember, Prosper," said M. Verduret in a warning tone, "not one word to this man about your plans, or about me. Pretend to be discouraged, helpless, and undecided what to do."

And he disappeared behind the curtain, as Prosper ran to open the door.

Prosper's portrait of M. de Lagors had not been an exaggerated one. So handsome a face and manly a figure could belong only to a noble character.

Although Raoul said that he was twenty-four, he appeared to be not more than twenty. He had a superb figure, well knit and supple; a beautiful white brow, shaded by soft chestnut curly hair, soft blue eyes which beamed with frankness.

His first impulse was to throw himself into Prosper's arms.

"My poor, dear friend!" he said, "my poor Prosper!"

But beneath these affectionate demonstrations there was a certain constraint, which, if it escaped the cashier, was noticed by M. Verduret.

"Your letter, my dear Prosper," said Raoul, "made me almost ill, I was so frightened by it. I asked myself if you could have lost your mind. Then I left everything, to fly to your assistance; and here I am."

Prosper did not seem to hear him; he was pre-occupied about the letter which he had not written. What were its contents? Who was this stranger whose assistance he had accepted?

"You must not feel discouraged," continued M. de Lagors: "you are young enough to commence life anew. Your friends are still left to you. I have come to say to you, Rely upon me; I am rich, half of my fortune is at your disposal."

This generous offer, made at a moment like this with such frank simplicity, deeply touched Prosper.

"Thanks, Raoul," he said with emotion, "thank you! But unfortunately all the money in the world would be of no use now."

"Why so? What are you going to do? Do you propose to remain in Paris?"

"I know not, Raoul. I have made no plans yet. My mind is too confused for me to think."

"I will tell you what to do," replied Raoul quickly, "you must start afresh; until this mysterious robbery is explained you must keep away from Paris. It will never do for you to remain here."

"And suppose it never should be explained?"

"Only the more reason for your remaining in oblivion. I have been talking about you to de Clameran. 'If I were in Prosper's place,' he said, 'I would turn everything into money, and embark for America; there I would make a fortune, and return to crush with my millions those who have suspected me.'"

This advice offended Prosper's pride, but he said nothing. He was thinking of what the stranger had said to him.

"I will think it over," he finally forced himself to say. "I will see. I would like to know what M. Fauvel says."

"My uncle? I suppose you know that I have declined the offer he made me to enter his banking-house, and we have almost quarrelled. I have not set foot in his house for over a month; but I hear of him occasionally."

"Through whom?"

"Through your friend Cavaillon. My uncle, they say, is more distressed by this affair than you are. He does not attend to his business, and wanders about as if he had lost every friend on earth."

"And Madame Fauvel, and"—Prosper hesitated—"and Mademoiselle Madeleine, how are they?"

"Oh," said Raoul lightly, "my aunt is as pious as ever; she has mass said for the benefit of the sinner. As to my handsome, icy cousin, she cannot bring herself down to common matters, because she is entirely absorbed in preparing for the fancy ball to be given day after tomorrow by Mm. Jandidier. She has discovered, so one of her friends told me, a wonderful dressmaker, a stranger who has suddenly appeared from no one knows where, who is making a costume of Catherine de Medici's maid of honour; and it is to be a marvel of beauty."

Excessive suffering brings with it a sort of dull insensibility and stupor; and Prosper thought that there was nothing left to be inflicted upon him, and had reached that state of impassibility from which he never expected to be aroused, when this last remark of M. de Lagors made him cry out with pain:

"Madeleine! Oh, Madeleine!"

M. de Lagors, pretending not to have heard him, rose from his chair, and said:

"I must leave you now, my dear Prosper; on Saturday I will see these ladies at the ball, and will bring you news of them. Now, do have courage, and remember that, whatever happens, you have a friend in me."

Raoul shook Prosper's hand, closed the door after him, and hurried up the street, leaving Prosper standing immovable and overcome by disappointment.

He was aroused from his gloomy reverie by hearing the red-whiskered man say, in a bantering tone:

"So these are your friends."

"Yes," said Prosper with bitterness. "You heard him offer me half his fortune?"

M. Verduret shrugged his shoulders with an air of compassion.

"That was very stingy on his part," he said, "why did he not offer the whole? Offers cost nothing; although I have no doubt that this sweet youth would cheerfully give ten thousand *francs* to put the ocean between you and him."

"*Monsieur*! what reason?"

"Who knows? Perhaps for the same reason that he had not set foot in his uncle's house for a month."

"But that is the truth, *monsieur*, I am sure of it."

"Naturally," said M. Verduret with a provoking smile. "But," he continued with a serious air, "we have devoted enough time to this Adonis. Now, be good enough to change your dress, and we will go and call on M. Fauvel."

This proposal seemed to stir up all of Prosper's anger.

"Never!" he exclaimed with excitement, "no, never will I voluntarily set eyes on that wretch!"

This resistance did not surprise M. Verduret.

"I can understand your feelings toward him," said he, "but at the same time I hope you will change your mind. For the same reason that I wished to see M. de Lagors, do I wish to see M. Fauvel; it is necessary, you understand. Are you so very weak that you cannot put a constraint upon yourself for five minutes? I shall introduce myself as one of your relatives, and you need not open your lips."

"If it is positively necessary," said Prosper, "if—"

"It is necessary; so come on. You must have confidence, put on a brave face. Hurry and fix yourself up a little; it is getting late, and I am hungry. We will breakfast on our way there."

Prosper had hardly passed into his bedroom when the bell rang again. M. Verduret opened the door. It was the porter, who handed him a thick letter, and said:

"This letter was left this morning for M. Bertomy; I was so flustered when he came that I forgot to hand it to him. It is a very odd-looking letter; is it not, *monsieur*?"

It was indeed a most peculiar missive. The address was not written, but formed of printed letters, carefully cut from a book, and pasted on the envelope.

"Oh, ho! what is this?" cried M. Verduret; then turning toward the porter he cried, "Wait."

He went into the next room, and closed the door behind him; there he found Prosper, anxious to know what was going on.

"Here is a letter for you," said M. Verduret.

He at once tore open the envelope.

Some bank-notes dropped out; he counted them; there were ten.

Prosper's face turned purple.

"What does this mean?" he asked.

"We will read the letter and find out," replied M. Verduret.

The letter, like the address, was composed of printed words cut out and pasted on a sheet of paper.

It was short but explicit:

"My Dear Prosper—A friend, who knows the horror of your situation, sends you this succour. There is one heart, be assured, that shares your sufferings. Go away; leave France; you are young; the future is before you. Go, and may this money bring you happiness!"

As M. Verduret read the note, Prosper's rage increased. He was angry and perplexed, for he could not explain the rapidly succeeding events which were so calculated to mystify his already confused brain.

"Everybody wishes me to go away," he cried; "then there must be a conspiracy against me."

M. Verduret smiled with satisfaction.

"At last you begin to open your eyes, you begin to understand. Yes, there are people who hate you because of the wrong they have done you; there are people to whom your presence in Paris is a constant danger, and who will not feel safe till they are rid of you."

"But who are these people, *monsieur*? Tell me, who dares send this money?"

"If I knew, my dear Prosper, my task would be at an end, for then I would know who committed the robbery. But we will continue our searches. I have finally procured evidence which will sooner or later become convincing proof. I have heretofore only made deductions more or less probable; I now possess knowledge which proves that I was not mistaken. I walked in darkness: now I have a light to guide me."

As Prosper listened to M. Verduret's reassuring words, he felt hope arising in his breast.

"Now," said M. Verduret, "we must take advantage of this evidence, gained by the imprudence of our enemies, without delay. We will begin with the porter."

He opened the door and called out:

"I say, my good man, step here a moment."

The porter entered, looking very much surprised at the authority exercised over his lodger by this stranger.

"Who gave you this letter?" said M. Verduret.

"A messenger, who said he was paid for bringing it."

"Do you know him?"

"I know him well; he is the errand-runner who keeps his cart at the corner of the Rue Pigalle."

"Go and bring him here."

After the porter had gone, M. Verduret drew from his pocket his diary, and compared a page of it with the notes which he had spread over the table.

"These notes were not sent by the thief," he said, after an attentive examination of them.

"Do you think so, *monsieur*?"

"I am certain of it; that is, unless the thief is endowed with extraordinary penetration and forethought. One thing is certain: these ten thousand *francs* are not part of the three hundred and fifty thousand which were stolen from the safe."

"Yet," said Prosper, who could not account for this certainty on the part of his protector, "yet—"

"There is no doubt about it: I have the numbers of all the stolen notes."

"What! When even I did not have them?"

"But the bank did, fortunately. When we undertake an affair we must anticipate everything, and forget nothing. It is a poor excuse for a man to say, 'I did not think of it' when he commits some oversight. I thought of the bank."

If, in the beginning, Prosper had felt some repugnance about confiding in his father's friend, the feeling had now disappeared.

He understood that alone, scarcely master of himself, governed only by the inspirations of inexperience, never would he have the patient perspicacity of this singular man.

Verduret continued talking to himself, as if he had absolutely forgotten Prosper's presence:

"Then, as this package did not come from the thief, it can only come from the other person, who was near the safe at the time of the robbery, but could not prevent it, and now feels remorse. The probability of two persons assisting at the robbery, a probability suggested by the scratch, is now converted into undeniable certainty. *Ergo*, I was right."

Prosper listening attentively tried hard to comprehend this monologue, which he dared not interrupt.

"Let us seek," went on the fat man, "this second person, whose conscience pricks him, and yet who dares not reveal anything."

He read the letter over several times, scanning the sentences, and weighing every word.

"Evidently this letter was composed by a woman," he finally said. "Never would one man doing another man a service, and sending him money, use the word 'succour.' A man would have said, loan, money, or some other equivalent, but succour, never. No one but a woman, ignorant of masculine susceptibilities, would have naturally made use of this word to express the idea it represents. As to the sentence, 'There is one heart,' and so on, it could only have been written by a woman."

"You are mistaken, *monsieur*," said Prosper: "no woman is mixed up in this affair."

M. Verduret paid no attention to this interruption, perhaps he did not hear it; perhaps he did not care to argue the matter.

"Now, let us see if we can discover whence the printed words were taken to compose this letter."

He approached the window, and began to study the pasted words with all the scrupulous attention which an antiquarian would devote to an old, half-effaced manuscript.

"Small type," he said, "very slender and clear; the paper is thin and glossy. Consequently, these words have not been cut from a newspaper, magazine, or even a novel. I have seen type like this, I recognise it at once; Didot often uses it, so does Madame de Tours."

He stopped with his mouth open, and eyes fixed, appealing laboriously to his memory.

Suddenly he struck his forehead exultantly.

"Now I have it!" he cried; "now I have it! Why did I not see it at once? These words have all been cut from a prayer-book. We will look, at least, and then we shall be certain."

He moistened one of the words pasted on the paper with his tongue, and, when it was sufficiently softened, he detached it with a pin. On the other side of this word was printed a Latin word, *Deus*.

"Ah, ha," he said with a little laugh of satisfaction. "I knew it. Father Taberet would be pleased to see this. But what has become of the mutilated prayer-book? Can it have been burned? No, because a heavy-bound book is not easily burned. It is thrown in some corner."

M. Verduret was interrupted by the porter, who returned with the messenger from the Rue Pigalle.

"Ah, here you are," he said encouragingly. Then he showed the envelope of the letter, and said:

"Do you remember bringing this letter here this morning?"

"Perfectly, *monsieur*. I took particular notice of the direction; we don't often see anything like it."

"Who told you to bring it? a gentleman, or a lady?"

"Neither, *monsieur*; it was a porter."

This reply made the porter laugh very much, but not a muscle of M. Verduret's face moved.

"A porter? Well, do you know this colleague of yours."

"I never even saw him before."

"How does he look?"

"He was neither tall nor short; he wore a green vest, and his medal."

"Your description is so vague that it would suit every porter in the city; but did your colleague tell you who sent the letter?"

"No, *monsieur*. He only put ten *sous* in my hand, and said, 'Here, carry this to No. 39, Rue Chaptal: a coachman on the boulevard handed it to me.' Ten *sous*! I warrant you he made more than that by it."

This answer seemed to disconcert M. Verduret. So many precautions taken in sending the letter disturbed him, and disarranged his plans.

"Do you think you would recognise the porter again?"

"Yes, *monsieur*, if I saw him."

"How much do you gain a day as a porter?"

"I can't tell exactly; but my corner is a good stand, and I am busy doing errands nearly all day. I suppose I make from eight to ten *francs*."

"Very well; I will give you ten *francs* a day if you will walk about the streets, and look for the porter who brought this letter. Every evening, at eight o'clock, come to the Archangel, on the Quai Saint Michel, give me a report of your search, and receive your pay. Ask for M. Verduret. If you find the man I will give you fifty *francs*. Do you accept?"

"I rather think I will, *monsieur*."

"Then don't lose a minute. Start off!"

Although ignorant of M. Verduret's plans, Prosper began to comprehend the sense of his investigations. His fate depended upon their success, and yet he almost forgot this fact in his admiration of this singular man; for his energy, his bantering coolness when he wished to discover anything, the surety of his deductions, the fertility of his expedients, and the rapidity of his movements, were astonishing.

"*Monsieur*," said Prosper when the porter had left the room, "do you still think you see a woman's hand in this affair?"

"More than ever; and a pious woman too, and a woman who has two prayer-books, since she could cut up one to write to you."

"And you hope to find the mutilated book?"

"I do, thanks to the opportunity I have of making an immediate search; which I will set about at once."

Saying this, he sat down, and rapidly scratched off a few lines on a slip of paper, which he folded up, and put in his vest-pocket.

"Are you ready to go to M. Fauvel's? Yes? Come on, then; we have certainly earned our lunch today."

Chapter 8

When Raoul de Lagors spoke of M. Fauvel's extraordinary dejection, he had been guilty of no exaggeration.

Since the fatal day when, upon his denunciation, his cashier had been arrested, the banker, this active, energetic man of business, had been a prey to the most gloomy melancholy, and absolutely refused to take any interest in his affairs, seldom entering the banking-house.

He, who had always been so domestic, never came near his family except at meals, when he would swallow a few mouthfuls, and hastily leave the room.

Shut up in his study, he would deny himself to visitors. His anxious countenance, his indifference to everybody and everything, his constant reveries and fits of abstraction, betrayed the preoccupation of some fixed idea, or the tyrannical empire of some hidden sorrow.

The day of Prosper's release, about three o'clock, M. Fauvel was, as usual, seated in his study, with his elbows resting on the table, and his face buried in his hands, when his office-boy rushed in, and with a frightened look said:

"*Monsieur*, the former cashier, M. Bertomy, is here with one of his relatives; he says he must see you on business."

The banker at these words started up as if he had been shot.

"Prosper!" he cried in a voice choked by anger, "what! does he dare—"

Then remembering that he ought to control himself before his servant, he waited a few moments, and then said, in a tone of forced calmness:

"Ask them to walk in."

If M. Verduret had counted upon witnessing a strange and affecting sight, he was not disappointed.

Nothing could be more terrible than the attitude of these two men as they stood confronting each other. The banker's face was almost purple with suppressed anger, and he looked as if about to be struck by apoplexy. Prosper was as pale and motionless as a corpse.

Silent and immovable, they stood glaring at each other with mortal hatred.

M. Verduret curiously watched these two enemies, with the indifference and coolness of a philosopher, who, in the most violent outbursts of human passion, merely sees subjects for meditation and study.

Finally, the silence becoming more and more threatening, he decided to break it by speaking to the banker:

"I suppose you know, *monsieur*, that my young relative has just been released from prison."

"Yes," replied M. Fauvel, making an effort to control himself, "yes, for want of sufficient proof."

"Exactly so, *monsieur*, and this want of proof, as stated in the decision of 'Not proven,' ruins the prospects of my relative, and compels him to leave here at once for America."

M. Fauvel's features relaxed as if he had been relieved of some fearful agony.

"Ah, he is going away," he said, "he is going abroad."

There was no mistaking the resentful, almost insulting intonation of the words, "going away!"

M. Verduret took no notice of M. Fauvel's manner.

"It appears to me," he continued, in an easy tone, "that Prosper's determination is a wise one. I merely wished him, before leaving Paris, to come and pay his respects to his former chief."

The banker smiled bitterly.

"M. Bertomy might have spared us both this painful meeting. I have nothing to say to him, and of course he can have nothing to tell me."

This was a formal dismissal; and M. Verduret, understanding it thus, bowed to M. Fauvel, and left the room, accompanied by Prosper, who had not opened his lips.

They had reached the street before Prosper recovered the use of his tongue.

"I hope you are satisfied, *monsieur*," he said, in a gloomy tone; "you exacted this painful step, and I could only acquiesce. Have I gained anything by adding this humiliation to the others which I have suffered?"

"You have not, but I have," replied M. Verduret. "I could find no way of gaining access to M. Fauvel, save through you; and now I have found out what I wanted to know. I am convinced that M. Fauvel had nothing to do with the robbery."

"Oh, *monsieur*!" objected Prosper, "innocence can be feigned."

"Certainly, but not to this extent. And this is not all. I wished to find out if M. Fauvel would be accessible to certain suspicions. I am now confident that he is."

Prosper and his companion had stopped to talk more at their ease, near the corner of the Rue Lafitte, in the middle of a large space which had lately been cleared by pulling down an old house.

M. Verduret seemed to be anxious, and was constantly looking around as if he expected someone.

He soon uttered an exclamation of satisfaction.

At the other end of the vacant space, he saw Cavaillon, who was bareheaded and running.

He was so excited that he did not even stop to shake hands with Prosper, but darted up to M. Verduret, and said:

"They have gone, *monsieur*!"

"How long since?"

"They went about a quarter of an hour ago."

"The deuce they did! Then we have not an instant to lose."

He handed Cavaillon the note he had written some hours before at Prosper's house.

"Here, send him this, and then return at once to your desk; you might be missed. It was very imprudent in you to come out without your hat."

Cavaillon ran off as quickly as he had come. Prosper was stupefied.

"What!" he exclaimed. "You know Cavaillon?"

"So it seems," answered M. Verduret with a smile, "but we have no time to talk; come on, hurry!"

"Where are we gong now?"

"You will soon know; walk fast!"

And he set the example by striding rapidly toward the Rue Lafayette. As they went along he continued talking more to himself than to Prosper.

"Ah," said he, "it is not by putting both feet in one shoe, that one wins a race. The track once found, we should never rest an instant. When the savage discovers the footprints of an enemy, he follows it persistently, knowing that falling rain or a gust of wind may efface the footprints at any moment. It is the same with us: the most trifling incident may destroy the traces we are following up."

M. Verduret suddenly stopped before a door bearing the number 81.

"We are going in here," he said to Prosper; "come."

They went up the steps, and stopped on the second floor, before a door over which was a large sign, "Fashionable Dressmaker."

A handsome bell-rope hung on the wall, but M. Verduret did not touch it. He tapped with the ends of his fingers in a peculiar way, and the door instantly opened as if someone had been watching for his signal on the other side.

The door was opened by a neatly dressed woman of about forty. She quietly ushered M. Verduret and Prosper into a neat dining-room with several doors opening into it.

This woman bowed humbly to M. Verduret, as if he were some superior being.

He scarcely noticed her salutation, but questioned her with a look. His look said:

"Well?"

She bowed affirmatively:

"Yes."

"In there?" asked M. Verduret in a low tone, pointing to one of the doors.

"No," said the woman in the same tone, "over there, in the little parlour."

M. Verduret opened the door pointed out, and pushed Prosper into the little parlour, whispering, as he did so:

"Go in, and keep your presence of mind."

But his injunction was useless. The instant he cast his eyes around the room into which he had so unceremoniously been pushed without any warning, Prosper exclaimed, in a startled voice:

"Madeleine!"

It was indeed M. Fauvel's niece, looking more beautiful than ever. Hers was that calm, dignified beauty which imposes admiration and respect.

Standing in the middle of the room, near a table covered with silks and satins, she was arranging a skirt of red velvet embroidered in gold; probably the dress she was to wear as maid of honour to Catherine de Medicis.

At sight of Prosper, all the blood rushed to her face, and her beautiful eyes half closed, as if she were about to faint; she clung to the table to prevent herself from falling.

Prosper well knew that Madeleine was not one of those cold-hearted women whom nothing could disturb, and who feel sensations, but never a true sentiment.

Of a tender, dreamy nature, she betrayed in the minute details of her life the most exquisite delicacy. But she was also proud, and incapable of in any way violating her conscience. When duty spoke, she obeyed.

She recovered from her momentary weakness, and the soft expression of her eyes changed to one of haughty resentment. In an offended tone she said:

"What has emboldened you, *monsieur*, to be watching my movements? Who gave you permission to follow me, to enter this house?"

Prosper was certainly innocent. He would have given worlds to explain what had just happened, but he was powerless, and could only remain silent.

"You promised me upon your honour, *monsieur*," continued Madeleine, "that you would never again seek my presence. Is this the way you keep your word?"

"I did promise, *mademoiselle*, but—"

He stopped.

"Oh, speak!"

"So many things have happened since that terrible day, that I think I am excusable in forgetting, for one hour, an oath torn from me in a moment of blind weakness. It is to chance, at least to another will than my own, that I am indebted for the happiness of once more finding myself near you. Alas! the instant I saw you my heart bounded with joy. I did not think, no I could not think, that you would prove more pitiless than strangers have been, that you would cast me off when I am so miserable and heartbroken."

Had not Prosper been so agitated he could have read in the eyes of Madeleine—those beautiful eyes which had so long been the arbiters of his destiny—the signs of a great inward struggle.

It was, however, in a firm voice that she replied:

"You know me well enough, Prosper, to be sure than no blow can strike you without reaching me at the same time. You suffer, I suffer with you: I pity you as a sister would pity a beloved brother."

"A sister!" said Prosper, bitterly. "Yes, that was the word you used the day you banished me from your presence. A sister! Then why during three years did you delude me with vain hopes? Was I a brother to you the day we went to Notre Dame de Fourvieres, that day when, at the foot of the altar, we swore to love each other for ever and ever, and you fastened around my neck a holy relic and said, 'Wear this always for my sake, never part from it, and it will bring you good fortune'?"

Madeleine attempted to interrupt him by a supplicating gesture: he would not heed it, but continued with increased bitterness:

"One month after that happy day—a year ago—you gave me back my promise, told me to consider myself free from any engagement, and never to come near you again. If I could have discovered in what way I had offended you—But no, you refused to explain. You drove me away, and to obey you I told everyone that I had left you of my own accord. You told me that an invincible obstacle had arisen between us, and I believed you, fool that I was! The obstacle was your own heart, Madeleine. I have always worn the medal; but it has not brought me happiness or good fortune."

As white and motionless as a statue, Madeleine stood with bowed head before this storm of passionate reproach.

"I told you to forget me," she murmured.

"Forget!" exclaimed Prosper, excitedly, "forget! Can I forget! Is it in my power to stop, by an effort of will, the circulation of my blood? Ah, you have never loved! To forget, as to stop the beatings of the heart, there is but one means—death!"

This word, uttered with the fixed determination of a desperate, reckless man, caused Madeleine to shudder.

"Miserable man!" she exclaimed.

"Yes, miserable man, and a thousand times more miserable than you can imagine! You can never understand the tortures I have suffered, when for a year I would awake every morning, and say to myself, 'It is all over, she has ceased to love me!' This great sorrow stared me in the face day and night in spite of all my efforts to dispel it. And you speak of forgetfulness! I sought it at the bottom of poisoned cups, but found it not. I tried to extinguish this memory of the past, that tears my heart to shreds like a devouring flame; in vain. When the body succumbed, the pitiless heart kept watch. With this corroding torture making life a burden, do you wonder that I should seek rest which can only be obtained by suicide?"

"I forbid you to utter that word."

"You forget, Madeleine, that you have no right to forbid me, unless you love me. Love would make you all powerful, and me obedient."

With an imperious gesture Madeleine interrupted him as if she wished to speak, and perhaps to explain all, to exculpate herself.

But a sudden thought stopped her; she clasped her hands despairingly, and cried:

"My God! this suffering is beyond endurance!"

Prosper seemed to misconstrue her words.

"Your pity comes too late," he said. "There is no happiness in store for one like myself, who has had a glimpse of divine felicity, had the cup of bliss held to his lips, and then dashed to the ground. There is nothing left to attach me to life. You have destroyed my holiest beliefs; I came forth from prison disgraced by my enemies; what is to become of me? Vainly do I question the future; for me there is no hope of happiness. I look around me to see nothing but abandonment, ignominy, and despair!"

"Prosper, my brother, my friend, if you only knew—"

"I know but one thing, Madeleine, and that is, that you no longer love me, and that I love you more madly than ever. Oh, Madeleine, God only knows how I love you!"

He was silent. He hoped for an answer. None came.

But suddenly the silence was broken by a stifled sob.

It was Madeleine's maid, who, seated in a corner, was weeping bitterly.

Madeleine had forgotten her presence.

Prosper had been so surprised at finding Madeleine when he entered the room, that he kept his eyes fastened upon her face, and never once looked about him to see if anyone else were present.

He turned in surprise and looked at the weeping woman.

He was not mistaken: this neatly dressed waiting-maid was Nina Gypsy.

Prosper was so startled that he became perfectly dumb. He stood there with ashy lips, and a chilly sensation creeping through his veins.

The horror of the situation terrified him. He was there, between the two women who had ruled his fate; between Madeleine, the proud heiress who spurned his love, and Nina Gypsy, the poor girl whose devotion to himself he had so disdainfully rejected.

And she had heard all; poor Gypsy had witnessed the passionate avowal of her lover, had heard him swear that he could never love any woman but Madeleine, that if his love were not reciprocated he would kill himself, as he had nothing else to live for.

Prosper could judge of her sufferings by his own. For she was wounded not only in the present, but in the past. What must be her humiliation and danger on hearing the miserable part which Prosper, in his disappointed love, had imposed upon her?

He was astonished that Gypsy—violence itself—remained silently weeping, instead of rising and bitterly denouncing him.

Meanwhile Madeleine had succeeded in recovering her usual calmness.

Slowly and almost unconsciously she had put on her bonnet and shawl, which were lying on the sofa.

Then she approached Prosper, and said:

"Why did you come here? We both have need of all the courage we can command. You are unhappy, Prosper; I am more than unhappy, I am most wretched. You have a right to complain: I have not the right to shed a tear. While my heart is slowly breaking, I must wear a smiling face. You can seek consolation in the bosom of a friend: I can have no confidant but God."

Prosper tried to murmur a reply, but his pale lips refused to articulate; he was stifling.

"I wish to tell you," continued Madeleine, "that I have forgotten nothing. But oh! let not this knowledge give you any hope; the future is blank for us, but if you love me you will live. You will not, I know, add to my already heavy burden of sorrow, the agony of mourning your death. For my sake, live; live the life of a good man, and perhaps the day will come when I can justify myself in your eyes. And now, oh, my brother, oh, my only friend, *adieu*! *adieu*!"

She pressed a kiss upon his brow, and rushed from the room, followed by Nina Gypsy.

Prosper was alone. He seemed to be awaking from a troubled dream. He tried to think over what had just happened, and asked himself if he were losing his mind, or whether he had really spoken to Madeleine and seen Gypsy?

He was obliged to attribute all this to the mysterious power of the strange man whom he had seen for the first time that very morning.

How did he gain this wonderful power of controlling events to suit his own purposes?

He seemed to have anticipated everything, to know everything. He was acquainted with Cavaillon, he knew all Madeleine's movements; he had made even Gypsy become humble and submissive.

Thinking all this, Prosper had reached such a degree of exasperation, that when M. Verduret entered the little parlour, he strode toward him white with rage, and in a harsh, threatening voice, said to him:

"Who are you?"

The stout man did not show any surprise at this burst of anger, but quietly answered:

"A friend of your father's; did you not know it?"

"That is no answer, *monsieur*; I have been surprised into being influenced by a stranger, and now—"

"Do you want my biography, what I have been, what I am, and what I may be? What difference does it make to you? I told you that I would save you; the main point is that I am saving you."

"Still I have the right to ask by what means you are saving me."

"What good will it do you to know what my plans are?"

"In order to decide whether I will accept or reject them?"

"But suppose I guarantee success?"

"That is not sufficient, *monsieur*. I do not choose to be any longer deprived of my own free will, to be exposed without warning to trials like those I have undergone today. A man of my age must know what he is doing."

"A man of your age, Prosper, when he is blind, takes a guide, and does not undertake to point out the way to his leader."

The half-bantering, half-commiserating tone of M. Verduret was not calculated to calm Prosper's irritation.

"That being the case, *monsieur*," he cried, "I will thank you for your past services, and decline them for the future, as I have no need of them. If I attempted to defend my honour and my life, it was because I hoped that Madeleine would be restored to me. I have been convinced today that all is at an end between us; I retire from the struggle, and care not what becomes of me now."

Prosper was so decided, that M. Verduret seemed alarmed.

"You must be mad," he finally said.

"No, unfortunately I am not. Madeleine has ceased to love me, and of what importance is anything else?"

His heart-broken tone aroused M. Verduret's sympathy, and he said, in a kind, soothing tone:

"Then you suspect nothing? You did not fathom the meaning of what she said?"

"You were listening," cried Prosper fiercely.

"I certainly was."

"*Monsieur!*"

"Yes. It was a presumptuous thing to do, perhaps; but the end justified the means in this instance. I am glad I did listen, because it has enabled me to say to you, Take courage, Prosper: Mademoiselle Madeleine loves you; she has never ceased to love you."

Like a dying man who eagerly listens to deceitful promises of recovery, although he feels himself sinking into the grave, did Prosper feel his sad heart cheered by M. Verduret's assertion.

"Oh," he murmured, suddenly calmed, "if only I could hope!"

"Rely upon me, I am not mistaken. Ah, I could see the torture endured by this generous girl, while she struggled between her love, and what she believed to be her duty. Were you not convinced of her love when she bade you farewell?"

"She loves me, she is free, and yet she shuns me."

"No, she is not free! In breaking off her engagement with you, she was governed by some powerful, irrepressible event. She is sacrificing herself—for whom? We shall soon know; and the secret of her self-sacrifice will discover to us the secret of her plot against you."

As M.Verduret spoke, Prosper felt all his resolutions of revolt slowly melting away, and their place taken by confidence and hope.

"If what you say were true!" he mournfully said.

"Foolish young man! Why do you persist in obstinately shutting your eyes to the proof I place before you? Can you not see that Mademoiselle Madeleine knows who the thief is? Yes, you need not look so shocked; she knows the thief, but no human power can tear it from her. She sacrifices you, but then she almost has the right, since she first sacrificed herself."

Prosper was almost convinced; and it nearly broke his heart to leave this little parlour where he had seen Madeleine.

"Alas!" he said, pressing M.Verduret's hand, "you must think me a ridiculous fool! but you don't know how I suffer."

The man with the red whiskers sadly shook his head, and his voice sounded very unsteady as he replied, in a low tone:

"What you suffer, I have suffered. Like you, I loved, not a pure, noble girl, yet a girl fair to look upon. For three years I was at her feet, a slave to her every whim; when, one day she suddenly deserted me who adored her, to throw herself in the arms of a man who despised her. Then, like you, I wished to die. Neither threats nor entreaties could induce her to return to me. Passion never reasons, and she loved my rival."

"And did you know this rival?"

"I knew him."

"And you did not seek revenge?"

"No," replied M.Verduret with a singular expression, "no: fate took charge of my vengeance."

For a minute Prosper was silent; then he said:

"I have finally decided, *monsieur*. My honour is a sacred trust for which I must account to my family. I am ready to follow you to the end of the world; dispose of me as you judge proper."

That same day Prosper, faithful to his promise, sold his furniture, and wrote a letter to his friends announcing his intended departure to San Francisco.

In the evening he and M. Verduret installed themselves in the

"Archangel."

Madame Alexandre gave Prosper her prettiest room, but it was very ugly compared with the *coquettish* little parlour on the Rue Chaptal. His state of mind did not permit him, however, to notice the difference between his former and present quarters. He lay on an old sofa, meditating upon the events of the day, and feeling a bitter satisfaction in his isolated condition.

About eleven o'clock he thought he would raise the window, and let the cool air fan his burning brow; as he did so a piece of paper was blown from among the folds of the window-curtain, and lay at his feet on the floor.

Prosper mechanically picked it up, and looked at it.

It was covered with writing, the handwriting of Nina Gypsy; he could not be mistaken about that.

It was the fragment of a torn letter; and, if the half sentences did not convey any clear meaning, they were sufficient to lead the mind into all sorts of conjectures.

The fragment read as follows:

> . . . of M. Raoul, I have been very im . . . plotted against him, of whom never . . . warn Prosper, and then . . . best friend. he . . . hand of Mademoiselle Ma . . .

Prosper never closed his eyes all that night.

Chapter 9

Not far from the Palais Royal, in the Rue St. Honore, is the sign of *La Bonne Foi*, a small establishment, half *café* and half fruiterer's shop, much frequented by the work-people of the neighbourhood.

It was in the smoking-room of this modest *café* that Prosper, the day after his release, awaited M. Verduret, who had promised to meet him at four o'clock.

Just as the clock struck four, M. Verduret, who was punctuality itself, appeared. He was more red-faced and self-satisfied, if possible, than the day before.

As soon as the waiter, of whom he ordered a glass of beer, had left the room M. Verduret said to Prosper:

"Well, are our commissions executed?"

"Yes, *monsieur*."

"Have you seen the *costumier*?"

"I gave him your letter, and everything you ordered will be sent to the Archangel tomorrow."

"Very good; you have not lost time, neither have I. I have good news for you."

The *Bonne Foi* is almost deserted at four o'clock. The hour for coffee is passed, and the hour for *absinthe* has not yet come. M. Verduret and Prosper could talk at their ease without fear of being overheard by gossiping neighbours.

M. Verduret drew forth his memorandum-book, the precious diary which, like the enchanted book in the fairytale, had an answer for every question.

"While awaiting our emissaries whom I appointed to meet here, let us devote a little time to M. de Lagors."

At this name Prosper did not protest, as he had done the night previous. Like those imperceptible insects which, having once penetrated the root of a tree, devour it in a single night, suspicion, when it invades our mind, soon develops itself, and destroys our firmest beliefs.

The visit of Lagors, and Gypsy's torn letter, had filled Prosper with suspicions which had grown stronger and more settled as time passed.

"Do you know, my dear friend," said M. Verduret, "what part of France this devoted friend of yours comes from?"

"He was born at St. Remy, which is also Madame Fauvel's native town."

"Are you certain of that?"

"Oh, perfectly so, *monsieur*! He has not only often told me so, but I have heard him tell M. Fauvel; and he would talk to Madame Fauvel by the hour about his mother, who was cousin to Madame Fauvel, and dearly beloved by her."

"Then you think there is no possible mistake or falsehood about this part of his story?"

"None in the least, *monsieur*."

"Well, things are assuming a queer look."

And he began to whistle between his teeth; which, with M. Verduret, was a sign of intense inward satisfaction.

"What seems so, *monsieur*?" inquired Prosper.

"What has just happened; what I have been tracing. *Parbleu*!" he exclaimed, imitating the manner of a showman at a fair, "here is a lovely town, called St. Remy, six thousand inhabitants; charming boulevards on the site of the old fortifications; handsome hotel; numerous fountains; large charcoal market, silk factories, famous hospital, and so on."

Prosper was on thorns.

"Please be so good, *monsieur*, as to explain what you—"

"It also contains," continued M. Verduret, "a Roman triumphal arch, which is of unparalleled beauty, and a Greek mausoleum; but no Lagors. St. Remy is the native town of Nostradamus, but not of your friend."

"Yet I have proofs."

"Naturally. But proofs can be fabricated; relatives can be improvised. Your evidence is open to suspicion. My proofs are undeniable, perfectly authenticated. While you were pining in prison, I was preparing my batteries and collecting munitions to open fire. I wrote to St. Remy, and received answers to my questions."

"Will you let me know what they were?"

"Have patience," said M. Verduret as he turned over the leaves of his memoranda. "Ah, here is number one. Bow respectfully to it, 'tis official."

He then read:

> Lagors.—Very old family, originally from Maillane, settled at St. Remy about a century ago.

"I told you so," cried Prosper.

"Pray allow me to finish," said M. Verduret.

"'The last of the Lagors (Jules-Rene-Henri) bearing without warrant the title of count, married in 1829 Mademoiselle Rosalie-Clarisse Fontanet, of Tarascon; died December 1848, leaving no male heir, but left two daughters. The registers make no mention of any person in the district bearing the name of Lagors.'

"Now what do you think of this information?" queried the fat man with a triumphant smile.

Prosper looked amazed.

"But why did M. Fauvel treat Raoul as his nephew?"

"Ah, you mean as his wife's nephew! Let us examine note number two: it is not official, but it throws a valuable light upon the twenty thousand *livres* income of your friend."

> Jules-Rene-Henri de Lagors, last of his name, died at St. Remy on the 29th of December, 1848, in a state of great poverty. He at one time was possessed of a moderate fortune, but invested it in a silk-worm nursery, and lost it all.
>
> He had no son, but left two daughters, one of whom is a teacher at Aix, and the other married a retail merchant at Orgon. His widow, who lives at Montagnette, is supported entirely by one

of her relatives, the wife of a rich banker in Paris. No person of the name of Lagors lives in the district of Arles.

"That is all," said M. Verduret; "don't you think it enough?"

"Really, *monsieur*, I don't know whether I am awake or dreaming."

"You will be awake after a while. Now I wish to remark one thing. Some people may assert that the widow Lagors had a child born after her husband's death. This objection has been destroyed by the age of your friend. Raoul is twenty-four, and M. de Lagors has not been dead twenty years."

"But," said Prosper thoughtfully, "who can Raoul be?"

"I don't know. The fact is, I am more perplexed to find out who he is, than to know whom he is not. There is one man who could give us all the information we seek, but he will take good care to keep his mouth shut."

"You mean M. de Clameran?"

"Him, and no one else."

"I have always felt the most inexplicable aversion toward him. Ah, if we could only get his account in addition to what you already have!"

"I have been furnished with a few notes concerning the de Clameran family by your father, who knew them well; they are brief, but I expect more."

"What did my father tell you?"

"Nothing favourable, you may be sure. I will read you the synopsis of this information:

Louis de Clameran was born at the Château de Clameran, near Tarascon. He had an elder brother named Gaston, who, in consequence of an affray in which he had the misfortune to kill one man and badly wound another, was compelled to fly the country in 1842. Gaston was an honest, noble youth, universally beloved. Louis, on the contrary, was a wicked, despicable fellow, detested by all who knew him.

Upon the death of his father, Louis came to Paris, and in less than two years had squandered not only his own patrimony, but also the share of his exiled brother.

Ruined and harassed by debt, Louis entered the army, but behaved so disgracefully that he was dismissed.

After leaving the army we lose sight of him; all we can discover is, that he went to England, and thence to a German gambling resort, where he became notorious for his scandalous conduct. In 1865 we find him again at Paris. He was in great poverty, and his associates were among the most depraved classes.

But he suddenly heard of the return of his brother Gaston to Paris. Gaston had made a fortune in Mexico; but being still a young man, and accustomed to a very active life, he purchased, near Orloron, an iron-mill, intending to spend the remainder of his life in working at it. Six months ago he died in the arms of his brother Louis. His death provided our de Clameran an immense fortune, and the title of *marquis*.

"Then," said Prosper, "from all this I judge that M. de Clameran was very poor when I met him for the first time at M. Fauvel's?"

"Evidently."

"And about that time Lagors arrived from the country?"

"Precisely."

"And about a month after his appearance Madeleine suddenly banished me?"

"Well," exclaimed M. Verduret, "I am glad you are beginning to understand the state of affairs."

He was interrupted by the entrance of a stranger.

The new-comer was a dandified-looking coachman, with elegant black whiskers, shining boots with fancy tops; buff breeches, and a yellow waistcoat with red and black stripes.

After cautiously looking around the room, he walked straight up to the table where M. Verduret sat.

"What is the news, Master Joseph Dubois?" said the stout man eagerly.

"Ah, patron, don't speak of it!" answered the servant: "things are getting warm."

Prosper concentrated all his attention upon this superb domestic. He thought he recognised his face. He had certainly somewhere seen that retreating forehead and those little restless black eyes, but where and when he could not remember.

Meanwhile, Master Joseph had taken a seat at a table adjoining the one occupied by M. Verduret and Prosper; and, having called for some *absinthe*, was preparing it by holding the water aloft and slowly dropping it in the glass.

"Speak!" said M. Verduret.

"In the first place, patron, I must say that the position of valet and coachman to M. de Clameran is not a bed of roses."

"Go on: come to the point. You can complain tomorrow."

"Very good. Yesterday my master walked out at two o'clock. I, of course, followed him. Do you know where he went? The thing was as good as a farce. He went to the Archangel to keep the appointment made by 'Nina Gypsy.'"

"Well, make haste. They told him she was gone. Then?"

"Then? Ah! he was not at all pleased, I can tell you. He hurried back to the hotel where the other, M. de Lagors, awaited him. And, upon my soul, I have never heard so much swearing in my life! M. Raoul asked him what had happened to put him in such a bad humour. 'Nothing,' replied my master, 'except that little devil has run off, and no one knows where she is; she has slipped through our fingers.' Then they both appeared to be vexed and uneasy. Lagors asked if she knew anything serious. 'She knows nothing but what I told you,' replied de Clameran; 'but this nothing, falling in the ear of a man with any suspicions, will be more than enough to work on.'"

M. Verduret smiled like a man who had his reasons for appreciating at their just value de Clameran's fears.

"Well, your master is not without sense, after all; don't you think he showed it by saying that?"

"Yes, patron. Then Lagors exclaimed, 'If it is as serious as that, we must get rid of this little serpent!' But my master shrugged his shoulders, and laughing loudly said, 'You talk like an idiot; when one is annoyed by a woman of this sort, one must take measures to get rid of her administratively.' This idea seemed to amuse them both very much."

"I can understand their being entertained by it," said M. Verduret; "it is an excellent idea; but the misfortune is, it is too late to carry it out. The nothing which made de Clameran uneasy has already fallen into a knowing ear."

With breathless curiosity, Prosper listened to this report, every word of which seemed to throw light upon past events. Now, he thought, he understood the fragment of Gypsy's letter. He saw that this Raoul, in whom he had confided so deeply, was nothing more than a scoundrel. A thousand little circumstances, unnoticed at the time, now recurred to his mind, and made him wonder how he could have been so blind so long.

Master Joseph Dubois continued his report:

"Yesterday, after dinner, my master decked himself out like a bridegroom. I shaved him, curled his hair, and perfumed him with special care, after which I drove him to the Rue de Provence to call on Madame Fauvel."

"What!" exclaimed Prosper, "after the insulting language he used the day of the robbery, did he dare to visit the house?"

"Yes, *monsieur*, he not only dared this, but he also stayed there until midnight, to my great discomfort; for I got as wet as a rat, waiting for him."

"How did he look when he came out?" asked M. Verduret.

"Well, he certainly looked less pleased then when he went in. After putting away my carriage, and rubbing down my horses, I went to see if he wanted anything; I found the door locked, and he swore at me like a trooper, through the key-hole."

And, to assist the digestion of this insult, Master Joseph here gulped down a glass of *absinthe*.

"Is that all?" questioned M. Verduret.

"All that occurred yesterday, patron; but this morning my master rose late, still in a horrible bad humour. At noon Raoul arrived, also in a rage. They at once began to dispute, and such a row! why, the most abandoned housebreakers and pickpockets would have blushed to hear such Billingsgate. At one time my master seized the other by the throat and shook him like a reed. But Raoul was too quick for him; he saved himself from strangulation by drawing out a sharp-pointed knife, the sight of which made my master drop him in a hurry, I can tell you."

"But what did they say?"

"Ah, there is the rub, patron," said Joseph in a piteous tone; "the scamps spoke English, so I could not understand them. But I am sure they were disputing about money."

"How do you know that?"

"Because I learned at the Exposition that the word 'argent' means money in every language in Europe; and this word they constantly used in their conversation."

M. Verduret sat with knit brows, talking in an undertone to himself; and Prosper, who was watching him, wondered if he was trying to understand and construct the dispute by mere force of reflection.

"When they had done fighting," continued Joseph, "the rascals began to talk in French again; but they only spoke of a fancy ball which is to be given by some banker. When Raoul was leaving, my master said, 'Since this thing is inevitable, and it must take place today, you had better remain at home, at Vesinet, this evening.' Raoul replied, 'Of course.'"

Night was approaching, and the smoking-room was gradually filling with men who called for *absinthe* or bitters, and youths who perched themselves up on high stools, and smoked their pipes.

"It is time to go," said M. Verduret; "your master will want you, Joseph; besides, here is someone come for me. I will see you tomorrow."

The newcomer was no other than Cavaillon, more troubled and frightened than ever. He looked uneasily around the room, as if he expected the whole police force to appear, and carry him off to prison.

He did not sit down at M. Verduret's table, but stealthily gave his hand to Prosper, and, after assuring himself that no one was observing them, handed M. Verduret a package, saying:

"She found this in a cupboard."

It was a handsomely bound prayer-book. M. Verduret rapidly turned over the leaves, and soon found the pages from which the words pasted on Prosper's letter had been cut.

"I had moral proofs," he said, handing the book to Prosper, "but here is material proof sufficient in itself to save you."

When Prosper looked at the book he turned pale as a ghost. He recognised this prayer-book instantly. He had given it to Madeleine in exchange for the medal.

He opened it, and on the fly-leaf Madeleine had written:

Souvenir of Notre Dame de Fourvieres, 17 January, 1866.

"This book belongs to Madeleine," he cried.

M. Verduret did not reply, but walked toward a young man dressed like a brewer, who had just entered the room.

He glanced at the note which this person handed to him, and hastened back to the table, and said, in an agitated tone:

"I think we have got them now!"

Throwing a five-*franc* piece on the table, and without saying a word to Cavaillon, he seized Prosper's arm, and hurried from the room.

"What a fatality!" he said, as he hastened along the street: "we may miss them. We shall certainly reach the St. Lazare station too late for the St. Germain train."

"For Heaven's sake, where are you going?" asked Prosper.

"Never mind, we can talk after we start. Hurry!"

Reaching Palais Royal Place, M. Verduret stopped before one of the hacks belonging to the railway station, and examined the horses at a glance.

"How much for driving us to Vesinet?" he asked of the driver.

"I don't know the road very well that way."

The name of Vesinet was enough for Prosper.

"Well," said the driver, "at this time of night, in such dreadful weather, it ought to be—twenty-five *francs*."

"And how much more for driving very rapidly?"

"Bless my soul! Why, *monsieur*, I leave that to your generosity; but if you put it at thirty-five *francs*—"

"You shall have a hundred," interrupted M. Verduret, "if you overtake a carriage which has half an hour's start of us."

"Tonnerre de Brest!" cried the delighted driver; "jump in quick: we are losing time!"

And, whipping up his lean horses, he galloped them down the Rue de Valois at a fearful speed.

Chapter 10

On quitting the little station of Vesinet, we come upon two roads. One, to the left, macadamized and kept in perfect repair, leads to the village, of which there are glimpses here and there through the trees. The other, newly laid out, and just covered with gravel, leads through the woods.

Along the latter, which before the lapse of five years will be a busy street, are built a few houses, hideous in design, and at some distance apart; rural summer retreats of city merchants, but unoccupied during the winter.

It was at the junction of these two roads that Prosper stopped the hack.

The driver had gained his hundred *francs*. The horses were completely worn out, but they had accomplished all that was expected of them; M. Verduret could distinguish the lamps of a hack similar to the one he occupied, about fifty yards ahead of him.

M. Verduret jumped out, and, handing the driver a bank-note, said:

"Here is what I promised you. Go to the first tavern you find on the right-hand side of the road as you enter the village. If we do not meet you there in an hour, you are at liberty to return to Paris."

The driver was overwhelming in his thanks; but neither Prosper nor his friend heard them. They had already started up the new road.

The weather, which had been inclement when they set out, was now fearful. The rain fell in torrents, and a furious wind howled dismally through the dense woods.

The intense darkness was rendered more dreary by the occasional glimmer of the lamps at the distant station, which seemed about to be extinguished by every new gust of wind.

M. Verduret and Prosper had been running along the muddy road for about five minutes, when suddenly the latter stopped and said:

"This is Raoul's house."

Before the gate of an isolated house stood the hack which M. Verduret had followed. Reclining on his seat, wrapped in a thick cloak, was the driver, who, in spite of the pouring rain, was already asleep, evidently waiting for the person whom he had brought to this house a few minutes ago.

M. Verduret pulled his cloak, and said, in a low voice:

"Wake up, my good man."

The driver started, and, mechanically gathering his reins, yawned out:

"I am ready: come on!"

But when, by the light of the carriage-lamps, he saw two men in this lonely spot, he imagined that they wanted his purse, and perhaps his life.

"I am engaged!" he cried out, as he cracked his whip in the air; "I am waiting here for someone."

"I know that, you fool," replied M. Verduret, "and only wish to ask you a question, which you can gain five *francs* by answering. Did you not bring a middle-aged lady here?"

This question, this promise of five *francs*, instead of reassuring the coachman, increased his alarm.

"I have already told you I am waiting for someone," he said, "and, if you don't go away and leave me alone, I will call for help."

M. Verduret drew back quickly.

"Come away," he whispered to Prosper, "the cur will do as he says; and, alarm once given, farewell to our projects. We must find some other entrance than by this gate."

They then went along the wall surrounding the garden, in search of a place where it was possible to climb up.

This was difficult to discover, the wall being twelve feet high, and the night very dark. Fortunately, M. Verduret was very agile; and, having decided upon the spot to be scaled, he drew back a few feet, and making a sudden spring, seized one of the projecting stones above him, and, drawing himself up by aid of his hands and feet, soon found himself on top of the wall.

It was now Prosper's turn to climb up; but, though much younger than his companion, he had not his agility and strength, and would never have succeeded if M. Verduret had not pulled him up, and then helped him down on the other side.

Once in the garden, M. Verduret looked about him to study the situation.

The house occupied by M. de Lagors was built in the middle of an immense garden. It was narrow, two storeys high, and with garrets.

Only one window, in the second story, was lighted.

"As you have often been here," said M. Verduret, "you must know all about the arrangement of the house: what room is that where we see the light?"

"That is Raoul's bedchamber."

"Very good. What rooms are on the first floor?"

"The kitchen, pantry, billiard-room, and dining-room."

"And on the floor above?"

"Two drawing-rooms separated by folding doors, and a library."

"Where do the servants sleep?"

"Raoul has none at present. He is waited on by a man and his wife, who live at Vesinet; they come in the morning, and leave after dinner."

M. Verduret rubbed his hands gleefully.

"That suits our plans exactly," he said; "there is nothing to prevent our hearing what Raoul has to say to this person who has come from Paris at ten o'clock at night, to see him. Let us go in."

Prosper seemed averse to this, and said:

"It is a serious thing for us to do, *monsieur*."

"Bless my soul! what else did we come here for? Did you think it was a pleasure-trip, merely to enjoy this lovely weather?" he said in a bantering tone.

"But we might be discovered."

"Suppose we are? If the least noise betrays our presence, you have only to advance boldly as a friend come to visit a friend, and, finding the door open walked in."

But unfortunately the heavy oak door was locked. M. Verduret shook it in vain.

"How foolish!" he said with vexation, "I ought to have brought my instruments with me. A common lock which could be opened with a nail, and I have not even a piece of wire!"

Thinking it useless to attempt the door, he tried successively every window on the ground-floor. Alas! each blind was securely fastened on the inside.

M.Verduret was provoked. He prowled around the house like a fox around a hen-coop, seeking an entrance, but finding none. Despairingly he came back to the spot in front of the house, whence he had the best view of the lighted window.

"If I could only look in," he cried. "Just to think that in there," and he pointed to the window, "is the solution of the mystery; and we are cut off from it by thirty or forty feet of cursed blank wall!"

Prosper was more surprised than ever at his companion's strange behaviour. He seemed perfectly at home in this garden; he ran about without any precaution; so that one would have supposed him accustomed to such expeditions, especially when he spoke of picking the lock of an occupied house, as if he were talking of opening a snuff-box. He was utterly indifferent to the rain and sleet driven in his face by the gusts of wind as he splashed about in the mud trying to find some way of entrance.

"I must get a peep into that window," he said, "and I will, cost what it may!"

Prosper seemed to suddenly remember something.

"There is a ladder here," he cried.

"Why did you not tell me that before? Where is it?"

"At the end of the garden, under the trees."

They ran to the spot, and in a few minutes had the ladder standing against the wall.

But to their chagrin they found the ladder six feet too short. Six long feet of wall between the top of the ladder and the lighted window was a very discouraging sight to Prosper; he exclaimed:

"We cannot reach it."

"We *can* reach it," cried M.Verduret triumphantly.

And he quickly placed himself a yard off from the house, and, seizing the ladder, cautiously raised it and rested the bottom round on his shoulders, at the same time holding the two uprights firmly and steadily with his hands. The obstacle was overcome.

"Now mount," he said to his companion.

Prosper did not hesitate. The enthusiasm of difficulties so skilfully conquered, and the hope of triumph, gave him a strength and agility which he had never imagined he possessed. He made a sudden spring, and, seizing the lower rounds, quickly climbed up the ladder, which swayed and trembled beneath his weight.

But he had scarcely looked in the lighted window when he uttered a cry which was drowned in the roaring tempest, and dropped like a log down on the wet grass, exclaiming:

"The villain! the villain!"

With wonderful promptness and vigour M.Verduret laid the ladder on the ground, and ran toward Prosper, fearing that he was dead or dangerously injured.

"What did you see? Are you hurt?" he whispered.

But Prosper had already risen. Although he had had a violent fall, he was unhurt; he was in a state when mind governs matter so absolutely that the body is insensible to pain.

"I saw," he answered in a hoarse voice, "I saw Madeleine—do you understand, Madeleine—in that room, alone with Raoul!"

M.Verduret was confounded. Was it possible that he, the infallible expert, had been mistaken in his deductions?

He well knew that M. de Lagors's visitor was a woman; but his own conjectures, and the note which Madame Gypsy had sent to him at the tavern, had fully assured him that this woman was Madame Fauvel.

"You must be mistaken," he said to Prosper.

"No, *monsieur*, no. Never could I mistake another for Madeleine. Ah! you who heard what she said to me yesterday, answer me: was I to expect such infamous treason as this? You said to me then, 'She loves you, she loves you!' Now do you think she loves me? speak!"

M.Verduret did not answer. He had first been stupefied by his mistake, and was now racking his brain to discover the cause of it, which was soon discerned by his penetrating mind.

"This is the secret discovered by Nina," continued Prosper. "Madeleine, this pure and noble Madeleine, whom I believed to be as immaculate as an angel, is in love with this thief, who has even stolen the name he bears; and I, trusting fool that I was, made this scoundrel my best friend. I confided to him all my hopes and fears; and he was her lover! Of course they amused themselves by ridiculing my silly devotion and blind confidence!"

He stopped, overcome by his violent emotions. Wounded vanity is the worst of miseries. The certainty of having been so shamefully deceived and betrayed made Prosper almost insane with rage.

"This is the last humiliation I shall submit to," he fiercely cried. "It shall not be said that I was coward enough to stand by and let an insult like this go unpunished."

He started toward the house; but M.Verduret seized his arm and said:

"What are you going to do?"

"Have my revenge! I will break down the door; what do I care for the noise and scandal, now that I have nothing to lose? I shall not attempt to creep into the house like a thief, but as a master, as one who has a right to enter; as a man who, having received an insult which can only be washed out with blood, comes to demand satisfaction."

"You will do nothing of the sort, Prosper."

"Who will prevent me?"

"I will."

"You? do not hope that you will be able to deter me. I will appear before them, put them to the blush, kill them both, then put an end to my own wretched existence. That is what I intend to do, and nothing shall stop me!"

If M. Verduret had not held Prosper with a vice-like grip, he would have escaped, and carried out his threat.

"If you make any noise, Prosper, or raise an alarm, all your hopes are ruined."

"I have no hopes now."

"Raoul, put on his guard, will escape us, and you will remain dishonoured forever."

"What difference is it to me?"

"It makes a great difference to me. I have sworn to prove your innocence. A man of your age can easily find a wife, but can never restore lustre to a tarnished name. Let nothing interfere with the establishing of your innocence."

Genuine passion is uninfluenced by surrounding circumstances. M. Verduret and Prosper stood foot-deep in mud, wet to the skin, the rain pouring down on their heads, and yet seemed in no hurry to end their dispute.

"I will be avenged," repeated Prosper with the persistency of a fixed idea, "I will avenge myself."

"Well, avenge yourself like a man, and not like a child!" said M. Verduret angrily.

"*Monsieur!*"

"Yes, I repeat it, like a child. What will you do after you get into the house? Have you any arms? No. You rush upon Raoul, and a struggle ensues; while you two are fighting, Madeleine jumps in her carriage, and drives off. What then? Which is the stronger, you or Raoul?"

Overcome by the sense of his powerlessness, Prosper was silent.

"And arms would be of no use," continued M.Verduret: "it is fortunate you have none with you, for it would be very foolish to shoot a man whom you can send to the galleys."

"What must I do?"

"Wait. Vengeance is a delicious fruit, that must ripen in order that we may fully enjoy it."

Prosper was unsettled in his resolution; M. Verduret seeing this brought forth his last and strongest argument.

"How do we know," he said, "that Mademoiselle Madeleine is here on her own account? Did we not come to the conclusion that she was sacrificing herself for the benefit of someone else? That superior will which compelled her to banish you may have constrained this step tonight."

That which coincides with our secret wishes is always eagerly welcomed. This supposition, apparently improbable, struck Prosper as possibly true.

"That might be the case," he murmured, "who knows?"

"I would soon know," said M. Verduret, "if I could see them together in that room."

"Will you promise me, *monsieur*, to tell me the exact truth, all that you see and hear, no matter how painful it may be for me?"

"I swear it, upon my word of honour."

Then, with a strength of which a few minutes before he would not have believed himself possessed, Prosper raised the ladder, placed the last round on his shoulders, and said to M.Verduret:

"Mount!"

M.Verduret rapidly ascended the ladder without even shaking it, and had his head on a level with the window.

Prosper had seen but too well. There was Madeleine at this hour of the night, alone with Raoul de Lagors in his room!

M.Verduret observed that she still wore her shawl and bonnet.

She was standing in the middle of the room, talking with great animation. Her look and gestures betrayed indignant scorn. There was an expression of ill-disguised loathing upon her beautiful face.

Raoul was seated by the fire, stirring up the coals with a pair of tongs. Every now and then, he would shrug his shoulders, like a man resigned to everything he heard, and had no answer, except, "I cannot help it. I can do nothing for you."

M. Verdure would willingly have given the diamond ring on his finger to be able to hear what was said; but the roaring wind completely drowned their voices.

"They are evidently quarrelling," he thought; "but it is not a lovers' quarrel."

Madeleine continued talking; and it was by closely watching the face of Lagors, clearly revealed by the lamp on the mantel, that M. Verduret hoped to discover the meaning of the scene before him.

At one moment Lagors would start and tremble in spite of his apparent indifference; the next, he would strike at the fire with the tongs, as if giving vent to his rage at some reproach uttered by Madeleine.

Finally Madeleine changed her threats into entreaties, and, clasping her hands, almost fell at his knees.

He turned away his head, and refused to answer save in monosyllables.

Several times she turned to leave the room, but each time returned, as if asking a favour, and unable to make up her mind to leave the house till she had obtained it.

At last she seemed to have uttered something decisive; for Raoul quickly rose and opened a desk near the fireplace, from which he took a bundle of papers, and handed them to her.

"Well," thought M. Verduret, "this looks bad. Can it be a compromising correspondence which the fair one wants to secure?"

Madeleine took the papers, but was apparently still dissatisfied. She again entreated him to give her something else. Raoul refused; and then she threw the papers on the table.

The papers seemed to puzzle M. Verduret very much, as he gazed at them through the window.

"I am not blind," he said, "and I certainly am not mistaken; those papers, red, green, and yellow, are pawnbroker's tickets!"

Madeleine turned over the papers as if looking for some particular ones. She selected three, which she put in her pocket, disdainfully pushing the others aside.

She was evidently preparing to take her departure, for she said a few words to Raoul, who took up the lamp as if to escort her downstairs.

There was nothing more for M. Verduret to see. He carefully descended the ladder, muttering to himself. "Pawnbroker's tickets! What infamous mystery lies at the bottom of all this?"

The first thing he did was to remove the ladder.

Raoul might take it into his head to look around the garden, when he came to the door with Madeleine, and if he did so the ladder could scarcely fail to attract his attention.

M. Verduret and Prosper hastily laid it on the ground, regardless of the shrubs and vines they destroyed in doing so, and then concealed themselves among the trees, whence they could watch at once the front door and the outer gate.

Madeleine and Raoul appeared in the doorway. Raoul set the lamp on the bottom step, and offered his hand to the girl; but she refused it with haughty contempt, which somewhat soothed Prosper's lacerated heart.

This scornful behaviour did not, however, seem to surprise or hurt Raoul. He simply answered by an ironical gesture which implied, "As you please!"

He followed her to the gate, which he opened and closed after her; then he hurried back to the house, while Madeleine's carriage drove rapidly away.

"Now, *monsieur*," said Prosper, "you must tell me what you saw. You promised me the truth no matter how bitter it might be. Speak; I can bear it, be it what it may!"

"You will only have joy to bear, my friend. Within a month you will bitterly regret your suspicions of tonight. You will blush to think that you ever imagined Mademoiselle Madeleine to be intimate with a man like Lagors."

"But, *monsieur*, appearances—"

"It is precisely against appearances that we must be on our guard. Always distrust them. A suspicion, false or just, is always based on something. But we must not stay here forever; and, as Raoul has fastened the gate, we shall have to climb back again." "But there is the ladder."

"Let it stay where it is; as we cannot efface our footprints, he will think thieves have been trying to get into the house."

They scaled the wall, and had not walked fifty steps when they heard the noise of a gate being unlocked. The stood aside and waited; a man soon passed on his way to the station.

"That is Raoul," said M. Verduret, "and Joseph will report to us that he has gone to tell de Clameran what has just taken place. If they are only kind enough to speak French!"

He walked along quietly for some time, trying to connect the broken chain of his deductions.

"How in the deuce," he abruptly asked, "did this Lagors, who is devoted to gay society, come to choose a lonely country house to live in?"

"I suppose it was because M. Fauvel's villa is only fifteen minutes' ride from here, on the Seine."

"That accounts for his staying here in the summer; but in winter?"

"Oh, in winter he has a room at the Hotel du Louvre, and all the year round keeps an apartment in Paris."

This did not enlighten M. Verduret much; he hurried his pace.

"I hope our driver has not gone. We cannot take the train which is about to start, because Raoul would see us at the station."

Although it was more than an hour since M. Verduret and Prosper left the hack at the branch road, they found it waiting for them in front of the tavern.

The driver could not resist the desire to change his five-*franc* piece; he had ordered dinner, and, finding his wine very good, was calling for more, when he looked up and saw his employers.

"Well, you are in a strange state!" he exclaimed.

Prosper replied that they had gone to see a friend, and, losing their way, had fallen into a pit; as if there were pits in Vesinet forest.

"Ah, that is the way you got covered with mud, is it?" exclaimed the driver, who, though apparently contented with this explanation, strongly suspected that his two customers had been engaged in some nefarious transaction.

This opinion seemed to be entertained by everyone present, for they looked at Prosper's muddy clothes and then at each other in a knowing way.

But M. Verduret stopped all comment by saying:

"Come on."

"All right, *monsieur*: get in while I settle my bill; I will be there in a minute."

The drive back was silent and seemed interminably long. Prosper at first tried to draw his strange companion into conversation, but, as he received nothing but monosyllables in reply, held his peace for the rest of the journey. He was again beginning to feel irritated at the absolute empire exercised over him by this man.

Physical discomfort was added to his other troubles. He was stiff and numb; every bone in him ached with the cold.

Although mental endurance may be unlimited, bodily strength must in the end give way. A violent effort is always followed by reaction.

Lying back in a corner of the carriage, with his feet upon the front seat, M. Verduret seemed to be enjoying a nap; yet he was never more wide awake.

He was in a perplexed state of mind. This expedition, which, he had been confident, would resolve all his doubts, had only added mystery to mystery. His chain of evidence, which he thought so strongly linked, was completely broken.

For him the facts remained the same, but circumstances had changed. He could not imagine what common motive, what moral or material complicity, what influences, could have existed to make the four actors in his drama, Madame Fauvel, Madeleine, Raoul, and de Clameran, seem to have the same object in view.

He was seeking in his fertile mind, that encyclopaedia of craft and subtlety, for some combination which would throw light on the problem before him.

The midnight bells were ringing when they reached the Archangel, and for the first time M.Verduret remembered that he had not dined.

Fortunately Madame Alexandre was still up, and in the twinkling of an eye had improvised a tempting supper. It was more than attention, more than respect, that she showed her guest. Prosper observed that she gazed admiringly at M.Verduret all the while he was eating his supper.

"You will not see me tomorrow," said M. Verduret to Prosper, when he had risen to leave the room; "but I will be here about this time tomorrow night. Perhaps I shall discover what I am seeking at Mm. Jandidier's ball."

Prosper was dumb with astonishment. What! would M. Verduret think of appearing at a ball given by the wealthiest and most fashionable bankers in Paris? This accounted for his sending to the costumer.

"Then you are invited to this ball?"

The expressive eyes of M.Verduret danced with amusement.

"Not yet," he said, "but I shall be."

Oh, the inconsistency of the human mind! Prosper was tormented by the most serious preoccupations. He looked sadly around his chamber, and, as he thought of M.Verduret's projected pleasure at the ball, exclaimed:

"Ah, how fortunate he is! Tomorrow he will see Madeleine more lovely than ever."

Chapter 11

About the middle of the Rue St. Lazare are the almost regal residences of the brothers Jandidier, two celebrated financiers, who, if deprived of the prestige of immense wealth, would still be looked up to as remarkable men. Why cannot the same be said of all men?

These two mansions, which were thought marvels at the time they were built, were entirely distinct from each other, but so planned that they could be turned into one immense house when so desired.

When Mm. Jandidier gave parties, they always had the movable partitions taken away, and thus obtained the most superb salon in Paris.

Princely magnificence, lavish hospitality, and an elegant, graceful manner of receiving their guests, made these entertainments eagerly sought after by the fashionable circles of the capital.

On Saturday, the Rue St. Lazare was blocked up by a file of carriages, whose fair occupants were impatiently awaiting their turn to drive up to the door, through which they could catch the tantalizing strains of a waltz.

It was a fancy ball; and nearly all of the costumes were superb, though some were more original than elegant.

Among the latter was a clown. Everything was in perfect keeping: the insolent eye, coarse lips, high cheek-bones, and a beard so red that it seemed to emit flames in the reflection of the dazzling lights.

He wore top-boots, a dilapidated hat on the back of his head, and a shirt-ruffle trimmed with torn lace.

He carried in his left hand a canvas banner, upon which were painted six or eight pictures, coarsely designed like those found in strolling fairs. In his right he waved a little switch, with which he would every now and then strike his banner, like a quack retailing his wares.

Quite a crowd surrounded this clown, hoping to hear some witty speeches and puns; but he kept near the door, and remained silent.

About half-past ten he quitted his post.

M. and Madame Fauvel, followed by their niece Madeleine, had just entered.

A compact group immediately formed near the door.

During the last ten days, the affair of the Rue de Provence had been the universal topic of conversation; and friends and enemies were alike glad to seize this opportunity of approaching the banker, some to tender their sympathy, and others to offer equivocal condolence, which of all things is the most exasperating and insulting.

Belonging to the battalion of grave, elderly men, M. Fauvel had not assumed a fancy costume, but merely threw over his shoulders a short silk *domino*.

On his arm leaned Madame Fauvel, *nee* Valentine de la Verberie, bowing and gracefully greeting her numerous friends.

She had once been remarkably beautiful; and tonight the effect of the soft wax-lights, and her very becoming dress, half restored her youthful freshness and comeliness. No one would have supposed her to be forty-eight years old.

She wore a dress of the later years of Louis the Fourteenth's reign, magnificent and severe, of embroidered satin and black velvet, without the adornment of a single jewel.

She looked so graceful and elegant in this court dress and powdered hair, that some ill-natured gossips said it was a pity to see a real La Verberie, so well fitted to adorn a queen's drawing-room, as all her ancestors had done before her, thrown away upon a man whom she had only married for his money.

But Madeleine was the object of universal admiration, so dazzlingly beautiful and queen-like did she appear in her costume of maid of honour, which seemed to have been especially invented to set forth her beautiful figure.

Her loveliness expanded in the perfumed atmosphere and soft light of the ball-room. Never had her hair looked so black, her complexion so exquisite, or her large eyes so brilliant.

Having greeted the hosts, Madeleine took her aunt's arm, while M. Fauvel wandered through the rooms in search of the card-table, the usual refuge of bored men, when they are enticed to the ball-room by their womankind.

The ball was now at its height.

Two orchestras, led by Strauss and one of his lieutenants, filled the two mansions with intoxicating music. The motley crowd whirled in the waltz until they presented a curious confusion of velvets, satins, laces, and diamonds. Almost every head and bosom sparkled with jewels; the palest cheeks were rosy; heavy eyes now shone like stars; and the glistening shoulders of fair women were like drifted snow in an April sun.

Forgotten by the crowd, the clown had taken refuge in the embrasure of a window, and seemed to be meditating upon the gay scene before him; at the same time, he kept his eye upon a couple not far off.

It was Madeleine, dancing with a splendidly dressed doge. The doge was the Marquis de Clameran.

He appeared to be radiant, rejuvenated, and well satisfied with the impression he was making upon his partner; at the end of a quadrille he leaned over her, and whispered compliments with the most unbounded admiration; and she seemed to listen, if not with pleasure, at least without repugnance. She now and then smiled, and *coquettishly* shrugged her shoulders.

"Evidently," muttered the clown, "this noble scoundrel is paying court to the banker's niece; so I was right yesterday. But how can Mademoiselle Madeleine resign herself to so graciously receive his insipid flattery? Fortunately, Prosper is not here now."

He was interrupted by an elderly man wrapped in a Venetian mantle, who said to him:

"You remember, M. Verduret,"—this name was uttered half seriously, half banteringly—"what you promised me?"

The clown bowed with great respect, but not the slightest shade of humility.

"I remember," he replied.

"But do not be imprudent, I beg you."

"M. the Count need not be uneasy; he has my promise."

"Very good. I know the value of it."

The count walked off; but during this short colloquy the quadrille had ended, and M. de Clameran and Madeleine were lost to sight.

"I shall find them near Madame Fauvel," said the clown.

And he at once started in search of the banker's wife.

Incommoded by the stifling heat of the room, Madame Fauvel had sought a little fresh air in the grand picture-gallery, which, thanks to the talisman called gold, was now transformed into a fairy-like garden, filled with orange-trees, japonicas, laurel, and many rare exotics.

The clown saw her seated near a grove, not far from the door of the card-room. Upon her right was Madeleine, and near her stood Raoul de Lagors, dressed in a costume of Henri III.

"I must confess," muttered the clown from his post of observation, "that the young scamp is a very handsome man."

Madeleine appeared very sad. She had plucked a japonica from a tree near by, and was mechanically pulling it to pieces as she sat with her eyes downcast.

Raoul and Madame Fauvel were engaged in earnest conversation. Their faces were composed, but the gestures of one and the trembling of the other betrayed a serious discussion.

In the card-room sat the doge, M. de Clameran, so placed as to have full view of Madame Fauvel and Madeleine, although himself concealed by an angle of the room.

"It is the continuation of yesterday's scene," thought the clown. "If I could only get behind the oleander-tree, I might hear what they are saying."

He pushed his way through the crowd, and, just as he had reached the desired spot, Madeleine arose, and, taking the arm of a bejewelled Persian, walked away.

At the same moment Raoul went into the card-room, and whispered a few words to de Clameran.

"There they go," muttered the clown. "The two scoundrels certainly hold these poor women in their power; and they are determined to make them suffer before releasing them. What can be the secret of their power?"

His attention was attracted by a commotion in the picture-gallery; it was caused by the announcement of a wonderful minuet to be danced in the ball-room; the arrival of the Countess de Commarin as Aurora; and the presence of the Princess Korasoff, with her superb emeralds, which were reported to be the finest in the world.

In an instant the gallery became almost deserted. Only a few forlorn-looking people remained; mostly sulky husbands, and some melancholy youths looking awkward and unhappy in their gay fancy dresses.

The clown thought it a favourable opportunity for carrying out his project.

He abruptly left his corner, flourishing his switch, and beating his banner, and, crossing the gallery, seated himself in a chair between Madame Fauvel and the door. As soon as the people had collected in a circle around him, he commenced to cough in an affected manner, like a stump orator about to make a speech.

Then he struck a comical attitude, standing up with his body twisted sideways, and his hat on one ear, and with great buffoonery and volubility made the following remarks:

"Ladies and gentlemen, this very morning I obtained a license from the authorities of this town. And what for? Why gentlemen, for the purpose of exhibiting to you a spectacle which has already won the admiration of the four quarters of the globe, and several universities besides. Inside of this booth, ladies, is about to commence the representation of a most remarkable drama, acted for the first time at Pekin, and translated into several languages by our most celebrated authors. Gentlemen, you can take your seats; the lamps are lighted, and the actors are changing their dress."

Here he stopped speaking, and imitated to perfection the feats which *mountebanks* play upon horns and kettle-drums.

"Now, ladies and gentlemen," he resumed, "you wish to know what I am doing outside, if the piece is to be performed under the tent. The fact is, gentlemen, that I wish to give you a foretaste of the agitations, sensations, emotions, palpitations, and other entertainments which you may enjoy by paying the small sum of ten *sous*. You see this superb picture? It represents eight of the most thrilling scenes in the drama. Ah, I see you begin to shudder already; and yet this is nothing compared to the play itself. This splendid picture gives you no more idea of the acting than a drop of water gives an idea of the sea, or a spark of fire of the sun. My picture, gentlemen, is merely to give you a foretaste of what is in the tent; as the steam oozing from a restaurant gives you a taste, or rather a smell, of what is within."

"Do you know this clown?" asked an enormous Turk of a melancholy Punch.

"No, but he can imitate a trumpet splendidly."

"Oh, very well indeed! But what is he driving at?"

The clown was endeavouring to attract the attention of Madame Fauvel, who, since Raoul and Madeleine had left her, sat by herself in a mournful reverie.

He succeeded in his object.

The showman's shrill voice brought the banker's wife back to a sense of reality; she started, and looked quickly about her, as if suddenly awakened from a troubled dream.

"Now, ladies, we are in China. The first picture on my canvas, here, in the left corner"—here he touched the top daub—"represents the celebrated Mandarin Li-Fo, in the bosom of his family. This pretty woman leaning over him is his wife; and these children playing on the carpet are the bonds of love between this happy pair. Do you not inhale the odour of sanctity and happiness emanating from this speaking picture, gentlemen?

"Madame Li-Fo is the most virtuous of women, adoring her husband and idolizing her children. Being virtuous she is happy; for the wise Confucius says, 'The ways of virtue are more pleasant than the ways of vice.'"

Madame Fauvel had left her seat, and approached nearer to the clown.

"Do you see anything on the banner like what he is describing?" asked the melancholy Punch of his neighbour.

"No, not a thing. Do you?"

The fact is, that the daubs of paint on the canvas represented one thing as well as another, and the clown could call them whatever he pleased.

"Picture No. 2!" he cried, after a flourish of music. "This old lady, seated before a mirror tearing out her hair—especially the gray ones—you have seen before; do you recognise her? No, you do not. She is the fair Mandarine of the first picture. I see the tears in your eyes, ladies and gentlemen. Ah! you have cause to weep; for she is no longer virtuous, and her happiness has departed with her virtue. Alas, it is a sad tale! One fatal day she met, on the streets of Pekin, a young ruffian, fiendish, but beautiful as an angel, and she loved him—the unfortunate woman loved him!"

The last words were uttered in the most tragic tone as he raised his clasped hands to heaven.

During this tirade he had whirled around, so that he found himself facing the banker's wife, whose countenance he closely watched while he was speaking.

"You are surprised, gentlemen," he continued; "I am not. The great Bilboquet has proved to us that the heart never grows old, and that the most vigorous wall-flowers flourish on old ruins. This unhappy woman is nearly fifty years old—fifty years old, and in love with a youth! Hence this heart-rending scene which should serve as a warning to us all."

"Really!" grumbled a cook dressed in white satin, who had passed the evening in carrying around bills of fare, which no one read, "I thought he was going to amuse us."

"But," continued the clown, "you must go inside of the booth to witness the effects of the Mandarine's folly. At times a ray of reason penetrates her diseased brain, and then the sight of her anguish would soften a heart of stone. Enter, and for the small sum of ten *sous* you shall hear sobs such as the Odeon never echoed in its halcyon days. The unhappy woman has waked up to the absurdity and inanity of her blind passion; she confesses to herself that she is madly pursuing a phantom. She knows but too well that he, in the vigour and beauty of youth, cannot love a faded old woman like herself, who vainly makes pitiable efforts to retain the last remains of her once entrancing beauty. She feels that the sweet words he once whispered in her charmed ear were deceitful falsehoods. She knows that the day is near when she will be left alone, with nothing save his mantle in her hand."

As the clown addressed this voluble description to the crowd before him, he narrowly watched the countenance of the banker's wife.

But nothing he had said seemed to affect her. She leaned back in her armchair perfectly calm, and occasionally smiled at the tragic manner of the showman.

"Good heavens!" muttered the clown uneasily, "can I be on the wrong track?"

He saw that his circle of listeners was increased by the presence of the doge, M. de Clameran.

"The third picture," he said, after a roll of drums, "depicts the old Mandarine after she has dismissed that most annoying of guests—remorse—from her bosom. She promises herself that interest shall supply the place of love in chaining the too seductive youth to her side. It is with this object that she invests him with false honours and dignity, and introduces him to the chief mandarins of the capital of the Celestial Empire; then, since so handsome a youth must cut a fine figure in society, and as a fine figure cannot be cut without money, the lady must needs to sacrifice all of her possessions for his sake. Necklaces, rings, bracelets, diamonds, and pearls, all are surrendered. The monster carries all these jewels to the pawnbrokers on Tien-Tsi Street, and then has the cruelty to refuse her the tickets, so that she may have a chance of redeeming her treasures."

The clown thought that at last he had hit the mark. Madame Fauvel began to betray signs of agitation.

Once she made an attempt to rise from her chair; but it seemed as if her strength failed her, and she sank back, forced to listen to the end.

"Finally, ladies and gentlemen," continued the clown, "the richly stored jewel-cases became empty. The day came when the Mandarine had nothing more to give. It was then that the young scoundrel conceived the project of carrying off the jasper button belonging to the Mandarin Li-Fo—a splendid jewel of incalculable value, which, being the badge of his dignity, was kept in a granite chest, and guarded by three soldiers night and day. Ah! the Mandarine resisted a long time! She knew the innocent soldiers would be accused and crucified, as is the custom in Pekin; and this thought restrained her. But her lover besought her so tenderly, that she finally yielded to his entreaties; and—the jasper button was stolen. The fourth picture represents the guilty couple stealthily creeping down the private stairway: see their frightened look—see—"

He abruptly stopped. Three or four of his auditors rushed to the assistance of Madame Fauvel, who seemed about to faint; and at the same time he felt his arm roughly seized by someone behind him.

He turned around and faced de Clameran and Lagors, both of whom were pale with anger.

"What do you want, gentlemen?" he inquired politely.

"To speak to you," they both answered.

"I am at your service."

And he followed them to the end of the picture-gallery, near a window opening on a balcony.

Here they were unobserved except by the man in the Venetian cloak, whom the clown had so respectfully addressed as "M. the Count."

The minuet having ended, the orchestras were resting, and the crowd began to rapidly fill the gallery.

The sudden faintness of Madame Fauvel had passed off unnoticed save by a few, who attributed it to the heat of the room. M. Fauvel had been sent for; but when he came hurrying in, and found his wife composedly talking to Madeleine, his alarm was dissipated, and he returned to the card-tables.

Not having as much control over his temper as Raoul, M. de Clameran angrily said:

"In the first place, *monsieur,* I would like to know who you are."

The clown determined to answer as if he thought the question were a jest, replied in the bantering tone of a buffoon:

"You want my passport, do you, my lord *doge?* I left it in the hands of the city authorities; it contains my name, age, profession, domicile, and every detail—"

With an angry gesture, M. de Clameran interrupted him.

"You have just committed a gross insult!"

"I, my lord *doge?*"

"Yes, you! What do you mean by telling this abominable story in this house?"

"Abominable! You may call it abominable; but I, who composed it, have a different opinion of it."

"Enough, *monsieur;* you will at least have the courage to acknowledge that your performance was a vile insinuation against Madame Fauvel?"

The clown stood with his head thrown back, and mouth wide open, as if astounded at what he heard.

But anyone who knew him would have seen his bright black eyes sparkling with malicious satisfaction.

"Bless my heart!" he cried, as if speaking to himself. "This is the strangest thing I ever heard of! How can my drama of the Mandarine

Li-Fo have any reference to Madame Fauvel, whom I don't know from Adam or Eve? I can't think how the resemblance—unless—but no, that is impossible."

"Do you pretend," said M. de Clameran, "to be ignorant of M. Fauvel's misfortune?"

The clown looked very innocent, and asked:

"What misfortune?"

"The robbery of which M. Fauvel was the victim. It has been in everyone's mouth, and you must have heard of it."

"Ah, yes, yes; I remember. His cashier ran off with three hundred and fifty thousand *francs*. *Pardieu*! It is a thing that almost daily happens. But, as to discovering any connection between this robbery and my play, that is another matter."

M. de Clameran made no reply. A nudge from Lagors had calmed him as if by enchantment.

He looked quietly at the clown, and seemed to regret having uttered the significant words forced from him by angry excitement.

"Very well," he finally said in his usual haughty tone; "I must have been mistaken. I accept your explanation."

But the clown, hitherto so humble and silly-looking, seemed to take offence at the word, and, assuming a defiant attitude, said:

"I have not made, nor do I intend making, any explanation."

"*Monsieur*," began de Clameran.

"Allow me to finish, if you please. If, unintentionally, I have offended the wife of a man whom I highly esteem, it is his business to seek redress, and not yours. Perhaps you will tell me he is too old to demand satisfaction: if so, let him send one of his sons. I saw one of them in the ballroom tonight; let him come. You asked me who I am; in return I ask you who are you—you who undertake to act as Madame Fauvel's champion? Are you her relative, friend, or ally? What right have you to insult her by pretending to discover an allusion to her in a play invented for amusement?"

There was nothing to be said in reply to this. M. de Clameran sought a means of escape.

"I am a friend of M. Fauvel," he said, "and this title gives me the right to be as jealous of his reputation as if it were my own. If this is not a sufficient reason for my interference, I must inform you that his family will shortly be mine: I regard myself as his nephew."

"Ah!"

"Next week, *monsieur*, my marriage with Madeleine will be publicly announced."

This news was so unexpected, so startling that for a moment the clown was dumb; and now his surprise was genuine.

But he soon recovered himself, and, bowing with deference, said, with covert irony:

"Permit me to offer my congratulations, *monsieur*. Besides being the *belle* tonight, Mademoiselle Madeleine is worth, I hear, half a million."

Raoul de Lagors had anxiously been watching the people near them, to see if they overheard this conversation.

"We have had enough of this gossip," he said, in a disdainful tone; "I will only say one thing more, master clown, and that is, that your tongue is too long."

"Perhaps it is, my pretty youth, perhaps it is; but my arm is still longer."

De Clameran here interrupted them by saying:

"It is impossible for one to seek an explanation from a man who conceals his identity under the guise of a fool."

"You are at liberty, my lord doge, to ask the master of the house who I am—if you dare."

"You are," cried de Clameran, "you are—"

A warning look from Raoul checked the forge-master from using an epithet which would have led to an affray, or at least a scandalous scene. The clown stood by with a sardonic smile, and, after a moment's silence, stared M. de Clameran steadily in the face, and in measured tones said:

"I was the best friend, *monsieur*, that your brother Gaston ever had. I was his adviser, and the confidant of his last wishes."

These few words fell like a clap of thunder upon de Clameran.

He turned deadly pale, and stared back with his hands stretched out before him, as if shrinking from a phantom.

He tried to answer, to protest against this assertion, but the words froze on his lips. His fright was pitiable.

"Come, let us go," said Lagors, who was perfectly cool.

And he dragged de Clameran away, half supporting him, for he staggered like a drunken man, and clung to every object he passed, to prevent falling.

"Oh," exclaimed the clown, in three different tones, "oh, oh!"

He himself was almost as much astonished as the forge-master, and remained rooted to the spot, watching the latter as he slowly left the room.

It was with no decided object in view that he had ventured to use the last mysteriously threatening words, but he had been inspired to do so by his wonderful instinct, which with him was like the scent of a blood-hound.

"What can this mean?" he murmured. "Why was he so frightened? What terrible memory have I awakened in his base soul? I need not boast of my penetration, or the subtlety of my plans. There is a great master, who, without any effort, in an instant destroys all my chimeras; he is called 'Chance.'"

His mind had wandered far from the present scene, when he was brought back to his situation by someone touching him on the shoulder. It was the man in the Venetian cloak.

"Are you very satisfied, M. Verduret?" he inquired.

"Yes, and no, M. the Count. No, because I have not completely achieved the object I had in view when I asked you for an invitation here tonight; yes, because these two rascals behaved in a manner which dispels all doubt."

"And yet you complain—"

"I do not complain, M. the Count: on the contrary, I bless chance, or rather Providence, which has just revealed to me the existence of a secret that I did not before even suspect."

Five or six people approached the count, and he went off with them after giving the clown a friendly nod.

The latter instantly threw aside his banner, and started in pursuit of Madame Fauvel. He found her sitting on a sofa in the large salon, engaged in an animated conversation with Madeleine.

"Of course they are talking over the scene; but what has become of Lagors and de Clameran?"

He soon saw them wandering among the groups scattered about the room, and eagerly asking questions.

"I will bet my head these honourable gentlemen are trying to find out who I am. Keep it up, my friends, ask everybody in the room; I wish you success!"

They soon gave it up, but were so preoccupied, and anxious to be alone in order to reflect and deliberate, that, without waiting for supper, they took leave of Madame Fauvel and her niece, saying they were going home.

The clown saw them go up to the dressing-room for their cloaks, and in a few minutes leave the house.

"I have nothing more to do here," he murmured; "I might as well go too."

He completely covered his dress with a *domino*, and started for home, thinking the cold frosty air would cool his confused brain.

He lit a cigar, and, walking up the Rue St. Lazare, crossed the Rue Notre Dame de Lorette, and struck into the Faubourg Montmartre.

A man suddenly started out from some place of concealment, and rushed upon him with a dagger.

Fortunately the clown had a cat-like instinct, which enabled him to protect himself against immediate danger, and detect any which threatened.

He saw, or rather divined, the man crouching in the dark shadow of a house, and had the presence of mind to strike an attitude which enabled him to ward off the assassin by spreading out his arms before him.

This movement certainly saved his life; for he received in his arm a furious stab, which would have instantly killed him had it penetrated his breast.

Anger, more than pain, made him cry out:

"Ah, you villain!"

And recoiling a few feet, he put himself on the defensive.

But the precaution was useless.

Seeing his blow miss, the assassin did not return to the attack, but made rapidly off.

"That was certainly Lagors," said the clown, "and de Clameran must be somewhere near. While I walked around one side of the church, they must have gone the other and lain in wait for me."

His wound began to pain him; he stood under a gas-lamp to examine it.

It did not appear to be dangerous, but the arm was cut through to the bone.

He tore his handkerchief into four bands, and tied his arm up with the dexterity of a surgeon.

"I must be on the track of some great crime, since these fellows are resolved upon murder. When such cunning rogues are only in danger of the police court, they do not gratuitously risk the chance of being tried for murder."

He thought by enduring a great deal of pain he might still use his arm; so he started in pursuit of his enemy, taking care to keep in the middle of the road, and avoid all dark corners.

Although he saw no one, he was convinced that he was being pursued.

He was not mistaken. When he reached the Boulevard Montmartre, he crossed the street, and, as he did so, distinguished two shadows which he recognised. They crossed the same street a little higher up.

"I have to deal with desperate men," he muttered. "They do not even take pains to conceal their pursuit of me. They seem to be accustomed to this kind of adventure, and the carriage trick which fooled Fanferlot would never succeed with them. Besides, my light hat is a perfect beacon to lead them on in the night." He continued his way up the boulevard, and, without turning his head, was sure that his enemies were thirty feet behind him.

"I must get rid of them somehow," he said to himself. "I can neither return home nor to the Archangel with these devils at my heels. They are following me to find out where I live, and who I am. If they discover that the clown is M. Verduret, and that M. Verduret is M. Lecoq, my plans will be ruined. They will escape abroad with the money, and I shall be left to console myself with a wounded arm. A pleasant ending to all my exertions!"

The idea of Raoul and de Clameran escaping him so exasperated him that for an instant he thought of having them arrested at once.

This was easy; for he had only to rush upon them, scream for help, and they would all three be arrested, carried to the watch-house, and consigned to the commissary of police.

The police often resort to this ingenious and simple means of arresting a malefactor for whom they are on the lookout, and whom they cannot seize without a warrant.

The next day there is a general explanation, and the parties, if innocent, are dismissed.

The clown had sufficient proof to sustain him in the arrest of Lagors. He could show the letter and the mutilated prayer-book, he could reveal the existence of the pawnbroker's tickets in the house at Vesinet, he could display his wounded arm. He could force Raoul to confess how and why he had assumed the name of Lagors, and what his motive was in passing himself off for a relative of M. Fauvel.

On the other hand, in acting thus hastily, he was insuring the safety of the principal plotter, de Clameran. What proofs had he against him? Not one. He had strong suspicions, but no well-grounded charge to produce against him.

On reflection the clown decided that he would act alone, as he had thus far done, and that alone and unaided he would discover the truth of all his suspicions.

Having reached this decision, the first step to be taken was to put his followers on the wrong scent.

He walked rapidly up the Rue Sebastopol, and, reaching the square of the Arts et Metiers, he abruptly stopped, and asked some insignificant questions of two constables who were standing talking together.

The manoeuvre had the result he expected; Raoul and de Clameran stood perfectly still about twenty steps off, not daring to advance.

Twenty steps! That was as much start as the clown wanted. While talking with the constables, he had pulled the bell of the door before which they were standing, and its hollow sound apprised him that the door was open. He bowed, and entered the house.

A minute later the constables had passed on, and Lagors and de Clameran in their turn rang the bell. When the *concierge* appeared, they asked who it was that had just gone in disguised as a clown.

They were told that no such person had entered, and that none of the lodgers had gone out disguised that night. "However," added the *concierge*, "I am not very sure, for this house has a back door which opens on the Rue St. Denis."

"We are tricked," interrupted Lagors, "and will never know who the clown is."

"Unless we learn it too soon for our own good," said de Clameran musingly.

While Lagors and de Clameran were anxiously trying to devise some means of discovering the clown's identity, Verduret hurried up the back street, and reached the Archangel as the clock struck three.

Prosper, who was watching from his window, saw him in the distance, and ran down to open the door for him.

"What have you learned?" he said; "what did you find out? Did you see Madeleine? Were Raoul and de Clameran at the ball?"

But M. Verduret was not in the habit of discussing private affairs where he might be overheard.

"First of all, let us go into your room, and get some water to wash this cut, which burns like fire."

"Heavens! Are you wounded?"

"Yes, it is a little souvenir of your friend Raoul. Ah, I will soon teach him the danger of chopping up a man's arm!"

Prosper was surprised at the look of merciless rage on his friend's face, as he calmly washed and dressed his arm.

"Now, Prosper, we will talk as much as you please. Our enemies are on the alert, and we must crush them instantly, or not at all. I have made a mistake. I have been on the wrong track; it is an accident liable to happen to any man, no matter how intelligent he may be. I took the effect for the cause. The day I was convinced that culpable relations existed between Raoul and Madame Fauvel, I thought I held the end of the thread that must lead us to the truth. I should have been more mistrustful; this solution was too simple, too natural."

"Do you suppose Madame Fauvel to be innocent?"

"Certainly not. But her guilt is not such as I first supposed. I imagined that, infatuated with a seductive young adventurer, Madame Fauvel had first bestowed upon him the name of one of her relatives, and then introduced him as her nephew. This was an adroit stratagem to gain him admission to her husband's house.

"She began by giving him all the money she could dispose of; later she let him take her jewels to the pawnbrokers; when she had nothing more to give, she allowed him to steal the money from her husband's safe. That is what I first thought."

"And in this way everything was explained?"

"No, this did not explain everything, as I well knew at the time, and should, consequently, have studied my characters more thoroughly. How is de Clameran's position to be accounted for, if my first idea was the correct one?"

"De Clameran is Lagors's accomplice of course."

"Ah, there is the mistake! I for a long time believed Lagors to be the principal person, when, in fact, he is not. Yesterday, in a dispute between them, the forge-master said to his dear friend, 'And, above all things, my friend, I would advise you not to resist me, for if you do I will crush you to atoms.' That explains all. The elegant Lagors is not the lover of Madame Fauvel, but the tool of de Clameran. Besides, did our first suppositions account for the resigned obedience of Madeleine? It is de Clameran, and not Lagors, whom Madeleine obeys."

Prosper began to remonstrate.

M. Verduret shrugged his shoulders. To convince Prosper he had only to utter one word: to tell him that three hours ago de Clameran had announced his intended marriage with Madeleine; but he did not.

"De Clameran," he continued, "de Clameran alone has Madame Fauvel in his power. Now, the question is, what is the secret of this terrible influence he has gained over her? I have positive proof that they have not met since their early youth until fifteen months ago; and, as

Madame Fauvel's reputation has always been above the reach of slander, we must seek in the past for the cause of her resigned obedience to his will."

"We can never discover it," said Prosper mournfully.

"We can discover it as soon as we know de Clameran's past life. Ah, tonight he turned as white as a sheet when I mentioned his brother Gaston's name. And then I remembered that Gaston died suddenly, while his brother Louis was making a visit."

"Do you think he was murdered?"

"I think the men who tried to assassinate me would do anything. The robbery, my friend, has now become a secondary detail. It is quite easily explained, and, if that were all to be accounted for, I would say to you, My task is done, let us go ask the judge of instruction for a warrant of arrest."

Prosper started up with sparkling eyes.

"Ah, you know—is it possible?"

"Yes, I know who gave the key, and I know who told the secret word."

"The key might have been M. Fauvel's. But the word—"

"The word you were foolish enough to give. You have forgotten, I suppose. But fortunately Gypsy remembered. You know that, two days before the robbery, you took Lagors and two other friends to sup with Madame Gypsy? Nina was sad, and reproached you for not being more devoted to her."

"Yes, I remember that."

"But do you remember what you replied to her?"

"No, I do not," said Prosper after thinking a moment.

"Well, I will tell you: 'Nina, you are unjust in reproaching me with not thinking constantly of you; for at this very moment your dear name guards M. Fauvel's safe.'"

The truth suddenly burst upon Prosper like a thunderclap. He wrung his hands despairingly, and cried:

"Yes, oh, yes! I remember now."

"Then you can easily understand the rest. One of the scoundrels went to Madame Fauvel, and compelled her to give up her husband's key; then, at a venture, placed the movable buttons on the name of Gypsy, opened the safe, and took the three hundred and fifty thousand *francs*. And Madame Fauvel must have been terribly frightened before she yielded. The day after the robbery the poor woman was near dying; and it was she who at the greatest risk sent you the ten thousand *francs*."

"But which was the thief, Raoul or de Clameran? What enables them to thus tyrannize over Madame Fauvel? And how does Madeleine come to be mixed up in the affair?"

"These questions, my dear Prosper, I cannot yet answer; therefore I postpone seeing the judge. I only ask you to wait ten days; and, if I cannot in that time discover the solution of this mystery, I will return and go with you to report to M. Patrigent all that we know."

"Are you going to leave the city?"

"In an hour I shall be on the road to Beaucaire. It was from that neighbourhood that de Clameran came, as well as Madame Fauvel, who was a Mademoiselle de la Verberie before marriage."

"Yes, I knew both families."

"I must go there to study them. Neither Raoul nor de Clameran can escape during my absence. The police are watching them. But you, Prosper, must be prudent. Promise me to remain a prisoner here during my trip."

All that M. Verduret asked, Prosper willingly promised. But he did not wish to be left in complete ignorance of his projects for the future, or of his motives in the past.

"Will you not tell me, *monsieur*, who you are, and what reasons you had for coming to my rescue?"

The extraordinary man smiled sadly, and said:

"I tell, in the presence of Nina, on the day before your marriage with Madeleine."

Once left to his own reflections, Prosper began to appreciate the powerful assistance rendered by his friend.

Recalling the field of investigation gone over by his mysterious protector, he was amazed at its extent.

How many facts had been discovered in a week, and with what precision, although he had pretended to be on the wrong track! Verduret had grouped his evidence, and reached a result which Prosper felt he never could have hoped to attain by his own exertions.

He was conscious that he possessed neither Verduret's penetration nor his subtlety. He did not possess this art of compelling obedience, of creating friends at every step, and the science of making men and circumstances unite in the attainment of a common result.

He began to regret the absence of his friend, who had risen up in the hour of adversity. He missed the sometimes rough but always kindly voice, which had encouraged and consoled him.

He felt woefully lost and helpless, not daring to act or think for himself, more timid than a child when deserted by his nurse.

He had the good sense to follow the recommendations of his mentor. He remained shut up in the Archangel, not even appearing at the windows.

Twice he had news of M. Verduret. The first time he received a letter in which this friend said he had seen his father, and had had a long talk with him. Afterward, Dubois, M. de Clameran's valet, came to tell him that his "patron" reported everything as progressing finely.

On the ninth day of his voluntary seclusion, Prosper began to feel restless, and at ten o'clock at night set forth to take a walk, thinking the fresh air would relieve the headache which had kept him awake the previous night.

Madame Alexandre, who seemed to have some knowledge of M. Verduret's affairs, begged Prosper to remain at home.

"What can I risk by taking a walk at this time, in a quiet part of the city?" he asked. "I can certainly stroll as far as the Jardin des Plantes without meeting anyone."

Unfortunately he did not strictly follow this programme; for, having reached the Orleans railway station, he went into a cafe near by, and called for a glass of ale.

As he sat sipping his glass, he picked up a daily paper, *The Sun*, and under the head of "Fashionable Gossip," signed Jacques Durand, read the following:

> We understand that the niece of one of our most prominent bankers, M. Andre Fauvel, will shortly be married to M. le Marquis Louis de Clameran. The engagement has been announced.

This news, coming upon him so unexpectedly, proved to Prosper the justness of M. Verduret's calculations.

Alas! why did not this certainty inspire him with absolute faith? why did it not give him courage to wait, the strength of mind to refrain from acting on his own responsibility?

Frenzied by distress of mind, he already saw Madeleine indissolubly united to this villain, and, thinking that M. Verduret would perhaps arrive too late to be of use, determined at all risks to throw an obstacle in the way of the marriage.

He called for pen and paper, and forgetting that no situation can excuse the mean cowardice of an anonymous letter, wrote in a disguised hand the following lines to M. Fauvel:

Dear Sir—

You consigned your cashier to prison; you acted prudently, since you were convinced of his dishonesty and faithlessness.

But, even if he stole three hundred and fifty thousand *francs* from your safe, does it follow that he also stole Madame Fauvel's diamonds, and pawned them at the Mont-de-Piete, where they now are?

Warned as you are, if I were you, I would not be the subject of public scandal. I would watch my wife, and would be distrustful of handsome cousins.

Moreover, I would, before signing the marriage contract of Mademoiselle Madeleine, inquire at the Prefecture of Police, and obtain some information concerning the noble Marquis de Clameran.

A Friend

Prosper hastened off to post his letter. Fearing that it would not reach M. Fauvel in time, he walked up to the Rue Cardinal Lemoine, and put it in the main letter-box, so as to be certain of its speedy delivery.

Until now he had not doubted the propriety of his action.

But now when too late, when he heard the sound of his letter falling into the box, a thousand scruples filled his mind. Was it not wrong to act thus hurriedly? Would not this letter interfere with M. Verduret's plans? Upon reaching the hotel, his doubts were changed into bitter regrets.

Joseph Dubois was waiting for him; he had received a despatch from his patron, saying that his business was finished, and that he would return the next evening at nine o'clock.

Prosper was wretched. He would have given all he had to recover the anonymous letter.

And he had cause for regret.

At that very hour M. Verduret was taking his seat in the cars at Tarascon, meditating upon the most advantageous plan to be adopted in pursuance of his discoveries.

For he had discovered everything, and now must bring matters to a crisis.

Adding to what he already knew, the story of an old nurse of Mademoiselle de la Verberie, the affidavit of an old servant who had always lived in the de Clameran family, and the depositions of the Vesinet husband and wife who attended M. Lagors at his country house, the latter having been sent to him by Dubois (Fanferlot), with a good deal of information obtained from the prefecture of police, he had worked up a complete case, and could now act upon a chain of evidence without a missing link.

As he had predicted, he had been compelled to search into the distant past for the first causes of the crime of which Prosper had been the victim.

The following is the drama, as written out by him for the benefit of the examining magistrate with the certainty that it contained sufficient grounds for preferring an indictment.

Chapter 12

The Drama

About six miles from Tarascon, on the left bank of the Rhone, not far from Messrs Audibert's wonderful gardens, stood the Château of Clameran, a weather-stained, neglected, but massive structure.

Here lived, in 1841, the old Marquis de Clameran and his two sons, Gaston and Louis.

The *marquis* was an eccentric old man. He belonged to the race of nobles, now almost extinct, whose watches stopped in 1789, and who kept time with the past century.

More attached to his illusions than to his life, the old *marquis* insisted upon considering all the stirring events which had happened since the first revolution as a series of deplorable practical jokes.

Emigrating with the Count d'Artois, he did not return to France until 1815, with the allies.

He should have been thankful to Heaven for the recovery of a portion of his immense family estates; a comparatively small portion, to be sure, but full enough to support him comfortably: he said, however, that he did not think the few paltry acres were worth thanking God for.

At first, he tried every means to obtain an appointment at court; but seeing all his efforts fail, he resolved to retire to his *château*, which he did, after cursing and pitying his king, whom he had worshipped.

He soon became accustomed to the free and indolent life of a country gentleman.

Possessing fifteen thousand *francs* a year, he spent twenty-five or thirty thousand, borrowing from every source, saying that a genuine restoration would soon take place, and that then he would regain possession of all his properties.

Following his example, his younger son lived extravagantly. Louis was always in pursuit of adventure, and idled away his time in drinking and gambling. The elder son, Gaston, anxious to participate in the stirring events of the time, prepared himself for action by quietly working, studying, and reading certain papers and pamphlets surreptitiously received, the very mention of which was considered a hanging matter by his father.

Altogether the old *marquis* was the happiest of mortals, living well, drinking high, hunting much, tolerated by the peasants, and execrated by the gentlemen of the neighbourhood, who regarded him with contempt and raillery.

Time never hung heavy on his hands, except in mid-summer, when the valley of the Rhone was intensely hot; and even then he had infallible means of amusement, always new, though ever the same.

He detested, above all, his neighbour the Countess de la Verberie.

The Countess de la Verberie, the *bete noire* of the *marquis*, as he ungallantly termed her, was a tall, dry woman, angular in appearance and character, cold and arrogant toward her equals, and domineering over her inferiors.

Like her noble neighbour, she too had emigrated; and her husband was afterward killed at Lutzen, but unfortunately not in the French ranks.

In 1815, the countess came back to France. But while the Marquis de Clameran returned to comparative ease, she could obtain nothing from royal munificence, but the small estate and Château of La Verberie.

It is true that the Château of La Verberie would have contented most people; but the countess never ceased to complain of her unmerited poverty, as she called it.

The pretty *château* was more modest in appearance than the manor of the de Clamerans; but it was equally comfortable, and much better regulated by its proud mistress.

It was built in the middle of a beautiful park, one of the wonders of that part of the country. It reached from the Beaucaire road to the river-bank, a marvel of beauty, with its superb old oaks, yoke-elms, and lovely groves, its meadow, and clear stream of water winding in among the trees.

The countess had but one child—a lovely girl of eighteen, named Valentine; fair, slender, and graceful, with large, soft eyes, beautiful enough to make the stone saints of the village church thrill in their niches, when she knelt piously at their feet.

The renown of her great beauty, carried on the rapid waters of the Rhone, was spread far and wide.

Often the bargemen and the robust wagoners, driving their powerful horses along the road, would stop to gaze with admiration upon Valentine seated under some grand old tree on the banks of the river, absorbed in her book.

At a distance her white dress and flowing tresses made her seem a mysterious spirit from another world, these honest people said; they thought it a good omen when they caught a glimpse of her as they passed up the river. All along between Arles and Valence she was spoken of as the "lovely fairy" of La Verberie.

If M. de Clameran detested the countess, Madame de la Verberie execrated the *marquis*. If he nicknamed her "the witch," she never called him anything but "the old gander."

And yet they should have agreed, for at heart they cherished the same opinions, with different ways of viewing them.

He considered himself a philosopher, scoffed at everything, and had an excellent digestion. She nursed her rancour, and grew yellow and thin from rage and envy.

Nevertheless, they might have spent many pleasant evenings together, for, after all, they were neighbours. From Clameran could be seen Valentine's greyhound running about the park of La Verberie; from La Verberie glimpses were had of the lights in the dining-room windows of Clameran.

And, as regularly as these lights appeared, every evening, the countess would say, in a spiteful tone:

"Ah, now their orgies are about to commence!"

The two *châteaux* were only separated by the fast-flowing Rhone, which at this spot was rather narrow.

But between the two families existed a hatred deeper and more difficult to avert than the course of the Rhone.

What was the cause of this hatred?

The countess, no less than the *marquis*, would have found it difficult to tell.

It was said that under the reign of Henri IV. or Louis XIII. a La Verberie betrayed the affections of a fair daughter of the de Clamerans.

This misdeed led to a duel and bloodshed.

This groundwork of facts had been highly embellished by fiction; handed down from generation to generation, it had now become a long tragic history of robbery, murder, and rapine, which precluded any intercourse between the two families.

The usual result followed, as it always does in real life, and often in romances, which, however exaggerated they may be, generally preserve a reflection of the truth which inspires them.

Gaston met Valentine at an entertainment; he fell in love with her at first sight.

Valentine saw Gaston, and from that moment his image filled her heart.

But so many obstacles separated them!

For over a year they both religiously guarded their secret, buried like a treasure in the inmost recesses of their hearts.

And this year of charming, dangerous reveries decided their fate. To the sweetness of the first impression succeeded a more tender sentiment; then came love, each having endowed the other with superhuman qualities and ideal perfections.

Deep, sincere passion can only expand in solitude; in the impure air of a city it fades and dies, like the hardy plants which lose their colour and perfume when transplanted to hot-houses.

Gaston and Valentine had only seen each other once, but seeing was to love; and, as the time passed, their love grew stronger, until at last the fatality which had presided over their first meeting brought them once more together. They both happened to be spending the day with the old Duchess d'Arlange, who had returned to the neighbourhood to sell her property. They spoke to each other, and like old friends, surprised to find that they both entertained the same thoughts and echoed the same memories.

Again they were separated for months. But soon, as if by accident, they happened to be at a certain hour on the banks of the Rhone, and would sit and gaze across at each other. Finally, one mild May evening, when Madame de la Verberie had gone to Beaucaire, Gaston ventured into the park, and appeared before Valentine.

She was not surprised or indignant. Genuine innocence displays none of the startled modesty assumed by conventional innocence. It never occurred to Valentine that she ought to bid Gaston to leave her.

She leaned upon his arm, and strolled up and down the grand old avenue of oaks. They did not say they loved each other, they felt it; but they did say that their love was hopeless. They well knew that the inveterate family feud could never be overcome, and that it would be folly to attempt it. They swore never, never to forget each other, and tearfully resolved never to meet again; never, not even once more!

Alas! Valentine was not without excuse. With a timid, loving heart, her expansive affection was repressed and chilled by a harsh mother. Never had there been one of those long private talks between the Countess de la Verberie and Valentine which enabled a good mother to read her daughter's heart like an open book.

Madame de la Verberie saw nothing but her daughter's beauty. She was wont to rub her hands, and say:

"Next winter I will borrow enough money to take the child to Paris, and I am much mistaken if her beauty does not win her a rich husband who will release me from poverty."

She called this loving her daughter!

The second meeting was not the last. Gaston dared not trust to a boatman, so he was obliged to walk a league in order to cross the bridge. Then he thought it would be shorter to swim the river; but he could not swim well, and to cross the Rhone where it ran so rapidly was rash for the most skilful swimmers.

One evening, however, Valentine was startled by seeing him rise out of the water at her feet.

She made him promise never to attempt this exploit again. He repeated the feat and the promise the next evening and every successive evening.

As Valentine always imagined he was being drowned in the furious current, they agreed upon a signal. At the moment of starting, Gaston would put a light in his window at Clameran, and in fifteen minutes he would be at his idol's feet.

What were the projects and hopes of the lovers? Alas! they projected nothing, they hoped for nothing.

Blindly, thoughtlessly, almost fearlessly, they abandoned themselves to the dangerous happiness of a daily rendezvous; regardless of the storm that must erelong burst over their devoted heads, they revelled in their present bliss.

Is not every sincere passion thus? Passion subsists upon itself and in itself; and the very things which ought to extinguish it, absence and obstacles, only make it burn more fiercely. It is exclusive and undisturbed; reflects neither of the past nor of the future; excepting the present, it sees and cares for nothing.

Moreover, Valentine and Gaston believed everyone ignorant of their secret.

They had always been so cautious! they had kept such strict watch! They had flattered themselves that their conduct had been a masterpiece of dissimulation and prudence.

Valentine had fixed upon the hour when she was certain her mother would not miss her. Gaston had never confided to anyone, not even to his brother Louis. They never breathed each other's name. They denied themselves a last sweet word, a last kiss, when they felt it would be more safe.

Poor blind lovers! As if anything could be concealed from the idle curiosity of country gossips; from the slanderous and ever-watchful enemies who are incessantly on the lookout for some new bit of tittle-tattle, good or bad, which they improve upon, and eagerly spread far and near.

They believed their secret well kept, whereas it had long since been made public; the story of their love, the particulars of their rendezvous, were topics of conversation throughout the neighbourhood.

Sometimes, at dusk, they would see a bark gliding along the water, near the shore, and would say to each other:

"It is a belated fisherman, returning home."

They were mistaken. The boat contained malicious spies, who delighted in having discovered them, and hastened to report, with a thousand false additions, the result of their expedition.

One dreary November evening, Gaston was awakened to the true state of affairs. The Rhone was so swollen by heavy rains that an inundation was daily expected. To attempt to swim across this impetuous torrent, would be tempting God. Therefore Gaston went to Tarascon, intending to cross the bridge there, and walk along the bank to the usual place of meeting at La Verberie. Valentine expected him at eleven o'clock.

Whenever Gaston went to Tarascon, he dined with a relative living there; but on this occasion a strange fatality led him to accompany a friend to the hotel of the "Three Emperors."

After dinner, they went not the Café Simon, their usual resort, but to the little *café* in the market-place, where the fairs were held.

The small dining-hall was filled with young men. Gaston and his friend called for a bottle of beer, and began to play billiards.

After they had been playing a short time, Gaston's attention was attracted by peals of laughter from a party at the other end of the room.

From this moment, preoccupied by this continued laughter, of which he was evidently the subject, he knocked the balls carelessly in every direction. His conduct surprised his friend, who said to him:

"What is the matter? You are missing the simplest shots."

"It is nothing."

The game went on a while longer, when Gaston suddenly turned as white as a sheet, and, throwing down his cue, strode toward the table which was occupied by five young men, playing dominoes and drinking wine.

He addressed the eldest of the group, a handsome man of twenty-six, with fierce-looking eyes, and a heavy black moustache, named Jules Lazet.

"Repeat, if you dare," he said, in a voice trembling with passion, "the remark you just now made!"

"I certainly will repeat it," said Lazet, calmly. "I said, and I say it again, that a nobleman's daughter is no better than a mechanic's daughter; that virtue does not always accompany a titled name."

"You mentioned a particular name!"

Lazet rose from his chair as if he knew his answer would exasperate Gaston, and that from words they would come to blows.

"I did," he said, with an insolent smile: "I mentioned the name of the pretty little fairy of La Verberie."

All the coffee-drinkers, and even two travelling agents who were dining in the cafe, rose and surrounded the two young men.

The provoking looks, the murmurs, or rather shouts, which welcomed him as he walked up to Lazet, proved to Gaston that he was surrounded by enemies.

The wickedness and evil tongue of the old *marquis* were bearing their fruit. Rancour ferments quickly and fiercely among the people of Provence.

Gaston de Clameran was not a man to yield, even if his foes were a hundred, instead of fifteen or twenty.

"No one but a coward," he said, in a clear, ringing voice, which the pervading silence rendered almost startling, "no one but a contemptible coward would be infamous enough to calumniate a young girl who has neither father nor brother to defend her honour."

"If she has no father or brother," sneered Lazet, "she has her lovers, and that suffices."

The insulting words, "her lovers," enraged Gaston beyond control; he slapped Lazet violently in the face.

Everyone in the *café* simultaneously uttered a cry of terror. Lazet's violence of character, his herculean strength and undaunted courage, were well known. He sprang across the table between them, and seized Gaston by the throat. Then arose a scene of excitement and confusion.

De Clameran's friend, attempting to assist him, was knocked down with billiard-cues, and kicked under a table.

Equally strong and agile, Gaston and Lazet struggled for some minutes without either gaining an advantage.

Lazet, as loyal as he was courageous, would not accept assistance from his friends. He continually called out:

"Keep away; let me fight it out alone!"

But the others were too excited to remain inactive spectators of the scene.

"A quilt!" cried one of them, "a quilt to make the *marquis* jump!"

Five or six young men now rushed upon Gaston, and separated him from Lazet. Some tried to throw him down, others to trip him up.

He defended himself with the energy of despair, exhibiting in his furious struggles a strength of which he himself had not been conscious. He struck right and left as he showered fierce epithets upon his adversaries for being twelve against one.

He was endeavouring to get around the billiard-table so as to be near the door, and had almost succeeded, when an exultant cry arose:

"Here is the quilt! the quilt!" they cried.

"Put him in the quilt, the pretty fairy's lover!"

Gaston heard these cries. He saw himself overcome, and suffering an ignoble outrage at the hands of these enraged men.

By a dexterous movement he extricated himself from the grasp of the three who were holding him, and felled a fourth to the ground.

His arms were free; but all his enemies returned to the charge.

Then he seemed to lose his head, and, seizing a knife which lay on the table where the travelling agents had been dining, he plunged it into the breast of the first man who rushed upon him.

This unfortunate man was Jules Lazet. He dropped to the ground.

There was a second of silent stupor.

Then four or five of the young men rushed forward to raise Lazet. The landlady ran about wringing her hands, and screaming with fright. Some of the assailants rushed into the street shouting, "Murder! Murder!"

The others once more turned upon Gaston with cries of "Vengeance! kill him!"

He saw that he was lost. His enemies had seized the first objects they could lay their hands upon, and he received several wounds. He jumped upon the billiard-table, and, making a rapid spring, dashed through the large glass window of the cafe. He was fearfully cut by the broken glass and splinters, but he was free.

Gaston had escaped, but he was not yet saved. Astonished and disconcerted at his desperate feat, the crowd for a moment were stupefied; but, recovering their presence of mind, they started in pursuit of him.

The weather was bad, the ground wet and muddy, and heavy black clouds were rolling westward; but the night was not dark.

Gaston ran on from tree to tree, making frequent turnings, every moment on the point of being seized and surrounded, and asking himself what course he should take. Finally he determined, if possible, to regain Clameran. With incredible rapidity he darted diagonally across the fair-ground, in the direction of the levee which protected the valley of Tarascon from inundations.

Unfortunately, upon reaching this levee, planted with magnificent trees which made it one of the most charming walks of Provence, Gaston forgot that the entrance was closed by a gate with three steps, such as are always placed before walks intended for foot-passengers, and rushed against it with such violence that he was thrown back and badly bruised.

He quickly sprang up; but his pursuers were upon him.

This time he could expect no mercy. The infuriated men at his heels yelled that fearful cry which in the evil days of lawless bloodshed had often echoed in that valley: "In the Rhone with him! In the Rhone with the *marquis*!"

His reason had abandoned him; he no longer knew what he did. His forehead was cut, and the blood trickled from the wound into his eyes, and blinded him.

He must escape, or die in the attempt.

He had tightly clasped the bloody knife with which he had stabbed Lazet. He struck his nearest foe; the man fell to the ground with a heavy groan.

A second blow gained him a moment's respite, which gave him time to open the gate and rush along the levee.

Two men were kneeling over their wounded companion, and five others resumed the pursuit.

But Gaston flew fast, for the horror of his situation tripled his energy; excitement deadened the pain of his wounds; with elbows held tight to his sides, and holding his breath, he went along at such a speed that he soon distanced his pursuers; the noise of their feet became gradually more indistinct, and finally ceased.

Gaston ran on for a mile, across fields and over hedges; fences and ditches were leaped without effort and when he knew he was safe from capture he sank down at the foot of a tree to rest.

This terrible scene had taken place with inconceivable rapidity. Only forty minutes had elapsed since Gaston and his friend entered the *café*.

But during this short time how much had happened! These forty minutes had given more cause for sorrow and remorse than the whole of his previous life put together.

Entering this tavern with head erect and a happy heart, enjoying present existence, and looking forward to a yet better future, he left it ruined; for he was a murderer! Henceforth he would be under a ban—an outcast!

He had killed a man, and still convulsively held the murderous instrument; he cast it from him with horror. He tried to account for the dreadful circumstances which had just taken place; as if it were of any importance to a man lying at the bottom of an abyss to know which stone had slipped, and precipitated him from the summit.

Still, if he alone had been ruined! But Valentine was dragged down with him: she was disgraced yet more than himself; her reputation was gone. And it was his want of self-command which had cast to the winds this honour, confided to his keeping, and which he held far dearer than his own.

But he could not remain here bewailing his misfortune. The police must soon be on his track. They would certainly go to the Château of Clameran to seek him; and before leaving home, perhaps forever, he wished to say goodbye to his father, and once more press Valentine to his heart.

He started to walk, but with great pain, for the reaction had come, and his nerves and muscles, so violently strained, had now begun to relax; the intense heat caused by his struggling and fast running was replaced by a cold perspiration, aching limbs, and chattering teeth. His hip and shoulder pained him almost beyond endurance. The cut on his forehead had stopped bleeding, but the coagulated blood around his eyes blinded him.

After a painful walk he reached his door at ten o'clock.

The old valet who admitted him started back terrified.

"Good heavens, *monsieur*! what is the matter?"

"Silence!" said Gaston in the brief, compressed tone always inspired by imminent danger, "silence! where is my father?"

"M. the Marquis is in his room with M. Louis. He has had a sudden attack of the gout, and cannot put his foot to the ground; but you, *monsieur*—"

Gaston did not stop to listen further. He hurried to his father's room.

The old *marquis*, who was playing backgammon with Louis, dropped his dice-box with a cry of horror, when he looked up and saw his eldest son standing before him covered with blood.

"What is the matter? what have you been doing, Gaston?"

"I have come to embrace you for the last time, father, and to ask for assistance to escape abroad."

"Do you wish to fly the country?"

"I must fly, father, and instantly; I am pursued, the police may be here at any moment. I have killed two men."

The *marquis* was so shocked that he forgot the gout, and attempted to rise; a violent twinge made him drop back in his chair.

"Where? When?" he gasped.

"At Tarascon, in a *café*, an hour ago; fifteen men attacked me, and I seized a knife to defend myself."

"The old tricks of '93," said the *marquis*. "Did they insult you, Gaston? What was the cause of the attack?"

"They insulted in my presence the name of a noble young girl."

"And you punished the rascals? *Jarnibleu*! You did well. Who ever heard of a gentleman allowing insolent puppies to speak disrespectfully of a lady of quality in his presence? But who was the lady you defended?"

"Mademoiselle Valentine de la Verberie."

"What!" cried the *marquis*, "what! the daughter of that old witch! Those accursed de la Verberies have always brought misfortune upon us."

He certainly abominated the countess; but his respect for her noble blood was greater than his resentment toward her individually, and he added:

"Nevertheless, Gaston, you did your duty."

Meanwhile, the curiosity of St. Jean, the *marquis's* old valet, made him venture to open the door, and ask:

"Did M. the *marquis* ring?"

"No, you rascal," answered M. de Clameran: "you know very well I did not. But, now you are here, be useful. Quickly bring some clothes for M. Gaston, some fresh linen, and some warm water: hasten and dress his wounds."

These orders were promptly executed, and Gaston found he was not so badly hurt as he had thought. With the exception of a deep stab in his left shoulder, his wounds were not serious.

After receiving all the attentions which his condition required, Gaston felt like a new man, ready to brave any peril. His eyes sparkled with renewed energy and excitement.

The *marquis* made a sign to the servants to leave the room.

"Do you still think you ought to leave France?" he asked Gaston.

"Yes, father."

"My brother ought not to hesitate," interposed Louis: "he will be arrested here, thrown into prison, vilified in court, and—who knows?"

"We all know well enough that he will be convicted," grumbled the old *marquis*. "These are the benefits of the immortal revolution, as it is called. Ah, in my day we three would have taken our swords, jumped on our horses, and, dashing into Tarascon, would soon have—. But those good old days are passed. Today we have to run away."

"There is no time to lose," observed Louis.

"True," said the *marquis*, "but to fly, to go abroad, one must have money; and I have none by me to give him."

"Father!"

"No, I have none. Ah, what a prodigal old fool I have been! If I only had a hundred *louis*!"

Then he told Louis to open the secretary, and hand him the money-box.

The box contained only nine hundred and twenty *francs* in gold.

"Nine hundred and twenty *francs*," cried the *marquis*: "it will never do for the eldest son of our house to fly the country with this paltry sum."

He sat lost in reflection. Suddenly his brow cleared, and he told Louis to open a secret drawer in the secretary, and bring him a small casket.

Then the *marquis* took from his neck a black ribbon, to which was suspended the key of the casket.

His sons observed with what deep emotion he unlocked it, and slowly took out a necklace, a large cross, several rings, and other pieces of jewellery.

His countenance assumed a solemn expression.

"Gaston, my dear son," he said, "at a time like this your life may depend upon bought assistance; money is power."

"I am young, father, and have courage."

"Listen to me. The jewels belonged to the *marquise*, your sainted mother, a noble, holy woman, who is now in heaven watching over us. These jewels have never left me. During my days of misery and want, when I was compelled to earn a livelihood by teaching music in London, I piously treasured them. I never thought of selling them; and to mortgage them, in the hour of direst need, would have seemed to be a sacrilege. But now you must take them, my son, and sell them for twenty thousand *livres*."

"No, father no; I cannot take them!"

"You must, Gaston. If your mother were on earth, she would tell you to take them, as I do now. I command you to take and use them. The salvation, the honour, of the heir of the house of Clameran, must not be imperilled for want of a little gold."

With tearful eyes, Gaston sank on his knees, and, carrying his father's hand to his lips, said:

"Thanks, father, thanks! In my heedless, ungrateful presumption I have hitherto misjudged you. I did not know your noble character. Forgive me. I accept; yes, I accept these jewels worn by my dear mother; but I take them as a sacred deposit, confided to my honour, and for which I will some day account to you."

In their emotion, the *marquis* and Gaston forgot the threatened danger. But Louis was not touched by the affecting scene.

"Time presses," he said: "you had better hasten."

"He is right," cried the *marquis*: "go, Gaston, go, my son; and God protect the heir of the de Clamerans!"

Gaston slowly got up and said, with an embarrassed air:

"Before leaving you, my father, I must fulfil a sacred duty. I have not told you everything. I love Valentine, the young girl whose honour I defended this evening."

"Oh!" cried the *marquis*, thunderstruck, "oh, oh!"

"And I entreat you, father, to ask Madame de la Verberie for the hand of her daughter. Valentine will gladly join me abroad, and share my exile."

Gaston stopped, frightened at the effect of his words. The old *marquis* had become crimson, or rather purple, as if struck by apoplexy.

"Preposterous!" he gasped. "Impossible! Perfect folly!"

"I love her, father, and have promised her never to marry another."

"Then always remain a bachelor."

"I shall marry her!" cried Gaston, excitedly. "I shall marry her because I have sworn I would, and I will not be so base as to desert her."

"Nonsense!"

"I tell you, Mademoiselle de la Verberie must and shall be my wife. It is too late for me to draw back. Even if I no longer loved her, I would still marry her, because she has given herself to me; because, can't you understand—what was said at the cafe tonight was true: I have but one way of repairing the wrong I have done Valentine—by marrying her."

Gaston's confession, forced from him by circumstances, produced a very different impression from that which he had expected. The enraged *marquis* instantly became cool, and his mind seemed relieved of an immense weight. A wicked joy sparkled in his eyes, as he replied:

"Ah, ha! she yielded to your entreaties, did she? *Jarnibleu*! I am delighted. I congratulate you, Gaston: they say she is a pretty little fool."

"*Monsieur*," interrupted Gaston, indignantly; "I have told you that I love her, and have promised to marry her. You seem to forget."

"Ta, ta ta!" cried the *marquis*, "your scruples are absurd. You know full well that her great-grandfather led our great-grandmother astray. Now we are quits! I am delighted at the retaliation, for the old witch's sake."

"I swear by the memory of my mother, that Valentine shall be my wife!"

"Do you dare assume that tone toward me?" cried the exasperated *marquis*. "Never, understand me clearly; never will I give my consent. You know how dear to me is the honour of our house. Well, I would rather see you tried for murder, and even chained to the galleys, than married to this worthless jade!"

This last word was too much for Gaston.

"Then your wish shall be gratified, *monsieur*. I will remain here, and be arrested. I care not what becomes of me! What is life to me without the hope of Valentine? Take back these jewels: they are useless now."

A terrible scene would have taken place between the father and son, had they not been interrupted by a domestic who rushed into the room, and excitedly cried:

"The *gendarmes!* here are the *gendarmes!*"

At this news the old *marquis* started up, and seemed to forget his gout, which had yielded to more violent emotions.

"*Gendarmes!*" he cried, "in my house at Clameran! They shall pay dear for their insolence! You will help me, will you not, my men?"

"Yes, yes," answered the servants. "Down with the *gendarmes!* down with them!"

Fortunately Louis, during all this excitement, preserved his presence of mind.

"To resist would be folly," he said. "Even if we repulsed the *gendarmes* tonight, they would return tomorrow with reinforcements."

"Louis is right," said the *marquis*, bitterly. "Might is right, as they said in '93. The *gendarmes* are all powerful. Do they not even have the impertinence to come up to me while I am hunting, and ask to see my shooting-license?—I, a Clameran, show a license!"

"Where are they?" asked Louis of the servants.

"At the outer gate," answered La Verdure, one of the grooms. "Does not *monsieur* hear the noise they are making with their sabres?"

"Then Gaston must escape over the garden wall."

"It is guarded, *monsieur*," said La Verdure, "and the little gate in the park besides. There seems to be a regiment of them. They are even stationed along the park walls."

This was only too true. The rumour of Lazet's death had spread like wildfire throughout the town of Tarascon, and everybody was in a state of excitement. Not only mounted *gendarmes*, but a platoon of hussars from the garrison, had been sent in pursuit of the murderer.

At least twenty young men of Tarascon were volunteer guides to the armed force.

"Then," said the *marquis*, "we are surrounded?"

"Not a single chance for escape," groaned St. Jean.

"We shall see about that, *Jarnibleu*!" cried the *marquis*. "Ah, we are not the strongest, but we can be the most adroit. Attention! Louis, my son, you and La Verdure go down to the stable, and mount the fastest horses; then as quietly as possible station yourselves, you, Louis, at the park gate, and you, La Verdure, at the outer gate. Upon the signal I shall give you by firing a pistol, let every door be instantly opened, while Louis and Verdure dash through the gates, and make the *gendarmes* pursue them."

"I will make them fly," said La Verdure.

"Listen. During this time, Gaston, aided by St. Jean, will scale the park wall, and hasten along the river to the cabin of Pilorel, the fisherman. He is an old sailor of the republic, and devoted to our house. He will take Gaston in his boat; and, when they are once on the Rhone, there is nothing to be feared save the wrath of God. Now go, all of you: fly!"

Left alone with his son, the old man slipped the jewellery into a silk purse, and, handing them once more to Gaston, said, as he stretched out his arms toward him:

"Come here, my son, and let me embrace you, and bestow my blessing."

Gaston hesitated.

"Come," insisted the old man in broken tones, "I must embrace you for the last time: I may never see you again. Save yourself, save your name, Gaston, and then—you know how I love you, my son: take back the jewels. Come."

For an instant the father and son clung to each other, overpowered by emotion.

But the continued noise at the gates now reaches their ears.

"We must part!" said M. de Clameran, "go!" And, taking from his desk a little pair of pistols, he handed them to his son, and added, with averted eyes, "You must not be captured alive, Gaston!"

Gaston did not immediately descend to the park.

He yearned to see Valentine, and give her one last kiss before leaving France, and determined to persuade Pilorel to stop the boat as they went by the park of La Verberie.

He hastened to his room, placed the signal in the window so that Valentine might know he was coming, and waited for an answering light.

"Come, M. Gaston," entreated old St. Jean, who could not understand the strange conduct. "For God's sake make haste! your life is at stake!"

At last he came running down the stairs, and had just reached the vestibule when a pistol-shot, the signal given by the *marquis*, was heard.

The loud swinging open of the large gate, the rattling of the sabres of the *gendarmes*, the furious galloping of many horses, and a chorus of loud shouts and angry oaths, were next heard.

Leaning against the window, his brow beaded with cold perspiration, the Marquis de Clameran breathlessly awaited the issue of this expedient, upon which depended the life of his eldest son.

His measures were excellent, and deserved success. As he had ordered, Louis and La Verdure dashed out through the gate, one to the right, the other to the left, each one pursued by a dozen mounted men. Their horses flew like arrows, and kept far ahead of the pursuers.

Gaston would have been saved, but for the interference of fate; but was it fate, or was it malice?

Suddenly Louis's horse stumbled, and fell to the ground with his rider. The *gendarmes* rode up, and at once recognised the second son of M. de Clameran.

"This is not the assassin!" they cried. "Let us hurry back, else he will escape!"

They returned just in time to see, by the uncertain light of the moon peeping from behind a cloud, Gaston climbing the garden wall.

"There is our man!" exclaimed the corporal. "Keep your eyes open, and gallop after him!"

They spurred their horses, and hastened to the spot where Gaston had jumped from the wall.

On a wooded piece of ground, even if it be hilly, an agile man, if he preserves his presence of mind, can escape a number of horsemen. The ground on this side of the park was favourable to Gaston. He found himself in an immense madder-field; and, as is well known, as this valuable root must remain in the ground three years, the furrows are necessarily ploughed very deep. Horses cannot even walk over its uneven surface; indeed, they can scarcely stand steadily upon it.

This circumstance brought the *gendarmes* to a dead halt.

Four rash hussars ventured in the field, but they and their beasts were soon rolling between hillocks.

Jumping from ridge to ridge, Gaston soon reached a large field, freshly ploughed, and planted with young chestnuts.

As his chances of escape increased, the excitement grew more intense. The pursuers urged each other on, and called out to head him off, every time they saw Gaston run from one clump of trees to another.

Being familiar with the country, young de Clameran was confident of eluding his pursuers. He knew that the next field was a thistle-field, and was separated from the chestnut by a long, deep ditch. He resolved to jump into this ditch, run along the bottom, and climb out at the farther end, while they were looking for him among the trees. But he had forgotten the swelling of the river. Upon reaching the ditch, he found it full of water. Discouraged but not disconcerted, he was about to jump across, when three horsemen appeared on the opposite side.

They were *gendarmes* who had ridden around the madder-field and chestnut-trees, knowing they could easily catch him on the level ground of the thistle-field.

At the sight of these three men, Gaston stood perplexed.

He should certainly be captured if he attempted to run through the field, at the end of which he could see the cabin of Pilorel the ferryman.

To retrace his steps would be surrendering to the hussars.

At a little distance on his right was a forest, but he was separated from it by a road upon which he heard the sound of approaching horses. He would certainly be caught there.

Foes in front of him, foes behind him, foes on the right of him! What was on his left?

On his left was the surging, foaming river.

What hope was left? The circle of which he was the centre was fast narrowing.

Must he, then, fall back upon suicide? Here in an open field, tracked by police like a wild beast, must he blow his brains out? What a death for a de Clameran!

No! He would seize the one chance of salvation left him: a forlorn, desperate, perilous chance, but still a chance—the river.

Holding a pistol in either hand, he ran and leaped upon the edge of a little promontory, projecting three yards into the Rhone. This cape of refuge was formed by the immense trunk of a fallen tree. The tree swayed and cracked fearfully under Gaston's weight, as he stood on the extreme end, and looked around upon his pursuers; there were fifteen of them, some on the right, some on the left, all uttering cries of joy.

"Do you surrender?" called out the corporal.

Gaston did not answer; he was weighing his chances. He was above the park of La Verberie; would he be able to swim there, granting that he was not swept away and drowned the instant he plunged into the angry torrent before him?

He pictured Valentine, at this very moment, watching, waiting, and praying for him on the other shore.

"For the last time I command you to surrender!" cried the corporal.

The unfortunate man did not hear; he was deafened by the waters which were roaring and rushing around him.

In a supreme moment like this, with his foot upon the threshold of another world, a man sees his past life rise before him, and seldom does he find cause for self-approval.

Although death stared him in the face, Gaston calmly considered which would be the best spot to plunge into, and commended his soul to God.

"He will stand there until we go after him," said a *gendarme*: "so we might as well advance."

Gaston had finished his prayer.

He flung his pistols in the direction of the *gendarmes*: he was ready.

He made the sign of the cross, then, with outstretched arms, dashed head foremost into the Rhone.

The violence of his spring detached the few remaining roots of the old tree; it oscillated a moment, whirled over, and then drifted away.

The spectators uttered a cry of horror and pity; anger seemed to have deserted them in their turn.

"That is an end of him," muttered one of the *gendarmes*. "It is useless for one to fight against the Rhone; his body will be picked up at Arles tomorrow."

The hussars seemed really remorseful at the tragic fate of the brave, handsome young man, whom a moment before they had pursued with so much bitter zeal. They admired his spirited resistance, his courage, and especially his resignation, his resolution to die.

True French soldiers, their sympathies were now all upon the side of the vanquished, and every man of them would have done all in his power to assist in saving the drowning man, and aiding his escape.

"An ugly piece of work!" grumbled the old quartermaster who had command of the hussars.

"*Bast*!" exclaimed the philosophic corporal, "the Rhone is no worse than the court of assizes: the result would be the same. Right about, men; march! The thing that troubles me is the idea of that poor old man waiting to hear his son's fate. I would not be the one to tell him what has happened. March!"

Chapter 13

Valentine knew, that fatal evening, that Gaston would have to walk to Tarascon, to cross the Rhone by the suspension bridge which connects Tarascon with Beaucaire, and did not expect to see him until eleven o'clock, the time which they had agreed upon the previous evening.

But, happening to look up at the windows of Clameran, she saw lights hurrying to and fro in an unusual manner, even in rooms that she knew to be unoccupied. A presentiment of impending misfortune chilled her blood, and stopped the beatings of her heart. A secret and imperious voice within told her that something extraordinary was going on at the Château of Clameran.

What was it? She could not imagine; but she knew, she felt, that some dreadful misfortune had happened.

With her eyes fastened upon the dark mass of stone looming in the distance, she watched the going and coming of the lights, as if their movements would give her a clew to what was taking place within those walls.

She raised her window, and tried to listen, fancying she could hear an unusual sound, even at such a distance. Alas! she heard nothing but the rushing roar of the angry river.

Her anxiety grew more insufferable every moment; and she felt as if she would faint were this torturing suspense to last much longer, when the well-known, beloved signal appeared suddenly in Gaston's window, and told her that her lover was about to swim across the Rhone. She could scarcely believe her eyes; she must be under the influence of a dream; her amazement prevented her answering the signal, until it had been repeated three times. Then, more dead than alive, with trembling limbs she hastened along the park to the river-bank.

Never had she seen the Rhone so furious. Since Gaston was risking his life in order to see her, she could no longer doubt that something fearful had occurred at Clameran.

She fell on her knees, and with clasped hands, and her wild eyes fixed upon the dark waters, besought the pitiless waves to yield up her dear Gaston.

Every dark object which she could distinguish floating in the middle of the torrent assumed the shape of a human form.

At one time, she thought she heard, above the roaring of the water, the terrible, agonized cry of a drowning man.

She watched and prayed, but her lover came not.

Still she waited.

While the *gendarmes* and hussars slowly and silently returned to the Château of Clameran, Gaston experienced one of those miracles which would seem incredible were they not confirmed by the most convincing proof.

When he first plunged into the river, he rolled over five or six times, and was then drawn toward the bottom. In a swollen river the current is unequal, being much stronger in some places than in others; hence the great danger. Gaston knew it, and guarded against it. Instead of wasting his strength in vain struggles, he held his breath, and kept still. About twenty-five yards from the spot where he had plunged in, he made a violent spring which brought him to the surface. Rapidly drifting by him was the old tree.

For an instant, he was entangled in the mass of weeds and debris which clung to its roots, and followed in its wake; an eddy set him free. The tree and its clinging weeds swept on. It was the last familiar friend, gone.

Gaston dared not attempt to reach the opposite shore. He would have to land where the waves dashed him.

With great presence of mind he put forth all his strength and dexterity to slowly take an oblique course, knowing well that there was no hope for him if the current took him crosswise. This fearful current is as capricious as a woman, which accounts for the strange effects of inundations; sometimes it rushes to the right, sometimes to the left, sparing one shore and ravaging the other. Gaston was familiar with every turn of the river; he knew that just below Clameran was an abrupt turning, and relied upon the eddy formed thereby, to sweep him in the direction of La Verberie.

His hopes were not deceived. An oblique current suddenly swept him toward the right shore, and, if he had not been on his guard, would have sunk him.

But the eddy did not reach as far as Gaston supposed, and he was still some distance from the shore, when, with the rapidity of lightning, he was swept by the park of La Verberie. As he floated by, he caught a glimpse of a white shadow among the trees; Valentine still waited for him. He was gradually approaching the bank, as he reached the end of La Verberie, and attempted to land.

Feeling a foothold, he stood up twice, and each time was thrown down by the violence of the waves. He escaped being swept away by seizing some willow branches, and, clinging to them, raised himself, and climbed up the steep bank.

He was safe at last.

Without taking time to breathe, he darted in the direction of the park. He came just in time. Overcome by the intensity of her emotions, Valentine had fainted, and lay apparently lifeless on the damp river-bank.

Gaston's entreaties and kisses aroused her from her stupor.

"Gaston!" she cried, in a tone that revealed all the love she felt for him. "Is it indeed you? Then God heard my prayers, and had pity on us."

"No, Valentine," he murmured. "God has had no pity."

The sad tones of Gaston's voice convinced her that her presentiment of evil was true.

"What new misfortune strikes us now?" she cried. "Why have you thus risked your life—a life far dearer to me than my own? What has happened?"

"This is what has happened, Valentine: our love-affair is the jest of the country around; our secret is a secret no longer."

She shrank back, and, burying her face in her hands, moaned piteously.

"This," said Gaston, forgetting everything but his present misery, "this is the result of the blind enmity of our families. Our noble and pure love, which ought to be a glory in the eyes of God and man, has to be concealed, and, when discovered, becomes a reproach as though it were some evil deed."

"Then all is known—all is discovered!" murmured Valentine. "Oh, Gaston, Gaston!"

While struggling for his life against furious men and angry elements, Gaston had preserved his self-possession; but the heart-broken tone of his beloved Valentine overcame him. He swung his arms above his head, and exclaimed:

"Yes, they know it; and oh, why could I not crush the villains for daring to utter your adored name? Ah, why did I only kill two of the scoundrels!"

"Have you killed someone, Gaston?"

Valentine's tone of horror gave Gaston a ray of reason.

"Yes," he replied with bitterness, "I have killed two men. It was for that that I have crossed the Rhone. I could not have my father's name disgraced by being tried and convicted for murder. I have been tracked like a wild beast by mounted police. I have escaped them, and now I am flying my country."

Valentine struggled to preserve her composure under this last unexpected blow.

"Where do you hope to find an asylum?" she asked.

"I know not. Where I am to go, what will become of me, God only knows! I only know that I am going to some strange land, to assume a false name and a disguise. I shall seek some lawless country which offers a refuge to murderers."

Gaston waited for an answer to this speech. None came, and he resumed with vehemence:

"And before disappearing, Valentine, I wished to see you, because now, when I am abandoned by everyone else, I have relied upon you, and had faith in your love. A tie unites us, my darling, stronger and more indissoluble than all earthly ties—the tie of love. I love you more than life itself, my Valentine; before God you are my wife; I am yours and you are mine, for ever and ever! Would you let me fly alone, Valentine? To the pain and toil of exile, to the sharp regrets of a ruined life, would you, could you, add the torture of separation?"

"Gaston, I implore you—"

"Ah, I knew it," he interrupted, mistaking the sense of her exclamation; "I knew you would not let me go off alone. I knew your sympathetic heart would long to share the burden of my miseries. This moment effaces the wretched suffering I have endured. Let us go! Having our happiness to defend, having you to protect, I fear nothing; I can brave all, conquer all. Come, my Valentine, we will escape, or die together! This is the long-dreamed-of happiness! The glorious future of love and liberty open before us!"

He had worked himself into a state of delirious excitement. He seized Valentine around the waist, and tried to draw her toward the gate.

As Gaston's exaltation increased, Valentine became composed and almost stolid in her forced calmness.

Gently, but with a quiet firmness, she withdrew herself from his embrace, and said sadly, but resolutely:

"What you wish is impossible, Gaston!"

This cold, inexplicable resistance confounded her lover.

"Impossible? Why, Valentine—"

"You know me well enough, Gaston, to be convinced that sharing the greatest hardships with you would to me be the height of happiness. But above the tones of your voice to which I fain would yield, above the voice of my own heart which urges me to follow the one being upon whom all its affections are centred, there is another voice—a powerful, imperious voice—which bids me to stay: the voice of duty."

"What! Would you think of remaining here after the horrible affair of tonight, after the scandal that will be spread tomorrow?"

"What do you mean? That I am lost, dishonoured? Am I any more so today than I was yesterday? Do you think that the jeers and scoffs of the world could make me suffer more than do the pangs of my guilty conscience? I have long since passed judgment upon myself, Gaston; and, although the sound of your voice and the touch of your hand would make me forget all save the bliss of your love, no sooner were you away than I would weep tears of shame and remorse."

Gaston listened immovable, stupefied. He seemed to see a new

Valentine standing before him, an entirely different woman from the one whose tender soul he thought he knew so well.

"Your mother, what will she say?" he asked.

"It is my duty to her that keeps me here. Do you wish me to prove an unnatural daughter, and desert a poor, lonely, friendless old woman, who has nothing but me to cling to? Could I abandon her to follow a lover?"

"But our enemies will inform her of everything, Valentine, and think how she will make you suffer!"

"No matter. The dictates of conscience must be obeyed. Ah, why can I not, at the price of my life, spare her the agony of hearing that her only daughter, her Valentine, has disgraced her name? She may be hard, cruel, pitiless toward me; but have I not deserved it? Oh, my only friend, we have been revelling in a dream too beautiful to last! I have long dreaded this awakening. Like two weak, credulous fools we imagined that happiness could exist beyond the pale of duty. Sooner or later stolen joys must be dearly paid for. After the sweet comes the bitter; we must bow our heads, and drink the cup to the dregs."

This cold reasoning, this sad resignation, was more than the fiery nature of Gaston could bear.

"You shall not talk thus!" he cried. "Can you not feel that the bare idea of your suffering humiliation drives me mad?"

"Alas! I see nothing but disgrace, the most fearful disgrace, staring me in the face."

"What do you mean, Valentine?"

"I have not told you, Gaston, I am—"

Here she stopped, hesitated, and then added:

"Nothing! I am a fool."

Had Gaston been less excited, he would have suspected some new misfortune beneath this reticence of Valentine; but his mind was too full of one idea—that of possessing her.

"All hope is not lost," he continued. "My father is kind-hearted, and was touched by my love and despair. I am sure that my letters, added to the intercession of my brother Louis, will induce him to ask Madame de la Verberie for your hand."

This proposition seemed to frighten Valentine.

"Heaven forbid that the *marquis* should take this rash step!"

"Why, Valentine?"

"Because my mother would reject his offer; because, I must confess it now, she has sworn I shall marry none but a rich man; and your father is not rich, Gaston, so you will have very little."

"Good heavens!" cried Gaston, with disgust, "is it to such an unnatural mother that you sacrifice me?"

"She is my mother; that is sufficient. I have not the right to judge her. My duty is to remain with her, and remain I shall."

Valentine's manner showed such determined resolution, that Gaston saw that further prayers would be in vain.

"Alas!" he cried, as he wrung his hands with despair, "you do not love me; you have never loved me!"

"Gaston, Gaston! you do not think what you say! Have you no mercy?"

"If you loved me," he cried, "you could never, at this moment of separation, have the cruel courage to coldly reason and calculate. Ah, far different is my love for you. Without you the world is void; to lose you is to die. What have I to live for? Let the Rhone take back this worthless life, so miraculously saved; it is now a burden to me!"

And he rushed toward the river, determined to bury his sorrow beneath its waves; Valentine seized his arm, and held him back.

"Is this the way to show your love for me?" she asked.

Gaston was absolutely discouraged.

"What is the use of living?" he said, dejectedly. "What is left to me now?"

"God is left to us, Gaston; and in his hands lies our future."

As a shipwrecked man seizes a rotten plank in his desperation, so Gaston eagerly caught at the word "*future*," as a beacon in the gloomy darkness surrounding him.

"Your commands shall be obeyed," he cried with enthusiasm. "Away with weakness! Yes, I will live, and struggle, and triumph. Madame de la Verberie wants gold; well, she shall have it; in three years I will be rich, or I shall be dead."

With clasped hands Valentine thanked Heaven for this sudden determination, which was more than she had dared hope for.

"But," said Gaston, "before going away I wish to confide to you a sacred deposit."

He drew from his pocket the purse of jewels, and, handing them to Valentine, added:

"These jewels belonged to my poor mother; you, my angel, are alone worthy of wearing them. I thought of you when I accepted them from my father. I felt that you, as my affianced wife, were the proper person to have them."

Valentine refused to accept them.

"Take them, my darling, as a pledge of my return. If I do not come back within three years, you may know that I am dead, and then you must keep them as a souvenir of him who so much loved you."

She burst into tears, and took the purse.

"And now," said Gaston, "I have a last request to make. Everybody believes me dead, but I cannot let my poor old father labour under this impression. Swear to me that you will go yourself tomorrow morning, and tell him that I am still alive."

"I will tell him, myself," she said.

Gaston felt that he must now tear himself away before his courage failed him; each moment he was more loath to leave the only being who bound him to this world; he enveloped Valentine in a last fond embrace, and started up.

"What is your plan of escape?" she asked.

"I shall go to Marseilles, and hide in a friend's house until I can procure a passage to America."

"You must have assistance; I will secure you a guide in whom I have unbounded confidence; old Menoul, the ferryman, who lives near us. He owns the boat which he plies on the Rhone."

The lovers passed through the little park gate, of which Gaston had the key, and soon reached the boatman's cabin.

He was asleep in an easy-chair by the fire. When Valentine stood before him with Gaston, the old man jumped up, and kept rubbing his eyes, thinking it must be a dream.

"Pere Menoul," said Valentine, "M. Gaston is compelled to fly the country; he wants to be rowed out to sea, so that he can secretly embark. Can you take him in your boat as far as the mouth of the Rhone?"

"It is impossible," said the old man, shaking his head; "I would not dare venture on the river in its present state."

"But, Pere Menoul, it would be of immense service to me; would you not venture for my sake?"

"For your sake? certainly I would, Mademoiselle Valentine: I will do anything to gratify you. I am ready to start."

He looked at Gaston, and, seeing his clothes wet and covered with mud, said to him:

"Allow me to offer you my dead son's clothes, *monsieur*; they will serve as a disguise: come this way."

In a few minutes Pere Menoul returned with Gaston, whom no

one would have recognised in his sailor dress.

Valentine went with them to the place where the boat was moored. While the old man was unfastening it, the disconsolate lovers tearfully embraced each other for the last time.

"In three years, my own Valentine; promise to wait three years for me! If alive, I will then see you."

"*Adieu, mademoiselle*," interrupted the boatman; "and you, *monsieur*, hold fast, and keep steady."

Then with a vigorous stroke of the boat-hook he sent the bark into the middle of the stream.

Three days later, thanks to the assistance of old Menoul, Gaston was concealed onboard the American three-master, *Tom Jones*, Captain Warth, which was to start the next day for Valparaiso.

Chapter 14

Cold and white like a marble statue, Valentine stood on the bank of the river, watching the frail bark which was carrying her lover away. It flew along the Rhone like a bird in a tempest, and after a few seconds appeared like a black speck in the midst of the heavy fog which floated over the water, then was lost to view.

Now that Gaston was gone, Valentine had no motive for concealing her despair; she wrung her hands and sobbed as if her heart would break. All her forced calmness, her bravery and hopefulness, were gone. She felt crushed and lost, as if the sharp pain in her heart was the forerunner of the torture in store for her; as if that swiftly gliding bark had carried off the better part of herself.

While Gaston treasured in the bottom of his heart a ray of hope, she felt there was nothing to look forward to but shame and sorrow.

The horrible facts which stared her in the face convinced her that happiness in this life was over; the future was worse than blank. She wept and shuddered at the prospect.

She slowly retraced her footsteps through the friendly little gate which had so often admitted poor Gaston; and, as she closed it behind her, she seemed to be placing an impassable barrier between herself and happiness.

Before entering, Valentine walked around the *château*, and looked up at the windows of her mother's chamber.

They were brilliantly lighted, as usual at this hour, for Madame de la Verberie passed half the night in reading, and slept till late in the day.

Enjoying the comforts of life, which are little costly in the country, the selfish countess disturbed herself very little about her daughter.

Fearing no danger in their isolation, she left her at perfect liberty; and day and night Valentine might go and come, take long walks, and sit under trees for hours at a time, without restriction.

But on this night Valentine feared being seen. She would be called upon to explain the torn, muddy condition of her dress, and what answer could she give? Fortunately she could reach her room without meeting anyone. She needed solitude in order to collect her thoughts, and to pray for strength to bear the heavy burden of her sorrows, and to withstand the angry storm about to burst over her head.

Seated before her little work-table, she emptied the purse of jewels, and mechanically examined them. It would be a sweet, sad comfort to wear the simplest of the rings, she thought, as she slipped the sparkling gem on her finger; but her mother would ask her where it came from. What answer could she give? Alas, none.

She kissed the purse, in memory of Gaston, and then concealed the sacred deposit in her bureau.

When she thought of going to Clameran, to inform the old *marquis* of the miraculous preservation of his son's life, her heart sank.

Blinded by his passion, Gaston did not think, when he requested this service, of the obstacles and dangers to be braved in its performance.

But Valentine saw them only too clearly; yet it did not occur to her for an instant to break her promise by sending another, or by delaying to go herself. At sunrise she dressed herself. When the bell was ringing for early mass, she thought it a good time to start on her errand.

The servants were all up, and one of them named Mihonne, who always waited on Valentine, was scrubbing the vestibule.

"If mother asks for me," said Valentine to the girl, "tell her I have gone to early mass."

She often went to church at this hour, so there was nothing to be feared thus far; Mihonne looked at her sadly, but said nothing.

Valentine knew that she would have difficulty in returning to breakfast. She would have to walk a league before reaching the bridge, and it was another league thence to Clameran; in all she must walk four leagues.

She set forth at a rapid pace. The consciousness of performing an extraordinary action, the feverish anxiety of peril incurred, increased her haste. She forgot that she had worn herself out weeping all night; that this fictitious strength could not last.

In spite of her efforts, it was after eight o'clock when she reached the long avenue leading to the main entrance of the Château of Clameran.

She had only proceeded a few steps, when she saw old St. Jean coming down the path.

She stopped and waited for him; he hastened his steps at sight of her, as if having something to tell her. He was very much excited, and his eyes were swollen with weeping. To Valentine's surprise, he did not take off his hat to bow, and when he came up to her, he said, rudely:

"Are you going up to the *château, mademoiselle?*"

"Yes."

"If you are going after M. Gaston," said the servant, with an insolent sneer, "you are taking useless trouble. M. the count is dead, *mademoiselle*; he sacrificed himself for the sake of a worthless woman."

Valentine turned white at this insult, but took no notice of it. St. Jean, who expected to see her overcome by the dreadful news, was bewildered at her composure.

"I am going to the *château*," she said, quietly, "to speak to the *marquis*."

St. Jean stifled a sob, and said:

"Then it is not worth while to go any farther."

"Why?"

"Because the Marquis of Clameran died at five o'clock this morning."

Valentine leaned against a tree to prevent herself from falling.

"Dead!" she gasped.

"Yes," said St. Jean, fiercely; "yes, dead!"

A faithful servant of the old regime, St. Jean shared all the passions, weaknesses, friendships, and enmities of his master. He had a horror of the La Verberies. And now he saw in Valentine the woman who had caused the death of the *marquis* whom he had served for forty years, and of Gaston whom he worshipped.

"I will tell you how he died," said the bitter old man. "Yesterday evening, when those hounds came and told the *marquis* that his eldest son was dead, he who was as hardy as an oak, and could face any danger, instantly gave way, and dropped as if struck by lightning. I was there. He wildly beat the air with his hands, and fell without opening his lips; not one word did he utter. We put him to bed, and M. Louis galloped into Tarascon for a doctor. But the blow had struck too deeply. When Dr. Raget arrived he said there was no hope.

"At daybreak, the *marquis* recovered consciousness enough to ask for M. Louis, with whom he remained alone for some minutes. The last words he uttered were, 'Father and son the same day; there will be rejoicing at La Verberie.'"

Valentine might have soothed the sorrow of the faithful servant, by telling him Gaston still lived; but she feared it would be indiscreet, and, unfortunately, said nothing.

"Can I see M. Louis?" she asked after a long silence.

This question seemed to arouse all the anger slumbering in the breast of poor St. Jean.

"You! You would dare take such a step, Mademoiselle de la Verberie? What! would you presume to appear before him after what has happened? I will never allow it! And you had best, moreover, take my advice, and return home at once. I will not answer for the tongues of the servants here, when they see you."

And, without waiting for an answer, he hurried away.

What could Valentine do? Humiliated and miserable, she could only wearily drag her aching limbs back the way she had so rapidly come early that morning. On the road, she met many people coming from the town, where they had heard of the events of the previous night; and the poor girl was obliged to keep her eyes fastened to the ground in order to escape the insulting looks and mocking salutations with which the gossips passed her.

When Valentine reached La Verberie, she found Mihonne waiting for her.

"Ah, *mademoiselle*," she said, "make haste, and go in the house. *Madame* had a visitor this morning, and ever since she left has been crying out for you. Hurry; and take care what you say to her, for she is in a violent passion."

Much has been said in favour of the patriarchal manners of our ancestors. Their manners may have been patriarchal years and years ago; but our mothers and wives nowadays certainly have not such ready hands and quick tongues, and are sometimes, at least, elegant in manner, and choice in their language.

Madame de La Verberie had preserved the manners of the good old times, when grand ladies swore like troopers, and impressed their remarks by slaps in the face.

When Valentine appeared, she was overwhelmed with coarse epithets and violent abuse.

The countess had been informed of everything, with many gross additions added by public scandal. An old dowager, her most intimate friend, had hurried over early in the morning, to offer her this poisoned dish of gossip, seasoned with her own pretended condolences.

In this sad affair, Madame de la Verberie mourned less over her daughter's loss of reputation, than over the ruin of her own projects—projects of going to Paris, making a grand marriage for Valentine, and living in luxury the rest of her days.

A young girl so compromised would not find it easy to get a husband. It would now be necessary to keep her two years longer in the country, before introducing her into Parisian society. The world must have time to forget this scandal.

"You worthless wretch!" cried the countess with fury; "is it thus you respect the noble traditions of our family? Heretofore it has never been considered necessary to watch the La Verberies; they could take care of their honour: but you must take advantage of your liberty to cover our name with disgrace!"

With a sinking heart, Valentine had foreseen this tirade. She felt that it was only a just punishment for her conduct. Knowing that the indignation of her mother was just, she meekly hung her head like a repentant sinner at the bar of justice.

But this submissive silence only exasperated the angry countess.

"Why do you not answer me?" she screamed with flashing eyes and a threatening gesture. "Speak! you—"

"What can I say, mother?"

"Say, miserable girl? Say that they lied when they accused a La Verberie of disgracing her name! Speak: defend yourself!"

Valentine mournfully shook her head, but said nothing.

"It is true, then?" shrieked the countess, beside herself with rage; "what they said is true?"

"Forgive me, mother: have mercy! I am so miserable!" moaned the poor girl.

"Forgive! have mercy! Do you dare to tell me I have not been deceived by this gossip today? Do you have the insolence to stand there and glory in your shame? Whose blood flows in your veins? You seem to be ignorant that some faults should be persistently denied, no matter how glaring the evidence against them. And you are my daughter! Can you not understand that an ignominious confession like this should never be forced from a woman by any human power? But no, you have lovers, and unblushingly avow it. Why not run over the town and tell everybody? Boast of it, glory in it: it would be something new!"

"Alas! you are pitiless, mother!"

"Did you ever have any pity on me, my dutiful daughter? Did it ever occur to you that your disgrace would kill me? No: I suppose you and your lover have often laughed at my blind confidence; for I had confidence in you: I had perfect faith in you. I believed you to be as innocent as when you lay in your cradle. And it has come to this: drunken men make a jest of your name in a billiard-room, then fight about you, and kill each other. I entrusted to you the honour of our name, and what did you do with it? You handed it over to the first-comer!"

This was too much for Valentine. The words, "first-comer," wounded her pride more than all the other abuse heaped upon her. She tried to protest against this unmerited insult.

"Ah, I have made a mistake in supposing this to be the first one," said the countess. "Among your many lovers, you choose the heir of our worst enemy, the son of those detested Clamerans. Among all, you select a coward who publicly boasted of your favours; a wretch who tried to avenge himself for the heroism of our ancestors by ruining you and me—an old woman and a child!"

"No, mother, you do him wrong. He loved me, and hopes for your consent."

"Wants to marry you, does he? Never, never shall that come to pass! I would rather see you lower than you are, in the gutter, laid in your coffin, than see you the wife of that man!"

Thus the hatred of the countess was expressed very much in the terms which the old *marquis* had used to his son.

"Besides," she added, with a ferocity of which only a bad woman is capable, "your lover is drowned, and the old *marquis* is dead. God is just; we are avenged."

The words of St. Jean, "There will be rejoicing at La Verberie," rung in Valentine's ears, as she saw the countess's eyes sparkle with wicked joy.

This was too much for the unfortunate girl.

For half an hour she had been exerting all of her strength to bear this cruel violence from her mother; but her physical endurance was not equal to the task. She turned pale, and with half-closed eyes tried to seize a table, as she felt herself falling; but her head fell against a bracket, and with bleeding forehead she dropped at her mother's feet.

The cold-hearted countess felt no revival of maternal love, as she looked at her daughter's lifeless form. Her vanity was wounded, but no other emotion disturbed her. Hers was a heart so full of anger and hatred that there was no room for any nobler sentiment.

She rang the bell; and the affrighted servants, who were trembling in the passage at the loud and angry tones of that voice, of which they all stood in terror, came running in.

"Carry *mademoiselle* to her room," she ordered: "lock her up, and bring me the key."

The countess intended keeping Valentine a close prisoner for a long time.

She well knew the mischievous, gossiping propensities of country people, who, from mere idleness, indulge in limitless scandal. A poor fallen girl must either leave the country, or drink to the very dregs the chalice of premeditated humiliations, heaped up and offered her by her neighbours. Each clown delights in casting a stone at her.

The plans of the countess were destined to be disconcerted.

The servants came to tell her that Valentine was restored to consciousness, but seemed to be very ill.

She replied that she would not listen to such absurdities, that it was all affectation; but Mihonne insisted upon her going up and judging for herself. She unwillingly went to her daughter's room, and saw that her life was in danger.

The countess betrayed no apprehension, but sent to Tarascon for Dr. Raget, who was the oracle of the neighbourhood; he was with the Marquis de Clameran when he died.

Dr. Raget was one of those men who leave a blessed memory, which lives long after they have left this world.

Intelligent, noble-hearted, and wealthy, he devoted his life to his art; going from the mansions of the rich to the hovels of the poor, without ever accepting remuneration for his services.

At all hours of the night and day, his grey horse and old buggy might be seen, with a basket of wine and soup under the seat, for his poorer patients.

He was a little, bald-headed man of fifty, with a quick, bright eye, and pleasant face.

The servant fortunately found him at home; and he was soon standing at Valentine's bedside, with a grave, perplexed look upon his usually cheerful face.

Endowed with profound perspicacity, quickened by practice, he studied Valentine and her mother alternately; and the penetrating gaze which he fastened on the old countess so disconcerted her that she felt her wrinkled face turning very red.

"This child is very ill," he abruptly said.

Madame de la Verberie made no reply.

"I desire," continued the doctor, "to remain alone with her for a few minutes."

The countess dared not resist the authority of a man of Dr. Raget's character, and retired to the next room, apparently calm, but in reality disturbed by the most gloomy forebodings.

At the end of half an hour—it seemed a century—the doctor entered the room where she was waiting. He, who had witnessed so much suffering and misery all his life, was agitated and nervous after talking with Valentine.

"Well," said the countess, "what is the matter?"

"Summon all your courage, *madame*," he answered sadly, "and be prepared to grant indulgence and pardon to your suffering child. Mademoiselle Valentine will soon become a mother."

"The worthless creature! I feared as much."

The doctor was shocked at this dreadful expression of the countess's eye. He laid his hand on her arm, and gave her a penetrating look, beneath which she instantly quailed.

The doctor's suspicions were correct.

A dreadful idea had flashed across Madame de la Verberie's mind—the idea of destroying this child which would be a living proof of Valentine's sin.

Feeling that her evil intention was divined, the proud woman's eyes fell beneath the doctor's obstinate gaze.

"I do not understand you, Dr. Raget," she murmured.

"But I understand you, *madame*; and I simply tell you that a crime does not obliterate a fault."

"Doctor!"

"I merely say what I think, *madame*. If I am mistaken in my impression, so much the better for you. At present, the condition of your daughter is serious, but not dangerous. Excitement and distress of mind have unstrung her nerves, and she now has a high fever; but I hope by great care and good nursing that she will soon recover."

The countess saw that the good doctor's suspicions were not dissipated; so she thought she would try affectionate anxiety, and said:

"At least, doctor, you can assure me that the dear child's life is not in danger?"

"No, *madame*," answered Dr. Raget with cutting irony, "your maternal tenderness need not be alarmed. All the poor child needs is rest of mind, which you alone can give her. A few kind words from you will do her more good than all of my prescriptions. But remember, *madame*, that the least shock or nervous excitement will produce the most fatal consequences."

"I am aware of that," said the hypocritical countess, "and shall be very careful. I must confess that I was unable to control my anger upon first hearing your announcement."

"But now that the first shock is over, *madame*, being a mother and a Christian, you will do your duty. My duty is to save your daughter and her child. I will call tomorrow."

Madame de la Verberie had no idea of having the doctor go off in this way. She called him back, and, without reflecting that she was betraying herself, cried out:

"Do you pretend to say, *monsieur*, that you will prevent my taking every means to conceal this terrible misfortune that has fallen upon me? Do you wish our shame to be made public, to make me the laughing-stock of the neighbourhood?"

The doctor reflected without answering; the condition of affairs was grave.

"No, *madame*," he finally said; "I cannot prevent your leaving La Verberie: that would be overstepping my powers. But it is my duty to hold you to account for the child. You are at liberty to go where you please; but you must give me proof of the child's living, or at least that no attempts have been made against its life."

After uttering these threatening words he left the house, and it was in good time; for the countess was choking with suppressed rage.

"Insolent upstart!" she said, "to presume to dictate to a woman of my rank! Ah, if I were not completely at his mercy!"

But she was at his mercy, and she knew well enough that it would be safest to obey.

She stamped her foot with anger, as she thought that all her ambitious plans were dashed to the ground.

No more hopes of luxury, of a millionaire son-in-law, of splendid carriages, rich dresses, and charming card-parties where she could lose money all night without disturbing her mind.

She would have to die as she had lived, neglected and poor; and this future life of deprivation would be harder to bear than the past, because she no longer had bright prospects to look forward to. It was a cruel awakening from her golden dreams.

And it was Valentine who brought this misery upon her.

This reflection aroused all her inherent bitterness, and she felt toward her daughter one of those implacable hatreds which, instead of being quenched, are strengthened by time.

She wished she could see Valentine lying dead before her; above all would she like the accursed infant to come to grief.

But the doctor's threatening look was still before her, and she dared not attempt her wicked plans. She even forced herself to go and say a few forgiving words to Valentine, and then left her to the care of the faithful Mihonne.

Poor Valentine! she prayed that death might kindly end her sufferings. She had neither the moral nor physical courage to fight against her fate, but hopelessly sank beneath the first blow, and made no attempt to rally herself.

She was, however, getting better. She felt that dull, heavy sensation which always follows violent mental or physical suffering; she was still able to reflect, and thought:

"Well, it is over; my mother knows everything. I no longer have her anger to fear, and must trust to time for her forgiveness."

This was the secret which Valentine had refused to reveal to Gaston, because she feared that he would refuse to leave her if he knew it; and she wished him to escape at any price of suffering to herself. Even now she did not regret having followed the dictates of duty, and remained at home.

The only thought which distressed her was Gaston's danger. Had he succeeded in embarking? How would she find out? The doctor had allowed her to get up; but she was not well enough to go out, and she did not know when she should be able to walk as far as Pere Menoul's cabin.

Happily the devoted old boatman was intelligent enough to anticipate her wishes.

Hearing that the young lady at the *château* was very ill, he set about devising some means of informing her of her friend's safety. He went to La Verberie several times on pretended errands, and finally succeeded in seeing Valentine. One of the servants was present, so he could not speak to her; but he made her understand by a significant look that Gaston was out of danger.

This knowledge contributed more toward Valentine's recovery than all the medicines administered by the doctor, who, after visiting her daily for six weeks, now pronounced his patient sufficiently strong to bear the fatigues of a journey.

The countess had waited with the greatest impatience for this decision. In order to prevent any delay, she had already sold at a discount half of her incoming rents, supposing that the sum thus raised, twenty-five thousand *francs*, would suffice for all contingent expenses.

For a fortnight she had been calling on all of her neighbours to bid them farewell, saying that her daughter had entirely recovered her health, and that she was going to take her to England to visit a rich old uncle, who had repeatedly written for her.

Valentine looked forward to this journey with terror, and shuddered when, on the evening that the doctor gave her permission to set out, her mother came to her room, and said:

"We will start the day after tomorrow."

Only one day left! And Valentine had been unable to let Louis de Clameran know that his brother was still living.

In this extremity she was obliged to confide in Mihonne, and sent her with a letter to Louis.

But the faithful servant had a useless walk.

The Château of Clameran was deserted; all the servants had been dismissed, and M. Louis, whom they now called the *marquis*, had gone abroad.

At last they started. Madame de la Verberie, feeling that she could trust Mihonne, decided to take her along; but first made her sacredly promise eternal secrecy.

It was in a little village near London that the countess, under the assumed name of Mrs. Wilson, took up her abode with her daughter and maid-servant.

She selected England, because she had lived there a long time, and was well acquainted with the manners and habits of the people, and spoke their language as well as she did her own.

She had also kept up her acquaintanceship with some of the English nobility, and often dined and went to the theatre with her friends in London. On these occasions she always took the humiliating precaution of locking up Valentine until she should return.

It was in this sad, solitary house, in the month of May, that the son of Valentine de la Verberie was born. He was taken to the parish priest, and christened Valentin-Raoul Wilson. The countess had prepared everything, and engaged an honest farmer's wife to adopt the child, bring him up as her own, and, when old enough, have him taught a trade. For doing this the countess paid her five hundred pounds.

Little Raoul was given over to his adopted parent a few hours after his birth.

The good woman thought him the child of an English lady, and there seemed no probability that he would ever discover the secret of his birth.

Restored to consciousness, Valentine asked for her child. She yearned to clasp it to her bosom; she implored to be allowed to hold her babe in her arms for only one minute.

But the cruel countess was pitiless.

"Your child!" she cried, "you must be dreaming; you have no child. You have had brain fever, but no child."

And as Valentine persisted in saying that she knew the child was alive, and that she must see it, the countess was forced to change her tactics.

"Your child is alive, and shall want for nothing," she said sharply; "let that suffice; and be thankful that I have so well concealed your disgrace. You must forget what has happened, as you would forget a painful dream. The past must be ignored—wiped out forever. You know me well enough to understand that I will be obeyed."

The moment had come when Valentine should have asserted her maternal rights, and resisted the countess's tyranny.

She had the idea, but not the courage to do so.

If, on one side, she saw the dangers of an almost culpable resignation—for she, too, was a mother!—on the other she felt crushed by the consciousness of her guilt.

She sadly yielded; surrendered herself into the hands of a mother whose conduct she refrained from questioning, to escape the painful necessity of condemning it.

But she secretly pined, and inwardly rebelled against her sad disappointment; and thus her recovery was delayed for several months.

Toward the end of July, the countess took her back to La Verberie. This time the mischief-makers and gossips were skilfully deceived. The countess went everywhere, and instituted secret inquiries, but heard no suspicions of the object of her long trip to England. Everyone believed in the visit to the rich uncle.

Only one man, Dr. Raget, knew the truth; and, although Madame de la Verberie hated him from the bottom of her heart, she did him the justice to feel sure that she had nothing to fear from his indiscretion.

Her first visit was paid to him.

When she entered the room, she abruptly threw on the table the official papers which she had procured especially for him.

"These will prove to you, *monsieur*, that the child is living, and well cared for at a cost that I can ill afford."

"These are perfectly right, *madame*," he replied, after an attentive examination of the papers, "and, if your conscience does not reproach you, of course I have nothing to say."

"My conscience reproaches me with nothing, *monsieur*."

The old doctor shook his head, and gazing searchingly into her eyes, said:

"Can you say that you have not been harsh, even to cruelty?"

She turned away her head, and, assuming her grand air, answered:

"I have acted as a woman of my rank should act; and I am surprised to find in you an advocate and abettor of misconduct."

"Ah, *madame*," said the doctor, "it is your place to show kindness to the poor girl; and if you feel none yourself, you have no right to complain of it in others. What indulgence do you expect from strangers toward your unhappy daughter, when you, her mother, are so pitiless?"

This plain-spoken truth offended the countess, and she rose to leave.

"Have you finished what you have to say, Dr. Raget?" she asked, haughtily.

"Yes, *madame*; I have done. My only object was to spare you eternal remorse. Good-day."

The good doctor was mistaken in his idea of Madame de la Verberie's character. She was utterly incapable of feeling remorse; but she suffered cruelly when her selfish vanity was wounded, or her comfort disturbed.

She resumed her luxurious mode of living, but, having disposed of a part of her income, found it difficult to make both ends meet.

This furnished her with an inexhaustible text for complaint; and at every meal she reproached Valentine so unmercifully, that the poor girl shrank from coming to the table.

She seemed to forget her own command, that the past should be buried in oblivion, and constantly recurred to it for food for her anger; a day seldom passed, that she did not say to Valentine:

"Your conduct has ruined me."

One day her daughter could not refrain from replying:

"I suppose you would have pardoned the fault, had it enriched us."

But these revolts of Valentine were rare, although her life was a series of tortures inflicted with inquisitorial cruelty.

Even the memory of Gaston had become a suffering.

Perhaps, discovering the uselessness of her sacrifice, of her courage, and her devotion to what she had considered her duty, she regretted not having followed him. What had become of him? Might he not have contrived to send her a letter, a word to let her know that he was still alive? Perhaps he was not dead. Perhaps he had forgotten her. He had sworn to return a rich man before the lapse of three years. Would he ever return?

There was a risk in his returning under any circumstances. His disappearance had not ended the terrible affair of Tarascon. He was supposed to be dead; but as there was no positive proof of his death, and his body could not be found, the law was compelled to yield to the clamour of public opinion.

The case was brought before the assize court; and, in default of appearance, Gaston de Clameran was sentenced to several years of close confinement.

As to Louis de Clameran, no one knew positively what had become of him. Some people said he was leading a life of reckless extravagance in Paris.

Informed of these facts by her faithful Mihonne, Valentine became more gloomy and hopeless than ever. Vainly did she question the dreary future; no ray appeared upon the dark horizon of her life.

Her elasticity was gone; and she had finally reached that state of passive resignation peculiar to people who are oppressed and cowed at home.

In this miserable way, passed four years since the fatal evening when Gaston left her.

Madame de la Verberie had spent these years in constant discomfort. Seeing that she could not live upon her income, and having too much pride to sell her land, which was so badly managed that it only brought her in two *per cent*, she mortgaged her estate in order to raise money only to be spent as soon as borrowed.

In such matters, it is the first step that costs; and, after having once commenced to live upon her capital, the countess made rapid strides in extravagance, saying to herself, "After me, the deluge!" Very much as her neighbour, the late Marquis de Clameran, had managed his affairs, she was now conducting hers, having but one object in view—her own comfort and pleasure.

She made frequent visits to the neighbouring towns of Nimes and Avignon; she sent to Paris for the most elegant toilets, and entertained a great deal of company. All the luxury that she had hoped to obtain by the acquisition of a rich son-in-law, she determined to give herself, utterly regardless of the fact that she was reducing her child to beggary. Great sorrows require consolation!

The summer that she returned from London, she did not hesitate to indulge her fancy for a horse; it was rather old, to be sure, but, when harnessed to a second-hand carriage bought on credit at Beaucaire, made quite a good appearance.

She would quiet her conscience, which occasionally reproached her for this constant extravagance, by saying, "I am so unhappy!"

The unhappiness was that this luxury cost her dear, very dear.

After having sold the rest of her rents, the countess first mortgaged the estate of La Verberie, and then the *château* itself.

In less than four years she owed more than forty thousand *francs*, and was unable to pay the interest of her debt.

She was racking her mind to discover some means of escape from her difficulties, when chance came to her rescue.

For some time a young engineer, employed in surveys along the Rhone, had made the village of Beaucaire the centre of his operations.

Being handsome, agreeable, and of polished manners, he had been warmly welcomed by the neighbouring society, and the countess frequently met him at the houses of her friends where she went to play cards in the evenings.

This young engineer was named Andre Fauvel.

The first time he met Valentine he was struck by her beauty, and after once looking into her large, melancholy eyes, his admiration deepened into love; a love so earnest and passionate, that he felt that he could never be happy without her.

Before being introduced to her, his heart had surrendered itself to her charms.

He was wealthy; a splendid career was open to him, he was free; and he swore that Valentine should be his.

He confided all his matrimonial plans to an old friend of Madame de la Verberie, who was as noble as a Montmorency, and as poor as Job.

With the precision of a graduate of the polytechnic school, he had enumerated all his qualifications for being a model son-in-law.

For a long time the old lady listened to him without interruption; but, when he had finished, she did not hesitate to tell him that his pretensions were presumptuous.

What! he, a man of no pedigree, a Fauvel, a common surveyor, to aspire to the hand of a La Verberie!

After having enumerated all the superior advantages of that superior order of beings, the nobility, she condescended to take a common-sense view of the case, and said:

"However, you may succeed. The poor countess owes money in every direction; not a day passes without the bailiffs calling upon her; so that, you understand, if a rich suitor appeared, and agreed to her terms for settlements—well, well, there is no knowing what might happen."

Andre Fauvel was young and sentimental: the insinuations of the old lady seemed to him preposterous.

On reflection, however, when he had studied the character of the nobility in the neighbourhood, who were rich in nothing but prejudices, he clearly saw that pecuniary considerations alone would be strong enough to decide the proud Countess de la Verberie to grant him her daughter's hand.

This certainly ended his hesitations, and he turned his whole attention to devising a plan for presenting his claim.

He did not find this an easy thing to accomplish. To go in quest of a wife with her purchase-money in his hand was repugnant to his feelings, and contrary to his ideas of delicacy. But he had no one to urge his suit for him on his own merits; so he was compelled to shut his eyes to the distasteful features of his task, and treat his passion as a matter of business.

The occasion so anxiously awaited, to explain his intentions, soon presented itself.

One day he entered a hotel at Beaucaire, and, as he sat down to dinner, he saw that Madame de la Verberie was at the adjoining table. He blushed deeply, and asked permission to sit at her table, which was granted with a most encouraging smile.

Did the countess suspect the love of the young engineer? Had she been warned by her friend?

At any rate, without giving Andre time to gradually approach the subject weighing on his mind, she began to complain of the hard times, the scarcity of money, and the grasping meanness of the tradespeople.

She had come to Beaucaire, indeed, to borrow money, and found every bank and cash-box closed against her; and her lawyer had advised her to sell her land for what it would bring. This made her very angry.

Temper, joined to that secret instinct of the situation of affairs which is the sixth sense of a woman, loosened her tongue, and made her more communicative to this comparative stranger than she had ever been to her bosom friends. She explained to him the horror of her situation, her present needs, her anxiety for the future, and, above all, her great distress at not being able to marry off her beloved daughter. If she only had a dowry for her child!

Andre listened to these complaints with becoming commiseration, but in reality he was delighted.

Without giving her time to finish her tale, he began to state what he called his view of the matter.

He said that, although he sympathized deeply with the countess, he could not account for her uneasiness about her daughter.

What? Could she be disturbed at having no dowry for her? Why, the rank and beauty of Mademoiselle Valentine were a fortune in themselves, of which any man might be proud.

He knew more than one man who would esteem himself only too happy if Mademoiselle Valentine would accept his name, and confer upon him the sweet duty of relieving her mother from all anxiety and care. Finally, he did not think the situation of the countess's affairs nearly so desperate as she imagined. How much money would be necessary to pay off the mortgages upon La Verberie? About forty thousand *francs*, perhaps? Indeed! That was but a mere trifle.

Besides, this sum need not be a gift from the son-in-law; if she chose, it might be a loan, because the estate would be his in the end, and in time the land would be double its present value; it would be a pity to sell now. A man, too, worthy of Valentine's love could never let his wife's mother want for the comforts and luxuries due to a lady of her age, rank, and misfortunes. He would be only too glad to offer her a sufficient income, not only to provide comfort, but even luxury.

As Andre spoke, in a tone too earnest to be assumed, it seemed to the countess that a celestial dew was dropping upon her pecuniary wounds. Her countenance was radiant with joy, her fierce little eyes beamed with the most encouraging tenderness, her thin lips were wreathed in the most friendly smiles.

One thought disturbed the young engineer.

"Does she understand me seriously?" he thought.

She certainly did, as her subsequent remarks proved. He saw that the would-be sentimental old lady had an eye to business.

"Alas!" she sighed, "La Verberie cannot be saved by forty thousand *francs*; the principal and interest of the debt amount to sixty thousand."

"Oh, either forty or sixty thousand is nothing worth speaking of."

"Four thousand *francs* is not enough to support a lady respectably," she said after a pause. "Everything is so dear in this section of the country! But with six thousand *francs*—yes, six thousand *francs* would make me happy!"

The young man thought that her demands were becoming excessive, but with the generosity of an ardent lover he said:

"The son-in-law of whom we are speaking cannot be very devoted to Mademoiselle Valentine, if the paltry sum of two thousand *francs* were objected to for an instant."

"You promise too much!" muttered the countess.

"The imaginary son-in-law," she finally added, "must be an honourable man who will fulfil his promises. I have my daughter's happiness too much at heart to give her to a man who did not produce—what do you call them?—securities, guarantees."

"Decidedly," thought Fauvel with mortification, "we are making a bargain and sale."

Then he said aloud:

"Of course, your son-in-law would bind himself in the marriage contract to—"

"Never! *monsieur*, never! Put such an agreement in the marriage contract! Think of the impropriety of the thing! What would the world say?"

"Permit me, *madame*, to suggest that your pension should be mentioned as the interest of a sum acknowledged to have been received from you."

"Well, that might do very well; that is very proper."

The countess insisted upon taking Andre home in her carriage. During the drive, no definite plan was agreed upon between them; but they understood each other so well, that, when the countess set the young engineer down at his own door, she invited him to dinner the next day, and held out her skinny hand which Andre kissed with devotion, as he thought of the rosy fingers of Valentine.

When Madame de la Verberie returned home, the servants were dumb with astonishment at her good-humour: they had not seen her in this happy frame of mind for years.

And her day's work was of a nature to elevate her spirits: she had been unexpectedly raised from poverty to affluence. She, who boasted of such proud sentiments, never stopped to think of the infamy of the transaction in which she had been engaged: it seemed quite right in her selfish eyes.

"A pension of six thousand *francs*!" she thought, "and a thousand crowns from the estate, that makes nine thousand *francs* a year! My daughter will live in Paris after she is married, and I can spend the winters with my dear children without expense."

At this price, she would have sold, not only one, but three daughters, if she had possessed them.

But suddenly her blood ran cold at a sudden thought, which crossed her mind.

"Would Valentine consent?"

Her anxiety to set her mind at rest sent her straightway to her daughter's room. She found Valentine reading by the light of a flickering candle.

"My daughter," she said abruptly, "an estimable young man has demanded your hand in marriage, and I have promised it to him."

On this startling announcement, Valentine started up and clasped her hands.

"Impossible!" she murmured, "impossible!"

"Will you be good enough to explain why it is impossible?"

"Did you tell him, mother, who I am, what I am? Did you confess—"

"Your past fully? No, thank God, I am not fool enough for that, and I hope you will have the sense to imitate my example, and keep silent on the subject."

Although Valentine's spirit was completely crushed by her mother's tyranny, her sense of honour made her revolt against this demand.

"You certainly would not wish me to marry an honest man, mother, without confessing to him everything connected with the past? I could never practise a deception so base."

The countess felt very much like flying into a passion; but she knew that threats would be of no avail in this instance, where resistance would be a duty of conscience with her daughter. Instead of commanding, she entreated.

"Poor child," she said, "my poor, dear Valentine. If you only knew the dreadful state of our affairs, you would not talk in this heartless way. Your folly commenced our ruin; now it is at its last stage. Do you know that our creditors threaten to drive us away from La Verberie?

Then what will become of us, my poor child? Must I in my old age go begging from door to door? We are on the verge of ruin, and this marriage is our only hope of salvation."

These tearful entreaties were followed by plausible arguments.

The fair-spoken countess made use of strange and subtle theories. What she formerly regarded as a monstrous crime, she now spoke of as a *peccadillo*.

She could understand, she said, her daughter's scruples if there were any danger of the past being brought to light; but she had taken such precautions that there was no fear of that.

Would it make her love her husband any the less? No. Would he be made any happier for hearing that she had loved before? No. Then why say anything about the past?

Shocked, bewildered, Valentine asked herself if this was really her mother? The haughty woman, who had always been such a worshipper of honour and duty, to contradict every word she had uttered during her life! Valentine could not understand the sudden change.

But she would have understood it, had she known to what base deeds a mind blunted by selfishness and vanity can lend itself.

The countess's subtle arguments and shameful sophistry neither moved nor convinced her; but she had not the courage to resist the tearful entreaties of her mother, who ended by falling on her knees, and with clasped hands imploring her child to save her from worse than death.

Violently agitated, distracted by a thousand conflicting emotions, daring neither to refuse nor to promise, fearing the consequences of a decision thus forced from her, the unhappy girl begged her mother for a few hours to reflect.

Madame de la Verberie dared not refuse this request, and acquiesced.

"I will leave you, my daughter," she said, "and I trust your own heart will tell you how to decide between a useless confession and your mother's salvation."

With these words she left the room indignant but hopeful.

And she had grounds for hope. Placed between two obligations equally sacred, equally binding, but diametrically opposite, Valentine's troubled mind could no longer clearly discern the path of duty. Could she reduce her mother to want and misery? Could she basely deceive the confidence and love of an honourable man? However she decided, her future life would be one of suffering and remorse.

Alas! why had she not a wise and kind adviser to point out the right course to pursue, and assist her in struggling against evil influences? Why had she not that gentle, discreet friend who had inspired her with hope and courage in her first dark sorrow—Dr. Raget?

Formerly the memory of Gaston had been her guiding star: now this far-off memory was nothing but a faint mist—a sort of vanishing dream.

In romance we meet with heroines of lifelong constancy: real life produces no such miracles.

For a long time Valentine's mind had been filled with the image of Gaston. As the hero of her dreams she dwelt fondly on his memory; but the shadows of time had gradually dimmed the brilliancy of her idol, and now only preserved a cold relic, over which she sometimes wept.

When she arose the next morning, pale and weak from a sleepless, tearful night, she had almost resolved to confess everything to her suitor.

But when evening came, and she went down to see Andre Fauvel, the presence of her mother's threatening, supplicating eye destroyed her courage.

She said to herself, "I will tell him tomorrow." Then she said, "I will wait another day; one more day can make no difference."

The countess saw all these struggles, but was not made uneasy by them.

She knew by experience that, when a painful duty is put off, it is never performed.

There was some excuse for Valentine in the horror of her situation. Perhaps, unknown to herself, she felt a faint hope arise within her. Any marriage, even an unhappy one, offered the prospect of a change, of a new life, a relief from the insupportable suffering she was now enduring.

Sometimes, in her ignorance of human life, she imagined that time and close intimacy would take it easier for her to confess her terrible fault; that it would be the most natural thing in the world for Andre to pardon her, and insist upon marrying her, since he loved her so deeply.

That he sincerely loved her, she knew full well. It was not the impetuous passion of Gaston, with its excitements and terrors, but a calm, steady affection, more lasting than the intoxicating love of Gaston was ever likely to be. She felt a sort of blissful rest in its legitimacy and constancy.

Thus Valentine gradually became accustomed to Andre's soothing presence, and was surprised into feeling very happy at the constant delicate attentions and looks of affection that he lavished upon her. She did not feel any love for him yet; but a separation would have distressed her deeply.

During the courtship the countess's conduct was a masterpiece.

She suddenly ceased to importune her daughter, and with tearful resignation said she would not attempt to influence her decision, that her happy settlement in life was the only anxiety that weighed upon her mind.

But she went about the house sighing and groaning as if she were upon the eve of starving to death. She also made arrangements to be tormented by the bailiffs. Attachments and notices to quit poured in at La Verberie, which she would show to Valentine and, with tears in her eyes, say:

"God grant we may not be driven from the home of our ancestors before your marriage, my darling!"

Knowing that her presence was sufficient to freeze any confession on her daughter's lips, she never left her alone with Andre.

"Once married," she thought, "they can settle the matter to suit themselves. I shall not then be disturbed by it."

She was as impatient as Andre, and hastened the preparations for the wedding. She gave Valentine no opportunity for reflection. She kept her constantly busy, either in driving to town to purchase some article of dress, or in paying visits.

At last the eve of the wedding-day found her anxious and oppressed with fear lest something should prevent the consummation of her hopes and labours. She was like a gambler who had ventured his last stake.

On this night, for the first time, Valentine found herself alone with the man who was to become her husband.

She was sitting at twilight, in the parlour, miserable and trembling, anxious to unburden her mind, and yet frightened at the very thought of doing so, when Andre entered. Seeing that she was agitated, he pressed her hand, and gently begged her to tell him the cause of her sorrow.

"Am I not your best friend," he said, "and ought I not to be the confidant of your troubles, if you have any? Why these tears, my darling?"

Now was the time for her to confess, and throw herself upon his generosity. But her trembling lips refused to open when she thought of his pain and anguish, and the anger of her mother, which would be caused by the few words she would utter. She felt that it was too late; and, bursting into tears, she cried out, "I am afraid—What shall I do?"

Imagining that she was merely disturbed by the vague fears experienced by most young girls when about to marry, he tried, with tender, loving words, to console and reassure her, promising to shield her from every care and sorrow, if she would only trust to his devoted love. But what was his surprise to find that his affectionate words only increased her distress; she buried her face in her hands, and wept as if her heart would break.

While she was thus summoning her courage, and he was entreating her confidence, Madame de la Verberie came hurrying into the room for them to sign the contract.

The opportunity was lost; Andre Fauvel was left in ignorance.

The next day, a lovely spring morning, Andre Fauvel and Valentine de la Verberie were married at the village church.

Early in the morning, the *château* was filled with the bride's friends, who came, according to custom, to assist at her wedding toilet.

Valentine forced herself to appear calm, even smiling; but her face was whiter than her veil; her heart was torn by remorse. She felt as though the sad truth were written upon her brow; and this pure white dress was a bitter irony, a galling humiliation.

She shuddered when her most intimate school-mate placed the wreath of orange-blossoms upon her head. These emblems of purity seemed to burn her like a band of red-hot iron. One of the wire stems of the flowers scratched her forehead, and a drop of blood fell upon her snowy robe.

What an evil omen! Valentine was near fainting when she thought of the past and the future connected by this bloody sign of woe.

But presages are deceitful, as it proved with Valentine; for she became a happy woman and a loving wife.

Yes, at the end of her first year of married life, she confessed to herself that her happiness would be complete if she could only forget the terrible past.

Andre adored her. He had been wonderfully successful in his business affairs; he wished to be immensely rich, not for himself, but for the sake of his beloved wife, whom he would surround with every luxury. He thought her the most beautiful woman in Paris, and determined that she should be the most superbly dressed.

Eighteen months after her marriage, Madame Fauvel presented

her husband with a son. But neither this child, nor a second son born a year later, could make her forget the first one of all, the poor, forsaken babe who had been thrown upon strangers, mercenaries, who valued the money, but not the child for whom it was paid.

She would look at her two sons, surrounded by every luxury which money could give, and murmur to herself:

"Who knows if the abandoned one has bread to eat?"

If she only knew where he was: if she only dared inquire! But she was afraid.

Sometimes she would be uneasy about Gaston's jewels, constantly fearing that their hiding-place would be discovered. Then she would think, "I may as well be tranquil; misfortune has forgotten me."

Poor, deluded woman! Misfortune is a visitor who sometimes delays his visits, but always comes in the end.

Chapter 15

Louis de Clameran, the second son of the *marquis*, was one of those self-controlled men who, beneath a cool, careless manner, conceal a fiery temperament, and ungovernable passions.

All sorts of extravagant ideas had begun to ferment in his disordered brain, long before the occurrence which decided the destiny of the Clameran family.

Apparently occupied in the pursuit of pleasure, this precocious hypocrite longed for a larger field in which to indulge his evil inclinations, secretly cursing the stern necessity which chained him down to this dreary country life, and the old *château*, which to him was more gloomy than a prison, and as lifeless as the grave.

This existence, dragged out in the country and the small neighbouring towns, was too monotonous for his restless nature. The paternal authority, though so gently expressed, exasperated his rebellious temper. He thirsted for independence, riches, excitement, and all the unknown pleasures that pall upon the senses simultaneously with their attainment.

Louis did not love his father, and he hated his brother Gaston.

The old *marquis*, in his culpable thoughtlessness, had kindled this burning envy in the heart of his second son.

A strict observer of traditional rights, he had always declared that the eldest son of a noble house should inherit all the family possessions, and that he intended to leave Gaston his entire fortune.

This flagrant injustice and favouritism inspired Louis with envious hatred for his brother.

Gaston always said that he would never consent to profit by this paternal partiality, but would share equally with his brother. Judging others by himself, Louis placed no faith in this assertion, which he called an ostentatious affectation of generosity.

Although this hatred was unsuspected by the *marquis* and Gaston, it was betrayed by acts significant enough to attract the attention of the servants, who often commented upon it.

They were so fully aware of Louis's sentiments toward his brother that, when he was prevented from escaping because of the stumbling horse, they refused to believe it an accident; and, whenever Louis came near would mutter, "Fratricide!"

A deplorable scene took place between Louis and St. Jean, who was allowed, on account of his fifty years' faithful service, to take liberties which he sometimes abused by making rough speeches to his superiors.

"It is a great pity," said the old servant, "that a skilful rider like yourself should have fallen at the very moment when your brother's life depended upon your horsemanship."

At this broad insinuation, Louis turned pale, and threateningly cried out:

"You insolent dog, what do you mean?"

"You know well enough what I mean, *monsieur*," the old man said, significantly.

"I do not know! Explain your impertinence: speak, I tell you!"

The man only answered by a meaning look, which so incensed Louis that he rushed toward him with upraised whip, and would have beaten him unmercifully, had not the other servants interfered, and dragged St. Jean from the spot.

This altercation occurred while Gaston was in the madder-field trying to escape his pursuers.

After a while the *gendarmes* and hussars returned, with slow tread and sad faces, to say that Gaston de Clameran had plunged into the Rhone, and was instantly drowned.

This melancholy news was received with groans and tears by everyone save Louis, who remained calm and unmoved: not a single muscle of his face quivered.

But his eyes sparkled with triumph. A secret voice cried within him, "Now you are assured of the family fortune, and a *marquis*'s coronet."

He was no longer the poverty-stricken younger son, but the sole heir of the Clamerans.

The corporal of the *gendarmes* had said:

"I would not be the one to tell the poor old man that his son is drowned."

Louis felt none of the tender-hearted scruples of the brave old soldier. He instantly went to his father's sick-room, and said, in a firm voice:

"My brother had to choose between disgrace and death; he is dead."

Like a sturdy oak stricken by lightning, the *marquis* tottered and fell when these fatal words sounded in his ears. The doctor soon arrived, but alas! only to say that science was of no avail.

Toward daybreak, Louis, without a tear, received his father's last sigh.

Louis was now the master.

All the unjust precautions taken by the *marquis* to elude the law, and insure beyond dispute the possession of his entire fortune to his eldest son, turned against him.

By means of a fraudulent deed of trust drawn by his dishonest lawyer, M. de Clameran had disposed everything so that, on the day of his death, every farthing he owned would be Gaston's.

Louis alone was benefited by this precaution. He came into possession without even being called upon for the certificate of his brother's death.

He was now Marquis de Clameran; he was free, he was comparatively rich. He who had never had twenty-five crowns in his pocket at once, now found himself the possessor of two hundred thousand *francs*.

This sudden, unexpected fortune so completely turned his head that he forgot his skilful dissimulation. His demeanour at the funeral of the *marquis* was much censured. He followed the coffin, with his head bowed and his face buried in a handkerchief; but this did not conceal the buoyancy of his spirit, and the joy which sparkled in his eyes.

The day after the funeral, Louis sold everything that he could dispose of, horses, carriages, and family plate.

The next day he discharged all the old servants, who had hoped to end their days beneath the hospitable roof of Clameran. Several, with tears in their eyes, took him aside, and entreated him to let them stay without wages. He roughly ordered them to be gone, and never appear before his eyes again.

He sent for his father's lawyer, and gave him a power of attorney to sell the estate, and received in return the sum of twenty thousand *francs* as the first payment in advance.

At the close of the week, he locked up the *château*, with a vow never to cross its sill again, and left the keys in the keeping of St. Jean, who owned a little house near Clameran, and would continue to live in the neighbourhood.

Poor St. Jean! little did he think that, in preventing Valentine from seeing Louis, he had ruined the prospects of his beloved Gaston.

On receiving the keys he asked one question:

"Shall we not search for your brother's body, M. the Marquis?" he inquired in broken-hearted tones. "And, if it is found, what must be done with it?"

"I shall leave instructions with my notary," replied Louis. And he hurried away from Clameran as if the ground burnt his feet. He went to Tarascon, where he had already forwarded his baggage, and took the stage-coach which travelled between Marseilles and Paris, the railroad not yet being finished.

At last he was off. The lumbering old stage rattled along, drawn by six horses; and the deep gullies made by the wheels seemed so many abysses between the past and the future.

Lying back in a corner of the stage, Louis de Clameran enjoyed in anticipation the fields of pleasure spread before his dazzled eyes. At the end of the journey, Paris rose up before him, radiant, brilliantly dazzling as the sun.

Yes, he was going to Paris, the promised land, the city of wonders, where every Aladdin finds a lamp. There all ambitions are crowned, all dreams realised, all passions, all desires, good and evil, can be satisfied.

There the fast-fleeting days are followed by nights of ever-varied pleasure and excitement. In twenty theatres tragedy weeps, or comedy laughs; whilst at the opera the most beautiful women in the world, sparkling with diamonds, are ready to die with ecstasy at the sound of divine music; everywhere noise, excitement, luxury, and pleasure.

What a dream! The heart of Louis de Clameran was swollen with desire, and he felt that he should go mad if the horses crawled with such torturing slowness: he would like to spring from the old stage, and fly to his haven of delight.

He never once thought of the past with a pang of regret. What mattered it to him how his father and brother had died? All his energies were devoted to penetrating the mysterious future that now awaited him.

Was not every chance in his favour? He was young, rich, handsome, and a *marquis*. He had a constitution of iron; he carried twenty thousand *francs* in his pocket, and would soon have ten times as many more.

He, who had always been poor, regarded this sum as an exhaustless treasure.

And at nightfall, when he jumped from the stage upon the brilliantly lighted street of Paris, he seemed to be taking possession of the grand city, and felt as though he could buy everything in it.

His illusions were those natural to all young men who suddenly come into possession of a patrimony after years of privation.

It is this ignorance of the real value of money that squanders fortunes, and fritters away accumulated patrimonies so laboriously earned and saved in the frugal provinces.

Imbued with his own importance, accustomed to the deference of the country people, the young *marquis* came to Paris with the expectation of being a lion, supposing that his name and fortune were sufficient to place him upon any pinnacle he might desire.

He was mortified to discover his error. To his great surprise he discovered that he possessed nothing which constituted a position in this immense city. He found that in the midst of this busy, indifferent crowd, he was lost, as unnoticed as a drop of water in a torrent.

But this unflattering reality could not discourage a man who was determined to gratify his passion at all costs. His ancestral name gained him but one privilege, disastrous for his future: it opened to him the doors of the Faubourg St. Germain.

There he became intimate with men of his own age and rank, whose incomes were larger than his principal.

Nearly all of them confessed that they only kept up their extravagant style of living by dint of skilful economy behind the scenes, and by regulating their vices and follies as judiciously as a hosier would manage his Sunday holidays.

This information astonished Louis, but did not open his eyes. He endeavoured to imitate the dashing style of these economically wasteful young men, without pretending to conform to their prudential rules. He learned how to spend, but not how to settle his accounts as they did.

He was Marquis de Clameran, and, having given himself a reputation of great wealth, he was welcomed by the *elite* of society; if he made no friends, he had at least many acquaintances. Among the set into which he was received immediately upon his arrival, he found ten satellites who took pleasure in initiating him into the secrets of fashionable life, and correcting any little provincialisms betrayed in his manners and conversation.

He profited well and quickly by their lessons. At the end of three months he was fairly launched; his reputation as a skilful gambler and one of the fastest men in Paris was fully established.

He had rented handsome apartments, with a coach-house and stable for three horses.

Although he only furnished this bachelor's establishment with what was necessary and comfortable, he found that comforts were very costly in this instance.

So that the day he took possession of his apartments, and looked over his bills, he made the startling discovery that this short apprenticeship of Paris had cost him fifty-thousand *francs*, one-fourth of his fortune.

Still he clung to his brilliant friends, although in a state of inferiority which was mortifying to his vanity, like a poor squire straining every nerve to make his nag keep up with blooded horses in a race.

Fifty thousand *francs*! For a moment Louis had a faint idea of retreating from the scene of temptation. But what a fall! Besides, his vices bloomed and flourished in this charming centre. He had heretofore considered himself fast; but the past was a state of unsophisticated verdancy, compared with the thousand attractive sins in which he now indulged.

Then the sight of suddenly acquired fortunes, and the many examples of the successful results of hazardous ventures, inflamed his mind, and persuaded him to try his fortune in the game of speculation.

He thought that in this great, rich city, he certainly could succeed in seizing a share of the loaves and fishes.

But how? He had no idea, and he did not seek to find one. He imagined that his good fortune would some day come, and that all he had to do was to wait for it.

This is one of the errors which it is time to destroy.

Fortune is not to be wasted upon idle fools.

In this furious race of self-interest, it requires great skill to bestride the capricious mare called Opportunity, and make her lead to the end in view. Every winner must possess a strong will and a dexterous hand.

But Louis did not devote much thought to the matter. Like the foolish man who wished to draw the prize without contributing to the raffle, he thought:

"*Bast*! opportunity, chance, a rich marriage will put me all right again!"

The rich bride failed to appear, and his last *louis* had gone the way of its predecessors.

To a pressing demand for money, his notary replied by a refusal.

"Your lands are all gone," he wrote; "you now possess nothing but the *château*. It is very valuable, but it is difficult, if not impossible, to find a purchaser of so large an amount of real estate, in its present condition. I will use every effort to make a good sale, and if successful, will inform you of the fact immediately." Louis was thunderstruck at this final catastrophe, as much surprised as if he could have expected any other result. But what could he do?

Ruined, with nothing to look forward to, the best course was to imitate the large number of poor fools who each year rise up, shine a moment, then suddenly disappear.

But Louis could not renounce this life of ease and pleasure which he had been leading for the last three years. After leaving his fortune on the battle-ground, he was willing to leave the shreds of his honour.

He first lived on the reputation of his dissipated fortune; on the credit remaining to a man who has spent much in a short space of time.

This resource was soon exhausted.

The day came when his creditors seized all they could lay their hands upon, the last remains of his opulence, his carriages, horses, and costly furniture.

He took refuge in a quiet hotel, but he could not keep away from the wealthy set whom he considered his friends.

He lived upon them as he had lived upon the tradesmen who furnished his supplies. Borrowing from one *louis* up to twenty-five, from anybody who would lend to him, he never pretended to pay them. Constantly betting, no one ever saw him pay a wager. He piloted all the raw young men who fell into his hands, and utilized, in rendering shameful services, an experience which had cost him two hundred thousand *francs*; he was half courtier, half adventurer.

He was not banished, but was made to cruelly expiate the favour of being tolerated. No one had the least regard for his feelings, or hesitated to tell him to his face what was thought of his unprincipled conduct.

Thus, when alone in his little den, he would give way to fits of violent rage. He had not yet reached a state of callousness to be able to endure these humiliations without the keenest torture to his false pride and vanity.

Envy and covetousness had long since stifled every sentiment of honour and self-respect in his base heart. For a few years of opulence he was ready to commit any crime.

And, though he did not commit a crime, he came very near it, and was the principal in a disgraceful affair of swindling and extortion, which raised such an outcry against him that he was obliged to leave Paris.

Count de Commarin, an old friend of his father, hushed up the matter, and furnished him with money to take him to England.

And how did he manage to live in London?

The detectives of the most corrupt capital in existence were the only people who knew his means of support.

Descending to the last stages of vice, the Marquis de Clameran finally found his level in a society composed of shameless women and gamblers.

Compelled to quit London, he travelled over Europe, with no other capital than his knavish audacity, deep depravity, and his skill at cards.

Finally, in 1865, he had a run of good luck at Homburg, and returned to Paris, where he imagined himself entirely forgotten.

Eighteen years had passed since he left Paris.

The first step which he took on his return, before even settling himself in Paris, was to make a visit to his old home.

Not that he had any relative or friend in that part of the country, from whom he could expect any assistance; but he remembered the old manor, which his notary had been unable to sell.

He thought that perhaps by this time a purchaser had appeared, and he determined to go himself and ascertain how much he should receive for this old *château*, which had cost one hundred thousand *francs* in the building.

On a beautiful October evening he reached Tarascon, and there learned that he was still the owner of the Château of Clameran. The next morning, he set out on foot to visit the paternal home, which he had not seen for twenty-five years.

Everything was so changed that he scarcely recognised this country, where he had been born, and passed his youth.

Yet the impression was so strong, that this man, tried by such varied, strange adventures, for a moment felt like retracing his steps.

He only continued his road because a secret, hopeful voice cried in him, "Onward, onward!"—as if, at the end of the journey, was to be found a new life and the long-wished-for good fortune.

As Louis advanced, the changes appeared less striking; he began to be familiar with the ground.

Soon, through the trees, he distinguished the village steeple, then the village itself, built upon the gentle rising of a hill, crowned by a wood of olive-trees.

He recognised the first houses he saw: the farrier's shed covered with ivy, the old parsonage, and farther on the village tavern, where he and Gaston used to play billiards.

In spite of what he called his scorn of vulgar prejudices, he felt a thrill of strange emotion as he looked on these once familiar objects.

He could not overcome a feeling of sadness as scenes of the past rose up before him.

How many events had occurred since he last walked along this path, and received a friendly bow and smile from every villager.

Then life appeared to him like a fairy scene, in which his every wish was gratified. And now, he had returned, dishonoured, worn out, disgusted with the realities of life, still tasting the bitter dregs of the cup of shame, stigmatized, poverty-stricken, and friendless, with nothing to lose, and nothing to look forward to.

The few villagers whom he met turned and stood gazing after this dust-covered stranger, and wondered who he could be.

Upon reaching St. Jean's house, he found the door open; he walked into the immense empty kitchen.

He rapped on the table, and was answered by a voice calling out:

"Who is there?"

The next moment a man of about forty years appeared in the doorway, and seemed much surprised at finding a stranger standing in his kitchen.

"What will you have, *monsieur*?" he inquired.

"Does not St. Jean, the old valet of the Marquis de Clameran, live here?"

"My father died five years ago, *monsieur*," replied the man in a sad tone.

This news affected Louis painfully, as if he had expected this old man to restore him some of his lost youth; the last link was gone. He sighed, and, after a silence, said:

"I am the Marquis de Clameran."

The farmer, at these words, uttered an exclamation of joy. He seized Louis's hand, and, pressing it with respectful attention, cried:

"You are the *marquis*! Alas!" he continued, "why is not my poor father alive to see you? he would be so happy! His last words were about his dear masters, and many a time did he sigh and mourn at not receiving any news of you. He is beneath the sod now, resting after a well-spent life; but I, Joseph, his son, am here to take his place, and devote my life to your service. What an honour it is to have you in my house! Ah, my wife will be happy to see you; she has all her life heard of the Clamerans."

Here he ran into the garden, and called: "Toinette! I say, Toinette! Come here quickly!"

This cordial welcome delighted Louis. So many years had gone by since he had been greeted with an expression of kindness, or felt the pressure of a friendly hand.

In a few moments a handsome, dark-eyed young woman entered the room, and stood blushing with confusion at sight of the stranger.

"This is my wife, *monsieur*," said Joseph, leading her toward Louis, "but I have not given her time to put on her finery. This is M. the Marquis, Antoinette."

The farmer's wife bowed, and, having nothing to say, gracefully uplifted her brow upon which the *marquis* pressed a kiss.

"You will see the children in a few minutes, M. the Marquis," said Joseph; "I have sent to the school for them."

The worthy couple overwhelmed the *marquis* with attentions.

After so long a walk he must be hungry, they said; he must take a glass of wine now, and breakfast would soon be ready; they would be so proud and happy if M. the Marquis would partake of a country breakfast!

Louis willingly accepted their invitation; and Joseph went to the cellar after the wine, while Toinette ran to catch her fattest pullet.

In a short time, Louis sat down to a table laden with the best of everything on the farm, waited upon by Joseph and his wife, who watched him with respectful interest and awe.

The children came running in from school, smeared with the juice of berries. After Louis had embraced them they stood off in a corner, and gazed at him with eyes wide open, as if he were a rare curiosity.

The important news had spread, and a number of villagers and countrymen appeared at the open door, to speak to the Marquis de Clameran.

"I am such a one, M. the Marquis; don't you remember me?"

"Ah! I should have recognised you anywhere."

"The late *marquis* was very good to me."

Another would say, "Don't you remember the time when you lent me your gun to go hunting?"

Louis welcomed with secret delight all these protestations and proofs of devotion which had not chilled with time.

The kindly voices of these honest people recalled many pleasant moments of the past, and made him feel once more the fresh sensations of his youth.

Here, at least, no echoes of his stormy life had been heard; no suspicions of his shameful career were entertained by these humble villagers on the borders of the Rhone.

He, the adventurer, the bully, the base accomplice of London swindlers, delighted in these marks of respect and veneration, bestowed upon him as the representative of the house of Clameran; it seemed to make him once more feel a little self-respect, as if the future were not utterly hopeless.

Ah, had he possessed only a quarter of his squandered inheritance, how happy he would be to peacefully end his days in this his native village!

But this rest after so many vain excitements, this haven after so many storms and shipwrecks, was denied him. He was penniless; how could he live here when he had nothing to live upon?

This thought of his pressing want gave him courage to ask Joseph for the key of the *château*, that he might go and examine its condition.

"You won't need the key, except the one to the front door, M. the *marquis*," replied Joseph.

It was but too true. Time had done its work, and the lordly manor of Clameran was nothing but a ruin. The rain and sun had rotted the shutters so that they were crumbling and dilapidated.

Here and there were traces of the friendly hand of St. Jean, who had tried to retard the total ruin of the old *château*; but of what use were his efforts?

Within, the desolation was still greater. All of the furniture which Louis had not dared to sell stood in the position he left it, but in what a state! All of the tapestry hangings and coverings were moth-eaten and in tatters; nothing seemed left but the dust-covered woodwork of the chairs and sofas.

Louis was almost afraid to enter these grand, gloomy rooms, where every footfall echoed until the air seemed to be filled with sounds strange and ominous.

He almost expected to see the angry old *marquis* start from some dark corner, and heap curses on his head for having dishonoured the name.

He turned pale with terror, when he suddenly recalled the scene of his fatal stumble and poor Gaston's death. The room was surely inhabited by the spirits of these two murdered men. His nerves could not bear it, and he hurried out into the open air and sunshine.

After a while, he recovered sufficiently to remember the object of his visit.

"Poor St. Jean was foolish to let the furniture in the *château* drop to pieces. Why did he not use it?"

"My father would not have dared to touch anything without receiving an order, M. the Marquis."

"He was very unwise to wait for an order, when anything was going to destruction without benefiting anyone. As the *château* is fast approaching the condition of the furniture, and my fortune does not permit me to repair it, I will sell it before the walls crumble away."

Joseph could scarcely believe his ears. He regarded the selling of the Château of Clameran as a sacrilege; but he was not bold of speech, like his father, so he dared not express an opinion.

"Would there be difficulty in selling this ruin?" continued Louis.

"That depends upon the price you ask, M. the Marquis; I know a man who would purchase the property if he could get it cheap."

"Who is he?"

"M. Fougeroux, who lives on the other side of the river. He came from Beaucaire, and twelve years ago married a servant-maid of the late Countess de la Verberie. Perhaps M. the *marquis* remembers her—a plump, bright-eyed brunette, named Mihonne."

Louis did not remember Mihonne.

"When can we see this Fougeroux?" he inquired.

"Today; I will engage a boat to take us over."

"Well, let us go now. I have no time to lose."

An entire generation has passed away since Louis had last crossed the Rhone in old Pilorel's boat.

The faithful ferryman had been buried many years, and his duties were now performed by his son, who, possessing great respect for traditional opinions, was delighted at the honour of rowing the Marquis de Clameran in his boat, and soon had it ready for Louis and Joseph to take their seats.

As soon as they were fairly started, Joseph began to warn the *marquis* against the wily Fougeroux.

"He is a cunning fox," said the farmer; "I have had a bad opinion of him ever since his marriage, which was a shameful affair altogether. Mihonne was over fifty years of age, and he was only twenty-four, when he married her; so you may know it was money, and not a wife, that he wanted. She, poor fool, believed that the young scamp really loved her, and gave herself and her money up to him. Women will be trusting fools to the end of time! And Fougeroux is not the man to let money lie idle. He speculated with Mihonne's gold, and is now very rich. But she, poor thing, does not profit by his wealth; one can easily understand his not feeling any love for her, when she looks like his grandmother; but he deprives her of the necessaries of life, and beats her cruelly."

"He would like to plant her six feet under ground," said the ferryman.

"Well, it won't be long before he has the satisfaction of burying her," said Joseph; "the poor old woman has been in almost a dying condition ever since Fougeroux brought a worthless jade to take charge of the house, and makes his wife wait upon her like a servant."

When they reached the opposite shore, Joseph asked young Pilorel to await their return.

Joseph knocked at the gate of the well-cultivated farm, and inquired for the master; the farm-boy said that "M. Fougeroux" was out in the field, but he would go and tell him.

He soon appeared. He was an ill-looking little man, with a red beard and small, restless eyes.

Although M. Fougeroux professed to despise the nobility and the clergy, the hope of driving a good bargain made him obsequious to Louis. He insisted upon ushering his visitor into "the parlour," with may bows and repetitions of "M. the Marquis."

Upon entering the room, he roughly ordered an old woman, who was crouching over some dying embers, to make haste and bring some wine for M. the Marquis de Clameran.

At this name, the old woman started as if she had received an electric shock. She opened her mouth to say something, but a look from her tyrant froze the words upon her lips. With a frightened air she hobbled out to obey his orders, and in a few minutes returned with a bottle of wine and three glasses.

Then she resumed her seat by the fire, and kept her eyes fastened upon the *marquis*.

Could this really be the merry, pretty Mihonne, who had been the confidant of the little fairy of Verberie?

Valentine herself would never have recognised this poor, shrivelled, emaciated old woman.

Only those who are familiar with country life know what hard work and worry can do to make a woman old.

The bargain, meanwhile, was being discussed between Joseph and Fougeroux, who offered a ridiculously small sum for the *château*, saying that he would only buy it to tear down, and sell the materials. Joseph enumerated the beams, joists, ashlars, and the iron-work, and volubly praised the old domain.

As for Mihonne, the presence of the *marquis* had a wonderful effect upon her.

If the faithful servant had hitherto never breathed the secret confided to her probity, it was none the less heavy for her to bear.

After marrying, and being so harshly treated that she daily prayed for death to come to her relief, she began to blame everybody but herself for her misfortunes.

Weakly superstitious, she traced back the origin of her sorrows to the day when she took the oath on the holy gospel during mass.

Her constant prayers that God would send her a child to soothe her wounded heart, being unanswered, she was convinced that she was cursed with barrenness for having assisted in the abandonment of an innocent, helpless babe.

She often thought, that by revealing everything, she could appease the wrath of Heaven, and once more enjoy a happy home. Nothing but her love for Valentine gave her strength to resist a constant temptation to confess everything.

But today the sight of Louis decided her to relieve her mind. She thought there could be no danger in confiding in Gaston's brother. Alas for woman's tongue!

The sale was finally concluded. It was agreed that Fougeroux should give five thousand two hundred and eighty *francs* in cash for the *château*, and land attached; and Joseph was to have the old furniture.

The *marquis* and the new owner of the *château* shook hands, and noisily called out the essential word:

"Agreed!"

Fougeroux went himself to get the "bargain bottle" of old wine.

The occasion was favourable to Mihonne; she walked quickly over to where the *marquis* stood, and said in a nervous whisper:

"M. the Marquis, I must speak with you apart."

"What can you want to tell me, my good woman?"

"It is a secret of life and death. This evening, at dusk, meet me in the walnut wood, and I will tell you everything."

Hearing her husband's approaching step, she darted back to her corner by the fire.

Fougeroux filled the glasses, and drank to the health of de Clameran.

As they returned to the boat, Louis tried to think what could be the object of this singular rendezvous.

"Joseph, what the deuce can that old witch want with me?" he said musingly.

"Who can tell? She used to be in the service of a lady who was very intimate with M. Gaston; so my father used to say. If I were in your place I would go and see what she wanted, *monsieur.* You can dine with me, and, after dinner, Pilorel will row you over."

Curiosity decided Louis to go, about seven o'clock, to the walnut wood, where he found Mihonne impatiently awaiting him.

"Ah, here you are, at last, M. the Marquis," she said, in a tone of relief. "I was afraid you would disappoint me."

"Yes, here I am, my good woman, to listen to what you have to say."

"I have many things to say. But first tell me some news of your brother."

Louis regretted having come, supposing from this request that the old woman was childish, and might bother him for hours with her senseless gabble.

"You know well enough that my poor brother was drowned in the Rhone."

"Good heavens!" cried Mihonne, "are you ignorant, then, of his escape? Yes, he did what has never been done before; he swam across the swollen Rhone. The next day Mademoiselle Valentine went to Clameran to tell the news; but St. Jean prevented her from seeing you. Afterward I carried a letter from her, but you had left the country."

Louis could not believe this strange revelation.

"Are you not mixing up dreams with real events, my good woman?" he said banteringly.

"No," she replied, mournfully shaking her head. "If Pere Menoul were alive, he would tell you how he took charge of your brother until he embarked for Marseilles. But that is nothing compared to the rest. M. Gaston has a son."

"My brother had a son! You certainly have lost your mind, my poor woman."

"Alas, no. Unfortunately for my happiness in this world and in the world to come, I am only telling the truth; he had a child, and Mademoiselle Valentine was its mother. I took the poor babe, and carried it to a woman whom I paid to take charge of it."

Then Mihonne described the anger of the countess, the journey to London, and the abandonment of little Raoul.

With the accurate memory natural to people unable to read and write, she related the most minute particulars—the names of the village, the nurse, the child's Christian name, and the exact date of everything which had occurred.

Then she told of Valentine's wretched suffering, of the impending ruin of the countess, and finally how everything was happily settled by the poor girl's marriage with an immensely rich man, who was now one of the richest bankers in Paris, and was named Fauvel.

A harsh voice calling, "Mihonne! Mihonne!" here interrupted the old woman.

"Heavens!" she cried in a frightened tone, "that is my husband, looking for me."

And, as fast as her trembling limbs could carry her, she hurried to the farm-house.

For several minutes after her departure, Louis stood rooted to the spot. Her recital had filled his wicked mind with an idea so infamous, so detestable, that even his vile nature shrank for a moment from its enormity.

He knew Fauvel by reputation, and was calculating the advantages he might gain by the strange information of which he was now possessed by means of the old Mihonne. It was a secret, which, if skilfully managed, would bring him in a handsome income.

The few faint scruples he felt were silenced by the thought of an old age spent in poverty. After the price of the *château* was spent, to what could he look forward? Beggary.

"But first of all," he thought, "I must ascertain the truth of the old woman's story; then I will decide upon a plan."

This was why, two days later having received the five thousand two hundred and eighty *francs* from Fougeroux, Louis de Clameran set out for London.

Chapter 16

During the twenty years of her married life, Valentine had experienced but one real sorrow; and this was one which, in the course of nature, must happen sooner or later.

In 1859 her mother died from inflammation of the lungs, during one of her frequent journeys to Paris, and, in spite of every attention which money could procure, she became worse, and died.

The countess preserved her faculties to the last, and with her dying breath said to her daughter:

"Ah, well! was I not wise in prevailing upon you to bury the past? Your silence has made my old age peaceful and happy, and I now thank you for having done your duty to yourself and to me. You will be rewarded on earth and in heaven, my dear daughter."

Madame Fauvel constantly said that, since the loss of her mother, she had never had cause to shed a tear. And what more could she wish for? As years rolled on, Andre's love remained steadfast; he was as devoted a husband as the most exacting woman could wish. To his great love was added that sweet intimacy which results from long conformity of ideas and unbounded confidence.

Everything prospered with this happy couple. Andre was twice as wealthy as he had ever hoped to be even in his wildest visions; every wish of Valentine was anticipated by Andre; their two sons, Lucien and Abel, were handsome, intelligent young men, whose honourable characters and graceful bearing reflected credit upon their parents, who had so carefully watched over their education.

Nothing seemed wanting to insure Valentine's felicity. When her husband and sons were at their business, her solitude was cheered by the intelligent, affectionate companionship of a young girl whom she loved as her own daughter, and who in return filled the place of a devoted child.

Madeleine was M. Fauvel's niece, and when an infant had lost both parents, who were poor but very worthy people. Valentine begged to adopt the babe, thinking she could thus, in a measure, atone for the desertion of the poor little creature whom she had abandoned to strangers. She hoped that this good work would bring down the blessings of God upon her.

The day of the little orphan's arrival, M. Fauvel invested for her ten thousand *francs*, which he presented to Madeleine as her dowry.

The banker amused himself by increasing this ten thousand *francs* in the most marvellous ways. He, who never ventured upon a rash speculation with his own money, always invested it in the most hazardous schemes, and was always so successful, that at the end of fifteen years the ten thousand *francs* had become half a million.

People were right when they said that the Fauvel family were to be envied.

Time had dulled the remorse and anxiety of Valentine. In the genial atmosphere of a happy home, she had found rest, and almost forgetfulness. She had suffered so much at being compelled to deceive Andre that she hoped she was now at quits with fate.

She began to look forward to the future, and her youth seemed buried in an impenetrable mist, and was, as it were, the memory of a painful dream.

Yes, she believed herself saved, and her very feeling of security made the impending danger more fearful in its shock.

One rainy November day, her husband had gone to Provence on business. She was sitting, gazing into the bright fire, and thankfully meditating upon her present happiness, when the servant brought her a letter, which had been left by a stranger, who refused to give his name.

Without the faintest presentiment of evil, she carelessly broke the seal, and in an instant was almost petrified by the words which met her terrified eye:

> *Madame*—
> Would it be relying too much upon the memories of the past to hope for half an hour of your time?
> Tomorrow, between two and three, I will do myself the honour of calling upon you.
>
> The Marquis de Clameran

Fortunately, Madame Fauvel was alone. Trembling like a leaf, she read the letter over and over again, as if to convince herself that she was not the victim of a horrible hallucination.

Half a dozen times, with a sort of terror, she whispered that name once so dear—Clameran! spelling it aloud as if it were a strange name which she could not pronounce. And the eight letters forming the name seemed to shine like the lightning which precedes a clap of thunder.

Ah! she had hoped and believed that the fatal past was atoned for, and buried in oblivion; and now it stood before her, pitiless and threatening.

Poor woman! As if all human will could prevent what was fated to be!

It was in this hour of security, when she imagined herself pardoned, that the storm was to burst upon the fragile edifice of her happiness, and destroy her every hope.

A long time passed before she could collect her scattered thoughts sufficiently to decide upon a course of conduct. Then she began to think she was foolish to be so frightened. This letter was written by Gaston, of course; therefore she need feel no apprehension. Gaston had returned to France, and wished to see her. She could understand this desire, and she knew too well this man, upon whom she had lavished her young affection, to attribute any bad motives to his visit.

He would come; and finding her the wife of another, the mother of grown sons, they would exchange thoughts of the past, perhaps a few regrets; she would restore the jewels which she had faithfully kept for him; he would assure her of his lifelong friendship, and—that would be all.

But one distressing doubt beset her agitated mind. Should she conceal from Gaston the birth of his son?

To confess was to expose herself to many dangers. It was placing herself at the mercy of a man—a loyal, honourable man to be sure—confiding to him not only her own peace, honour, and happiness, but the honour and happiness of her family, of her noble husband and loving sons.

Still silence would be a crime. She had abandoned her child, denied him the cares and affection of a mother; and now should she add to her sin by depriving him of the name and fortune of his father?

She was still undecided when the servant announced dinner.

But she had not the courage to meet the glance of her sons. She sent word that she was not well, and would not be down to dinner. For the first time in her life she rejoiced at her husband's absence.

Madeleine came hurrying into her aunt's room to see what was the matter; but Valentine dismissed her, saying she would try to sleep off her indisposition.

She wished to be alone in her trouble, and see if she could decide upon some plan for warding off this impending ruin.

The dreaded morrow came.

She counted the hours until two o'clock. After that, she counted the minutes.

At half-past two the servant announced:

"M. the Marquis de Clameran."

Madame Fauvel had promised herself to be calm, even cold. During a long, sleepless night, she had mentally arranged beforehand every detail of this painful meeting. She had even decided upon what she should say. She would reply this, and ask that; her words were all selected, and her speech ready.

But, at the dreaded moment, her strength gave way; she turned as cold as marble, and could not rise from her seat; she was speechless, and, with a frightened look, silently gazed upon the man who respectfully bowed, and stood in the middle of the room.

Her visitor was about fifty years of age, with iron-gray hair and moustache, and a cold, severe cast of countenance; his expression was one of haughty severity as he stood there in his full suit of black.

The agitated woman tried to discover in his face some traces of the man whom she had so madly loved, who had pressed her to his heart, and besought her to remain faithful until he should return from a foreign land, and lay his fortune at her feet—the father of her son.

She was surprised to discover no resemblance to the youth whose memory had haunted her life; no, never would she have recognised this stranger as Gaston.

As he continued to stand motionless before her, she faintly murmured:

"Gaston!"

He sadly shook his head, and replied:

"I am not Gaston, *madame*. My brother succumbed to the misery and suffering of exile: I am Louis de Clameran."

What! it was not Gaston, then, who had written to her; it was not Gaston who stood before her!

She trembled with terror; her head whirled, and her eyes grew dim.

It was not he! And she had committed herself, betrayed her secret by calling him "Gaston."

What could this man want?—this brother in whom Gaston had never confided? What did he know of the past? A thousand probabilities, each one more terrible than the other, flashed across her brain.

Yet she succeeded in overcoming her weakness so that Louis scarcely perceived it. The fearful strangeness of her situation, the very imminence of peril, inspired her with coolness and self-possession. Haughtily pointing to a chair, she said to Louis with affected indifference:

"Will you be kind enough, *monsieur*, to explain the object of this unexpected visit?"

The *marquis*, seeming not to notice this sudden change of manner, took a seat without removing his eyes from Madame Fauvel's face.

"First of all, *madame*," he began, "I must ask if we can be overheard by anyone?"

"Why this question? You can have nothing to say to me that my husband and children should not hear."

Louis shrugged his shoulders, and said:

"Be good enough to answer me, *madame*; not for my sake, but for your own."

"Speak, then, *monsieur*; you will not be heard."

In spite of this assurance, the *marquis* drew his chair close to the sofa where Madame Fauvel sat, so as to speak in a very low tone, as if almost afraid to hear his own voice.

"As I told you, *madame*, Gaston is dead; and it was I who closed his eyes, and received his last wishes. Do you understand?"

The poor woman understood only too well, but was racking her brain to discover what could be the purpose of this fatal visit. Perhaps it was only to claim Gaston's jewels.

"It is unnecessary to recall," continued Louis, "the painful circumstances which blasted my brother's life. However happy your own lot has been, you must sometimes have thought of this friend of your youth, who unhesitatingly sacrificed himself in defence of your honour."

Not a muscle of Madame Fauvel's face moved; she appeared to be trying to recall the circumstances to which Louis alluded.

"Have you forgotten, *madame*?" he asked with bitterness: "then I must explain more clearly. A long, long time ago you loved my unfortunate brother."

"*Monsieur!*"

"Ah, it is useless to deny it, *madame*: I told you that Gaston confided everything to me—everything," he added significantly.

But Madame Fauvel was not frightened by this information. This "everything" could not be of any importance, for Gaston had gone abroad in total ignorance of her secret.

She rose, and said with an apparent assurance she was far from feeling:

"You forget, *monsieur*, that you are speaking to a woman who is now advanced in life, who is married, and who has grown sons. If your brother loved me, it was his affair, and not yours. If, young and ignorant, I was led into imprudence, it is not your place to remind me of it. This past which you evoke I buried in oblivion twenty years ago."

"Thus you have forgotten all that happened?"

"Absolutely all; everything."

"Even your child, *madame*?"

This question, uttered in a sneer of triumph, fell upon Madame Fauvel like a thunder-clap. She dropped tremblingly into her seat, murmuring:

"My God! How did he discover it?"

Had her own happiness alone been at stake, she would have instantly thrown herself upon a Clameran's mercy. But she had her family to defend, and the consciousness of this gave her strength to resist him.

"Do you wish to insult me, *monsieur*?" she asked.

"Do you pretend to say you have forgotten Valentin-Raoul?"

She saw that this man did indeed know all. How? It little mattered. He certainly knew; but she determined to deny everything, even the most positive proofs, if he should produce them.

For an instant she had an idea of ordering the Marquis de Clameran to leave the house; but prudence stayed her. She thought it best to discover how much he really knew.

"Well," she said with a forced laugh, "will you be kind enough to state what you wish with me?"

"Certainly, *madame*. Two years ago the vicissitudes of exile took my brother to London. There, at the house of a friend, he met a young man by the name of Raoul. Gaston was so struck by the youth's appearance and intelligence, that he inquired who he was, and discovered that beyond a doubt this boy was his son, and your son, *madame*."

"This is quite a romance you are relating."

"Yes, *madame*, a romance the denouement of which is in your hands. Your mother certainly used every precaution to conceal your secret; but the best-laid plans always have some weak point. After your marriage, one of your mother's London friends came to Tarascon, and spread the report of what had taken place at the English village. This lady also revealed your true name to the nurse who was bringing up the child. Thus everything was discovered by my brother, who had no difficulty in obtaining the most positive proofs of the boy's parentage."

Louis closely watched Madame Fauvel's face to see the effect of his words.

To his astonishment she betrayed not the slightest agitation or alarm; she was smiling as if entertained by the recital of his romance.

"Well, what next?" she asked carelessly.

"Then, *madame*, Gaston acknowledged the child. But the de Clamerans are poor; my brother died on a pallet in a lodging-house; and I have only an income of twelve hundred *francs* to live upon. What is to become of Raoul, alone with no relations or friends to assist him? My brother's last moments were embittered by anxiety for the welfare of his child."

"Really, *monsieur*—"

"Allow me to finish," interrupted Louis. "In that supreme hour Gaston opened his heart to me. He told me to apply to you. 'Valentine,' said he, 'Valentine will remember the past, and will not let our son want for anything; she is wealthy, she is just and generous; I die with my mind at rest.'" Madame Fauvel rose from her seat, and stood, evidently waiting for her visitor to retire.

"You must confess, *monsieur*," she said, "that I have shown great patience."

This imperturbable assurance amazed Louis.

"I do not deny," she continued, "that I at one time possessed the confidence of M. Gaston de Clameran. I will prove it by restoring to you your mother's jewels, with which he entrusted me on his departure."

While speaking she took from beneath the sofa-cushion the purse of jewels, and handed it to Louis.

"These jewels would have been given to the owner the instant they were called for, *monsieur*, and I am surprised that your brother never reclaimed them."

Louis betrayed his astonishment at the sight of the jewels. He tried to cover his embarrassment by boldly saying:

"I was told not to mention this sacred trust."

Madame Fauvel, without making any reply, laid her hand on the bell-rope and quietly said:

"You will allow me to end this interview, *monsieur*, which was only granted for the purpose of placing in your hands these precious jewels."

Thus dismissed, M. de Clameran was obliged to take his leave without attaining his object.

"As you will, *madame*," he said, "I leave you; but before doing so I must tell you the rest of my brother's dying injunctions: 'If Valentine disregards the past, and refuses to provide for our son, I enjoin it upon you to compel her to do her duty.' Meditate upon these words, *madame*, for what I have sworn to do, upon my honour, shall be done!"

At last Madame Fauvel was alone. She could give vent to her despair.

Exhausted at her efforts at self-restraint during the presence of de Clameran, she felt weary and crushed in body and spirit. She had scarcely strength to drag herself up to her chamber, and lock the door.

Now there was no room for doubt; her fears had become realities. She could fathom the abyss into which she was about to be hurled, and knew that in her fall she would drag her family with her.

God alone, in this hour of danger, could help her, could save her from destruction. She prayed.

"Oh, my God!" she cried, "punish me for my great sin, and I will evermore adore thy chastising hand! I have been a bad daughter, an unworthy mother, and a perfidious wife. Smite me, oh, God, and only me! In thy just anger spare the innocent, have pity upon my husband and my children!"

What were her twenty years of happiness compared to this hour of misery? A bitter remorse; nothing more. Ah, why did she listen to her mother? Why had she committed moral suicide?

Hope had fled; despair had come.

This man who had left her presence with a threat upon his lips would return to torture her now. How could she escape him?

Today she had succeeded in subduing her heart and conscience; would she again have the strength to master her feelings?

She well knew that her calmness and courage were entirely due to the inaptness of de Clameran.

Why did he not use entreaties instead of threats?

When Louis spoke of Raoul, she could scarcely conceal her emotion; her maternal heart yearned toward the innocent child who was expiating his mother's faults.

A chill of horror passed over her at the idea of his enduring the pangs of hunger.

Her child wanting bread, when she, his mother, was rolling in wealth!

Ah, why could she not lay all her possessions at his feet? With what delight would she undergo the greatest privations for his sake! If she could but send him enough money to support him comfortably!

But no; she could not take this step without compromising herself and her family.

Prudence forbade her acceptance of the intervention of Louis de Clameran.

To confide in him, was placing herself, and all she held dear, at his mercy—at the mercy of a man who inspired her with instinctive terror.

Then she began to ask herself if he had spoken the truth, or had trumped up this story to frighten her?

In thinking over Louis's story, it seemed improbable and disconnected.

If Gaston had been living in Paris, in the poverty described by his brother, why had he not demanded of the married woman the deposit entrusted to the maiden?

Why, when anxious about the future of their child, had he not come to her, if he had such confidence in her generosity? If he entrusted her on his death-bed, why had he not shown this trust while living?

A thousand vague apprehensions beset her mind; she felt suspicion and distrust of everyone and everything.

She was aware that the time had come for her to take a decisive step, and upon this step depended her whole future peace and happiness. If she once yielded, what would not be exacted of her in the future? She would certainly be made to suffer if she refused to yield. If she had only some wise friend to advise her!

For a moment she thought of throwing herself at her husband's feet and confessing all.

Unfortunately, she thrust aside this means of salvation. She pictured to herself the mortification and sorrow that her noble-hearted husband would suffer upon discovering, after a lapse of twenty years, how shamefully he had been deceived, how his confidence and love had been betrayed.

Having been once deceived, would he ever trust her again? Would he believe in her fidelity as a wife, when he discovered that she had uttered her marriage vows to love and honour him, when her heart was already given to another?

She knew Andre was too magnanimous to ever allude to her horrible fault, and would use every means to conceal it. But his domestic happiness would be gone forever. His chair at the fireside would be left empty; his sons would shun her presence, and every family bond would be severed.

Then again, would peace be preserved by her silence? Would not de Clameran end by betraying her to Andre?

She thought of ending her doubts by suicide; but her death would not silence her implacable enemy, who, not being able to disgrace her while alive, would dishonour her memory.

Fortunately, the banker was still absent; and, during the two days succeeding Louis's visit, Madame Fauvel could keep her room under pretence of sickness.

But Madeleine, with her feminine instinct, saw that her aunt was troubled by something worse than nervous headache, for which the physician was prescribing all sorts of remedies, with no beneficial effect.

She remembered that this sudden illness dated from the visit of the melancholy looking stranger, who had been closeted for a long time with her aunt.

Madeleine supposed something was weighing upon the miserable woman's mind, and the second day of her sickness ventured to say:

"What makes you so sad, dear aunt? If you will not tell me, do let me bring our good cure to see you."

With a sharpness foreign to her nature, which was gentleness itself, Madame Fauvel refused to assent to her niece's proposition.

What Louis calculated upon happened.

After long reflection, not seeing any issue to her deplorable situation, Madame Fauvel determined to yield.

By consenting to everything demanded of her, she had a chance of saving her husband from suffering and disgrace.

She well knew that to act thus was to prepare a life of torture for herself; but she alone would be the victim, and, at any rate, she would be gaining time. Heaven might at last interpose, and save her from ruin.

In the meantime, M. Fauvel had returned home, and Valentine resumed her accustomed duties.

But she was no longer the happy mother and devoted wife, whose smiling presence was wont to fill the house with sunshine and comfort. She was melancholy, anxious, and at times irritable.

Hearing nothing of de Clameran, she expected to see him appear at any moment; trembling at every knock, and turning pale when a strange step was heard to enter, she dared not leave the house, for fear he should come during her absence.

Her agony was like that of a condemned man, who, each day as he wakes from his uneasy slumber, asks himself, "Am I to die today?"

De Clameran did not come; he wrote, or rather, as he was too prudent to furnish arms which could be used against him, he had a note written, which Madame Fauvel alone might understand, in which he said that he was quite ill, and unable to call upon her; and hoped she would be so good as to come to his room the next day; she had only to ask for 317, Hotel du Louvre.

The letter was almost a relief for Madame Fauvel. Anything was preferable to suspense. She was ready to consent to everything.

She burned the letter, and said, "I shall go."

The next day at the appointed hour, she dressed herself in a plain black silk, a large bonnet which concealed her face, and, putting a thick veil in her pocket to be used if she found it necessary, started forth.

After hurriedly walking several squares, she thought she might, without fear of being recognised, call a coach. In a few minutes she was set down at the Hotel du Louvre. Here her uneasiness increased. Her circle of acquaintances being large, she was in terror of being recognised. What would her friends think if they saw her at the Hotel du Louvre disguised in this old dress?

Anyone would naturally suspect an intrigue, a rendezvous; and her character would be ruined forever.

This was the first time since her marriage that she had had occasion for mystery; and her efforts to escape notice were in every way calculated to attract attention.

The porter said that the Marquis de Clameran's rooms were on the third floor.

She hurried up the stairs, glad to escape the scrutinizing glances of several men standing near; but, in spite of the minute directions given by the porter, she lost her way in one of the long corridors of the hotel.

Finally, after wandering about for some time, she found a door bearing the number sought—317.

She stood leaning against the wall with her hand pressed to her throbbing heart, which seemed bursting.

Now, at the moment of risking this decisive step, she felt paralyzed with fright. She would have given all she possessed to find herself safe in her own home.

The sight of a stranger entering the corridor ended her hesitation.

With a trembling hand she knocked at the door.

"Come in," said a voice from within.

She entered the room.

It was not the Marquis de Clameran who stood in the middle of the room, but a young man, almost a youth, who bowed to Madame Fauvel with a singular expression on his handsome face.

Madame Fauvel thought that she had mistaken the room.

"Excuse me, *monsieur*," she said, blushing deeply. "I thought that this was the Marquis de Clameran's room."

"It is his room, *madame*," replied the young man; then, seeing she was silent and about to leave, he added:

"I presume I have the honour of addressing Madame Fauvel?"

She bowed affirmatively, shuddering at the sound of her own name, frightened at this proof of de Clameran's betrayal of her secret to a stranger.

With visible anxiety she awaited an explanation.

"Reassure yourself, *madame*," said the young man: "you are as safe here as if you were in your own house. M. de Clameran desired me to make his excuses; he will not have the honour of seeing you today."

"But, *monsieur*, from an urgent letter sent by him yesterday, I was led to suppose—to infer—that he—"

"When he wrote to you, *madame*, he had projects in view which he has since renounced."

Madame Fauvel was too agitated and troubled to think clearly. Beyond the present she could see nothing.

"Do you mean," she asked with distrust, "that he has changed his intentions?"

The young man's face was expressive of sad compassion, as if he shared the sufferings of the unhappy woman before him.

"The *marquis* has renounced," he said, in a melancholy tone, "what he wrongly considered a sacred duty. Believe me, he hesitated a long time before he could decide to apply to you on a subject painful to you both. When he began to explain his apparent intrusion upon your private affairs, you refused to hear him, and dismissed him with indignant contempt. He knew not what imperious reasons dictated your conduct. Blinded by unjust anger, he swore to obtain by threats what you refused to give voluntarily. Resolved to attack your domestic happiness, he had collected overwhelming proofs against you. Pardon him: an oath given to his dying brother bound him.

"These convincing proofs," he continued, as he tapped his finger on a bundle of papers which he had taken from the mantel, "this evidence that cannot be denied, I now hold in my hand. This is the certificate of the Rev. Dr. Sedley; this is the declaration of Mrs. Dobbin, the farmer's wife; and these others are the statements of the physician and of several persons of high social position who were acquainted with Madame de la Verberie during her stay in London. Not a single link is missing. I had great difficulty in getting these papers away from M. de Clameran. Had he anticipated my intention of thus disposing of them, they would never have been surrendered to my keeping."

As he finished speaking, the young man threw the bundle of papers into the fire where they blazed up; and in a moment nothing remained of them but a little heap of ashes.

"All is now destroyed, *madame*," he said, with a satisfied air. "The past, if you desire it, is as completely annihilated as those papers. If anyone, thereafter, dares accuse you of having had a son before your marriage, treat him as a vile calumniator. No proof against you can be produced; none exists. You are free."

Madame Fauvel began to understand the sense of this scene; the truth dawned upon her bewildered mind.

This noble youth, who protected her from the anger of de Clameran, who restored her peace of mind and the exercise of her own free will, by destroying all proofs of her past, was, must be, the child whom she had abandoned: Valentin-Raoul.

In an instant, all was forgotten save the present. Maternal tenderness, so long restrained, now welled up and overflowed as with intense emotion she murmured:

"Raoul!"

At this name, uttered in so thrilling a tone, the youth started and tottered, as if overcome by an unhoped-for happiness.

"Yes, Raoul," he cried, "Raoul, who would a thousand times rather die than cause his mother a moment's pain; Raoul, who would shed his life's blood to spare her one tear."

She made no attempt to struggle against nature's yearnings; her longing to clasp to her heart this long-pined-for first-born must be gratified at all costs.

She opened her arms, and Raoul sprang forward with a cry of joy:

"Mother! my blessed mother! Thanks be to God for this first kiss!"

Alas! this was the sad truth. The deserted child had never been blest by a mother's kiss. This dear son whom she had never seen before, had been taken from her, despite her prayers and tears, without a mother's blessing, a mother's embrace. After twenty years waiting, should it be denied him now?

But joy so great, following upon so many contending emotions, was more than the excited mother could bear; she sank back in her chair almost fainting, and with distended eyes gazed in a bewildered, eager way upon her long-lost son, who was now kneeling at her feet.

With tenderness she stroked the soft chestnut curls, and drank in the tenderness of his soft dark eyes, and expressive mouth, as he murmured words of filial affection in her craving ear.

"Oh, mother!" he said, "words cannot describe my feelings of pain and anguish upon hearing that my uncle had dared to threaten you. He threaten you! He repents already of his cruelty; he did not know you as I do. Yes, my mother, I have known you for a long, long time. Often have my father and I hovered around your happy home to catch a glimpse of you through the window. When you passed by in your carriage, he would say to me, 'There is your mother, Raoul!' To look upon you was our greatest joy. When we knew you were going to a ball, we would wait near the door to see you enter, in your satin and diamonds. How often have I followed your fast horses to see you descend from the carriage and enter wealthy doors, which I could never hope to penetrate! And how my noble father loved you always! When he told his brother to apply to you in my behalf, he was unconscious of what he said; his mind was wandering."

Tears, the sweetest tears she had ever shed, coursed down Madame Fauvel's cheeks, as she listened to the musical tones of Raoul's voice.

This voice was so like Gaston's, that she seemed once more to be listening to the lover of her almost forgotten youth.

She was living over again those stolen meetings, those long hours of bliss, when Gaston was at her side, as they sat and watched the river rippling beneath the trees.

It seemed only yesterday that Gaston had pressed her to his faithful heart; she saw him still saying gently:

"In three years, Valentine! Wait for me!"

Andre, her two sons, Madeleine, all were forgotten in this new-found affection.

Raoul continued in tender tones:

"Only yesterday I discovered that my uncle had been to demand for me a few crumbs of your wealth. Why did he take such a step? I am poor, it is true, very poor; but I am too familiar with poverty to bemoan it. I have a clear brain and willing hands: that is fortune enough for a young man. You are very rich. What is that to me? Keep all your fortune, my beloved mother; but do not repel my affection; let me love you. Promise me that this first kiss shall not be the last. No one will ever know of my new-found happiness; not by word or deed will I do aught to let the world suspect that I possess this great joy."

And Madame Fauvel had dreaded this son! Ah, how bitterly did she now reproach herself for not having flown to meet him the instant she heard that he was living!

She questioned him regarding the past; she wished to know how he had lived, what he had been doing.

He replied that he had nothing to conceal; his existence had been that of every poor boy, who had nothing to look forward to but a life of labour and privation.

The farmer's wife who had brought him up was a kind-hearted woman, and had always treated him with affection. She had even given him an education superior to his condition in life, because, as she always said, he would make himself a great name, and attain to wealth, if he were taught.

When about sixteen years of age, she procured him a situation in a banking-house; and he was getting a salary, which, though small, was enough to support him and supply a few luxuries for his adopted mother.

One day a stranger came to him and said:

"I am your father: come with me."

Since then nothing was wanting to his happiness, save a mother's tenderness. He had suffered but one great sorrow, and that was the day when Gaston de Clameran, his father, had died in his arms.

"But now," he said, "all is forgotten, that one sorrow is forgotten in my present happiness. Now that I see you and possess your love, I forget the past, and ask for nothing more."

Madame Fauvel was oblivious of the lapse of time, and was startled when Raoul exclaimed:

"Why, it is seven o'clock!"

Seven o'clock! What would her family think of this long absence? Her husband must be even now awaiting dinner.

"Shall I see you again, mother?" asked Raoul in a beseeching tone, as they were about to separate.

"Oh, yes!" she replied, fondly, "yes, often; every day, tomorrow."

But now, for the first time since her marriage, Madame Fauvel perceived that she was not mistress of her actions. Never before had she had occasion to wish for uncontrolled liberty.

She left her heart and soul behind her in the Hotel du Louvre, where she had just found her son. She was compelled to leave him, to undergo the intolerable agony of composing her face to conceal this great happiness, which had changed her whole life and being. She was angry with fate because she could not remain with her first-born son.

Having some difficulty in procuring a carriage, it was half-past seven before she reached the Rue de Provence, when she found the family waiting for her.

She thought her husband silly, and even vulgar, when he joked her upon letting her poor children starve to death, while she was promenading the boulevards.

So strange are the sudden effects of a new passion, that she regarded almost with contempt this unbounded confidence reposed in her.

She replied to his jest with a forced calmness, as if her mind were really as free and undisturbed as it had been before de Clameran's visit.

So intoxicated had been her sensations while with Raoul, that in her joy she was incapable of desiring anything else, of dreaming of aught save the renewal of these delightful emotions.

No longer was she a devoted wife, an affectionate mother to this household which looked up to her as though she were a superior being. She took no interest in the two sons who were a short while since her chief pride and joy. They had always been petted and indulged in every way; they had a father, they were rich; whist the other, the other! oh, how much reparation was due to him!

She almost regarded her family as responsible for Raoul's sufferings, so blinded was she in her devotion to her martyr, as she called him.

Her folly was complete. No remorse for the past, no apprehensions for the future, disturbed the satisfied present. To her the future was tomorrow; eternity was the sixteen hours which must elapse before another interview.

She seemed to think that Gaston's death absolved the past, and changed the present.

Her sole regret was her marriage. Free, with no family ties, she could have consecrated herself exclusively to Raoul. How gladly would she have sacrificed her affluence to enjoy poverty with him!

She felt no fear that her husband and sons would suspect the thoughts which absorbed her mind; but she dreaded her niece.

She imagined that Madeleine looked at her strangely on her return from the Hotel du Louvre. She must suspect something; but did she suspect the truth?

For several days she asked embarrassing questions, as to where her aunt went, and with whom she had been during these long absences from home.

This disquietude and seeming curiosity changed the affection which Madame Fauvel had hitherto felt for her adopted daughter into positive dislike.

She regretted having placed over herself a vigilant spy from whom she could not escape. She pondered what means she could take to avoid the penetrating watchfulness of a girl who was accustomed to read in her face every thought that crossed her mind.

With unspeakable satisfaction she solved the difficulty in a way which she thought would please all parties.

During the last two years the banker's cashier and protege, Prosper Bertomy, had been devoted in his attentions to Madeleine. Madame Fauvel decided to do all in her power to hasten matters, so that, Madeleine once married and out of the house, there would be no one to criticise her own movements. She could then spend most of her time with Raoul without fear of detection.

That evening, with a duplicity of which she would have been incapable a few weeks before, she began to question Madeleine about her sentiments toward Prosper:

"Ah, ha, *mademoiselle*," she said, gaily, "I have discovered your secret. You are going on at a pretty rate! The idea of your choosing a husband without my permission!"

"Why, aunt! I thought you—"

"Yes, I know; you thought I had suspected the true state of affairs! That is precisely what I have done."

Then, in a serious tone, she said:

"Therefore nothing remains to be done except to obtain the consent of Master Prosper. Do you think he will grant it?"

"Oh, Aunt Valentine! he would be too happy."

"Ah, indeed! you seem to know all about it; perhaps you do not care for any assistance in carrying out your wishes?"

Madeleine, blushing and confused, hung her head, and said nothing. Madame Fauvel drew her toward her, and continued affectionately:

"My dear child, do not be distressed: you have done nothing wrong, and need fear no opposition to your wishes. Is it possible that a person of your penetration supposed us to be in ignorance of your secret? Did you think that Prosper would have been so warmly welcomed by your uncle and myself, had we not approved of him in every respect?"

Madeleine threw her arms around her aunt's neck, and said:

"Oh, my dear aunt, you make me so happy! I am very grateful for your love and kindness. I am very glad that you are pleased with my choice."

Madame Fauvel said to herself:

"I will make Andre speak to Prosper, and before two months are over the marriage must take place. Madeleine once married, I shall have nothing to fear."

Unfortunately, Madame Fauvel was so engrossed by her new passion that she put off from day to day her project of hastening the marriage, until it was too late. Spending a portion of each day at the Hotel du Louvre with Raoul, and, when separated from him, devoting her thoughts to insuring him an independent fortune and a good position, she could think of nothing else.

She had not yet spoken to him of money or business.

She imagined that she had discovered in him his father's noble qualities; that the sensitiveness which is so easily wounded was expressed in his every word and action.

She anxiously wondered if he would ever accept the least assistance from her. The Marquis de Clameran quieted her doubts on this point.

She had frequently met him since the day on which he had so frightened her, and to her first aversion had succeeded a secret sympathy. She felt kindly toward him for the affection he lavished on her son.

If Raoul, with the heedlessness of youth, mocked at the future, Louis, the man of the world, looked upon it with different eyes. He was anxious for the welfare of his nephew, and constantly complained of the idle life he was now leading.

One day, after praising the attractive qualities of Raoul, he said:

"This pleasant life is very well, as long as it lasts; but people cannot live upon air, and, as my handsome nephew has no fortune, it would be only prudent for us to procure him some employment."

"Ah, my dear uncle, do let me enjoy my present happiness. What is the use of any change? What do I want?"

"You want for nothing at present, Raoul; but when your resources are exhausted, and mine, too—which will be in a short time—what will become of you?"

"*Bast*! I will enter the army. All the de Clamerans are born soldiers; and if a war comes—"

Madame Fauvel laid her hand upon his lips, and said in a tone of reproachful tenderness:

"Cruel boy, become a soldier? would you, then, deprive me of the joy of seeing you?"

"No, my mother; no."

"You must agree to whatever plans we make for your good," said Louis; "and not be talking of any wild schemes of your own."

"I am ready to obey; but not yet. One of these days I will go to work, and make a fortune."

"How, poor, foolish boy? What can you do?"

"*Dame*! I don't know now; but set your mind at rest, I will find a way."

Finding it impossible to make this self-sufficient youth listen to reason, Louis and Madame Fauvel, after discussing the matter fully, decided that assistance must be forced upon him, and his path in life marked out for him.

It was difficult, however, to choose a profession; and de Clameran thought it prudent to wait awhile, and study the bent of the young man's mind. In the meanwhile it was decided that Madame Fauvel should place funds at de Clameran's disposal for Raoul's support.

Regarding Gaston's brother in the light of a father to her child, Madame Fauvel soon found him indispensable. She continually longed to see him, either to consult him concerning some step to be taken for Raoul's benefit, or to impress upon him some good advice to be given.

Thus she was well pleased, when one day he requested the honour of being allowed to call upon her at her own house.

Nothing was easier than to introduce the Marquis de Clameran to her husband as an old friend of her family; and, after once being admitted, he might come as often as he chose.

Madame Fauvel congratulated herself upon this arrangement.

Afraid to go to Raoul every day, and in constant terror lest her letters to him should be discovered, and his replies fall into her husband's hands, she was delighted at the prospect of having news of him from de Clameran.

For a month, things went on very smoothly, when one day the *marquis* confessed that Raoul was giving him a great deal of trouble. His hesitating, embarrassed manner frightened Madame Fauvel. She thought something dreadful had happened, and that he was trying to break the bad news gently.

"What is the matter?" she said, turning pale.

"I am sorry to say," replied de Clameran, "that this young man has inherited all the pride and passions of his ancestors. He is one of those natures who stop at nothing, who only find incitement in opposition; and I can think of no way of checking him in his mad career."

"Merciful Heaven! what has he been doing?"

"Nothing especially censurable; that is, nothing irreparable, thus far; but I am afraid of the future. He is unaware of the liberal allowance which you have placed in my hands for his benefit; and, although he thinks that I support him, there is not a single indulgence which he denies himself; he throws away money as if he were the son of a millionaire."

Like all mothers, Madame Fauvel attempted to excuse her son.

"Perhaps you are a little severe," she said. "Poor child, he has suffered so much! He has undergone so many privations during his childhood, that this sudden happiness and wealth has turned his head; he seizes it as a starving man seizes a piece of bread. Is it surprising that he should refuse to listen to reason until hungry nature shall have been gratified? Ah, only have patience, and he will soon return to the path of sober duty. He has too noble a heart to do anything really wrong."

"He has suffered so much!" was Madame Fauvel's constant excuse for Raoul. This was her invariable reply to M. de Clameran's complaints of his nephew's conduct.

And, having once commenced, he was now constant in his accusations against Raoul.

"Nothing restrains his extravagance and dissipation," Louis would say in a mournful voice; "the instant a piece of folly enters his head, it is carried out, no matter at what cost."

Madame Fauvel saw no reason why her son should be thus harshly judged.

"You must remember," she said in an aggrieved tone, "that from infancy he has been left to his own unguided impulses. The unfortunate boy never had a mother to tend and counsel him. You must remember, too, that he has never known a father's guidance."

"There is some excuse for him, to be sure; but nevertheless he must change his present course. Could you not speak seriously to him, *madame*? You have more influence over him than I."

She promised, but forgot her good resolution when with Raoul. She had so little time to devote to him, that it seemed cruel to spend it in reprimands. Sometimes she would hurry from home for the purpose of following the *marquis's* advice; but, the instant she saw Raoul, her courage failed; a pleading look from his soft, dark eyes silenced the rebuke upon her lips; the sound of his voice banished every anxious thought, and lulled her mind to the present happiness.

But de Clameran was not a man to lose sight of the main object, in what he considered a sentimental wasting of time. He would have no compromise of duty.

His brother had bequeathed to him, as a precious trust, his son Raoul; he regarded himself, he said, as his guardian, and would be held responsible in another world for his welfare.

He entreated Madame Fauvel to use her influence, when he found himself powerless in trying to check the heedless youth in his headlong career. She ought, for the sake of her child, to see more of him, study his disposition, and daily admonish him in his duty to himself and to her.

"Alas," the poor woman replied, "that would be my heart's desire. But how can I do it? Have I the right to ruin myself? I have other children, for whom I must be careful of my reputation."

This answer appeared to astonish de Clameran. A fortnight before, Madame Fauvel would not have alluded to her other sons.

"I will think the matter over," said Louis, "And perhaps when I see you next I shall be able to submit to you a plan which will reconcile everything."

The reflections of a man of so much experience could not be fruitless. He had a relieved, satisfied look, when he called to see Madame Fauvel on the following week.

"I think I have solved the problem," he said.

"What problem?"

"The means of saving Raoul."

He explained himself by saying, that as Madame Fauvel could not, without arousing her husband's suspicions, continue her daily visits to Raoul, she must receive him at her own house.

This proposition shocked Madame Fauvel; for though she had been imprudent, even culpable, she was the soul of honour, and naturally shrank from the idea of introducing Raoul into the midst of her family, and seeing him welcomed by her husband, and perhaps become the friend of his sons. Her instinctive sense of justice made her declare that she would never consent to such an infamous step.

"Yes," said the *marquis*, thoughtfully, "there is some risk; but then, it is the only chance of saving your child."

She resisted with so much firmness and indignation that Louis was astonished, and for a time nonplussed; though he by no means let the subject drop, but seized every opportunity of impressing upon her tortured mind that Raoul's salvation depended entirely upon her.

"No," she would always reply, "no! Never will I be so base and perfidious to my husband!"

Unfortunate woman! little did she know of the pitfalls which stand ever ready to swallow up wanderers from the path of virtue.

Before a week had passed, she listened to this project, which at first had filled her with horror, with a willing ear, and even began to devise means for its speedy execution.

Yes, after a cruel struggle, she finally yielded to the pressure of de Clameran's politely uttered threats and Raoul's wheedling entreaties.

"But how," she asked, "upon what pretext can I receive Raoul?"

"It would be the easiest thing in the world," replied de Clameran, "to admit him as an ordinary acquaintance, and, indeed, to place him on the same footing which I myself occupy—that of an intimate friend and *habitué* of your drawing-rooms. But Raoul must have more than this; he needs your constant care."

After torturing Madame Fauvel for a long time, he finally revealed his scheme.

"We have in our hands," he said, "the solution of this problem, which may be so easily reached that I regard it as an inspiration."

Madame Fauvel eagerly scanned his face as she listened with the pitiable resignation of a martyr.

"Have you not a cousin, a widow lady, who had two daughters, living at St. Remy?" asked Louis.

"Yes, Madame de Lagors."

"Precisely so. What fortune has she?"

"She is poor, *monsieur*, very poor."

"And, but for the assistance you render her secretly, she would be thrown upon the charity of the world."

Madame Fauvel was bewildered at finding the *marquis* so well informed of her private affairs.

"How could you have discovered this?" she asked.

"Oh, I know all about this affair, and many others besides. I know, for example, that your husband has never met any of your relatives, and that he is not even aware of the existence of your cousin De Lagors. Do you begin to comprehend my plan?"

She not only understood it, but also knew that she would end by being a party to it.

"All will succeed if you follow my instructions," said Louis. "To-morrow or next day, you will receive a letter from your cousin at St. Remy, telling you that she has sent her son to Paris on a visit, and begs you to receive and watch over him. Naturally you show this letter to your husband; and a few days afterward he warmly welcomes your nephew, Raoul de Lagors, a handsome, rich, attractive young man, who does everything he can to please you both."

"*Monsieur*," replied Madame Fauvel, "my cousin is a pious, honourable woman, and nothing would induce her to countenance so shameful a transaction."

The *marquis* smiled scornfully, and said:

"Who told you that I intended to confide in her?"

"But you would be obliged to do so! How else?"

"You are very simple, *madame*. The letter which you will receive, and show to your husband, will be dictated by me, and posted at St. Remy by a friend of mine. If I spoke of the obligations under which you have placed your cousin, it was merely to show you that, in case of accident, her own interest would make her serve you. Do you see any obstacle to this plan, *madame*?"

Madame Fauvel's eyes flashed with indignation.

"Is my will of no account?" she exclaimed. "You seem to have made your arrangements without consulting me at all."

"Excuse me," said the *marquis*, with ironical politeness, "but I knew that you would take the same view of the matter as myself. Your good sense would convince you of the necessity of using every possible means of rescuing your child from destruction."

"But it is a crime, *monsieur*, that you propose—an abominable crime! My mind revolts at the very idea of it!"

This speech seemed to arouse all the bad passions slumbering in de Clameran's bosom; and his pale face had a fiendish expression as he fiercely replied:

"We had better end this humbuggery, and come to a clear understanding at once. Before you begin to talk about crime, think over your past life. You were not so timid and scrupulous when you gave yourself up to your lover; neither did you hesitate to faithlessly refuse to share his exile, although for your sake he had just jeopardized his life by killing two men. You felt no scruples at abandoning your child in London; although rolling in wealth, you never even inquired if this poor waif had bread to eat. You felt no scruples about marrying M. Fauvel. Did you tell your confiding husband of the lines of shame concealed beneath that orange wreath? Did you hesitate to confirm and strengthen his happy delusion, that his lips had pressed the first kiss upon your brow? No! All these crimes you indulged in; and, when in Gaston's name I demand reparation, you indignantly refuse. But, mark my words, *madame*, it is too late! You ruined the father; but you shall save the son, or, by all the saints in heaven, I swear you shall no longer cheat the world of its esteem."

"I will obey you, *monsieur*," murmured the trembling, frightened woman.

The following week Raoul, now Raoul de Lagors, was seated at the banker's dinner-table, between Madame Fauvel and Madeleine.

Chapter 17

It was not without the most acute suffering and self-condemnation that Madame Fauvel submitted to the will of the relentless Marquis de Clameran.

She had used every argument and entreaty to soften him; but he merely looked upon her with a triumphant, sneering smile, when she knelt at his feet, implored him to be merciful and spare her the shame and remorse of committing another crime. Spare her this torture, and she would grant anything else he wished, give Raoul all she possessed while alive, and insure him a handsome competency after her death.

Alas! neither tears nor prayers moved him. Disappointed, and almost desperate, she sought the intercession of her son.

Raoul was in a state of furious indignation at the sight of his mother's distress, and hastened to demand an apology from de Clameran.

But he had reckoned without his host. He soon returned with downcast eyes, and moodily angry at his own powerlessness, declaring that safety demanded a complete surrender to the tyrant.

Now only did the wretched woman fully fathom the abyss into which she was being dragged, and clearly see the labyrinth of crime of which she was becoming the victim.

And all this suffering was the consequence of a fault, an interview granted to Gaston. Ever since that fatal day she had been vainly struggling against the implacable logic of events. Her life had been spent in trying to overcome the past, and now it had risen to crush her.

The hardest thing of all to do, the act that most wrung her heart, was showing to her husband the forged letter from St. Remy, and saying that she expected to see her rich young nephew in a day or two. 'Tis hard to deceive those who trust and love us.

But words cannot paint the torture she endured on the evening that she introduced Raoul to her family, and saw the honest banker cordially shake hands with this nephew of whom he had never heard before, and affectionately say to him:

"I am not surprised that a rich young fellow like yourself should prefer Paris to St. Remy, and nothing will give me more pleasure than your visit; for I seldom have an opportunity of welcoming a relative of my dear wife, for whose sake I take an interest in everyone coming from St. Remy."

Raoul exerted his utmost to deserve this warm reception.

If his early education had been neglected, and he lacked those delicate refinements of manner and conversation which home influence imparts, his superior tact concealed these defects.

He possessed the happy faculty of reading characters, and adapting his conversation to the minds of his listeners.

Before a week had gone by, he was a favourite with M. Fauvel, intimate with Abel and Lucien, and inseparable from Prosper Bertomy, the cashier, who spent all his evenings with the banker's family.

Charmed at the favourable impression made by Raoul, Madame Fauvel recovered comparative ease of mind, and at times almost congratulated herself upon having obeyed the *marquis*, as she saw all around her contented and happy. Once more she began to hope that peace had not deserted her, that God had forgiven her.

Alas! she rejoiced too soon.

Raoul's intimacy with his cousins threw him among a set of rich young men, whose extravagance he not only imitated, but surpassed. He daily grew more dissipated and reckless. Gambling, racing, expensive suppers, made money slip through his fingers like grains of sand.

This proud young man, whose sensitive delicacy not long since made him refuse to accept aught save affection from his mother, now never approached her without demanding large sums of money.

At first she gave with pleasure, not stopping to count the rolls of notes she would eagerly run to bring him. But as he each time increased his demands, until they finally reached a sum far larger than she could bestow, her eyes were opened to the ruinous effects of her lavish generosity.

This rich woman, whose magnificent diamonds, elegant toilets, and superb equipages were the admiration and envy of Paris, now suffered the keenest torture. She had no more money to give her son; and what so pains the female heart as being unable to gratify the wishes of a beloved being?

Her husband never thought of giving her a fixed sum for the year's expenses, or of asking how she disposed of her money. The day after the wedding he gave her a key to his secretary, and told her, that what was his was hers, to use as she thought best. And, ever since, she had been in the habit of freely taking all the money necessary for keeping up the hospitable, elegant house over which she so gracefully presided; for her own dress, and many charitable purposes that the world never knew of.

But the fact of her having always been so modest in her personal expenses that her husband used to jestingly say that he was afraid she would end by being a miser; and her judicious, well-regulated management of household expenditures, causing her to spend much the same amount each year—prevented her now being able to dispose of large sums, without giving rise to embarrassing questions.

M. Fauvel, the most generous of millionaires, delighted to see his wife indulge in any extravagance, no matter how foolish; but he would naturally expect to see traces of the money spent, something to show for it.

The banker might suddenly discover that double the usual amount of money was used in the house; and, if he should ask the cause of this astonishing outlay, what answer could she give?

In three months, Raoul had squandered a little fortune. In the first place, he was obliged to have bachelor's apartments, prettily furnished, and a handsome outfit from a fashionable tailor, besides the thousand little things indispensable to a society man; he must have a blooded horse and a *coupe*. His doting mother felt it her duty to give him these luxuries, when her other sons were enjoying everything of the sort, besides many other advantages of which her poor Raoul was deprived. But each day the extravagance of his fancies increased, and Madame Fauvel began to be alarmed when his demands far exceeded her ability to gratify them.

When she would gently remonstrate, Raoul's beautiful eyes would fill with tears, and in a sad, humble tone he would say:

"Alas! you are right to refuse me this gratification. What claim have I? I must not forget that I am only the poor son of Valentine, not the rich banker's child!"

This touching repentance wrung her heart, so that she always ended by granting him more than he had asked for. The poor boy had suffered so much that it was her duty to console him, and atone for her past neglect.

She soon discovered that he was jealous and envious of his two brothers—for, after all, they were his brothers—Abel and Lucien.

"You never refuse them anything," he would resentfully say: "they were fortunate enough to enter life by the golden gate. Their every wish is gratified; they enjoy wealth, position, home affection, and have a splendid future awaiting them."

"But what is lacking to your happiness, my son? Have you not everything that money can give? and are you not first in my affections?" asked his distressed mother.

"What do I want? Apparently nothing, in reality everything. Do I possess anything legitimately? What right have I to your affection, to the comforts and luxuries you heap upon me, to the name I bear? Is not my life an extortion, my very birth a fraud?"

When Raoul talked in this strain, she would weep, and overwhelm him with caresses and gifts, until she imagined that every jealous thought was vanished from his mind.

As spring approached, she told Raoul she designed him to spend the summer in the country, near her villa at St. Germain. She wanted to have him with her all the time, and this was the only way of gratifying her wish. She was surprised to find her proposal readily acquiesced in. In a few days he told her he had rented a little house at Vesinet, and intended having his furniture moved into it.

"Then, just think, dear mother, what a happy summer we will spend together!" he said, with beaming eyes.

She was delighted for many reasons, one of which was that the expenses of the prodigal son would necessarily be lessened. Anxiety as to the exhausted state of her finances made her bold enough to chide him at the dinner-table one day for having lost two thousand *francs* at the races that morning.

"You are severe, my dear," said M. Fauvel with the carelessness of a rich man, who considered this sum a mere trifle. "Mamma Lagors won't object to footing his bills; mammas are created for the special purpose of paying bills."

And, not observing that his wife had turned pale at these jocular words, he turned to Raoul, and added:

"Don't disturb yourself about a small sum like this, my boy; when you want money, come to me."

What could Madame Fauvel say? Had she not followed de Clameran's orders, and told her husband that Raoul was wealthy? She could not go now and tell him that he would never recover any money which he lent to a penniless spendthrift.

Why had she been made to tell this unnecessary lie?

She suspected the snare laid for her; but now it was too late to escape it: struggles would only more deeply entangle her in its meshes.

The banker's offer was soon accepted. That same week Raoul went to his uncle's bank, and boldly borrowed ten thousand *francs*.

When Madame Fauvel heard of this piece of audacity, she wrung her hands in despair.

"What can he want with so much money?" she moaned to herself: "what wicked extravagance is it for?" For some time de Clameran had kept away from Madame Fauvel's house. She decided to write and ask him to come and advise her as to what steps should be taken to check Raoul.

She hoped that this energetic, determined man, who was so fully awake to his duties as a guardian and an uncle, would make Raoul listen to reason, and instantly refund the borrowed money.

When de Clameran heard what his graceless nephew had done, his surprise and anger were unbounded. He expressed so much indignation against Raoul, that Madame Fauvel was frightened at the storm she had raised, and began to make excuses for her son.

While they were discussing the matter, Raoul came in, and a violent altercation ensued between him and de Clameran.

But the suspicions of Madame Fauvel were aroused; she watched them, and it seemed to her—could it be possible—that their anger was feigned; that, although they abused and even threatened each other in the bitterest language, their eyes twinkled with amusement.

She dared not breathe her doubts; but, like a subtle poison which disorganises everything with which it comes in contact, this new suspicion filled her thoughts, and added to her already intolerable sufferings.

Yet she never once thought of blaming Raoul; nor for a moment did she feel displeased with her idolized son. She accused the *marquis* of taking advantage of the youthful weakness and inexperience of his nephew.

She knew that she would have to suffer insolence and extortion from this man who had her completely in his power; but she could not imagine what object he now had in view, for she plainly saw that he was aiming at something more than his nephew's success in life. He constantly concealed some plan to benefit himself at her expense; but assuredly her darling Raoul could not be an accomplice in any plot to harass her.

De Clameran himself soon cleared her mind of all doubts.

One day, after complaining more bitterly than usual of Raoul, and proving to Madame Fauvel that it was impossible for this state of affairs to continue much longer, and a catastrophe was inevitable, he would up by saying there was one means of salvation left.

This was that he, de Clameran, must marry Madeleine!

Madame Fauvel was prepared for almost any base proposal save this one. She knew that his cupidity and insolence stopped at nothing, but never did she imagine he would have the wild presumption to aspire to Madeleine's hand.

If she had renounced all hope of happiness for herself, if she consented to the sacrifice of her own peace of mind, it was because she thus hoped to insure the undisturbed felicity of her household, of her husband, whom she had sinned against.

This unexpected declaration shocked her, and for a moment she was speechless.

"Do you suppose for an instant, *monsieur*," she indignantly exclaimed, "that I will consent to any such disgraceful project? Sacrifice Madeleine, and to you!"

"I certainly do suppose so, *madame*; in fact, I am certain of it," he answered with cool insolence.

"What sort of a woman do you think I am, *monsieur*? Alas, I am to eternally suffer for a fault committed twenty years ago; have I not already been more than adequately punished? And does it become you to be constantly reproaching me with my long-past imprudence? You have no right to be thus harassing me, till I dare not say my life is my own! Your power is at an end, and God only knows how deeply I regret having been insane enough to yield to its base sway! So long as I alone was to be the tool, you found me weak and timid; but, now that you seek the ruin of those I love, I rebel against your usurped authority. I have still a little conscience left, and nothing under heaven will force me to sacrifice my gentle, pure-hearted Madeleine!"

"May I inquire, *madame*, why you regard Mademoiselle Madeleine's becoming the Marchioness of Clameran as a disgrace and a sacrifice?"

"My niece chose, of her own free will, a husband whom she will shortly marry. She loves M. Prosper Bertomy."

The *marquis* disdainfully shrugged his shoulders.

"A schoolgirl love-affair," said he; "she will forget all about it, if you wish her to do so."

"I do not wish it. I wish her to marry him."

"Listen to me," he replied, in the low, suppressed tone of a man trying to control himself: "let us not waste time in these idle discussions. Hitherto you have always commenced by protesting against my proposed plans, and in the end acknowledge the good sense and justness of my arguments; now, for once why not yield without going through with the customary preliminaries? I ask it as a favour."

"Never," said Madame Fauvel, "never will I yield."

De Clameran paid no attention to this interruption, but went on:

"I insist upon this marriage, mainly on your account, although it will enable me to re-establish my own affairs, as well as yours and Raoul's. Of course you see that the allowance you give your son is insufficient for his extravagant style of living. The time approaches when, having nothing more to give him, you will have to encroach upon your husband's money-drawer to such an extent that longer concealment will be impossible. When that day comes what is to be done? Perhaps you have some feasible plan of escape?"

Madame Fauvel shuddered. The dreadful day of discovery could not be far off, and no earthly way was there to escape it.

The *marquis* went on:

"Assist me now, and, instead of having to make a shameful confession, you will thank me for having saved you. Mademoiselle Madeleine is rich: her dowry will enable me to supply the deficiency, and spare you all further anxiety about Raoul."

"I would rather be ruined than be saved by such means."

"But I will not permit you to ruin us all. Remember, *madame*, that we are associated in a common cause, the future welfare of Raoul; and, although you have a right to rush upon destruction yourself, you certainly shall not drag us with you."

"Cease your importunities," she said, looking him steadily in the eye. "I have made up my mind irrevocably."

"To what?"

"To do everything and anything to escape your shameful persecution. Oh! you need not smile. I shall throw myself at M. Fauvel's feet, and confess everything. He is noble-hearted and generous, and, knowing how I have suffered, will forgive me."

"Do you think so?" said de Clameran derisively.

"You mean to say that he will be pitiless, and banish me from his roof. So be it; it will only be what I deserve. There is no torture that I cannot bear, after what I have suffered through you."

This inconceivable resistance so upset all the *marquis's* plans that he lost all constraint, and, dropping the mask of politeness, appeared in his true character.

"Indeed!" he said in a fierce, brutal tone, "so you have decided to confess to your loving, magnanimous husband! A famous idea! What a pity you did not think of it before; it is rather late to try it now. Confessing everything the first day I called on you, you might have been forgiven. Your husband might have pardoned a youthful fault atoned for by twenty years of irreproachable conduct; for none can deny that you have been a faithful wife and a good mother. But picture the indignation of your trusting husband when you tell him that this pretended nephew, whom you imposed upon his family circle, who sat at his table, who borrowed his money, is your illegitimate son! M. Fauvel is, no doubt, an excellent, kind-hearted man; but I scarcely think he will pardon a deception of this nature, which betrays such depravity, duplicity, and audacity."

All that the angry *marquis* said was horribly true; yet Madame Fauvel listened unflinchingly, as if the coarse cruelty of his words strengthened her resolution to have nothing more to do with him, but to throw herself on her husband's mercy.

"Upon my soul," he went on, "you must be very much infatuated with this M. Bertomy! Between the honour of your husband's name, and pleasing this love-sick cashier, you refuse to hesitate. Well, I suppose he will console you. When M. Fauvel divorces you, and Abel and Lucien avert their faces at your approach, and blush at being your sons, you will be able to say, 'I have made Prosper happy!'"

"Happen what may, I shall do what is right," said Madame Fauvel.

"You shall do what I say!" cried de Clameran, threateningly. "Do you suppose that I will allow your sentimentality to blast all my hopes? I shall tolerate no such folly, *madame*, I can assure you. Your niece's fortune is indispensable to us, and, more than that—I love the fair Madeleine, and am determined to marry her."

The blow once struck, the *marquis* judged it prudent to await the result. With cool politeness, he continued:

"I will leave you now, *madame*, to think the matter over, and you cannot fail to view it in the same light as I do. You had better take my advice, and consent to this sacrifice of prejudice, as it will be the last required of you. Think of the honour of your family, and not of your niece's love-affair. I will return in three days for your answer."

"Your return is unnecessary, *monsieur*. I shall tell my husband everything tonight."

If Madame Fauvel had not been so agitated herself, she would have detected an expression of alarm upon de Clameran's face.

But this uneasiness was only momentary. With a shrug, which meant, "Just as you please," he said:

"I think you have sense enough to keep your secret."

He bowed ceremoniously, and left the room, but slammed the front door after him so violently as to prove that his restrained anger burst forth before leaving the house.

De Clameran had cause for fear. Madame Fauvel's determination was not feigned. She was firm in her resolve to confess.

"Yes," she cried, with the enthusiasm of a noble resolution, "yes, I will tell Andre everything!"

She believed herself to be alone, but turned around suddenly at the sound of footsteps, and found herself face to face with Madeleine, who was pale and swollen-eyed with weeping.

"You must obey this man, aunt," she quietly said.

Adjoining the parlour was a little card-room separated only by a heavy silk curtain, instead of a door.

Madeleine was sitting in this little room when the *marquis* arrived, and, as there was no egress save through the parlour, had remained, and thus overheard the conversation.

"Good Heaven!" cried Madame Fauvel with terror, "do you know—"

"I know everything, aunt."

"And you wish me to sacrifice you to this fiend?"

"I implore you to let me save you from misery."

"You certainly despise and hate M. de Clameran; how can you think I would let you marry him?"

"I do despise him, aunt, and shall always regard him as the basest of men; nevertheless I will marry him."

Madame Fauvel was overcome by the magnitude of this devotion.

"And what is to become of Prosper, my poor child—Prosper, whom you love?"

Madeleine stifled a sob, and said in a firm voice:

"Tomorrow I will break off my engagement with M. Bertomy."

"I will never permit such a wrong," cried Madame Fauvel. "I will not add to my sins by suffering an innocent girl to bear their penalty."

The noble girl sadly shook her head, and replied:

"Neither will I suffer dishonour to fall upon this house, which is my home, while I have power to prevent it. Am I not indebted to you for more than life? What would I now be had you not taken pity on me? A factory girl in my native village. You warmly welcomed the poor orphan, and became a mother to her. Is it not to your husband that I owe the fortune which excites the cupidity of this wicked de Clameran? Are not Abel and Lucien brothers to me? And now, when the happiness of all who have been loving and generous to me is at stake, do you suppose I would hesitate? No. I will become the wife of de Clameran."

Then began a struggle of self-sacrifice between Madame Fauvel and her niece, as to which should be the victim; only the more sublime, because each offered her life to the other, not from any sudden impulse, but deliberately and willingly.

But Madeleine carried the day, fired as she was by that holy enthusiasm of sacrifice which is the sustaining element of martyrs.

"I am responsible to none but myself," said she, well knowing this to be the most vulnerable point she could attack; "whilst you, dear aunt, are accountable to your husband and children. Think of the pain and sorrow of M. Fauvel if he should learn the truth; it would kill him."

The generous girl was right. She knew her uncle's heart.

After having sacrificed her husband to her mother, Madame Fauvel was about to immolate her husband and children for Raoul.

As a general thing, a first fault draws many others in its train. As an impalpable flake is the beginning of an avalanche, so an imprudence is often the prelude to a great crime.

To false situations there is but one safe issue: truth.

Madame Fauvel's resistance grew weaker and more faint, as her niece pointed out the line for her to pursue: the path of wifely duty.

"But," she faintly argued, "I cannot accept your sacrifice. What sort of a life will you lead with this man?"

"We can hope for the best," replied Madeleine with a cheerfulness she was far from feeling; "he loves me, he says; perhaps he will be kind to me."

"Ah, if I only knew where to obtain money! It is money that the grasping man wants; money alone will satisfy him."

"Does he not want it for Raoul? Has not Raoul, by his extravagant follies, dug an abyss which must be bridged over by money? If I could only believe M. de Clameran!"

Madame Fauvel looked at her niece with bewildered curiosity.

What! this inexperienced girl had weighed the matter in its different lights before deciding upon a surrender; whereas, she, a wife and a mother, had blindly yielded to the inspirations of her heart!

"What do you mean? Madeleine, what do you suspect?"

"I mean this, aunt: that I do not believe that de Clameran has any thought of his nephew's welfare. Once in possession of my fortune, he may leave you and Raoul to your fates. And there is another dreadful suspicion that tortures my mind."

"A suspicion?"

"Yes, and I would reveal it to you, if I dared; if I did not fear that you—"

"Speak!" insisted Madame Fauvel. "Alas! misfortune has given me strength to bear all things. There is nothing worse than has already happened. I am ready to hear anything."

Madeleine hesitated; she wished to enlighten her credulous aunt, and yet hesitated to distress her.

"I would like to be certain," she said, "that some secret understanding between M. de Clameran and Raoul does not exist. Do you not think they are acting a part agreed upon for the purpose of extorting money?"

Love is blind and deaf. Madame Fauvel would not remember the laughing eyes of the two men, upon the occasion of the pretended quarrel in her presence. Infatuation had drowned suspicion. She could not, she would not, believe in such hypocrisy. Raoul plot against the mother? Never!

"It is impossible," she said, "the *marquis* is really indignant and distressed at his nephew's mode of life, and he certainly would not countenance any disgraceful conduct. As to Raoul, he is vain, trifling, and extravagant; but he has a good heart. Prosperity has turned his head, but he loves me still. Ah, if you could see and hear him, when I reproach him for his faults, your suspicions would fly to the winds. When he tearfully promises to be more prudent, and never again give me trouble, he means to keep his word; but perfidious friends entice him away, and he commits some piece of folly without thinking of the consequences."

Mothers always blame themselves and everyone else for the sins of their sons. The innocent friends come in for the principal share of censure, each mother's son leading the other astray.

Madeleine had not the heart to undeceive her aunt.

"God grant that what you say may be true," she said; "if so, this marriage will not be useless. We will write to M. de Clameran to-night."

"Why tonight, Madeleine? We need not hurry so. Let us wait a little; something else might happen to save us."

These words, this confidence in chance, in a mere nothing, revealed Madame Fauvel's true character, and accounted for her troubles. Timid, hesitating, easily swayed, she never could come to a firm decision, form a resolution, and abide by it, in spite of all arguments brought to bear against it. In the hour of peril she would always shut her eyes and trust to chance for a relief which never came. Never once did she think to ward off trouble by her own exertions.

Quite different was Madeleine's character. Beneath her gentle timidity lay a strong, self-reliant will. Once decided upon what was right and just, nothing could change her. If it was her duty to make a sacrifice, it was to be carried out to the letter; no hesitation and sighs for what might have been; she shut out all deceitful illusions, and walked straight forward without one look back.

"We had better end the matter at once, dear aunt," she said, in a gentle, but firm tone. "Believe me, the reality of misfortune is not as painful as its apprehension. You cannot bear the shocks of sorrow, and delusive hopes of happiness, much longer. Do you know what anxiety of mind has done to you? Have you looked in the mirror during the last four months?"

She led her aunt up to the glass, and said:

"Look at yourself."

Madame Fauvel was indeed a mere shadow of her former self.

She had reached the perfidious age when a woman's beauty, like a full-blown rose, fades in a day.

Four months of trouble had made her an old woman. Sorrow had stamped its fatal seal upon her brow. Her fair, soft skin was wrinkled, her golden hair was streaked with silver, and her large, soft eyes had a painfully frightened look.

"Do you not agree with me," continued Madeleine, pityingly, "that peace of mind is necessary to you? Do you not see that you are a wreck of your former self? It is a miracle that M. Fauvel has not noticed this sad change in you!"

Madame Fauvel, who flattered herself that she had displayed wonderful dissimulation, shook her head.

"Alas, my poor aunt! you think you concealed your secret from all: you may have blinded my uncle, but I suspected all along that something dreadful was breaking your heart."

"You suspected what, Madeleine? Not the truth?"

"No, I was afraid—Oh, pardon an unjust suspicion, my dear aunt, but I was wicked enough to suppose—"

She stopped, too distressed to finish her sentence; then, making a painful effort, she added, as her aunt signed to her to go on:

"I was afraid that perhaps you loved another man than my uncle; it was the only construction that I could put upon your strange conduct."

Madame Fauvel buried her face, and groaned. Madeleine's suspicion was, no doubt, entertained by others.

"My reputation is gone," she moaned.

"No, dear aunt, no; do not be alarmed about that. No one has had occasion to observe you as I have; it was only a dreadful thought which penetrated my mind in spite of my endeavours to dispel it. Have courage: we two can fight the world and silence our enemies. You shall be saved, aunt: only trust in me."

The Marquis de Clameran was agreeably surprised that evening by receiving a letter from Madame Fauvel, saying that she consented to everything, but must have a little time to carry out the plan.

Madeleine, she said, could not break off her engagement with M. Bertomy in a day. M. Fauvel would make objections, for he had an affection for Prosper, and had tacitly approved of the match. It would be wiser to leave to time the smoothing away of certain obstacles which a sudden attack might render insurmountable.

A line from Madeleine, at the bottom of the letter, assured him that she fully concurred with her aunt.

Poor girl! she did not spare herself. The next day she took Prosper aside, and forced from him the fatal promise to shun her in the future, and to take upon himself the responsibility of breaking their engagement.

He implored Madeleine to at least explain the reason of this banishment, which destroyed all of his hopes for happiness.

She quietly replied that her peace of mind and honour depended upon his blind obedience to her will.

He left her with death in his soul.

As he went out of the house, the *marquis* entered.

Yes, he had the audacity to come in person, to tell Madame Fauvel that, now he had the promise of herself and Madeleine, he would consent to wait awhile.

He himself saw the necessity of patience, knowing that he was not liked by the banker.

Having the aunt and niece on his side, or rather in his power, he was certain of success. He said to himself that the moment would come when a deficit impossible to be paid would force them to hasten the wedding.

Raoul did all he could to bring matters to a crisis.

Madame Fauvel went sooner than usual to her country seat, and Raoul at once moved into his house at Vesinet. But living in the country did not lessen his expenses.

Gradually he laid aside all hypocrisy, and now only came to see his mother when he wanted money; and his demands were frequent and more exorbitant each time.

As for the *marquis*, he prudently absented himself, awaiting the propitious moment.

At the end of three weeks he met the banker at a friend's, and was invited to dinner the next day.

Twenty people were seated at the table; and, as the dessert was being served, the banker suddenly turned to de Clameran and said:

"I have a piece of news for you, *monsieur*. Have you any relatives of your name?"

"None that I know of, *monsieur*."

"I am surprised. About a week ago, I became acquainted with another Marquis de Clameran."

Although so hardened by crime, impudent enough to deny anything, de Clameran was so taken aback that he sat with pale face and a blank look, silently staring at M. Fauvel.

But he soon recovered enough self-control to say hurriedly:

"Oh, indeed! That is strange. A de Clameran may exist; but I cannot understand the title of *marquis*."

M. Fauvel was not sorry to have the opportunity of annoying a guest whose aristocratic pretensions had often piqued him.

"*Marquis* or not," he replied, "the de Clameran in question seems to be able to do honour to the title."

"Is he rich?"

"I have reason to suppose that he is very wealthy. I have been notified to collect for him four hundred thousand *francs*."

De Clameran had a wonderful faculty of self-control; he had so schooled himself that his face never betrayed what was passing in his mind. But this news was so startling, so strange, so pregnant of danger, that his usual assurance deserted him.

He detected a peculiar look of irony in the banker's eye.

The only persons who noticed this sudden change in the *marquis's* matter were Madeleine and her aunt. They saw him turn pale, and exchange a meaning look with Raoul.

"Then I suppose this new *marquis* is a merchant," said de Clameran after a moment's pause.

"That I don't know. All that I know is, that four hundred thousand *francs* are to be deposited to his account by some ship-owners at Havre, after the sale of the cargo of a Brazilian ship."

"Then he comes from Brazil?"

"I do not know, but I can give you his Christian name."

"I would be obliged."

M. Fauvel arose from the table, and brought from the next room a memorandum-book, and began to read over the names written in it.

"Wait a moment," he said, "let me see—the 22nd, no, it was later than that. Ah, here it is: Clameran, Gaston. His name is Gaston, *monsieur*."

But this time Louis betrayed no emotion or alarm; he had had sufficient time to recover his self-possession, and nothing could not throw him off his guard.

"Gaston?" he queried, carelessly. "I know who he is now. He must be the son of my father's sister, whose husband lived at Havana. I suppose, upon his return to France, he must have taken his mother's name, which is more sonorous than his father's, that being, if I recollect aright, Moirot or Boirot."

The banker laid down his memorandum-book, and, resuming his seat, went on:

"Boirot or Clameran," said he, "I hope to have the pleasure of inviting you to dine with him before long. Of the four hundred thousand *francs* which I was ordered to collect for him, he only wishes to draw one hundred, and tells me to keep the rest on running account.

I judge from this that he intends coming to Paris."

"I shall be delighted to make his acquaintance."

De Clameran broached another topic, and seemed to have entirely forgotten the news told him by the banker. Although apparently engrossed in the conversation of his neighbour at the table, he closely watched Madame Fauvel and her niece. He saw that they were unable to conceal their agitation, and stealthily exchanged significant looks.

Evidently the same terrible idea had crossed their minds. Madeleine seemed more nervous and startled than her aunt. When M. Fauvel uttered Gaston's name, she saw Raoul begin to draw back in his chair and glance in a frightened manner toward the window, like a detected thief looking for means of escape.

Raoul, less experienced than his uncle, was thoroughly discountenanced. He, the original talker, the lion of a dinner-party, never at a loss for some witty speech, was now perfectly dumb; he sat anxiously watching Louis.

At last the dinner ended, and as the guests passed into the drawing-room, de Clameran and Raoul managed to remain last in the dining-room. When they were alone, they no longer attempted to conceal their anxiety.

"It is he!" said Raoul.

"I have no doubt of it."

"Then all is lost; we had better make our escape."

But a bold adventurer like de Clameran had no idea of giving up the ship till forced to do so.

"Who knows what may happen?" he asked, thoughtfully. "There is hope yet. Why did not that muddle-headed banker tell us where this Clameran is to be found?"

Here he uttered a joyful exclamation. He saw M. Fauvel's memorandum-book lying on the table.

"Watch!" he said to Raoul.

Seizing the note-book, he hurriedly turned over the leaves, and, in an undertone, read:

"Gaston, Marquis de Clameran, Oloron, Lower Pyrenees."

"Well, does finding out his address assist us?" inquired Raoul, eagerly.

"It may save us: that is all. Let us return to the drawing-room; our absence might be observed. Exert yourself to appear unconcerned and gay. You almost betrayed us once by your agitation."

"The two women suspect something."

"Well, suppose they do?"

"The best thing that we can do is escape; the sooner we leave Paris, the better."

"Do you think we should do any better in London? Don't be so easily frightened. I am going to plant my batteries, and I warrant they will prove successful."

They joined the other guests. But, if their conversation had not been overheard their movements had been watched.

Madeleine looked through the half-open door, and saw de Clameran consulting her uncle's note-book, and whispering to Raoul. But what benefit would she derive from this proof of the *marquis's* villainy? She knew now that he was plotting to obtain her fortune, and she would be forced to yield it to him; that he had squandered his brother's fortune, and was now frightened at the prospect of having to account for it. Still this did not explain Raoul's conduct. Why did he show such fear?

Two hours later, de Clameran was on the road to Vesinet with Raoul, explaining to him his plans.

"It is my precious brother, and no mistake," he said. "But that need not alarm you so easily, my lovely nephew."

"Merciful powers! Doesn't the banker expect to see him any day? Is he not liable to pounce down on me tomorrow?"

"Don't be an idiot!" interrupted de Clameran. "Does he know that Fauvel is Valentine's husband? That is what we must find out. If he knows that little fact, we must take to our heels; if he is ignorant of it, our case is not desperate."

"How will you find out?"

"By simply asking him."

Raoul exclaimed at his ally's cunning:

"That is a dangerous thing to do," he said.

"'Tis not as dangerous as sitting down with our hands folded. And, as to running away at the first suspicion of alarm, it would be imbecility."

"Who is going to look for him?"

"I am."

"Oh, oh, oh!" exclaimed Raoul in three different tones. De Clameran's audacity confounded him.

"But what am I going to do?" he inquired after a moment's silence.

"You will oblige me by remaining here and keeping quiet. I will send you a despatch if there is danger; and then you can decamp."

As they parted at Raoul's door, de Clameran said:

"It is then understood you will remain here. But mind, so long as my absence lasts, become once more the best of sons. Set yourself against me, calumniate me if you can. But no nonsense. No demands for money. So now, goodbye. Tomorrow night I shall be at Oloron and shall have seen this de Clameran."

Chapter 18

After leaving Valentine de la Verberie, Gaston underwent great peril and difficulty in effecting his escape.

But for the experienced and faithful Menoul, he never would have succeeded in embarking.

Having left his mother's jewels with Valentine, his sole fortune consisted of not quite a thousand *francs*; and with this paltry sum in his pocket, the murderer of two men, a fugitive from justice, and with no prospect of earning a livelihood, he took passage for Valparaiso.

But Menoul was a bold and experienced sailor.

While Gaston remained concealed in a farm-house at Camargue, Menoul went to Marseilles, and that very evening discovered, from some of his sailor friends, that a three-masted American vessel was in the roadstead, whose commander, Captain Warth, a not over-scrupulous Yankee, would be glad to welcome on board an able-bodied man who would be of assistance to him at sea.

After visiting the vessel, and finding, during a conversation over a glass of rum with the captain, that he was quite willing to take a sailor without disturbing himself about his antecedents, Menoul returned to Gaston.

"Left to my own choice, *monsieur*," he said, "I should have settled this matter on the spot; but you might object to it."

"What suits you, suits me," interrupted Gaston.

"You see, the fact is, you will be obliged to work very hard. A sailor's life is not boy's play. You will not find much pleasure in it. And I must confess that the ship's company is not the most moral one I ever saw. You never would imagine yourself in a Christian company. And the captain is a regular swaggering bully."

"I have no choice," said Gaston. "Let us go on board at once."

Old Menoul's suspicions were correct.

Before Gaston had been on board the *Tom Jones* forty-eight hours, he saw that chance had cast him among a collection of the most depraved bandits and cut-throats.

The vessel, which seemed to have recruited at all points of the compass, possessed a crew composed of every variety of thievish knaves; each country had contributed a specimen.

But Gaston's mind was undisturbed as to the character of the people with whom his lot was cast for several months.

It was only his miserable wounded body, that the vessel was carrying to a new country. His heart and soul rested in the shady park of La Verberie, beside his lovely Valentine. He took no note of the men around him, but lived over again those precious hours of bliss beneath the old tree on the banks of the Rhone, where his beloved had confided her heart to his keeping, and sworn to love him forever.

And what would become of her now, poor child, when he was no longer there to love, console, and defend her?

Happily, he had no time for sad reflections.

His every moment was occupied in learning the rough apprenticeship of a sailor's life. All his energies were spent in bearing up under the heavy burden of labour allotted to him. Being totally unaccustomed to manual work, he found it difficult to keep pace with the other sailors, and for the first week or two he was often near fainting at his post, from sheer fatigue; but indomitable energy kept him up.

This was his salvation. Physical suffering calmed and deadened his mental agony. The few hours relaxation granted him were spent in heavy sleep; the instant his weary body touched his bunk, his eyes closed, and no moment did he have to mourn over the past.

At rare intervals, when the weather was calm, and he was relieved from his constant occupation of trimming the sails, he would anxiously question the future, and wonder what he should do when this irksome voyage was ended.

He had sworn that he would return before the end of three years, rich enough to satisfy the exactions of Madame de la Verberie. How should he be able to keep this boastful promise? Stern reality had convinced him that his projects could never be realised, except by hard work and long waiting. What he hoped to accomplish in three years was likely to require a lifetime.

Judging from the conversation of his companions, he was not now on the road to fortune.

The *Tom Jones* set sail for Valparaiso, but certainly went in a roundabout way to reach her destination.

The real fact was, that Captain Warth proposed visiting the Gulf of Guinea.

A friend of his, the "Black Prince," he said, with a loud laugh, was waiting for him at Badagri, to exchange a cargo of "*ebony*" for some pipes of rum, and a hundred flint-lock muskets which were on board the *Tom Jones.*

Gaston soon saw that he was serving his apprenticeship on a slaver, one of the many ships sent yearly by the free and philanthropic Americans, who made immense fortunes by carrying on the slave-trade. Although this discovery filled Gaston with indignation and shame, he was prudent enough to conceal his impressions.

His remonstrances, no matter how eloquent, would have made no change in the opinions of Captain Warth regarding a traffic which brought him in more than a hundred *per cent*, in spite of the French and English cruisers, the damages, sometimes entire loss of cargoes, and many other risks.

The crew admired Gaston when they learned that he had cut two men into mince-meat when they were insolent to him; this was the account of Gaston's affair, as reported to the captain by old Menoul.

Gaston wisely determined to keep on friendly terms with the villains, as long as he was in their power. To express disapproval of their conduct would have incurred the enmity of the whole crew, without bettering his own situation.

He therefore kept quiet, but swore mentally that he would desert on the first opportunity.

This opportunity, like everything impatiently longed for, came not.

By the end of three months, Gaston had become so useful and popular that Captain Warth found him indispensable.

Seeing him so intelligent and agreeable, he liked to have him at his own table, and would spend hours at cards with him or consulting about his business matters. The mate of the ship dying, Gaston was chosen to replace him. In this capacity he made two successful voyages to Guinea, bringing back a thousand blacks, whom he superintended during a trip of fifteen hundred leagues, and finally landed them on the coast of Brazil.

When Gaston had been with Captain Warth about three years, the *Tom Jones* stopped at Rio Janeiro for a month, to lay in supplies. He now decided to leave the ship, although he had become somewhat attached to the friendly captain, who was after all a worthy man, and never would have engaged in the diabolical traffic of human beings, but for his little angel daughter's sake. He said that his child was so good and beautiful, that she deserved a large fortune. Each time that he sold a black, he would quiet any faint qualms of conscience by saying, "It is for little Mary's good."

Gaston possessed twelve thousand *francs*, as his share of the profits, when he landed at Brazil.

As a proof that the slave-trade was repugnant to his nature, he left the slaver the moment he possessed a little capital with which to enter some honest business.

But he was no longer the high-minded, pure-hearted Gaston, who had so devotedly loved and periled his life for the little fairy of La Verberie.

It is useless to deny that evil examples are pernicious to morals. The most upright characters are unconsciously influenced by bad surroundings. As the exposure to rain, sun, and sea-air first darkened and then hardened his skin, so did wicked associates first shock and then destroy the refinement and purity of Gaston's mind. His heart had become as hard and coarse as his sailor hands. He still remembered Valentine, and sighed for her presence; but she was no longer the sole object of affection, the one woman in the world to him. Contact with sin had lowered his standard of women.

The three years, after which he had pledged himself to return, had passed; perhaps Valentine was expecting him. Before deciding on any definite project, he wrote to an intimate friend at Beaucaire to learn what had happened during his long absence. He expressed great anxiety about his family and neighbours.

He also wrote to his father, asking why he had never answered the many letters which he had sent to him by returning sailors, who would have safely forwarded the replies.

At the end of a year, he received an answer from his friend.

The letter almost drove him mad.

It told him that his father was dead; that his brother had left France, Valentine was lately married, and that he, Gaston, had been sentenced to ten years' imprisonment for murder.

Henceforth he was alone in the world; with no country, no family, no home, and disgraced by a public sentence.

Valentine was married, and he had no object in life! He would hereafter have faith in no one, since she, Valentine, had cast him off, forgotten him. What could he expect of others, when she had broken her troth, had lacked the courage to keep her promise and wait for him?—she, whom he had so trusted.

In his despair, he almost regretted the *Tom Jones*. Yes, he sighed for the wicked slaver crew, his life of excitement and peril. The dangers and triumphs of those bold pirates whose only care was to heap up money would have been preferable to his present wretchedness.

But Gaston was not a man to be long cast down.

"Money is the cause of it all!" he said with rage. "If the lack of money can bring such misery, its possession must bestow intense happiness. Henceforth I will devote all my energies to getting money."

He set to work with a greedy activity, which increased each day. He tried all the many speculations open to adventurers. Alternately he traded in furs, worked in a mine, and cultivated lands.

Five times he went to bed rich, and waked up ruined; five times, with the patience of the castor, whose hut is swept away by each returning tide, he recommenced the foundation of his fortune.

Finally, after long weary years of toil and struggle, he was worth a million in gold, besides immense tracts of land.

He had often said that he would never leave Brazil, that he wanted to end his days in Rio. He had forgotten that love for his native land never dies in the heart of a Frenchman. Now that he was rich, he wished to die in France.

He made inquiries, and found that the law of limitations would permit him to return without being disturbed by the authorities. He left his property in charge of an agent, and embarked for France, taking a large portion of his fortune with him.

Twenty-three years and four months had elapsed since he fled from home.

On a bright, crisp day in January, 1866, he once again stepped on French soil. With a sad heart, he stood upon the quays at Bordeaux, and compared the past with the present.

He had departed a young man, ambitious, hopeful, and beloved; he returned grey-haired, disappointed, trusting no one.

Gold could not supply the place of affection. He had said that riches would bring happiness: his wealth was immense, and he was miserable.

His health, too, began to suffer from this sudden change of climate. Rheumatism confined him to his bed for several months. As soon as he could sit up, the physicians sent him to the warm baths, where he recovered his health, but not his spirits. He felt his lonely condition more terribly in his own country than when in a foreign land.

He determined to divert his mind by engaging in some occupation which would keep him too busy to think of himself and his disappointment. Charmed with the beauty of the Pyrenees, and the lovely valley of Aspe, he resolved to take up his abode there.

An iron-mill was for sale near Oloron, on the borders of the Gara; he bought it with the intention of utilizing the immense quantity of wood, which, for want of means of transportation, was being wasted in the mountains.

He was soon settled comfortably in his new home, and enjoying a busy, active life.

One evening, as he was ruminating over the past, his servant brought him a card, and said the gentleman was waiting to see him.

He read the name on the card: *Louis de Clameran.*

Many years had passed since Gaston had experienced such violent agitation. His blood rushed to his face, and he trembled like a leaf.

The old home affections which he thought dead now sprung up anew in his heart. A thousand confused memories rushed through his mind. Like one in a dream, he tottered toward the door, gasping, in a smothered, broken voice:

"My brother! oh, my brother!"

Hurriedly passing by the frightened servant, he ran downstairs.

In the passage stood a man: it was Louis de Clameran.

Gaston threw his arms around his neck and held him in a close embrace for some minutes, and then drew him into the room.

Seated close beside him, with his two hands tightly clasped in those of Louis, Gaston gazed at his brother as a fond mother would gaze at her son just returned from the battle-field.

There was scarcely any danger and excitement which the mate of the redoubtable Captain Warth had not experienced; nothing had ever before caused him to lose his calm presence of mind, to force him to betray that he had a heart. The sight of this long unseen brother seemed to have changed his nature; he was like a woman, weeping and laughing at once.

"And is this really Louis?" he cried. "My dear brother! Why, I should have recognised you among a thousand; the expression of your face is just the same; your smile takes me back twenty-three years."

Louis did indeed smile, just as he smiled on that fatal night when his horse stumbled, and prevented Gaston's escape.

He smiled now as if he was perfectly happy at meeting his brother.

And he was much more at ease than he had been a few moments before. He had exerted all the courage he possessed to venture upon this meeting. Nothing but pressing necessity would have induced him to face this brother, who seemed to have risen from the dead to reproach him for his crimes.

His teeth chattered and he trembled in every limb when he rang Gaston's bell, and handed the servant his card, saying:

"Take this to your master."

The few moments before Gaston's appearance seemed to be centuries. He said to himself:

"Perhaps it is not he; if it is he, does he know? Does he suspect anything? How will he receive me?"

He was so anxious, that when he saw Gaston running downstairs, he felt like fleeing from the house without speaking to him.

Not knowing the nature of Gaston's feelings, whether he was hastening toward him in anger or brotherly love, he stood perfectly motionless. But one glance at his brother's face convinced him that he was the same affectionate, credulous, trusting Gaston of old; and, now that he was certain that his brother harboured no suspicions, he smilingly received the demonstrations lavished upon him.

"After all," continued Gaston, "I am not alone in the world; I shall have someone to love, someone to care for me."

Then, as if suddenly struck by a thought, he said:

"Are you married, Louis?"

"No."

"That is a pity, a great pity. It would so add to my happiness to see you the husband of a good, affectionate woman, the father of bright, lovely children! It would be a comfort to have a happy family about me. I should look upon them all as my own. To live alone, without a loving wife to share one's joys and sorrows, is not living at all: it is a sort of living death. There is no joy equal to having the affection of a true woman whose happiness is in your keeping. Oh the sadness of having only one's self to care for! But what am I saying? Louis, forgive me. I have you now, and ought not that to be enough? I have a brother, a kind friend who will be interested in me, and afford me company, instead of the weariness of solitude."

"Yes, Gaston, yes: I am your best friend."

"Of course you are. Being my brother, you are naturally my true friend. You are not married, you say. Then we will have to do the best we can, and keep house for ourselves. We will live together like two old bachelors, as we are, and be as happy as kings; we will lead a gay life, and enjoy everything that can be enjoyed. I feel twenty years younger already. The sight of your face renews my youth, and I feel as active and strong as I did the night I swam across the swollen Rhone. And that was long, long ago. The struggles, privations, and anxieties endured since, have been enough to age any man. I feel old, older than my years."

"What an idea!" interrupted Louis: "why, you look younger than I do."

"You are jesting."

"I swear I think you look the younger."

"Would you have recognised me?"

"Instantly. You are very little changed."

And Louis was right. He himself had an old, worn-out, used-up appearance; while Gaston, in spite of his gray hair and weather-beaten face, was a robust man, in the full maturity of his prime.

It was a relief to turn from Louis's restless eyes and crafty smile to Gaston's frank, honest face.

"But," said Gaston, "how did you know that I was living? What kind chance guided you to my house?"

Louis was prepared for this question. During his eighteen hours' ride by the railway, he had arranged all his answers, and had his story ready.

"We must thank Providence for this happy meeting," he replied. "Three days ago, a friend of mine returned from the baths, and mentioned that he had heard that a Marquis de Clameran was near there, in the Pyrenees. You can imagine my surprise. I instantly supposed that some impostor had assumed our name. I took the next train, and finally found my way here."

"Then you did not expect to see me?"

"My dear brother, how could I hope for that? I thought that you were drowned twenty-three years ago."

"Drowned! Mademoiselle de la Verberie certainly told you of my escape? She promised that she would go herself, the next day, and tell my father of my safety."

Louis assumed a distressed look, as if he hesitated to tell a sad truth, and said, in a regretful tone:

"Alas! she never told us."

Gaston's eyes flashed with indignation. He thought that perhaps Valentine had been glad to get rid of him.

"She did not tell you?" he exclaimed. "Did she have the cruelty to let you mourn my death? to let my old father die of a broken heart? Ah, she must have been very fearful of what the world says. She sacrificed me, then, for the sake of her reputation."

"But why did you not write to us?" asked Louis.

"I did write as soon as I had an opportunity; and Lafourcade wrote back, saying that my father was dead, and that you had left the country."

"I left Clameran because I believed you to be dead."

After a long silence, Gaston arose, and walked up and down the room as if to shake off a feeling of sadness; then he said, cheerfully:

"Well, it is of no use to mourn over the past. All the memories in the world, good or bad, are not worth one slender hope for the future; and thank God, we have a bright future before us. Let us bury the past, and enjoy life together."

Louis was silent. His footing was not sure enough to risk any questions.

"But here I have been talking incessantly for an hour," said Gaston, "and I dare say that you have not dined."

"No, I have not, I confess."

"Why did you not say so before? I forgot that I had not dined myself. I will not let you starve, the first day of your arrival. I will make amends by giving you some splendid old Cape wine."

He pulled the bell, and ordered the servant to hasten dinner, adding that it must be an excellent one; and within an hour the two brothers were seated at a sumptuous repast.

Gaston kept up an uninterrupted stream of questions. He wished to know all that had happened during his absence.

"What about Clameran?" he abruptly asked.

Louis hesitated a moment. Should he tell the truth, or not?

"I have sold Clameran," he finally said.

"The *château* too?"

"Yes."

"You acted as you thought best," said Gaston sadly; "but it seems to me that, if I had been in your place, I should have kept the old homestead. Our ancestors lived there for many generations, and our father lies buried there."

Then seeing Louis appear sad and distressed, he quickly added:

"However, it is just as well; it is in the heart that memory dwells, and not in a pile of old stones. I myself had not the courage to return to Provence. I could not trust myself to go to Clameran, where I would have to look into the park of La Verberie. Alas, the only happy moments of my life were spent there!"

Louis's countenance immediately cleared. The certainty that Gaston had not been to Provence relieved his mind of an immense weight.

The next day Louis telegraphed to Raoul:

"Wisdom and prudence. Follow my directions. All goes well. Be sanguine."

All was going well; and yet Louis, in spite of his skilfully applied questions, had obtained none of the information which he had come to obtain.

Gaston was communicative on every subject except the one in which Louis was interested. Was this silence premeditated, or simply unconscious? Louis, like all villains, was ever ready to attribute to others the bad motives by which he himself would be influenced.

Anything was better than this uncertainty; he determined to ask his brother plainly what his intentions were in regard to money matters.

He thought the dinner-table a favourable opportunity, and began by saying:

"Do you know, my dear Gaston, that thus far we have discussed every topic except the most important one?"

"Why do you look so solemn, Louis? What is the grave subject of which you speak?"

"Our father's estate. Supposing you to be dead, I inherited, and have disposed of it."

"Is that what you call a serious matter?" said Gaston with an amused smile.

"It certainly is very serious to me; as you have a right to half of the estate, I must account to you for it. You have—"

"I have," interrupted Gaston, "a right to ask you never to allude to the subject again. It is yours by limitation."

"I cannot accept it upon those terms."

"But you must. My father only wished to have one of us inherit his property; we will be carrying out his wishes by not dividing it."

Seeing that Louis's face still remained clouded, he went on:

"Ah, I see what annoys you, my dear Louis; you are rich, and think that I am poor, and too proud to accept anything from you. Is it not so?"

Louis started at this question. How could he reply so as not to commit himself?

"I am not rich," he finally said.

"I am delighted to hear it," cried Gaston. "I wish you were as poor as Job, so that I might share what I have with you."

Dinner over, Gaston rose and said:

"Come, I want to visit with you, my—that is, our property. You must see everything about the place."

Louis uneasily followed his brother. It seemed to him that Gaston obstinately shunned anything like an explanation.

Could all this brotherly confidence be assumed to blind him as to his real plans? Why did Gaston inquire into his brother's past and future, without revealing his own? Louis's suspicions were aroused, and he regretted his over-hasty seeking of Gaston.

But his calm, smiling face betrayed none of the anxious thoughts which filled his mind.

He was called upon to praise everything. First he was taken over the house and servants' quarters, then to the stable, kennels, and the vast, beautifully laid-out garden. Across a pretty meadow was the iron-foundry in full operation. Gaston, with all the enthusiasm of a new proprietor, explained everything, down to the smallest file and hammer.

He detailed all his projects; how he intended substituting wood for coal, and how, besides having plenty to work the forge, he could make immense profits by felling the forest trees, which had hitherto been considered impracticable. He would cut a hundred cords of wood that year.

Louis approved of everything; but only answered in monosyllables, "Ah, indeed! excellent idea; quite a success."

His mind was tortured by a new pain; he was paying no attention to Gaston's remarks, but enviously comparing all this wealth and prosperity with his own poverty.

He found Gaston rich, respected, and happy, enjoying the price of his own labour and industry; whilst he—Never had he so cruelly felt the misery of his own condition; and he had brought it on himself, which only made it more aggravating.

After a lapse of twenty-three years, all the envy and hate he had felt toward Gaston, when they were boys together, revived.

"What do you think of my purchase?" asked Gaston, when the inspection was over.

"I think you possess, my dear brother, a most splendid piece of property, and on the loveliest spot in the world. It is enough to excite the envy of any poor Parisian."

"Do you really think so?"

"Certainly."

"Then, my dear Louis," said Gaston joyfully, "this property is yours, as well as mine. You like this lovely Bearn more than the dusty streets of Paris? I am very glad that you prefer the comforts of living on your own estate, to the glitter and show of a city life. Everything you can possibly want is here, at your command. And, to employ our time, there is the foundry. Does my plan suit you?"

Louis was silent. A year ago this proposal would have been eagerly welcomed. How gladly he would have seized this offer of a comfortable, luxurious home, after having been buffeted about the world so long! How delightful it would have been to turn over a new leaf, and become an honest man!

But he saw with disappointment and rage that he would now be compelled to decline it.

He was no longer free. He could not leave Paris.

He had become entangled in one of those hazardous plots which are fatal if neglected, and whose failure generally leads the projector to the galleys.

Alone, he could easily remain where he was: but he was trammelled with an accomplice.

"You do not answer me," said Gaston with surprise; "are there any obstacles to my plans?"

"None."

"What is the matter, then?"

"The matter is, my dear brother, that the salary of an office which I hold in Paris is all that I have to support me."

"Is that your only objection? Yet you just now wanted to pay me back half of the family inheritance! Louis, that is unkind; you are not acting as a brother should."

Louis hung his head. Gaston was unconsciously telling the truth.

"I should be a burden to you, Gaston."

"A burden! Why, Louis, you must be mad! Did I not tell you I am very rich? Do you suppose that you have seen all I possess? This house and the iron-works do not constitute a fourth of my fortune. Do you think that I would have risked my twenty years' savings in an experiment of this sort? The forge may be a failure; and then what would become of me, if I had nothing else?

"I have invested money which yields me an income of eighty thousand *francs*. Besides, my grants in Brazil have been sold, and my agent has already deposited four hundred thousand *francs* to my credit as part payment."

Louis trembled with pleasure. He was, at last, to know the extent of the danger hanging over him. Gaston had finally broached the subject which had caused him so much anxiety, and he determined that it should now be explained before their conversation ended.

"Who is your agent?" he asked with assumed indifference.

"My old partner at Rio. He deposited the money at my Paris banker's."

"Is this banker a friend of yours?"

"No; I never heard of him until my banker at Pau recommended him to me as an honest, reliable man; he is immensely wealthy, and stands at the head of the financiers in Paris. His name is Fauvel, and he lives on the Rue de Provence."

Although prepared for hearing almost anything, and determined to betray no agitation, Louis turned deadly pale.

"Do you know this banker?" asked Gaston.

"Only by reputation."

"Then we can make his acquaintance together; for I intend accompanying you to Paris, when you return there to settle up your affairs before establishing yourself here to superintend the forge."

At this unexpected announcement of a step which would prove his utter ruin, Louis was stupefied. In answer to his brother's questioning look, he gasped out.

"You are going to Paris?"

"Certainly I am. Why should I not go?"

"There is no reason why."

"I hate Paris, although I have never been there. But I am called there by interest, by sacred duties," he hesitatingly said. "The truth is, I understand that Mademoiselle de la Verberie lives in Paris, and I wish to see her."

"Ah!"

Gaston was silent and thoughtful for some moments, and then said, nervously:

"I will tell you, Louis, why I wish to see her. I left our family jewels in her charge, and I wish to recover them."

"Do you intend, after a lapse of twenty-three years, to claim these jewels?"

"Yes—or rather no. I only make the jewels an excuse for seeing her. I must see her because—because—she is the only woman I ever really loved!"

"But how will you find her?"

"Oh! that is easy enough. Anyone can tell me the name of her husband, and then I will go to see her. Perhaps the shortest way to find out, would be to write to Beaucaire. I will do so tomorrow."

Louis made no reply.

Men of his character, when brought face to face with imminent danger, always weigh their words, and say as little as possible, for fear of committing themselves by some indiscreet remark.

Above all things, Louis was careful to avoid raising any objections to his brother's proposed trip to Paris. To oppose the wishes of a determined man has the effect of making him adhere more closely to them. Each argument is like striking a nail with a hammer. Knowing this, Louis changed the conversation, and nothing more during the day was said of Valentine or Paris.

At night, alone in his room, he brought his cunning mind to bear upon the difficulties of his situation, and wondered by what means he could extricate himself.

At first the case seemed hopeless, desperate. During twenty years, Louis had been at war with society, trusted by none, living upon his wits, and the credulity of foolish men enabling him to gain an income without labour; and, though he generally attained his ends, it was not without great danger and constant dread of detection.

He had been caught at the gaming-table with his hands full of duplicate cards; he had been tracked all over Europe by the police, and obliged to fly from city to city under an assumed name; he had sold to cowards his skilful handling of the sword and pistol; he had been repeatedly thrown into prison, and always made his escape. He had braved everything, and feared nothing. He had often conceived and carried out the most criminal plans, without the slightest hesitation or remorse. And now here he sat, utterly bewildered, unable to think clearly; his usual impudence and ready cunning seemed to have deserted him.

Thus driven to the wall, he saw no means of escape, and was almost tempted to confess all, and throw himself upon his brother's clemency. Then he thought that it would be wiser to borrow a large sum from Gaston, and fly the country.

Vainly did he think over the wicked experiences of the past: none of the former successful stratagems could be resorted to in the present case.

Fatally, inevitably, he was about to be caught in a trap laid by himself.

The future was fraught with danger, worse than danger—ruin and disgrace.

He had to fear the wrath of M. Fauvel, his wife and niece. Gaston would have speedy vengeance the moment he discovered the truth; and Raoul, his accomplice, would certainly turn against him, and become his most implacable enemy.

Was there no possible way of preventing a meeting between Valentine and Gaston?

None that he could think of.

Their meeting would be his destruction.

Lost in reflection, he paid no attention to the flight of time. Daybreak still found him sitting at the window with his face buried in his hands, trying to come to some definite conclusion what he should say and do to keep Gaston away from Paris.

"It is vain for me to think," he muttered. "The more I rack my brain, the more confused it becomes. There is nothing to be done but gain time, and wait for an opportunity."

The fall of the horse at Clameran was what Louis called "an opportunity."

He closed the window, and, throwing himself upon the bed, was soon in a sound sleep; being accustomed to danger, it never kept him awake.

At the breakfast-table, his calm, smiling face bore no traces of a wakeful, anxious night.

He was in a gayer, more talkative mood than usual, and said he would like to ride over the country, and visit the neighbouring towns. Before leaving the table, he had planned several excursions which were to take place during the week.

He hoped to keep Gaston so amused and occupied, that he would forget all about going to Paris in search of Valentine.

He thought that with time, and skilfully put objections, he could dissuade his brother from seeking out his former love. He relied upon being able to convince him that this absolutely unnecessary interview would be painful to both, embarrassing to him, and dangerous to her.

As to the jewels, if Gaston persisted in claiming them, Louis could safely offer to go and get them for him, as he had only to redeem them from the pawnbroker.

But his hopes and plans were soon scattered to the winds.

"You know," said Gaston, "I have written."

Louis knew well enough to what he alluded, but pretended to be very much surprised, and said:

"Written? To whom? Where? For what?"

"To Beaucaire, to ask Lafourcade the name of Valentine's husband."

"You are still thinking of her?"

"She is never absent from my thoughts."

"You have not given up your idea of going to see her?"

"Of course not."

"Alas, Gaston! you forget that she whom you once loved is now the wife of another, and possibly the mother of a large family. How do you know that she will consent to see you? Why run the risk of destroying her domestic happiness, and planting seeds of remorse in your own bosom?"

"I know I am a fool; but my folly is dear to me, and I would not cure it if I could."

The quiet determination of Gaston's tone convinced Louis that all remonstrances would be unavailing.

Yet he remained the same in his manner and behaviour, apparently engrossed in pleasure parties; but, in reality, his only thought was the mail. He always managed to be at the door when the postman came, so that he was the first to receive his brother's letters.

When he and Gaston were out together at the time of the postman's visit, he would hurry into the house first, so as to look over the letters which were always laid in a card-basket on the hall table.

His watchfulness was at last rewarded.

The following Sunday, among the letters handed to him by the postman, was one bearing the postmark of Beaucaire.

He quickly slipped it into his pocket; and, although he was on the point of mounting his horse to ride with Gaston, he said that he must run up to his room to get something he had forgotten; this was to gratify his impatient desire to read the letter.

He tore it open, and, seeing "Lafourcade" signed at the bottom of three closely written pages, hastily devoured the contents.

After reading a detailed account of events entirely uninteresting to him, Louis came to the following passage relating to Valentine:

"Mademoiselle de la Verberie's husband is an eminent banker named Andre Fauvel. I have not the honour of his acquaintance, but I intend going to see him shortly. I am anxious to submit to him a project that I have conceived for the benefit of this part of the country. If he approves of it, I shall ask him to invest in it, as his name will be of great assistance to the scheme. I suppose you have no objections to my referring him to you, should he ask for my endorsers."

Louis trembled like a man who had just made a narrow escape from death. He well knew that he would have to fly the country if Gaston received this letter.

But though the danger was warded off for the while, it might return and destroy him at any moment.

Gaston would wait a week for an answer, then he would write again; Lafourcade would instantly reply to express surprise that his first letter had not been received; all of this correspondence would occupy about twelve days. In those twelve days Louis would have to think over some plan for preventing Lafourcade's visit to Paris; since, the instant he mentioned the name of Clameran to the banker, everything would be discovered.

Louis's meditations were interrupted by Gaston, who called from the lower passage:

"What are you doing, Louis? I am waiting for you."

"I am coming now," he replied.

Hastily thrusting Lafourcade's letter into his trunk, Louis ran down to his brother.

He had made up his mind to borrow a large sum from Gaston, and go off to America; and Raoul might get out of the scrape as best he could.

The only thing which now disturbed him was the sudden failure of the most skilful combination he had ever conceived; but he was not a man to fight against destiny, and determined to make the best of the emergency, and hope for better fortune in his next scheme.

The next day about dusk, while walking along the pretty road leading from the foundry to Oloron, he commenced a little story which was to conclude by asking Gaston to lend him two hundred thousand *francs*.

As they slowly went along arm in arm, about half a mile from the foundry they met a young labourer who bowed as he passed them.

Louis dropped his brother's arm, and started back as if he had seen a ghost.

"What is the matter?" asked Gaston, with astonishment.

"Nothing, except I struck my foot against a stone, and it is very painful."

Gaston might have known by the tremulous tones of Louis's voice that this was a lie. Louis de Clameran had reason to tremble; in this workman he recognised Raoul de Lagors.

Instinctive fear paralyzed and overwhelmed him.

The story he had planned for the purpose of obtaining the two hundred thousand *francs* was forgotten; his volubility was gone; and he silently walked along by his brother's side, like an automaton, totally incapable of thinking or acting for himself.

He seemed to listen, he did listen; but the words fell upon his ear unmeaningly; he could not understand what Gaston was saying, and mechanically answered "yes" or "no," like one in a dream.

Whilst necessity, absolute necessity, kept him here at Gaston's side, his thoughts were all with the young man who had just passed by.

What had brought Raoul to Oloron? What plot was he hatching? Why was he disguised as a labourer? Why had he not answered the many letters which Louis had written him from Oloron? He had ascribed this silence to Raoul's carelessness, but now he saw it was premeditated. Something disastrous must have happened at Paris; and Raoul, afraid to commit himself by writing, had come himself to bring the bad news. Had he come to say that the game was up, and they must fly?

But, after all, perhaps he was mistaken in supposing this to be his accomplice. It might be some honest workman bearing a strong resemblance to Raoul.

If he could only run after this stranger, and speak to him! But no, he must walk on up to the house with Gaston, quietly, as if nothing had happened to arouse his anxiety. He felt as if he would go mad if his brother did not move faster; the uncertainty was becoming intolerable.

His mind filled with these perplexing thoughts, Louis at last reached the house; and Gaston, to his great relief, said that he was so tired that he was going directly to bed.

At last he was free!

He lit a cigar, and, telling the servant not to sit up for him, went out.

He knew that Raoul, if it was Raoul, would be prowling near the house, waiting for him.

His suspicions were well founded.

He had barely proceeded thirty yards, when a man suddenly sprang from behind a tree, and stood before him.

The night was clear, and Louis recognised Raoul.

"What is the matter?" he impatiently demanded; "what has happened?"

"Nothing."

"What! Do you mean to say that nothing has gone wrong in Paris—that no one is on our track?"

"Not the slightest danger of any sort. And moreover, but for your inordinate greed of gain, everything would have succeeded admirably; all was going on well when I left Paris."

"Then why have you come here?" cried Louis fiercely. "Who gave you permission to desert your post, when your absence might bring ruin upon us? What brought you here?"

"That is my business," said Raoul with cool impertinence.

Louis seized the young man's wrists, and almost crushed them in his vicelike grasp.

"Explain this strange conduct of yours," he said, in a tone of suppressed rage. "What do you mean by it?"

Without apparent effort Raoul released his hands from their imprisonment, and jeeringly said:

"Hein! Gently, my friend! I don't like being roughly treated; and, if you don't know how to behave yourself, I have the means of teaching you."

At the same time he drew a revolver from his pocket.

"You must and shall explain yourself," insisted Louis: "if you don't—"

"Well, if I don't? Now, you might just as well spare yourself the trouble of trying to frighten me. I intend to answer your questions when I choose; but it certainly won't be here, in the middle of the road, with the bright moonlight showing us off to advantage. How do you know people are not watching us this very minute? Come this way."

They strode through the fields, regardless of Gaston's plants, which were trampled under foot in order to take a short cut.

"Now," began Raoul, when they were at a safe distance from the road, "now, my dear uncle, I will tell you what brings me here. I have received and carefully read your letters. I read them over again. You wished to be prudent; and the consequence was, that your letters were unintelligible. Only one thing did I understand clearly: we are in danger."

"Only the more reason for your watchfulness and obedience."

"Very well put: only, before braving danger, my venerable and beloved uncle, I want to know its extent. I am not a man to retreat in the hour of peril, but I want to know exactly how much risk I am running."

"I told you to keep quiet, and follow my directions."

"But to do this would imply that I have perfect confidence in you, my dear uncle," said Raoul, sneeringly.

"And why should you not? What reasons for distrust have you after all that I have done for you? Who went to London, and rescued you from a state of privation and ignominy? I did. Who gave you a name and position when you had neither? I did. And who is working now to maintain your present life of ease, and insure you a splendid future? I am. And how do you repay me?"

"Superb, magnificent, inimitable!" said Raoul, with mocking derision. "But, while on the subject, why don't you prove that you have sacrificed yourself for my sake? You did not need me as a tool for carrying out plans for your own benefit; did you? oh no, not at all! Dear, kind, generous, disinterested uncle! You ought to have the Montyon prize; I think I must recommend you as the most deserving person I have ever met!"

De Clameran was so angry at these jeering words that he feared to trust himself to speak.

"Now, my good uncle," continued Raoul more seriously, "we had better end this child's play, and come to a clear understanding. I follow you here, because I thoroughly understand your character, and have just as much confidence in you as you deserve, and not a particle more. If it were for your advantage to ruin me, you would not hesitate one instant. If danger threatened us, you would fly alone, and leave your dutiful nephew to make his escape the best way he could. Oh! don't look shocked, and pretend to deny it; your conduct is perfectly natural, and in your place I would act the same way. Only remember this, that I am not a man to be trifled with. Now let us cease these unnecessary recriminations, and come to the point: what is your present plan?"

Louis saw that his accomplice was too shrewd to be deceived, and that the safest course was to trust all to him, and to pretend that he had intended doing so all along.

Without any show of anger, he briefly and clearly related all that had occurred at his brother's.

He told the truth about everything except the amount of his brother's fortune, the importance of which he lessened as much as possible.

"Well," said Raoul, when the report was ended, "we are in a nice fix. And do you expect to get out of it?"

"Yes, if you don't betray me."

"I wish you to understand, *marquis*, that I have never betrayed anyone yet; don't judge me by yourself, I beg. What steps will you take to get free of this entanglement?"

"I don't know; but something will turn up. Oh, don't be alarmed; I'll find some means of escape: so you can return home with your mind at rest. You run no risk in Paris, and 'tis the best place for you. I will stay here to watch Gaston."

Raoul reflected for some moments, and then said:

"Are you sure I am not in danger at Paris?"

"What are you afraid of? We have Madame Fauvel so completely in our power that she would not dare speak a word against you; even if she knew the whole truth, what no one but you and I know, she would not open her lips, but be only too glad to hush up matters so as to escape punishment for her fault from her deceived husband and a censuring world."

"I know we have a secure hold on her," said Raoul. "I am not afraid of her giving any trouble."

"Who, then?"

"An enemy of your own making, my respected uncle; a most implacable enemy—Madeleine."

"Fiddlesticks!" replied de Clameran, disdainfully.

"It is very well for you to treat her with contempt," said Raoul, gravely; "but I can tell you, you are much mistaken in your estimate of her character. I have studied her lately, and see that she is devoted to her aunt, and ready to make any sacrifice to insure her happiness. But she has no idea of doing anything blindly, of throwing herself away if she can avoid it. She has promised to marry you. Prosper is broken-hearted at being discarded, it is true; but he has not given up hope. You imagine her to be weak and yielding, easily frightened? It's a great mistake. She is self-reliant and fearless. More than that, she is in love, my good uncle; and a woman will defend her lover as a tigress defends her young. She will fight to the bitter end before marrying anyone save Prosper."

"She is worth five hundred thousand *francs*."

"So she is; and at five *per cent* we would each have an income of twelve thousand five hundred *francs*. But, for all that, you had better take my advice, and give up Madeleine."

"Never; I swear by Heaven!" exclaimed de Clameran. "Rich or poor, she shall be mine! I first wanted her money, but now I want her; I love her for herself, Raoul!"

Raoul seemed to be amazed at this declaration of his uncle.

He raised his hands, and started back with astonishment.

"Is it possible," he said, "that you are in love with Madeleine?—you!"

"Yes," replied Louis, sullenly. "Is there anything so very extraordinary in it?"

"Oh, no, certainly not! only this sentimental view of the matter explains your strange behaviour. Alas, you love Madeleine! Then, my venerable uncle, we might as well surrender at once."

"Why so?"

"Because you know the axiom, 'When the heart is interested the head is lost.' Generals in love always lose their battles. The day is not far off when your infatuation of Madeleine will make you sell us both for a smile. And, mark my words, she is shrewd, and watching us as only an enemy can watch."

With a forced laugh de Clameran interrupted his nephew.

"Just see how you fire up for no cause," he said; "you must dislike the charming Madeleine very much, if you abuse her in this way."

"She will prove to be our ruin: that is all."

"You might as well be frank, and say you are in love with her yourself."

"I am only in love with her money," replied Raoul, with an angry frown.

"Then what are you complaining of? I shall give you half her fortune. You will have the money without being troubled with the wife; the profit without the burden."

"I am not over fifty years old," said Raoul conceitedly. "I can appreciate a pretty woman better than you."

"Enough of that," interrupted Louis angrily. "The day I relieved your pressing wants, and brought you to Paris, you promised to follow my directions, to help me carry out my plan; did you not?"

"Yes; but not the plot you are hatching now! You forget that my liberty, perhaps my life, is at stake. You may hold the cards, but I must have the right of advising you."

It was midnight before the accomplices separated.

"I won't stand idle," said Louis. "I agree with you that something must be done at once. But I can't decide what it shall be on the spur of the moment. Meet me here at this hour tomorrow night, and I will have some plan ready for you."

"Very good. I will be here."

"And remember, don't be imprudent!"

"My costume ought to convince you that I am not anxious to be recognised by anyone. I left such an ingenious alibi, that I defy anybody to prove that I have been absent from my house at Vesinet. I even took the precaution to travel in a third-class car. Well, goodnight. I am going to the inn."

Raoul went off after these words, apparently unconscious of having aroused suspicion in the breast of his accomplice.

During his adventurous life, de Clameran had transacted "business" with too many scamps not to know the precise amount of confidence to place in a man like Raoul.

The old adage, "Honour among thieves," seldom holds good after the "stroke." There is always a quarrel over the division of the spoils.

This distrustful de Clameran foresaw a thousand difficulties and counter-plots to be guarded against in his dealings with Raoul.

"Why," he pondered, "did the villain assume this disguise? Why this alibi at Paris? Can he be laying a trap for me? It is true that I have a hold upon him; but then I am completely at his mercy. Those accursed letters which I have written to him, while here, are so many proofs against me. Can he be thinking of cutting loose from me, and making off with all the profits of our enterprise?"

Louis never once during the night closed his eyes; but by daybreak he had fully made up his mind how to act, and with feverish impatience waited for evening to come, to communicate his views with Raoul.

His anxiety made him so restless that the unobserving Gaston finally noticed it, and asked him what the matter was; if he was sick, or troubled about anything.

At last evening came, and, at the appointed hour, Louis went to the field where they had met the night previous, and found Raoul lying on the grass smoking a fragrant cigar, as if he had no other object in life except to blow little clouds of smoke in the air, and count the stars in the clear sky above him.

"Well?" he carelessly said, as Louis approached, "have you decided upon anything?"

"Yes. I have two projects, either of which would probably accomplish our object."

"I am listening."

Louis was silently thoughtful for a minute, as if arranging his thoughts so as to present them as clearly and briefly as possible.

"My first plan," he began, "depends upon your approval. What would you say, if I proposed to you to renounce the affair altogether?"

"What!"

"Would you consent to disappear, leave France, and return to London, if I paid you a good round sum?"

"What do you call a good round sum?"

"I will give you a hundred and fifty thousand *francs*."

"My respected uncle," said Raoul with a contemptuous shrug, "I am distressed to see how little you know me! You try to deceive me, to outwit me, which is ungenerous and foolish on your part; ungenerous, because it fails to carry out our agreement; foolish, because as you know well enough, my power equals yours."

"I don't understand you."

"I am sorry for it. I understand myself, and that is sufficient. Oh! I understand you, my dear uncle. I have watched you with careful eyes, which are not to be deceived; I see through you clearly. If you offer me one hundred and fifty thousand *francs*, it is because you intend to walk off with half a million for yourself."

"You are talking like a fool," said de Clameran with virtuous indignation.

"Not at all; I only judge the future by the past. Of all the large sums extorted from Madame Fauvel, often against my wishes, I never received a tenth part."

"But you know we have a reserve fund."

"All very good; but you have the keeping of it, my good uncle. It is very nice for you, but not so funny for me. If our little plot were to be discovered tomorrow, you would walk off with the money-box, and leave your devoted nephew to be sent to prison."

"Ingrate!" muttered Louis, as if distressed at these undeserved reproaches of his protege.

"You have hit on the very word I was trying to remember," cried Raoul: "'ingrate' is the name that just suits you. But we have not time for this nonsense. I will end the matter by proving how you have been trying to deceive me."

"I would like to hear you do so if you can."

"Very good. In the first place, you told me that your brother only possessed a modest competency. Now, I learn that Gaston has an income of at least sixty thousand *francs*. It is useless for you to deny it; and how much is this property worth? A hundred thousand crowns. He had four hundred thousand *francs* deposited in M. Fauvel's bank. Total, seven hundred thousand *francs*. And, besides all this, the broker in Oloron has orders to buy up a large amount of stocks and railroad shares, which will require large cash payments. I have not wasted my day, you see, and have obtained all the information I came for."

Raoul's information was too concise and exact for Louis to deny it.

"You might have sense enough," Raoul went on, "to know how to manage your forces if you undertake to be a commander. We had a splendid game in our hands; and you, who held the cards, have made a perfect muddle of it."

"I think—"

"That the game is lost? That is my opinion too, and all through you. You have no one to blame but yourself."

"I could not control events."

"Yes, you could, if you had been shrewd. Fools sit down and wait for an opportunity; sensible men make one. What did we agree upon in London? We were to implore my good mother to assist us a little, and, if she complied with our wishes, we were to be flattering and affectionate in our devotion to her. And what was the result? At the risk of killing the golden goose, you have made me torment the poor woman until she is almost crazy."

"It was prudent to hasten matters."

"You think so, do you? Was it also to hasten matters that you took it into your head to marry Madeleine? That made it necessary to let her into the secret; and, ever since, she has advised and set her aunt against us. I would not be surprised if she makes her confess everything to M. Fauvel, or even inform against us at the police-office."

"I love Madeleine!"

"You told me that before. And suppose you do love her. You led me into this piece of business without having studied its various bearings, without knowing what you were about. No one but an idiot, my beloved uncle, would go and put his foot into a trap, and then say, 'If I had only known about it!' You should have made it your business to know everything. You came to me, and said, 'Your father is dead,' which was a lie to start with; perhaps you call it a mistake. He is living; and, after what we have done, I dare not appear before him. He would have left me a million, and now I shall not get a *sou*. He will find his Valentine, and then goodbye."

"Enough!" angrily interrupted Louis. "If I have made a mistake, I know how to redeem it. I can save everything yet."

"You can? How so?"

"That is my secret," said Louis gloomily.

Louis and Raoul were silent for a minute. And this silence between them, in this lonely spot, at dead of night, was so horribly significant that both of them shuddered.

An abominable thought had flashed across their evil minds, and without a word or look they understood each other.

Louis broke the ominous silence, by abruptly saying:

"Then you refuse to disappear if I pay you a hundred and fifty thousand *francs*? Think it over before deciding: it is not too late yet."

"I have fully thought it over. I know you will not attempt to deceive me any more. Between certain ease, and the probability of an immense fortune, I choose the latter at all risks. I will share your success or your failure. We will swim or sink together."

"And you will follow my instructions?"

"Blindly."

Raoul must have been very certain of Louis's intentions of resorting to the most dangerous extremities, must have known exactly what he intended to do; for he did not ask him a single question. Perhaps he dared not. Perhaps he preferred doubt to shocking certainty, as if he could thus escape the remorse attendant upon criminal complicity.

"In the first place," said Louis, "you must at once return to Paris."

"I will be there in forty-eight hours."

"You must be very intimate at Madame Fauvel's, and keep me informed of everything that takes place in the family."

"I understand."

Louis laid his hand upon Raoul's shoulder, as if to impress upon his mind what he was about to say.

"You have a sure means of being restored to your mother's confidence and affection, by blaming me for everything that has happened to distress her. Abuse me constantly. The more odious you render me in her eyes and those of Madeleine, the better you will serve me. Nothing would please me more than to be denied admittance to the house when I return to Paris. You must say that you have quarrelled with me, and that, if I still come to see you, it is because you cannot prevent it, and you will never voluntarily have any intercourse with me. That is the scheme; you can develop it."

Raoul listened to these strange instructions with astonishment.

"What!" he cried: "you adore Madeleine, and take this means of showing it? An odd way of carrying on a courtship, I must confess. I will be shot if I can comprehend."

"There is no necessity for your comprehending."

"All right," said Raoul submissively; "if you say so."

Then Louis reflected that no one could properly execute a commission without having at least an idea of its nature.

"Did you ever hear," he asked Raoul, "of the man who burnt down his lady-love's house so as to have the bliss of carrying her out in his arms?"

"Yes: what of it?"

"At the proper time, I will charge you to set fire, morally, to Madame Fauvel's house; and I will rush in, and save her and her niece. Now, in the eyes of those women my conduct will appear more magnanimous and noble in proportion to the contempt and abuse they have heaped upon me. I gain nothing by patient devotion: I have everything to hope from a sudden change of tactics. A well-managed stroke will transform a demon into an angel."

"Very well, a good idea!" said Raoul approvingly, when his uncle had finished.

"Then you understand what is to be done?"

"Yes, but will you write to me?"

"Of course; and if anything should happen at Paris—"

"I will telegraph to you."

"And never lose sight of my rival, the cashier."

"Prosper? not much danger of our being troubled by him, poor boy! He is just now my most devoted friend. Trouble has driven him into a path of life which will soon prove his destruction. Every now and then I pity him from the bottom of my soul."

"Pity him as much as you like; but don't interfere with his dissipation."

The two men shook hands, and separated apparently the best friends in the world; in reality the bitterest enemies.

Raoul would not forgive Louis for having attempted to appropriate all the booty, and leave him in the lurch, when it was he who had risked the greatest dangers.

Louis, on his part, was alarmed at the attitude taken by Raoul. Thus far he had found his nephew tractable, and even blindly obedient; and now he had suddenly become rebellious and threatening. Instead of ordering Raoul, he was forced to consult and bargain with him.

What could be more wounding to his vanity and self-conceit than the reproaches, well founded though they were, to which he had been obliged to listen, from a mere youth?

As he walked back to his brother's house, thinking over what had just occurred, Louis swore that sooner or later he would be revenged, and that, as soon as he could get rid of Raoul he would do so, and would do him some great injury.

But, for the present, he was so afraid lest the young villain should betray him, or thwart his plans in some way, that he wrote to him the next day, and every succeeding day, full particulars of everything that happened. Seeing how important it was to restore his shaken confidence, Louis entered into the most minute details of his plans, and asked Raoul's advice about every step he took.

The situation remained the same. The dark cloud remained threateningly near, but grew no larger.

Gaston seemed to have forgotten that he had written to Beaucaire, and never mentioned Valentine's name once.

Like all men accustomed to a busy life, Gaston was miserable except when occupied, and spent his whole time in the foundry, which seemed to absorb him entirely.

When he began the experiment of felling the woods, his losses had been heavy; but he determined to continue the work until it should be equally beneficial to himself and the neighbouring land-owners.

He engaged the services of an intelligent engineer, and thanks to untiring energy, and the new improvements in machinery, his profits soon more than equalled his expenses.

"Now that we are doing so well," said Gaston joyously, "we shall certainly make twenty-five thousand *francs* next year."

Next year! Alas, poor Gaston!

Five days after Raoul's departure, one Saturday afternoon, Gaston was suddenly taken ill.

He had a sort of vertigo, and was so dizzy that he was forced to lie down.

"I know what is the matter," he said. "I have often been ill in this way at Rio. A couple of hours' sleep will cure me. I will go to bed, and you can send someone to awaken me when dinner is ready, Louis; I shall be all right by that time."

But, when the servant came to announce dinner, he found Gaston much worse. He had a violent headache, a choking sensation in his throat, and dimness of vision. But his worst symptom was *dysphonia*;

he would try to articulate one word, and find himself using another. His jaw-bones became so stiff that it was with the greatest difficulty that he opened his mouth.

Louis came up to his brother's room, and urged him to send for the physician.

"No," said Gaston, "I won't have any doctor to make me ill with all sorts of medicines; I know what is the matter with me, and my indisposition will be cured by a simple remedy which I have always used."

At the same time he ordered Manuel, his old Spanish servant, who had lived with him for ten years, to prepare him some lemonade.

The next day Gaston appeared to be much better. He ate his breakfast, and was about to take a walk, when the pains of the previous day suddenly returned, in a more violent form.

Without consulting his brother, Louis sent to Oloron for Dr. C—, whose wonderful cures at Eaux Bonnes had won him a wide reputation.

The doctor declared that there was no danger, and merely prescribed a dose of valerian, and a blister with some grains of morphine sprinkled on it.

But in the middle of the night, all the symptoms suddenly changed for the worse. The pain in the head was succeeded by a fearful oppression, and the sick man suffered torture in trying to get his breath; daybreak found him still tossing restlessly from pillow to pillow.

When Dr. C—came early in the morning, he appeared very much surprised at this change for the worse. He inquired if they had not administered an overdose of morphine. Manuel said that he had put the blister on his master, and the doctor's directions had been accurately followed.

The doctor, after having examined Gaston, and found his breathing heavy and irregular, prescribed a heavy dose of sulphate of quinine; he then retired, saying he would return the next day.

As soon as the doctor had gone, Gaston sent for a friend of his, a lawyer, to come to him as soon as possible.

"For Heaven's sake, what do you want with a lawyer?" inquired Louis.

"I want his advice, brother. It is useless to try and deceive ourselves; I know I am extremely ill. Only timid fools are superstitious about making their wills; if I defer it any longer, I may be suddenly taken without having arranged my affairs. I would rather have the lawyer at once, and then my mind will be at rest."

Gaston did not think he was about to die, but, knowing the uncertainty of life, determined to be prepared for the worst; he had too often imperilled his life, and been face to face with death, to feel any fear now.

He had made his will while ill at Bordeaux; but, now that he had found Louis, he wished to leave him all his property, and sent for his business man to advise as to the best means of disposing of his wealth for his benefit.

The lawyer was a shrewd, wiry little man, very popular because he had a faculty for always gaining suits which other attorneys had lost, or declined to try, because of their groundlessness. Being perfectly familiar with all the intricacies of the law, nothing delighted him more than to succeed in eluding some stringent article of the code; and often he sacrificed large fees for the sake of outwitting his opponent, and controverting the justness of a decision.

Once aware of his client's wishes and intentions, he had but one idea: and that was, to carry them out as inexpensively as possible, by skilfully evading the heavy costs to be paid by the inheritor of an estate.

He explained to Gaston that he could, by an act of partnership, associate Louis in his business enterprises, by signing an acknowledgment that half of the money invested in these various concerns, belonged to and had been advanced by his brother; so that, in the event of Gaston's death, Louis would only have to pay taxes on half the fortune.

Gaston eagerly took advantage of this fiction; not that he thought of the money saved by the transaction if he died, but this would be a favourable opportunity for sharing his riches with Louis, without wounding his delicate sensibility.

A deed of partnership between Gaston and Louis de Clameran, for the working of a cast-iron mill, was drawn up; this deed acknowledged Louis to have invested five hundred thousand *francs* as his share of the capital; therefore half of the iron-works was his in his own right.

When Louis was called in to sign the paper, he violently opposed his brother's project.

"Why do you distress me by making these preparations for death, merely because you are suffering from a slight indisposition? Do you think that I would consent to accept your wealth during your lifetime? If you die, I am your heir; if you live, I enjoy your property as if it were my own. What more can you wish? Pray do not draw up any papers; let things remain as they are, and turn all your attention to getting well."

Vain remonstrances. Gaston was not a man to be persuaded from accomplishing a purpose upon which he had fully set his heart. When, after mature deliberation, he made a resolution, he always carried it out in spite of all opposition.

After a long and heroic resistance, which betrayed great nobleness of character and rare disinterestedness, Louis, urged by the physician, finally yielded, and signed his name to the papers drawn up by the lawyer.

It was done. Now he was legally Gaston's partner, and possessor of half his fortune. No court of law could deprive him of what had been deeded with all the legal formalities, even if his brother should change his mind and try to get back his property.

The strangest sensations now filled Louis's breast.

He was in a state of delirious excitement often felt by persons suddenly raised from poverty to affluence.

Whether Gaston lived or died, Louis was the lawful possessor of an income of twenty-five thousand *francs*, without counting the eventual profits of the iron-works.

At no time in his life had he hoped for or dreamed of such wealth. His wildest wishes were surpassed. What more could he want?

Alas! he wanted the power of enjoying these riches; they had come too late.

This fortune, fallen from the skies, should have filled his heart with joy; whereas it only made him melancholy and angry.

This unlooked-for happiness seemed to have been sent by cruel fate as a punishment for his past sins. What could be more terrible than seeing this haven of rest open to him, and to be prevented from enjoying it because of his own vile plottings?

Although his conscience told him that he deserved this misery, he blamed Gaston entirely for his present torture. Yes, he held Gaston responsible for the horrible situation in which he found himself.

His letters to Raoul for several days expressed all the fluctuations of his mind, and revealed glimpses of coming evil.

"I have twenty-five thousand *livres* a year," he wrote to him, a few hours after signing the agreement of partnership; "and I possess in my own right five hundred thousand *francs*. One-fourth of this sum would have made me the happiest of men a year ago. Now it is of no use to me. All the gold on earth could not remove one of the difficulties of our situation. Yes, you were right. I have been imprudent; but I pay dear for my precipitation. We are now going down hill so rapidly that nothing can save us; we must fall to the very bottom. To attempt stopping half way would be madness. Rich or poor, I have cause to tremble as long as there is any risk of a meeting between Gaston and Valentine. How can they be kept apart? Will my brother renounce his plan of discovering the whereabouts of this woman whom he so loved?"

No; Gaston would never be turned from his search for his first love, as he proved by calling for her in the most beseeching tones when he was suffering his worst paroxysms of pain.

He grew no better. In spite of the most careful nursing his symptoms changed, but showed no improvement.

Each attack was more violent than the preceding.

Toward the end of the week the pains left his head, and he felt well enough to get up and partake of a slight nourishment.

But poor Gaston was a mere shadow of his former self. In one week he had aged ten years. His strong constitution was broken. He, who ten days ago was boasting of his vigorous health, was now weak and bent like an old man. He could hardly drag himself along, and shivered in the warm sun as if he were bloodless.

Leaning on Louis's arm, he slowly walked down to look at the forge, and, seating himself before a furnace at full blast, he declared that he felt very much better, that this intense heat revived him.

His pains were all gone, and he could breathe without difficulty.

His spirits rose, and he turned to the workmen gathered around, and said cheerfully:

"I was not blessed with a good constitution for nothing, my friends, and I shall soon be well again."

When the neighbours called to see him, and insisted that this illness was entirely owing to change of climate, Gaston replied that he supposed they were right, and that he would return to Rio as soon as he was well enough to travel.

What hope this answer roused in Louis's breast!

"Yes," he eagerly said, "I will go with you; a trip to Brazil would be charming! Let us start at once."

But the next day Gaston had changed his mind.

He told Louis that he felt almost well, and was determined not to leave France. He proposed going to Paris to consult the best physicians; and then he would see Valentine.

That night he grew worse.

As his illness increased, he became more surprised and troubled at not hearing from Beaucaire.

He wrote again in the most pressing terms, and sent the letter by a courier who was to wait for the answer.

This letter was never received by Lafourcade.

At midnight, Gaston's sufferings returned with renewed violence, and for the first time Dr. C—was uneasy.

A fatal termination seemed inevitable. Gaston's pain left him in a measure, but he was growing weaker every moment. His mind wandered, and his feet were as cold as ice. On the fourteenth day of his illness, after lying in a stupor for several hours, he revived sufficiently to ask for a priest, saying that he would follow the example of his ancestors, and die like a Christian.

The priest left him after half an hour's interview, and all the workmen were summoned to receive the farewell greeting of their master.

Gaston spoke a few kind words to them all, saying that he had provided for them in his will.

After they had gone, he made Louis promise to carry on the iron-works, embraced him for the last time, and sank back on his pillow in a dying state.

As the bell tolled for noon he quietly breathed his last, murmuring, softly, "In three years, Valentine; wait for me."

Now Louis was in reality Marquis de Clameran, and besides he was a millionaire.

Two weeks later, having made arrangements with the engineer in charge of the iron-works to attend to everything during his absence, he took his seat in the train for Paris.

He had sent the following significant telegram to Raoul the night previous: "I arrive tomorrow."

Chapter 19

Faithful to the program laid down by his accomplice, while Louis watched at Oloron, Raoul remained in Paris with the purpose of recovering Madame Fauvel's confidence and affection, and of lulling any suspicions which might have arisen in her breast.

The task was difficult, but not impossible.

Madame Fauvel had been distressed by Raoul's wild extravagance, but had never ceased to love him.

Whatever faults he had committed, whatever future follies he might indulge in, he would always remain her best-loved child, her first-born, the living image of her noble, handsome Gaston, the lover of her youth.

She adored her two sons, Lucien and Abel; but she could not overcome an indulgent weakness for the unfortunate child, torn from her arms the day of his birth, abandoned to the mercies of hired strangers, and for twenty years deprived of home influences and a mother's love.

She blamed herself for Raoul's misconduct, and accepted the responsibility of his sins, saying to herself, "It is my fault. But for me, he would not have been exposed to the temptations of the world."

Knowing these to be her sentiments, Raoul did not hesitate to take advantage of them.

Never were more irresistible fascinations employed for the accomplishment of a wicked object. Beneath an air of innocent frankness, this precocious scoundrel concealed wonderful astuteness and penetration. He could at will adorn himself with the confiding artlessness of youth, so that angels might have yielded to the soft look of his large dark eyes. There were few women living who could have resisted the thrilling tones of his sympathetic voice.

During the month of Louis's absence, Madame Fauvel was in a state of comparative happiness.

Never had this mother and wife—this pure, innocent woman, in spite of her first and only fault—enjoyed such tranquillity. She felt as one under the influence of enchantment, while revelling in the sunshine of filial love, which almost bore the character of a lover's passion; for Raoul's devotion was ardent and constant, his manner so tender and winning, that anyone would have taken him for Madame Fauvel's suitor.

As she was still at her country-seat, and M. Fauvel went into the city every morning at nine o'clock, and did not return till six, she had the whole of her time to devote to Raoul. When she had spent the morning with him at his house in Vesinet, she would often bring him home to dine and spend the evening with her.

All his past faults were forgiven, or rather the whole blame of them was laid upon de Clameran; for, now that he was absent, had not Raoul once more become her noble, generous, affectionate son, the pride and consolation of her life?

Raoul enjoyed the life he was leading, and took such an interest in the part that he was playing, that his acting was perfect. He possessed the faculty which makes cheats successful, faith in his own impostures.

Sometimes he would stop to think whether he was telling the truth, or acting a shameful comedy.

His success was wonderful. Even Madeleine, the prudent, distrustful Madeleine, without being able to shake off her prejudice against the young adventurer, confessed that perhaps she had been influenced by appearances, and had judged unjustly.

Raoul not only never asked for money, but even refused it when offered; saying that, now that his uncle was away, his expenses were but trifling.

Affairs were in this happy state when Louis arrived from Oloron.

Although now immensely rich, he resolved to make no change in his style of living, but returned to his apartments at the Hotel du Louvre.

His only outlay was the purchase of a handsome carriage; and this was driven by Manuel, who consented to enter his service, although Gaston had left him a handsome little fortune, more than sufficient to support him comfortably.

Louis's dream, the height of his ambition, was to be ranked among the great manufacturers of France.

He was prouder of being called "iron-founder" than of his *marquisate.*

During his adventurous life, he had met with so many titled gamblers and cut-throats, that he no longer believed in the prestige of nobility. It was impossible to distinguish the counterfeit from the genuine. He thought what was so easily imitated was not worth the having.

Dearly bought experience had taught him that our unromantic century attaches no value to armorial bearings, unless their possessor is rich enough to display them upon a splendid coach.

One can be a *marquis* without a *marquisate*, but it is impossible to be a forge-master without owning iron-works.

Louis now thirsted for the homage of the world. All the badly digested humiliations of the past weighed upon him.

He had suffered so much contempt and scorn from his fellow-men, that he burned to avenge himself. After a disgraceful youth, he longed to live a respected and honoured old age.

His past career disturbed him little. He was sufficiently acquainted with the world to know that the noise of his coach-wheels would silence the jeers of those who knew his former life.

These thoughts fermented in Louis's brain as he journeyed from Pau to Paris. He troubled his mind not in the least about Raoul, determined to use him as a tool so long as he needed his services, and then pay him a large sum if he would go back to England.

All these plans and thoughts were afterward found noted down in the diary which he had in his pocket at the time of the journey.

The first interview between the accomplices took place at the Hotel du Louvre.

Raoul, having a practical turn of mind, said he thought that they both ought to be contented with the result already obtained, and that it would be folly to try and grasp anything more.

"What more do we want?" he asked his uncle. "We now possess over a million; let us divide it and keep quiet. We had better be satisfied with our good luck, and not tempt Providence."

But this moderation did not suit Louis.

"I am rich," he replied, "but I desire more than wealth. I am determined to marry Madeleine: I swear she shall be my wife! In the first place, I madly love her, and then, as the nephew of the most eminent banker in Paris, I at once gain high position and public consideration."

"I tell you, uncle, your courtship will involve you in great risks."

"I don't care if it does. I choose to run them. My intention is to share my fortune with you; but I will not do so till the day after my wedding. Madeleine's fortune will then be yours."

Raoul was silent. De Clameran held the money, and was therefore master of the situation.

"You don't seem to anticipate any difficulty in carrying out your wishes," he said discontentedly; "how are you to account for your suddenly acquired fortune? M. Fauvel knows that a Clameran lived at Oloron, and had money in his bank. You tell him that you never heard of this person bearing your name, and then, at the end of the month, you come and say that you have inherited his fortune. People don't inherit fortunes from perfect strangers; so you had better trump up some relationship."

"You are an innocent youth, nephew; your ingenuousness is amusing."

"Explain yourself."

"Certainly. The banker, his wife, and Madeleine must be informed that the Clameran of Oloron was a natural son of my father, consequently my brother, born at Hamburg, and recognised during the emigration. Of course, he wished to leave his fortune to his own family. This is the story which you must tell Madame Fauvel tomorrow."

"That is a bold step to take."

"How so?"

"Inquiries might be made."

"Who would make them? The banker would not trouble himself to do so. What difference is it to him whether I had a brother or not? My title as heir is legally authenticated; and all he has to do is to pay the money he holds, and there his business ends."

"I am not afraid of his giving trouble."

"Do you think that Madame Fauvel and her niece will ask any questions? Why should they? They have no grounds for suspicion. Besides, they cannot take a step without compromising themselves. If they knew all our secrets I would not have the least fear of their making revelations. They have sense enough to know that they had best keep quiet."

Not finding any other objections to make, Raoul said:

"Very well, then, I obey you; but I am not to call upon Madame Fauvel for any more money, am I?"

"And why not, pray?"

"Because, my uncle, you are rich now."

"Suppose I am rich," replied Louis, triumphantly; "what is that to you? Have we not quarrelled about the means of making this money? and did you not heap abuse upon me until I consider myself justified in refusing you any assistance whatever? However, I will overlook the past. And, when I explain my present plan, you will feel ashamed of your former doubts and suspicion. You will say with me, 'Success is certain.'"

Louis de Clameran's scheme was very simple, and therefore unfortunately presented the strongest chances of success.

"We will go back and look at our balance-sheet. As heretofore, my brilliant nephew, you seem to have misunderstood my management of this affair; I will now explain it to you."

"I am listening."

"In the first place, I presented myself to Madame Fauvel, and said not, 'Your money or your life,' but 'Your money or your reputation!' It was a rude blow to strike, but effective. As I expected, she was frightened, and regarded me with the greatest aversion."

"Aversion is a mild term, uncle."

"I know that. Then I brought you upon the scene; and, without flattering you in the least, I must say that your opening act was a perfect success. I was concealed behind the curtain, and saw your first interview; it was sublime! She saw you, and loved you: you spoke a few words and won her heart."

"And but for you?"

"Let me finish. This was the first act of our comedy. Let us pass to the second. Your extravagant follies—your grandfather would have said, your dissoluteness—soon changed our respective situations. Madame Fauvel, without ceasing to worship you—you resemble Gaston so closely—was uneasy about you. She was so frightened that she was forced to come to me for assistance."

"Poor woman!"

"I acted my part very well, as you must confess. I was grave, cold, indignant, and represented the distressed uncle to perfection. I spoke of the old probity of the Clamerans, and bemoaned that the family honour should be dragged in the dust by a degenerate descendant. For a short time I triumphed at your expense; Madame Fauvel forgot her former prejudice against me, and soon showed that she esteemed and liked me."

"That must have been a long time ago."

Louis paid no attention to this ironical interruption.

"Now we come to the third scene," he went on to say, "the time when Madame Fauvel, having Madeleine for an adviser, judged us at our true value. Oh! you need not flatter yourself that she did not fear and despise us both. If she did not hate you, Raoul, it was because a mother's heart always forgives a sinful child. A mother can despise and worship her son at the same time."

"She has proved it to me in so many touching ways, that!—yes, even I, hardened as I am—was moved, and felt remorse."

"*Parbleu*! I have felt some pangs myself. Where did I leave off? Oh, yes! Madame Fauvel was frightened, and Madeleine, bent on sacrificing herself, had discarded Prosper, and consented to marry me, when the existence of Gaston was suddenly revealed. And what has happened since? You have succeeded in convincing Madame Fauvel that you are pure, and that I am blacker than hell. She is blinded by your noble qualities, and she and Madeleine regard me as your evil genius, whose pernicious influence led you astray."

"You are right, my venerated uncle; that is precisely the position you occupy."

"Very good. Now we come to the fifth act, and our comedy needs entire change of scenery. We must veer around."

"Change our tactics?"

"You think it difficult, I suppose? Nothing easier. Listen attentively, for the future depends upon your skilfulness."

Raoul leaned back in his chair, with folded arms, as if prepared for anything, and said:

"I am ready."

"The first thing for you to do," said Louis, "is to go to Madame Fauvel tomorrow, and tell her the story about my natural brother. She will not believe you, but that makes no difference. The important thing is, for you to appear convinced of the truth of what you tell her."

"Consider me convinced."

"Five days hence, I will call on M. Fauvel, and confirm the notification sent him by my notary at Oloron, that the money deposited in the bank now belongs to me. I will repeat, for his benefit, the story of the natural brother, and ask him to keep the money until I call for it, as I have no occasion for it at present. You, who are so distrustful, my good nephew, may regard this deposit as a guarantee of my sincerity."

"We will talk of that another time. Go on."

"Then I will go to Madame Fauvel, and say, 'Being very poor, my dear *madame*, necessity compelled me to claim your assistance in the support of my brother's son, who is also yours. This youth is worthless and extravagant.'"

"Thanks, my good uncle."

"'He has poisoned your life when he should have added to your happiness; he is a constant anxiety and sorrow to your maternal heart. I have come to offer my regrets for your past trouble, and to assure you that you will have no annoyance in the future. I am now rich, and henceforth take the whole responsibility of Raoul upon myself. I will provide handsomely for him.'"

"Is that what you call a scheme?"

"*Parbleu*, you will soon see whether it is. After listening to this speech, Madame Fauvel will feel inclined to throw herself in my arms, by way of expressing her gratitude and joy. She will refrain, however, on account of her niece. She will ask me to relinquish my claim on Madeleine's hand, now that I am rich. I will roundly tell her, No. I will make this an opportunity for an edifying display of magnanimity and disinterestedness. I will say, 'Madame, you have accused me of cupidity. I am now able to prove your injustice. I have been infatuated, as every man must be, by the beauty, grace, and intelligence of Mademoiselle Madeleine; and—I love her. If she were penniless, my devotion would only be the more ardent. She has been promised to me, and I must insist upon this one article of our agreement. This must be the price of my silence. And, to prove that I am not influenced by her fortune, I give you my sacred promise, that, the day after the wedding, I will send Raoul a stock receipt of twenty-five thousand *livres per annum*."

Louis expressed himself with such convincing candour, that Raoul, an artist in knavery, was charmed and astonished.

"Beautifully done," he cried, clapping his hands with glee. "That last sentence will create a chasm between Madame Fauvel and her niece. The promise of a fortune for me will certainly bring my mother over to our side."

"I hope so," said Louis with pretended modesty. "And I have strong reasons for hoping so, as I shall be able to furnish the good lady with excellent arguments for excusing herself in her own eyes. You know when someone proposes some little—what shall we call it?—transaction to an honest person, it must be accompanied by justifications sufficient to quiet all qualms of conscience. I shall prove to Madame Fauvel and her niece that Prosper has shamefully deceived them. I shall prove to them that he is cramped by debts, dissipated, and a reckless gambler, openly associating with a woman of no character."

"And very pretty, besides, by Jove! You must not neglect to expatiate upon the beauty and fascinations of the adorable Gypsy; that will be your strongest point."

"Don't be alarmed; I shall be more eloquent than a popular divine. Then I will explain to Madame Fauvel that if she really loves her niece, she will persuade her to marry, not an insignificant cashier, but a man of position, a great manufacturer, a *marquis*, and, more than this, one rich enough to establish you in the world."

Raoul was dazzled by this brilliant prospect.

"If you don't decide her, you will make her waver," he said.

"Oh! I don't expect a sudden change. I only intend planting the germ in her mind; thanks to you, it will develop, flourish, and bear fruit."

"Thanks to me?"

"Allow me to finish. After making my speeches I shall disappear from the scene, and your role will commence. Of course your mother will repeat the conversation to you, and then we can judge of the effect produced. But remember, you must scorn to receive any assistance from me. You must swear that you will brave all privation, want, famine even, rather than accept a cent from a base man whom you hate and despise; a man who—But you know exactly what you are to say. I can rely upon you for good acting."

"No one can surpass me when I am interested in my part. In pathetic roles I am always a success, when I have had time to prepare myself."

"I know you are. But this disinterestedness need not prevent you from resuming your dissipations. You must gamble, bet, and lose more money than you ever did before. You must increase your demands, and say that you must have money at all costs. You need not account to me for any money you can extort from her. All you get is your own to spend as you please."

"You don't say so! If you mean that—"

"You will hurry up matters, I'll be bound."

"I can promise you, no time shall be wasted."

"Now listen to what you are to do, Raoul. Before the end of three months, you must have exhausted the resources of these two women. You must force from them every *franc* they can raise, so that they will be wholly unable to procure money to supply your increasing demands. In three months I must find them penniless, absolutely ruined, without even a jewel left."

Raoul was startled at the passionate, vindictive tone of Louis's voice as he uttered these last words.

"You must hate these women, if you are so determined to make them miserable," he said.

"I hate them?" cried Louis. "Can't you see that I madly love Madeleine, love her as only a man of my age can love? Is not her image ever in my mind? Does not the very mention of her name fire my heart, and make me tremble like a school-boy?"

"Your great devotion does not prevent you planning the destruction of her present happiness."

"Necessity compels me to do so. Nothing but the most cruel deceptions and the bitterest suffering would ever induce her to become my wife, to take me as the lesser of two evils. The day on which you have led Madame Fauvel and her niece to the extreme edge of the precipice, pointed out its dark depths, and convinced them that they are irretrievably lost, I shall appear, and rescue them. I will play my part with such grandeur, such lofty magnanimity, that Madeleine will be touched, will forget her past enmity, and regard me with favourable eyes. When she finds that it is her sweet self, and not her money, that I want, she will soften, and in time yield to my entreaties. No true woman can be indifferent to a grand passion. I don't pretend to say that she will love me at first; but, if she will only consent to be mine,

I ask for nothing more; time will do much, even for a poor devil like myself."

Raoul was shocked at this cold-blooded perversity of his uncle; but de Clameran showed his immense superiority in wickedness, and the apprentice admired the master.

"You would certainly succeed, uncle," he said, "were it not for the cashier. Between you and Madeleine, Prosper will always stand; if not in person, certainly in memory."

Louis smiled scornfully, and, throwing away his cigar, which had died out, said:

"I don't mind Prosper, or attach any more importance to him than to that cigar."

"But she loves him."

"So much the worse for him. Six months hence, she will despise him; he is already morally ruined, and at the proper time I will make an end of him socially. Do you know whither the road of dissipation leads, my good nephew? Prosper supports Gypsy, who is extravagant; he gambles, keeps fast horses, and gives suppers. Now, you gamble yourself, and know how much money can be squandered in one night; the losses of *baccarat* must be paid within twenty-four hours. He has lost heavily, must pay, and—has charge of a money-safe."

Raoul protested against this insinuation.

"It is useless to tell me that he is honest, that nothing would induce him to touch money that does not belong to him. I know better. *Parbleu*! I was honest myself until I learned to gamble. Any man with a grain of sense would have married Madeleine long ago, and sent us flying bag and baggage. You say she loves him! No one but a coward would be defrauded of the woman he loved and who loved him. Ah, if I had once felt Madeleine's hand tremble in mine, if her rosy lips had once pressed a kiss upon my brow, the whole world could not take her from me. Woe to him who dared stand in my path! As it is, Prosper annoys me, and I intend to suppress him. With your aid I will so cover him with disgrace and infamy, that Madeleine will drive every thought of him from her mind, and her love will turn to hate."

Louis's tone of rage and vengeance startled Raoul, and made him regard the affair in a worse light than ever.

"You have given me a shameful, dastardly role to play," he said after a long pause.

"My honourable nephew has scruples, I suppose," said de Clameran sneeringly.

"Not exactly scruples; yet I confess—"

"That you want to retreat? Rather too late to sing that tune, my friend. You wish to enjoy every luxury, have your pockets filled with gold, cut a fine figure in high society, and remain virtuous. Are you fool enough to suppose a poor man can be honest? 'Tis a luxury pertaining to the wealthy. Did you ever see people such as we draw money from the pure fount of virtue? We must fish in muddy waters, and then wash ourselves clean, and enjoy the result of our labour."

"I have never been rich enough to be honest," said Raoul humbly; "but I must say it goes hard with me to torture two defenceless, frightened women, and ruin the character of a poor devil who regards me as his best friend. It is a low business!"

This resistance exasperated Louis to the last degree.

"You are the most absurd, ridiculous fool I ever met," he cried. "An opportunity occurs for us to make an immense fortune. All we have to do is to stretch out our hands and take it; when you must needs prove refractory, like a whimpering baby. Nobody but an ass would refuse to drink when he is thirsty, because he sees a little mud at the bottom of the bucket. I suppose you prefer theft on a small scale, stealing by driblets. And where will your system lead you? To the poor-house or the police-station. You prefer living from hand to mouth, supported by Madame Fauvel, having small sums doled out to you to pay your little gambling debts."

"I am neither ambitious nor cruel."

"And suppose Madame Fauvel dies tomorrow: what will become of you? Will you go cringing up to the widower, and implore him to continue your allowance?"

"Enough said," cried Raoul, angrily interrupting his uncle. "I never had any idea of retreating. I made these objections to show you what infamous work you expect of me, and at the same time prove to you that without my assistance you can do nothing."

"I never pretended to the contrary."

"Then, my noble uncle, we might as well settle what my share is to be. Oh! it is not worth while for you to indulge in idle protestations. What will you give me in case of success? and what if we fail?"

"I told you before. I will give you twenty-five thousand *livres* a year, and all you can secure between now and my wedding-day."

"This arrangement suits me very well; but where are your securities?"

This question was discussed a long time before it was satisfactorily settled by the accomplices, who had every reason to distrust each other.

"What are you afraid of?" asked de Clameran.

"Everything," replied Raoul. "Where am I to obtain justice, if you deceive me? From this pretty little poniard? No, thank you. I would be made to pay as dear for your hide, as for that of an honest man."

Finally, after long debate and much recrimination, the matter was arranged, and they shook hands before separating.

Alas! Madame Fauvel and her niece soon felt the evil effects of the understanding between the villains.

Everything happened as Louis had arranged.

Once more, when Madame Fauvel had begun to breathe freely, and to hope that her troubles were over, Raoul's conduct suddenly changed; he became more extravagant and dissipated than ever.

Formerly, Madame Fauvel would have said, "I wonder what he does with all the money I give him?" Now she saw where it went.

Raoul was reckless in his wickedness; he was intimate with actresses, openly lavishing money and jewellery upon them; he drove about with four horses, and bet heavily on every race. Never had he been so exacting and exorbitant in his demands for money; Madame Fauvel had the greatest difficulty in supplying his wants.

He no longer made excuses and apologies for spending so much; instead of coaxingly entreating, he demanded money as a right, threatening to betray Madame Fauvel to her husband if she refused him.

At this rate, all the possessions of Madame Fauvel and Madeleine soon disappeared. In one month, all their money had been squandered. Then they were compelled to resort to the most shameful expedients in the household expenses. They economized in every possible way, making purchases on credit, and making tradesmen wait; then they changed figures in the bills, and even invented accounts of things never bought.

These imaginary costly whims increased so rapidly, that M. Fauvel one day said, as he signed a large check, "Upon my word, ladies, you will buy out all the stores, if you keep on this way. But nothing pleases me better than to see you gratify every wish."

Poor women! For months they had bought nothing, but had lived upon the remains of their former splendour, having all their old dresses made over, to keep up appearances in society.

More clear-sighted than her aunt, Madeleine saw plainly that the day would soon come when everything would have to be explained.

Although she knew that the sacrifices of the present would avail nothing in the future, that all this money was being thrown away without securing her aunt's peace of mind, yet she was silent. A high-minded delicacy made her conceal her apprehensions beneath an assumed calmness.

The fact of her sacrificing herself made her refrain from uttering anything like a complaint or censure. She seemed to forget herself entirely in her efforts to comfort her aunt.

"As soon as Raoul sees we have nothing more to give," she would say, "he will come to his senses, and stop all this extravagance."

The day came when Madame Fauvel and Madeleine found it impossible to give another *franc*.

The evening previous, Madame Fauvel had a dinner-party, and with difficulty scraped together enough money to defray the expenses.

Raoul appeared, and said that he was in the greatest need of money, being forced to pay a debt of two thousand *francs* at once.

In vain they implored him to wait a few days, until they could with propriety ask M. Fauvel for money. He declared that he must have it now, and that he would not leave the house without it.

"But I have no way of getting it for you," said Madame Fauvel desperately; "you have taken everything from me. I have nothing left but my diamonds: do you want them? If they can be of use, take them."

Hardened as the young villain was, he blushed at these words.

He felt pity for this unfortunate woman, who had always been so kind and indulgent to him, who had so often lavished upon him her maternal caresses. He felt for the noble girl who was the innocent victim of a vile plot.

But he was bound by an oath; he knew that a powerful hand would save these women at the brink of the precipice. More than this, he saw an immense fortune at the end of his road of crime, and quieted his conscience by saying that he would redeem his present cruelty by honest kindness in the future. Once out of the clutches of de Clameran, he would be a better man, and try to return some of the kind affection shown him by these poor women.

Stifling his better impulses, he said harshly to Madame Fauvel, "Give me the jewels; I will take them to the pawnbroker's." Madame Fauvel handed him a box containing a set of diamonds. It was a present from her husband the day he became worth a million.

And so pressing was the want of these women who were surrounded by princely luxury, with their ten servants, beautiful blooded horses, and jewels which were the admiration of Paris, that they implored him to bring them some of the money which he would procure on the diamonds, to meet their daily wants.

He promised, and kept his word.

But they had revealed a new source, a mine to be worked; he took advantage of it.

One by one, all Madame Fauvel's jewels followed the way of the diamonds; and, when hers were all gone, those of Madeleine were given up.

A recent law-suit, which showed how a young and beautiful woman had been kept in a state of terror and almost poverty, by a rascal who had possession of her letters, a sad case which no honest man could read without blushing for his sex, has revealed to what depths human infamy can descend.

And such abominable crimes are not so rare as people suppose.

How many men are supported entirely by stolen secrets, from the coachman who claims ten *louis* every month of the foolish girl whom he drove to a rendezvous, to the elegant dandy in light kids, who discovered a financial swindle, and makes the parties interested buy his silence, cannot be known.

This is called the extortion of hush-money, the most cowardly and infamous of crimes, which the law, unfortunately, can rarely overtake and punish.

"Extortion of hush-money," said an old prefect of police, "is a trade which supports at least a thousand scamps in Paris alone. Sometimes we know the black-mailer and his victim, and yet we can do nothing. Moreover, if we were to catch the villain in the very act, and hand him over to justice, the victim, in her fright at the chance of her secret being discovered, would turn against us."

It is true, extortion has become a business. Very often it is the business of loafers, who spend plenty of money, when everyone knows they have no visible means of support, and of whom people ask, "What do they live upon?"

The poor victims do not know how easy it would be to rid themselves of their tyrants. The police are fully capable of faithfully keeping secrets confided to them. A visit to the Rue de Jerusalem, a confidential communication with a head of the bureau, who is as silent as a father confessor, and the affair is arranged, without noise, without publicity, without anyone ever being the wiser. There are traps for "master extortioners," which work well in the hands of the police.

Madame Fauvel had no defence against the scoundrels who were torturing her, save prayers and tears; these availed her little.

Sometimes Madame Fauvel betrayed such heart-broken suffering when Raoul begged her for money which she had no means of obtaining, that he would hurry away disgusted at his own brutal conduct, and say to de Clameran:

"You must end this dirty business; I cannot stand it any longer. I will blow any man's brains out, or fight a crowd of cut-throats, if you choose; but as to killing by agony and fright these two poor miserable women, whom I am really fond of, I am not going to do it. You ask for more than I can do. I am not quite the cowardly hound you take me for."

De Clameran paid no attention to these remonstrances: indeed, he was prepared for them.

"It is not pleasant, I know," he replied; "but necessity knows no law. Have a little more perseverance and patience; we have almost got to the end."

The end was nearer than de Clameran supposed. Toward the latter part of November, Madame Fauvel saw that it was impossible to postpone the catastrophe any longer, and as a last effort determined to apply to the *marquis* for assistance.

She had not seen him since his return from Oloron, except once, when he came to announce his accession to wealth. At that time, persuaded that he was the evil genius of Raoul, she had received him very coldly, and did not invite him to repeat his visit.

She hesitated about speaking to her niece of the step she intended taking, because she feared violent opposition.

To her great surprise Madeleine warmly approved of it.

Trouble had made her keen-sighted and suspicious. Reflecting on past events, comparing and weighing every act and speech of Raoul, she was now convinced that he was de Clameran's tool.

She thought that Raoul was too shrewd to be acting in this shameful way, ruinously to his own interests, if there were not some secret motive at the bottom of it all. She saw that this persecution was more feigned than real.

So thoroughly was she convinced of this, that, had it only concerned herself alone, she would have firmly resisted the oppression, certain that the threatened exposure would never take place.

Recalling, with a shudder, certain looks of de Clameran, she guessed the truth, that the object of all this underhand work was to force her to become his wife.

Determined on making the sacrifice, in spite of her repugnance toward the man, she wished to have the deed done at once; anything was preferable to this terrible anxiety, to the life of torture which Raoul made her lead. She felt that her courage might fail if she waited and suffered much longer.

"The sooner you see M. de Clameran the better for us, aunt," she said, after talking the project over.

The next day Madame Fauvel called on the *marquis* at the Hotel du Louvre, having sent him a note announcing her intended visit.

He received her with cold, studied politeness, like a man who had been misunderstood and had been unjustly wounded.

After listening to her report of Raoul's scandalous behaviour, he became very indignant, and swore that he would soon make him repent of his heartlessness.

But when Madame Fauvel told of the immense sums of money forced from her, de Clameran seemed confounded, as if he could not believe it.

"The worthless rascal!" he exclaimed, "the idea of his audacity! Why, during the last four months, I have given him more than twenty thousand *francs*, which I would not have done except to prevent him from applying to you, as he constantly threatened to do."

Seeing an expression of doubtful surprise upon Madame Fauvel's face, Louis arose, and took from his desk some receipts signed by Raoul. The total amount was twenty-three thousand five hundred *francs*.

Madame Fauvel was shocked and amazed.

"He has obtained forty thousand *francs* from me," she faintly said, "so that altogether he has spent sixty thousand *francs* in four months."

"I can't imagine what he does with it," said de Clameran, "unless he spends it on actresses."

"Good heavens! what can these creatures do with all the money lavished on them?"

"That is a question I cannot answer, *madame*."

He appeared to pity Madame Fauvel sincerely; he promised that he would at once see Raoul, and reason with him about the shameful life he was leading; perhaps he could be persuaded to reform. Finally, after many protestations of friendship, he wound up by placing his fortune at her disposal.

Although Madame Fauvel refused his offer, she appreciated the kindness of it, and on returning home said to Madeleine:

"Perhaps we have mistaken his character; he may be a good man after all."

Madeleine sadly shook her head. She had anticipated just what happened. De Clameran's magnanimity and generosity confirmed her presentiments.

Raoul came to see his uncle, and found him radiant.

"Everything is going on swimmingly, my smart nephew," said de Clameran; "your receipts acted like a charm. Ah, you are a partner worth having. I congratulate you upon your success. Forty thousand *francs* in four months!"

"Yes," said Raoul carelessly. "I got about that much from pawnbrokers."

"Pests! Then you must have a nice little sum laid by."

"That is my business, uncle, and not yours. Remember our agreement. I will tell you this much: Madame Fauvel and Madeleine have turned everything they could into money; they have nothing left, and I have had enough of my role."

"Your role is ended. I forbid you to hereafter ask for a single *centime*."

"What are you about to do? What has happened?"

"The mine is loaded, nephew, and I am awaiting an opportunity to set fire to it."

Louis de Clameran relied upon making his rival, Prosper Bertomy, furnish him this ardently desired opportunity.

He loved Madeleine too passionately to feel aught save the bitterest hate toward the man whom she had freely chosen, and who still possessed her heart.

De Clameran knew that he could marry her at once if he chose; but in what way? By holding a sword of terror over her head, and forcing her to be his. He became frenzied at the idea of possessing her person, while her heart and soul would always be with Prosper.

Thus he swore that, before marrying, he would so cover Prosper with shame and ignominy that no honest person would speak to him. He had first thought of killing him, but, fearing that Madeleine would enshrine and worship his memory, he determined to disgrace him.

He imagined that there would be no difficulty in ruining the unfortunate young man. He soon found himself mistaken.

Though Prosper led a life of reckless dissipation, he preserved order in his disorder. If in a state of miserable entanglement, and obliged to resort to all sorts of make-shifts to escape his creditors, his caution prevented the world from knowing it.

Vainly did Raoul, with his pockets full of gold, try to tempt him to play high; every effort to hasten his ruin failed.

When he played he did not seem to care whether he lost or won; nothing aroused him from his cold indifference.

His friend Nina Gypsy was extravagant, but her devotion to Prosper restrained her from going beyond certain limits.

Raoul's great intimacy with Prosper enabled him to fully understand the state of his mind; that he was trying to drown his disappointment in excitement, but had not given up all hope.

"You need not hope to beguile Prosper into committing any piece of folly," said Raoul to his uncle; "his head is as cool as a usurer's. He never goes beyond a certain degree of dissipation. What object he has in view I know not. Perhaps, when he has spent his last *napoleon*, he will blow his brains out; he certainly never will descend to any dishonourable act. As to tampering with the money-safe entrusted to his keeping—"

"We must force him on," replied de Clameran, "lead him into extravagances, make Gypsy call on him for costly finery, lend him plenty of money."

Raoul shook his head, as if convinced that his efforts would be vain.

"You don't know Prosper, uncle: we can't galvanise a dead man. Madeleine killed him the day she discarded him. He takes no interest in anything on the face of the earth."

"We can wait and see."

They did wait; and, to the great surprise of Madame Fauvel, Raoul once more became an affectionate and dutiful son, as he had been during de Clameran's absence. From reckless extravagance he changed to great economy. Under pretext of saving money, he remained at Vesinet, although it was very uncomfortable and disagreeable there in the winter. He said he wished to expiate his sins in solitude. The truth was, that, by remaining in the country, he insured his liberty, and escaped his mother's visits.

It was about this time that Madame Fauvel, charmed with the improvement in Raoul, asked her husband to give him some employment.

M. Fauvel was delighted to please his wife, and at once offered Raoul the place of corresponding clerk with a salary of five hundred *francs* a month.

The appointment pleased Raoul; but, in obedience to de Clameran's command, he refused it, saying his vocation was not banking.

This refusal so provoked the banker, that he told Raoul, if he was so idle and lazy, not to call on him for money again, or expect him to do anything to assist him. Raoul seized this pretext for ostensibly ceasing his visits.

When he wanted to see his mother, he would come in the afternoon, when he knew that M. Fauvel would be from home; and he only came often enough to keep informed of what was going on in the household.

This sudden lull after so many storms appeared ominous to Madeleine. She was more certain that ever that the plot was now ripe, and would suddenly burst upon them, without warning. She did not impart her presentiment to her aunt, but prepared herself for the worst.

"What can they be doing?" Madame Fauvel would say; "can they have ceased to persecute us?"

"Yes: what can they be doing?" Madeleine would murmur.

Louis and Raoul gave no signs of life, because, like expert hunters, they were silently hiding, and watching for a favourable opportunity of pouncing upon their victims.

Never losing sight of Prosper for a day, Raoul had exhausted every effort of his fertile mind to compromise his honour, to ensnare him into some inextricable entanglement. But, as he had foreseen, the cashier's indifference offered little hope of success.

De Clameran began to grow impatient at this delay, and had fully determined to bring matters to a crisis himself, when one morning, about three o'clock, he was aroused by Raoul.

He knew that some event of great importance must have happened, to make his nephew come to his house at this hour of the morning.

"What is the matter?" he anxiously inquired.

"Perhaps nothing; perhaps everything. I have just left Prosper."

"Well?"

"I had him, Madame Gypsy, and three other friends to dine with me. After dinner, I made up a game of *baccarat*, but Prosper took no interest in it, although he was quite tipsy."

"You must be drunk yourself to come here waking me up in the middle of the night, to hear this idle gabble," said Louis angrily. "What the devil do you mean by it?"

"Now, don't be in a hurry; wait until you hear the rest."

"*Morbleu*! speak, then!"

"After the game was over, we went to supper; Prosper became intoxicated, and betrayed the secret name with which he closes the money-safe."

At these words de Clameran uttered a cry of triumph.

"What was the word?"

"The name of his friend."

"Gypsy! Yes, that would be five letters."

Louis was so excited that he jumped out of bed, slipped on his dressing-gown, and began to stride up and down the chamber.

"Now we have got him!" he said with vindictive satisfaction. "There's no chance of escape for him now! Ah, the virtuous cashier won't touch the money confided to him: so we must touch it for him. The disgrace will be just as great, no matter who opens the safe. We have the word; you know where the key is kept."

"Yes; when M. Fauvel goes out he always leaves the key in the drawer of his secretary, in his chamber."

"Very good. Go and get this key from Madame Fauvel. If she does not give it up willingly, use force: so that you get it, that is the point; then open the safe, and take out every *franc* it contains. Ah, Master Bertomy, you shall pay dear for being loved by the woman whom I love!"

For five minutes de Clameran indulged in such a tirade of abuse against Prosper, mingled with rhapsodies of love for Madeleine, that Raoul thought him almost out of his mind.

"Before crying victory," he said, "you had better consider the drawbacks and difficulties. Prosper might change the word tomorrow."

"Yes, he might; but it is not probable he will; he will forget what he said while drunk; besides, we can hasten matters."

"That is not all. M. Fauvel has given orders that no large sum shall be kept in the safe overnight; before closing the bank everything is sent to the Bank of France."

"A large sum will be kept there the night I choose."

"You think so?"

"I think this: I have a hundred thousand crowns deposited with M. Fauvel: and if I desire the money to be paid over to me early some morning, directly the bank is opened, of course the money will be kept in the safe the previous night."

"A splendid idea!" cried Raoul admiringly.

It was a good idea; and the plotters spent several hours in studying its strong and weak points.

Raoul feared that he would never be able to overcome Madame Fauvel's resistance. And, even if she yielded the key, would she not go directly and confess everything to her husband? She was fond of Prosper, and would hesitate a long time before sacrificing him.

But Louis felt no uneasiness on this score.

"One sacrifice necessitates another," he said: "she has made too many to draw back at the last one. She sacrificed her adopted daughter; therefore she will sacrifice a young man, who is, after all, a comparative stranger to her."

"But *madame* will never believe any harm of Prosper; she will always have faith in his honour; therefore—"

"You talk like an idiot, my verdant nephew!"

Before the conversation had ended, the plan seemed feasible. The scoundrels made all their arrangements, and fixed the day for committing the crime.

They selected the evening of the 7th of February, because Raoul knew that M. Fauvel would be at a bank-director's dinner, and Madeleine was invited to a party on that evening.

Unless something unforeseen should occur, Raoul knew that he would find Madame Fauvel alone at half-past eight o'clock.

"I will ask M. Fauvel this very day," said de Clameran, "to have my money on hand for Tuesday."

"That is a very short notice, uncle," objected Raoul. "You know there are certain forms to be gone through, and he can claim a longer time wherein to pay it over."

"That is true, but our banker is proud of always being prepared to pay any amount of money, no matter how large; and if I say I am pressed, and would like to be accommodated on Tuesday, he will make a point of having it ready for me. Now, you must ask Prosper, as a personal favour to you, to have the money on hand at the opening of the bank."

Raoul once more examined the situation, to discover if possible a grain of sand which might be converted into a mountain at the last moment.

"Prosper and Gypsy are to be at Vesinet this evening," he said, "but I cannot ask them anything until I know the banker's answer. As soon as you arrange matters with him, send me word by Manuel."

"I can't send Manuel, for an excellent reason; he has left me; but I can send another messenger."

Louis spoke the truth; Manuel was gone. He had insisted on keeping Gaston's old servant in his service, because he thought it imprudent to leave him at Oloron, where his gossiping might cause trouble.

He soon became annoyed by Manuel's loyalty, who had shared the perils and good fortunes of an excellent master for many years; and determined to rid himself of this last link which constantly reminded him of Gaston. The evening before, he had persuaded Manuel to return to Arenys-de-mer, a little port of Catalonia, his native place; and Louis was looking for another servant.

After breakfasting together, they separated.

De Clameran was so elated by the prospect of success, that he lost sight of the great crime intervening. Raoul was calm, but resolute. The shameful deed he was about to commit would give him riches, and release him from a hateful servitude. His one thought was liberty, as Louis's was Madeleine.

Everything seemed to progress finely. The banker did not ask for the notice of time, but promised to pay the money at the specified hour. Prosper said he would have it ready early in the morning.

The certainty of success made Louis almost wild with joy. He counted the hours, and the minutes, which passed but too slowly.

"When this affair is ended," he said to Raoul, "I will reform and be a model of virtue. No one will dare hint that I have ever indulged in any sins, great or small."

But Raoul became more and more sad as the time approached. Reflection gradually betrayed the blackness of the contemplated crime.

Raoul was bold and determined in the pursuit of his own gratifications and wickedness; he could smile in the face of his best friend, while cheating him of his last *napoleon* at cards; and he could sleep well after stabbing his enemy in the heart; but he was young.

He was young in sin. Vice had not yet penetrated to his marrow-bones: corruption had not yet crowded into his soul enough to uproot and destroy every generous sentiment.

It had not been so very long since he had cherished a few holy beliefs. The good intentions of his boyhood were not quite obliterated from his sometimes reproachful memory.

Possessing the daring courage natural to youth, he despised the cowardly part forced upon him; this dark plot, laid for the destruction of two helpless women, filled him with horror and disgust. His heart revolted at the idea of acting the part of Judas toward his mother to betray her between two kisses.

Disgusted by the cool villainy of Louis, he longed for some unexpected danger to spring up, some great peril to be braved, so as to excuse himself in his own eyes, to give him the spirit to carry through the scheme; for he would like to reap the benefits without doing the revolting work.

But no; he well knew that he ran no risk, not even that of being arrested and sent to the galleys. For he was certain that, if M. Fauvel discovered everything, he would do his best to hush it up, to conceal every fact connected with the disgraceful story which would implicate his wife. Although he was careful not to breathe it to de Clameran, he felt a sincere affection for Madame Fauvel, and was touched by the indulgent fondness which she so unchangingly lavished upon him. He had been happy at Vesinet, while his accomplice, or rather his master, was at Oloron. He would have been glad to lead an honest life, and could not see the sense of committing a crime when there was no necessity for it. He hated de Clameran for not consenting to let the matter drop, now that he was rich enough to live in affluence the rest of his life, and who, for the sake of gratifying a selfish passion, was abusing his power, and endangering the safety and happiness of so many people. He longed for an opportunity of thwarting his plots, if it could be done without also ruining himself.

His resolution, which had been so firm in the beginning, was growing weaker and weaker as the hours rolled on: as the crisis approached, his horror of the deed increased.

Seeing this uncertain state of Raoul's mind, Louis never left him, but continued to paint for him a dazzling future, position, wealth, and freedom. Possessing a large fortune, he would be his own master, gratify his every wish, and make amends to his mother for his present undutiful conduct. He urged him to take pride in acting his part in this little comedy, which would soon be over without doing harm to anyone.

He prepared, and forced his accomplice to rehearse, the scene which was to be enacted at Madame Fauvel's, with as much coolness and precision as if it were to be performed at a public theatre. Louis said that no piece could be well acted unless the actor was interested and imbued with the spirit of his role.

But the more urgently Louis pressed upon him the advantages to be derived from success, the oftener he sounded in his ears the magic words, "five hundred thousand *francs*," the more loudly did Raoul's conscience cry out against the sinful deed.

On Monday evening, about six o'clock, Raoul felt so depressed and miserable, that he had almost made up his mind to refuse to move another step, and to tell Louis that he must find another tool to carry out his abominable plot.

"Are you afraid?" asked de Clameran, who had anxiously watched these inward struggles.

"Yes, I am afraid. I am not cursed with your ferocious nature and iron will. I am the most miserable dog living!"

"Come, cheer up, my boy! You are not yourself today. Don't fail me at the last minute, when everything depends upon you. Just think that we have almost finished; one more stroke of our oars, and we are in port. You are only nervous: come to dinner, and a bottle of Burgundy will soon set you right."

They were walking along the boulevard. De Clameran insisted upon their entering a restaurant, and having dinner in a private room.

Vainly did he strive, however, to chase the gloom from Raoul's pale face; he sat listening, with a sullen frown, to his friend's jests about "swallowing the bitter pill gracefully."

Urged by Louis, he drank two bottles of wine, in hopes that intoxication would inspire him with courage to do the deed, which de Clameran impressed upon his mind must and should be done before many more hours had passed over his head.

But the drunkenness he sought came not; the wine proved false; at the bottom of the last bottle he found disgust and rage.

The clock struck eight.

"The time has come," said Louis firmly.

Raoul turned livid; his teeth chattered, and his limbs trembled so that he was unable to stand on his feet.

"Oh, I cannot do it!" he cried in an agony of terror and rage.

De Clameran's eyes flashed with angry excitement at the prospect of all his plans being ruined at the last moment. But he dared not give way to his anger, for fear of exasperating Raoul, whom he knew to be anxious for an excuse to quarrel; so he quietly pulled the bell-rope. A boy appeared.

"A bottle of port," he said, "and a bottle of rum."

When the boy returned with the bottles, Louis filled a goblet with the two liquors mixed, and handed it to Raoul.

"Drink this," he said in a tone of command.

Raoul emptied the glass at one draught, and a faint colour returned to his ashy cheeks. He arose, and snatching up his hat, cried fiercely:

"Come along!"

But before he had walked half a square, the factitious energy inspired by drink deserted him.

He clung to de Clameran's arm, and was almost dragged along in the direction of the banker's house, trembling like a criminal on his way to the scaffold.

"If I can once get him in the house," thought Louis, "and make him begin, the excitement of his mother's opposition will make him carry it through successfully. The cowardly baby! I would like to wring his neck!"

Although his breast was filled with these thoughts and fears, he was careful to conceal them from Raoul, and said soothingly:

"Now, don't forget our arrangement, and be careful how you enter the house; everything depends upon your being unconcerned and cool, to avoid arousing suspicion in the eyes of anyone you may meet. Have you a pistol in your pocket?"

"Yes, yes! Let me alone!"

It was well that de Clameran had accompanied Raoul; for, when he got in sight of the door, his courage gave way, and he longed to retreat.

"A poor, helpless woman!" he groaned, "and an honest man who pressed my hand in friendship yesterday, to be cowardly ruined, betrayed by me! Ah, it is too base! I cannot!"

"Come, don't be a coward! I thought you had more nerve. Why, you might as well have remained virtuous and honest; you will never earn your salt in this sort of business."

Raoul overcame his weakness, and, silencing the clamours of his conscience, rushed up the steps, and pulled the bell furiously.

"Is Madame Fauvel at home?" he inquired of the servant who opened the door.

"Madame is alone in the sitting-room adjoining her chamber," was the reply.

And Raoul went upstairs.

Chapter 20

De Clameran's last injunction to Raoul was:

"Be very cautious how you enter the room; your appearance must tell everything, so you can avoid impossible explanations."

The recommendation was useless.

The instant that Raoul went into the little salon, the sight of his pale, haggard face and wild eyes caused Madame Fauvel to spring up with clasped hands, and cry out:

"Raoul! What has happened? Speak, my son!"

The sound of her tender, affectionate voice acted like an electric shock upon the young bandit. He shook like a leaf. But at the same time his mind seemed to change. Louis was not mistaken in his estimate of his companion's character. Raoul was on the stage, his part was to be played; his assurance returned to him; his cheating, lying nature assumed the ascendant, and stifled any better feeling in his heart.

"This misfortune is the last I shall ever suffer, mother!"

Madame Fauvel rushed toward him, and, seizing his hand, gazed searchingly into his eyes, as if to read his very soul.

"What is the matter? Raoul, my dear son, do tell me what troubles you."

He gently pushed her from him.

"The matter is, my mother," he said in a voice of heart-broken despair, "that I am an unworthy, degenerate son! Unworthy of you, unworthy of my noble father!"

She tried to comfort him by saying that his errors were all her fault, and that he was, in spite of all, the pride of her heart.

"Alas!" he said, "I know and judge myself. No one can reproach me for my infamous conduct more bitterly than does my own conscience. I am not naturally wicked, but only a miserable fool. At times I am like an insane man, and am not responsible for my actions. Ah, my dear mother, I would not be what I am, if you had watched over my childhood. But brought up among strangers, with no guide but my own evil passions, nothing to restrain me, no one to advise me, no one to love me, owning nothing, not even my stolen name, I am cursed with vanity and unbounded ambition. Poor, with no one to assist me but you, I have the tastes and vices of a millionaire's son.

"Alas for me! When I found you, the evil was done. Your affection, your maternal love, the only true happiness of my life, could not save me. I, who had suffered so much, endured so many privations, even the pangs of hunger, became spoiled by this new life of luxury and pleasure which you opened before me. I rushed headlong into extravagance, as a drunkard long deprived of liquor seizes and drains to the dregs the first bottle in his reach."

Madame Fauvel listened, silent and terrified, to these words of despair and remorse, which Raoul uttered with vehemence.

She dared not interrupt him, but felt certain some dreadful piece of news was coming.

Raoul continued in a sad, hopeless tone:

"Yes, I have been a weak fool. Happiness was within my reach, and I had not the sense to stretch forth my hand and grab it. I rejected a heavenly reality to eagerly pursue a vain phantom. I, who ought to have spent my life at your feet, and daily striven to express my gratitude for your lavish kindness, have made you unhappy, destroyed your peace of mind, and, instead of being a blessing, I have been a curse ever since the first fatal day you welcomed me to your kind heart. Ah, unfeeling brute that I was, to squander upon creatures whom I despised, a fortune, of which each gold piece must have cost you a tear! Too late, too late! With you I might have been a good and happy man!"

He stopped, as if overcome by the conviction of his evil deeds, and seemed about to burst into tears.

"It is never too late to repent, my son," murmured Madame Fauvel in comforting tones.

"Ah, if I only could!" cried Raoul; "but no, it is too late! Besides, can I tell how long my good resolutions will last? This is not the first time that I have condemned myself pitilessly. Stinging remorse for each new fault made me swear to lead a better life, to sin no more. What was the result of these periodical repentances? At the first temptation I forgot my remorse and good resolutions. I am weak and mean-spirited, and you are not firm enough to govern my vacillating nature. While my intentions are good, my actions are villainous. The disproportion between my extravagant desires, and the means of gratifying them, is too great for me to endure any longer. Who knows to what fearful lengths my unfortunate disposition may lead me? However, I will take my fate in my own hands!" he finally said with a reckless laugh.

"Oh, Raoul, my dear son," cried Madame Fauvel in an agony of terror, "explain these dreadful words; am I not your mother? Tell me what distresses you; I am ready to hear the worst."

He appeared to hesitate, as if afraid to crush his mother's heart by the terrible blow he was about to inflict. Then in a voice of gloomy despair he replied:

"I am ruined."

"Ruined?"

"Yes, ruined; and I have nothing more to expect or hope for. I am dishonoured, and all through my own fault; no one is to be blamed but myself."

"Raoul!"

"It is the sad truth, my poor mother; but fear nothing: I shall not trail in the dust the name which you bestowed upon me. I will at least have the courage not to survive my dishonour. Come, mother, don't pity me, or distress yourself; I am one of those miserable beings fated to find no peace save in the arms of death. I came into the world with misfortune stamped upon my brow. Was not my birth a shame and disgrace to you? Did not the memory of my existence haunt you day and night, filling your soul with remorse? And now, when I am restored to you after many years' separation, do I not prove to be a bitter curse instead of a blessing?"

"Ungrateful boy! Have I ever reproached you?"

"Never! Your poor Raoul will die with your beloved name on his lips; his last words a prayer to Heaven to heap blessings upon your head, and reward your long-suffering devotion."

"Die? You die, my son!"

"It must be, my dear mother; honour compels it. I am condemned by judges from whose decision no appeal can be taken—my conscience and my will."

An hour ago, Madame Fauvel would have sworn that Raoul had made her suffer all the torments that a woman could endure; but now she felt that all her former troubles were nothing compared with her present agony.

"My God! Raoul, what have you been doing?"

"Money was entrusted to me: I gambled and lost it."

"Was it a large sum?"

"No; but more than I can replace. My poor mother, have I not taken everything from you? Did you not give me your last jewel?"

"But M. de Clameran is rich. He placed his fortune at my disposal. I will order the carriage, and go to him."

"But M. de Clameran is absent, and will not return to Paris until next week; and if I do not have the money this evening, I am lost. Alas! I have thought deeply, and, although it is hard to die so young, still fate wills it so."

He pulled a pistol from his pocket, and, with a forced smile, said:

"This will settle everything."

Madame Fauvel was too excited and frightened to reflect upon the horror of Raoul's behaviour, and that these wild threats were a last resort for obtaining money. Forgetful of the past, careless of the future, her every thought concentrated upon the present, she comprehended but one fact: that her son was about to commit suicide, and that she was powerless to prevent the fearful deed.

"Oh, wait a little while my son!" she cried. "Andre will soon return home, and I will ask him to give me—How much did you lose?"

"Thirty thousand *francs*."

"You shall have them tomorrow."

"But I must have the money tonight."

Madame Fauvel wrung her hands in despair.

"Oh! why did you not come to me sooner, my son? Why did you not have confidence enough in me to come at once for help? This evening! There is no one in the house to open the money-safe; if it were not for that—if you had only come before Andre went out—"

"The safe!" cried Raoul, with sudden joy, as if this magic word had thrown a ray of light upon his dark despair; "do you know where the key is kept?"

"Yes: it is in the next room."

"Well!" he exclaimed, with a bold look that caused Madame Fauvel to lower her eyes, and keep silent.

"Give me the key, mother," he said in a tone of entreaty.

"Oh, Raoul, Raoul!"

"It is my life I am asking of you."

These words decided her; she snatched up a candle, rushed into her chamber, opened the secretary, and took out M. Fauvel's key.

But, when about to hand it to Raoul, she seemed to suddenly see the enormity of what she was doing.

"Oh, Raoul! my son," she murmured, "I cannot! Do not ask me to commit such a dreadful deed!"

He said nothing, but sadly turned to leave the room; then coming back to his mother said:

"Ah, well; it makes but little difference in the end! At least, you will give me one last kiss, before we part forever, my darling mother!"

"What could you do with the key, Raoul?" interrupted Madame Fauvel. "You do not know the secret word of the buttons."

"No; but I can try to open it without moving the buttons."

"You know that money is never kept in the safe over-night."

"Nevertheless, I can make the attempt. If I open the safe, and find money in it, it will be a miracle, showing that Heaven has pitied my misfortune, and provided relief."

"And if you are not successful, will you promise me to wait until tomorrow, to do nothing rash tonight?"

"I swear it, by my father's memory."

"Then take the key and follow me."

Pale and trembling, Raoul and Madame Fauvel passed through the banker's study, and down the narrow staircase leading to the offices and cash-room below.

Raoul walked in front, holding the light, and the key of the safe.

Madame Fauvel was convinced that it would be utterly impossible to open the safe, as the key was useless without the secret word, and of course Raoul had no way of discovering what that was.

Even granting that some chance had revealed the secret to him, he would find but little in the safe, since everything was deposited in the Bank of France. Everyone knew that no large sum was ever kept in the safe after banking hours.

The only anxiety she felt was, how Raoul would bear the disappointment, and how she could calm his despair.

She thought that she would gain time by letting Raoul try the key; and then, when he could not open the safe, he would keep his promise, and wait until the next day. There was surely no harm in letting him try the lock, when he could not touch the money.

"When he sees there is no chance of success," she thought, "he will listen to my entreaties; and tomorrow—tomorrow—"

What she could do tomorrow she knew not, she did not even ask herself. But in extreme situations the least delay inspires hope, as if a short respite meant sure salvation.

The condemned man, at the last moment, begs for a reprieve of a day, an hour, a few seconds. Raoul was about to kill himself: his mother prayed to God to grant her one day, not even a day, one night; as if in this space of time some unexpected relief would come to end her misery.

They reached Prosper's office, and Raoul placed the light on a high stool so that it lighted the whole room.

He then summoned up all his coolness, or rather that mechanical precision of movement, almost independent of will, of which men accustomed to peril avail themselves in time of need.

Rapidly, with the dexterity of experience, he slipped the buttons on the five letters composing the name of G, y, p, s, y.

His features, during this short operation, expressed the most intense anxiety. He was fearful that his nervous energy might give out; of not being able to open the safe; of not finding the money there when he opened it; of Prosper having changed the word; or perhaps having neglected to leave the money in the safe.

Madame Fauvel saw these visible apprehensions with alarm. She read in his eyes that wild hope of a man who, passionately desiring an object, ends by persuading himself that his own will suffices to overcome all obstacles.

Having often been present when Prosper was preparing to leave his office, Raoul had fifty times seen him move the buttons, and lock the safe, just before leaving the bank. Indeed, having a practical turn of mind, and an eye to the future, he had even tried to lock the safe himself on several occasions, while waiting for Prosper. He inserted the key softly, turned it around, pushed it farther in, and turned it a second time; then thrust it in suddenly, and turned it again. His heart beat so loudly that Madame Fauvel could hear its throbs.

The word had not been changed; the safe opened.

Raoul and his mother simultaneously uttered a cry; she of terror, he of triumph.

"Shut it again!" cried Madame Fauvel, frightened at the incomprehensible result of Raoul's attempt: "Come away! Don't touch anything, for Heaven's sake! Raoul!"

And, half frenzied, she clung to Raoul's arm, and pulled him away so abruptly, that the key was dragged from the lock, and, slipping along the glossy varnish of the safe-door, made a deep scratch some inches long.

But at a glance Raoul discovered, on the upper shelf of the safe, three bundles of bank-notes. He snatched them up with his left hand, and slipped them inside his vest.

Exhausted by the effort she had just made, Madame Fauvel dropped Raoul's arm, and, almost fainting with emotion, clung to the back of a chair.

"Have mercy, Raoul!" she moaned. "I implore you to put back that money and I solemnly swear that I will give you twice as much tomorrow. Oh, my son, have pity upon your unhappy mother!"

He paid no attention to these words of entreaty, but carefully examined the scratch on the safe. He was alarmed at this trace of the robbery, which it was impossible for him to cover up.

"At least you will not take all," said Madame Fauvel; "just keep enough to save yourself, and put back the rest."

"What good would that do? The discovery will be made that the safe has been opened; so I might as well take all as a part."

"Oh, no! not at all. I can account to Andre; I will tell him I had a pressing need for a certain sum, and opened the safe to get it."

In the meantime Raoul had carefully closed the safe.

"Come, mother, let us go back to the sitting-room. A servant might go there to look for you, and be astonished at our absence."

Raoul's cruel indifference and cold calculations at such a moment filled Madame Fauvel with indignation. She saw that she had no influence over her son, that her prayers and tears had no effect upon his hard heart.

"Let them be astonished," she cried: "let them come here and find us! I will be relieved to put an end to this tissue of crime. Then Andre will know all, and drive me from his house. Let come what will, I shall not sacrifice another victim. Prosper will be accused of this theft tomorrow. De Clameran defrauded him of the woman he loved, and now you would deprive him of his honour! I will have nothing to do with so base a crime."

She spoke so loud and angrily that Raoul was alarmed. He knew that the errand-boy slept in a room close by, and might be in bed listening to her, although it was early in the evening.

"Come upstairs!" he said, seizing Madame Fauvel's arm.

But she clung to a table and refused to move a step.

"I have been cowardly enough to sacrifice Madeleine," she said, "but I will not ruin Prosper."

Raoul had an argument in reserve which he knew would make Madame Fauvel submit to his will.

"Now, really," he said with a cynical laugh, "do you pretend that you do not know Prosper and I arranged this little affair together, and that he is to have half the booty?"

"Impossible! I never will believe such a thing of Prosper!"

"Why, how do you suppose I discovered the secret word? Who do you suppose disobeyed orders, and left the money in the safe?"

"Prosper is honest."

"Of course he is, and so am I too. The only thing is, that we both need money."

"You are telling a falsehood, Raoul!"

"Upon my soul, I am not. Madeleine rejected Prosper, and the poor fellow has to console himself for her cruelty; and these sorts of consolations are expensive, my good mother."

He took up the candle, and gently but firmly led Madame Fauvel toward the staircase.

She mechanically suffered herself to be led along, more bewildered by what she had just heard than she was at the opening of the safe-door.

"What!" she gasped, "can Prosper be a thief?"

She began to think herself the victim of a terrible nightmare, and that, when she waked, her mind would be relieved of this intolerable torture. She helplessly clung to Raoul's arm as he helped her up the narrow little staircase.

"You must put the key back in the secretary," said Raoul, as soon as they were in the chamber again.

But she did not seem to hear him; so he went and replaced the safe-key in the place from which he had seen her take it.

He then led, or rather carried, Madame Fauvel into the little sitting-room, and placed her in an easy-chair.

The set, expressionless look of the wretched woman's eyes, and her dazed manner, frightened Raoul, who thought that she had lost her mind, that her reason had finally given way beneath this last terrible shock.

"Come, cheer up, my dear mother," he said in coaxing tones as he rubbed her icy hands; "you have saved my life, and rendered an immense service to Prosper. Don't be alarmed; everything will come out right in the end. Prosper will be accused, perhaps arrested; he expects that, and is prepared for it; he will deny his culpability; and, as there is no proof against him, he will be set at liberty immediately."

But these falsehoods were wasted on Madame Fauvel, who was incapable of understanding anything said to her.

"Raoul," she moaned in a broken-hearted tone, "Raoul, my son, you have killed me."

Her gentle voice, kind even in its despairing accents, touched the very bottom of Raoul's perverted heart, and once more his soul was wrung by remorse; so that he felt inclined to put back the stolen money, and comfort the despairing woman whose life and reason he was destroying. The thought of de Clameran restrained him.

Finding his efforts to restore Madame Fauvel fruitless, that, in spite of all his affectionate regrets and promises, she still sat silent, motionless, and death-like; and fearing that M. Fauvel or Madeleine might enter at any moment, and demand an explanation, he hastily pressed a kiss upon his mother's brow, and hurried from the house.

At the restaurant, in the room where they had dined, de Clameran, tortured by anxiety, awaited his accomplice.

He wondered if at the last moment, when he was not near to sustain him, Raoul would prove a coward, and retreat; if any unforeseen trifle had prevented his finding the key; if any visitors were there; and, if so, would they depart before M. Fauvel's return from the dinner-party?

He had worked himself into such a state of excitement, that, when Raoul returned, he flew to him with ashy face and trembling all over, and could scarcely gasp out:

"Well?"

"The deed is done, uncle, thanks to you; and I am now the most miserable, abject villain on the face of the earth."

He unbuttoned his vest, and, pulling out the four bundles of bank-notes, angrily dashed them upon the table, saying, in a tone of scorn and disgust:

"Now I hope you are satisfied. This is the price of the happiness, honour, and perhaps the life of three people."

De Clameran paid no attention to these angry words. With feverish eagerness he seized the notes, and rattled them in his hand as if to convince himself of the reality of success.

"Now Madeleine is mine!" he cried excitedly.

Raoul looked at de Clameran in silent disgust. This exhibition of joy was a shocking contrast to the scene in which he had just been an actor. He was humiliated at being the tool of such a heartless scoundrel as he now knew de Clameran to be.

Louis misinterpreted this silence, and said gaily:

"Did you have much difficulty?"

"I forbid you ever to allude to this evening's work," cried Raoul fiercely. "Do you hear me? I wish to forget it."

De Clameran shrugged his shoulders at this outburst of anger, and said in a bantering tone:

"Just as you please, my handsome nephew: I rather think you will want to remember it though, when I offer you these three hundred and fifty thousand *francs*. You will not, I am sure, refuse to accept them as a slight souvenir. Take them: they are yours."

This generosity seemed neither to surprise nor satisfy Raoul.

"According to our agreement," he said sullenly, "I was to have more than this."

"Of course: this is only part of your share."

"And when am I to have the rest, if you please?"

"The day I marry Madeleine, and not before, my boy. You are too valuable an assistant to lose at present; and you know that, though I don't mistrust you, I am not altogether sure of your sincere affection for me."

Raoul reflected that to commit a crime, and not profit by it, would be the height of absurdity. He had come with the intention of breaking off all connection with de Clameran; but he now determined that he would not abandon his accomplice until he had been well paid for his services.

"Very well," he said, "I accept this on account; but remember, I will never do another piece of work like this tonight. You can do what you please; I shall flatly refuse."

De Clameran burst into a loud laugh, and said:

"That is sensible: now that you are rich, you can afford to be honest. Set your conscience at rest, for I promise you I will require nothing more of you save a few trifling services. You can retire behind the scenes now, while I appear upon the stage."

Chapter 21

For more than an hour after Raoul's departure, Madame Fauvel remained in a state of torpor bordering upon unconsciousness.

Gradually, however, she recovered her senses sufficiently to comprehend the horrors of her present situation; and, with the faculty of thought, that of suffering returned.

The dreadful scene in which she had taken part was still before her affrighted vision; all the attending circumstances, unnoticed at the time, now struck her forcibly.

She saw that she had been the dupe of a shameful conspiracy: that Raoul had tortured her with cold-blooded cruelty, had taken advantage of her tenderness, and had speculated upon her fright.

But had Prosper anything to do with the robbery? This Madame Fauvel had no way of finding out. Ah, Raoul knew how the blow would strike when he accused Prosper. He knew that Madame Fauvel would end by believing in the cashier's complicity.

The unhappy woman sat and thought over every possible way in which Raoul could find out the secret word without Prosper's knowledge. She rejected with horror the idea that the cashier was the instigator of the crime; but, in spite of herself, it constantly recurred. And finally she felt convinced that what Raoul said must be true; for who but Prosper could have betrayed the word? And who but Prosper could have left so large an amount of money in the safe, which, by order of the banker, was to be always left empty at night?

Knowing that Prosper was leading a life of extravagance and dissipation, she thought it very likely that he had, from sheer desperation, resorted to this bold step to pay his debts; her blind affection, moreover, made her anxious to attribute the crime to anyone, rather than to her darling son.

She had heard that Prosper was supporting one of those worthless creatures whose extravagance impoverishes men, and whose evil influence perverts their natures. When a young man is thus degraded, will he stop at any sin or crime? Alas! Madame Fauvel knew, from her own sad experience, to what depths even one fault can lead. Although she believed Prosper guilty, she did not blame him, but considered herself responsible for his sins.

Had she not herself banished the poor young man from the fireside which he had begun to regard as his own? Had she not destroyed his hopes of happiness, by crushing his pure love for a noble girl, whom he looked upon as his future wife, and thus driven him into a life of dissipation and sin?

She was undecided whether to confide in Madeleine, or bury the secret in her own breast.

Fatally inspired, she decided to keep silent.

When Madeleine returned home at eleven o'clock, Madame Fauvel not only was silent as to what had occurred, but even succeeded in so concealing all traces of her agitation, that she escaped any questions from her niece.

Her calmness never left her when M. Fauvel and Lucien returned, although she was in terror lest her husband should go down to the cash-room to see that everything was safely locked up. It was not his habit to open the money-safe at night, but he sometimes did.

As fate would have it, the banker, as soon as he entered the room, began to speak of Prosper, saying how distressing it was that so interesting a young man should be thus throwing himself away, and wondering what could have happened to make him suddenly cease his visits at the house, and resort to bad company.

If M. Fauvel had looked at the faces of his wife and niece while he harshly blamed the cashier, he would have been puzzled at their strange expressions.

All night long Madame Fauvel suffered the most intolerable agony. She counted each stroke of the town-clock, as the hours dragged on.

"In six hours," she said to herself, "in five hours—in four hours—

in three hours—in one hour—all will be discovered; and then what will happen? Heaven help me!"

At sunrise she heard the servants moving about the house. Then the office-shutters opened; then, later, she heard the clerks going into the bank.

She attempted to get up, but felt so ill and weak that she sank back on her pillow; and lying there, trembling like a leaf, bathed in cold perspiration, she awaited the discovery of the robbery.

She was leaning over the side of the bed, straining her ear to catch a sound from the cash-room, when Madeleine, who had just left her, rushed into the room.

The white face and wild eyes of the poor girl told Madame Fauvel that the crime was discovered.

"Do you know what has happened, aunt?" cried Madeleine, in a shrill, horrified tone. "Prosper is accused of robbery, and the police have come to take him to prison!"

A groan was Madame Fauvel's only answer.

"Raoul or the *marquis* is at the bottom of this," continued Madeleine excitedly.

"How can they be concerned in it, my child?"

"I can't tell yet; but I only know that Prosper is innocent. I have just seen him, spoken to him. He would never have looked me in the face had he been guilty."

Madame Fauvel opened her lips to confess all: fear kept her silent.

"What can these wretches want?" said Madeleine: "what new sacrifice do they demand? Dishonour Prosper! Good heavens! Why did they not kill him at once? He would rather be dead than disgraced!"

Here the entrance of M. Fauvel interrupted Madeleine. The banker was so angry that he could scarcely speak.

"The worthless scoundrel!" he cried; "to think of his daring to accuse me! To insinuate that I robbed my own safe! And that Marquis de Clameran must needs doubt my good faith in keeping my engagement to pay his money!"

Then, without noticing the effect of his story upon the two women, he proceeded to relate all that had occurred downstairs.

"I was afraid this extravagance would lead to something terrible," he said in conclusion; "you know I told you last night that Prosper was growing worse in his conduct, and that he would get into trouble."

Throughout the day Madeleine's devotion to her aunt was severely tried.

The generous girl saw disgrace heaped upon the man she loved. She had perfect faith in his innocence; she felt sure she knew who had laid the trap to ruin him; and yet she could not say a word in his defence.

Fearing that Madeleine would suspect her of complicity in the theft, if she remained in bed and betrayed so much agitation, Madame Fauvel arose and dressed for breakfast.

It was a dreary meal. No one tasted a morsel. The servants moved about on their tiptoes, as silently as if a death had occurred in the family.

About two o'clock, a servant came to M. Fauvel's study, and said that the Marquis de Clameran desired to see him.

"What!" cried the banker; "does he dare—"

Then, after a moment's reflection, he added:

"Ask him to walk up."

The very name of Clameran had sufficed to arouse all the slumbering wrath of M. Fauvel. The victim of a robbery, finding his safe empty at the moment that he was called upon to make a heavy payment, he had been constrained to conceal his anger and resentment; but now he determined to have his revenge upon his insolent visitor.

But the *marquis* declined to come upstairs. The messenger returned with the answer that the gentleman had a particular reason for seeing M. Fauvel in the office below, where the clerks were.

"What does this fresh impertinence mean?" cried the banker, as he angrily jumped up and hastened downstairs.

M. de Clameran was standing in the middle of the room adjoining the cash-room; M. Fauvel walked up to him, and said bluntly:

"What do you want now, *monsieur*? You have been paid your money, and I have your receipt."

To the surprise of all the clerks, and the banker himself, the *marquis* seemed not in the least offended at this rude greeting, but answered in a deferential but not at all humble manner:

"You are hard upon me, *monsieur*; but I deserve it, and that is why I am here. A gentleman always acknowledges when he is in the wrong: in this instance I am the offender; and I flatter myself that my past will permit me to say so without being accused of cowardice or lack of self-respect. I insisted upon seeing you here instead of in your study, because, having been rude to you in the presence of your clerks, I wished them to hear me apologise for my behaviour of this morning."

De Clameran's speech was so different from his usual overbearing, haughty conduct, that surprise almost stupefied the banker, and he could only answer:

"I must say that I was hurt by your doubts, insinuations, suspicions of my honour—"

"This morning," continued the *marquis*, "I was irritated, and thoughtlessly gave way to my temper. Although I am gray-headed, my disposition is as excitable as that of a fiery young man of twenty years; and I hope you will forget words uttered in a moment of excitement, and now deeply regretted."

M. Fauvel, being a kind-hearted though quick-tempered man, could appreciate de Clameran's feelings; and, knowing that his own high reputation for scrupulous honesty could not be affected by any hasty or abusive language uttered by a creditor, at once calmed down before so frank an apology; and, holding out his hand to de Clameran, said:

"Let us forget what happened, *monsieur*."

They conversed in a friendly manner for some minutes; and, after de Clameran had explained why he had such pressing need of the money at that particular hour of the morning, turned to leave, saying that he would do himself the honour of calling upon Madame Fauvel during the day.

"That is, if a visit from me would not be considered intrusive," he said with a shade of hesitation. "Perhaps, after the trouble of this morning, she does not wish to be disturbed."

"Oh, no!" said the banker; "come, by all means; I think a visit from you would cheer her mind. I shall be from home all day, trying to trace this unfortunate affair."

Madame Fauvel was in the same room where Raoul had threatened to kill himself the night previous; she looked very pale and ill as she lay on a sofa. Madeleine was bathing her forehead.

When M. de Clameran was announced, they both started up as if a phantom had appeared before them.

Although Louis had been gay and smiling when he parted from M. Fauvel downstairs, he now wore a melancholy aspect, as he gravely bowed, and refused to seat himself in the chair which Madame Fauvel motioned him to take.

"You will excuse me, ladies, for intruding at this time of your affliction; but I have a duty to fulfil."

The two women were silent; they seemed to be waiting for him to explain. He added in an undertone:

"I know all."

By an imploring gesture, Madame Fauvel tried to stop him. She saw that he was about to reveal her secret to Madeleine.

But Louis would not see this gesture; he turned his whole attention to Madeleine, who haughtily said:

"Explain yourself, *monsieur*."

"Only one hour ago," he replied, "I discovered that Raoul last night forced from his mother the key of the money-safe, and stole three hundred and fifty thousand *francs*."

Madeleine crimsoned with shame and indignation; she leaned over the sofa, and seizing her aunt's wrist shook it violently, and in a hollow voice cried:

"It is false, is it not, aunt? speak!"

"Alas! alas!" groaned Madame Fauvel. "What have I done?"

"You have allowed Prosper to be accused," cried Madeleine; "you have suffered him to be arrested, and disgraced for life."

"Forgive me," sighed Madame Fauvel. "He was about to kill himself; I was so frightened! Then you know—Prosper was to share the money: he gave Raoul the secret word—"

"Good Heavens! Aunt, how could you believe such a falsehood as that?"

De Clameran interrupted them.

"Unfortunately, what your aunt says of M. Bertomy is the truth," he said in a sad tone.

"Your proofs, *monsieur*; where are your proofs?"

"Raoul's confession."

"Raoul is false."

"That is only too true: but how did he find out the word, if M. Bertomy did not reveal it? And who left the money in the safe but M. Bertomy?"

These arguments had no effect upon Madeleine.

"And now tell me," she said scornfully, "what became of the money?"

There was no mistaking the significance of these words: they meant:

"You are the instigator of the robbery, and of course you have taken possession of the money."

This harsh accusation from a girl whom he so passionately loved, when, grasping bandit as he was, he gave up for her sake all the money gained by his crime, so cruelly hurt de Clameran that he turned livid.

But his mortification and anger did not prevent him from pursuing the part he had prepared and studied.

"A day will come, *mademoiselle*," he said, "when you will deeply regret having treated me so cruelly. I understand your insinuation; you need not attempt to deny it."

"I have no idea of denying anything, *monsieur*."

"Madeleine!" remonstrated Madame Fauvel, who trembled at the rising anger of the man who held her fate in his hands, "Madeleine, be careful!"

"*Mademoiselle* is pitiless," said de Clameran sadly; "she cruelly punishes an honourable man whose only fault is having obeyed his brother's dying injunctions. And I am here now, because I believe in the joint responsibility of all the members of a family."

Here he slowly drew from his pocket several bundles of bank-notes, and laid them on the mantel-piece.

"Raoul stole three hundred and fifty thousand *francs*," he said: "I return the same amount. It is more than half my fortune. Willingly would I give the rest to insure this being the last crime committed by him."

Too inexperienced to penetrate this bold, and yet simple plan of de Clameran's, Madeleine was dumb with astonishment; all her calculations were upset.

Madame Fauvel, on the contrary, accepted this restitution as salvation sent from heaven.

"Oh, thanks, *monsieur*, thanks!" she cried, gratefully clasping de Clameran's hand in hers; "you are goodness itself!"

Louis's eye lit up with pleasure. But he rejoiced too soon. A minute's reflection brought back all of Madeleine's distrust. She thought this magnanimity and generosity unnatural in a man whom she considered incapable of a noble sentiment, and at once concluded that it must conceal some snare beneath.

"What are we to do with the money?" she demanded.

"Restore it to M. Fauvel, *mademoiselle*."

"We restore it, *monsieur*, and how? Restoring the money is denouncing Raoul, and ruining my aunt. Take back your money, *monsieur*. We will not touch it."

De Clameran was too shrewd to insist; he took up the money, and prepared to leave.

"I comprehend your refusal, *mademoiselle*, and must find another way of accomplishing my wish. But, before retiring, let me say that your injustice pains me deeply. After the promise you made to me, I had reason to hope for a kinder welcome."

"I will keep my promise, *monsieur*; but not until you have furnished security."

"Security! And for what? Pray, explain yourself."

"Something to protect my aunt against the molestations of Raoul after my—marriage. What is to prevent his coming to extort money from his mother after he has squandered my dowry? A man who spends a hundred thousand *francs* in four months will soon run through my little fortune. We are making a bargain; I give you my hand in exchange for the honour and life of my aunt; and of course you must give me some guarantee to secure the performance of your promise."

"Oh! I will give you ample securities," cried de Clameran, "such as will quiet all your suspicious doubts of my good faith. Alas! you will not believe in my devotion; what shall I do to convince you of its sincerity? Shall I try to save M. Bertomy?"

"Thanks for the offer, *monsieur*," replied Madeleine disdainfully; "if Prosper is guilty, let him be punished by the law; if he is innocent, God will protect him."

Here Madeleine stood up, to signify that the interview was over.

De Clameran bowed, and left the room.

"What pride! What determination! The idea of her demanding securities of me!" he said to himself as he slowly walked away. "But the proud girl shall be humbled yet. She is so beautiful! and, if I did not so madly love her, I would kill her on the spot!"

Never had de Clameran been so irritated. Madeleine's quiet determination and forethought had unexpectedly thrown him off his well-laid track; not anticipating any such self assertion on her part, he was disconcerted, and at a loss how to proceed.

He knew that it would be useless to attempt deceiving a girl of Madeleine's character a second time; he saw that she had penetrated his motives sufficiently to put her on the defensive, and prepare her for any new surprise. Moreover, she would prevent Madame Fauvel from being frightened and forced into submission any longer.

With mortification and rage, Louis saw that after all his plotting, when success was in his reach, when his hopes were almost crowned, he had been foiled and scornfully set at defiance by a girl: the whole thing would have to be gone over again.

Although Madeleine had resigned herself to sacrifice, it was still evident that she had no idea of doing so blindly, and would not hazard her aunt's and her own happiness upon the uncertainty of a verbal promise.

De Clameran racked his brain to furnish guarantees; how could he convince her that Raoul had no idea or desire of annoying Madame Fauvel in the future?

He could not tell Madeleine that her dowry was to be the bribe received by Raoul for his future good behaviour and past crimes.

The knowledge of all the circumstances of this shameful criminal intrigue would have reassured her upon her aunt's peace of mind; but then it would never do to inform her of these details, certainly not before the marriage.

What securities could he give? Not one could he think of.

But de Clameran was not one of those slow-minded men who take weeks to consider a difficulty. When he could not untie a knot, he would cut it.

Raoul was a stumbling-block to his wishes, and he swore to rid himself of his troublesome accomplice as soon as possible.

Although it was not an easy matter to dispose of so cunning a knave, de Clameran felt no hesitation in undertaking to accomplish his purpose. He was incited by one of those passions which age renders terrible.

The more certain he was of Madeleine's contempt and dislike, the more determined he was to marry her. His love seemed to be a sort of insane desire to possess and call his own the one being whom he recognised as his superior in every way.

But he had sense enough to see that he might ruin his prospects by undue haste, and that the safest course would be to await the result of the robbery and its effect upon Prosper.

He waited in anxious expectation of a summons from Madame Fauvel. At last he concluded that Madeleine was waiting for him to make the next move in the direction of yielding.

He was right; Madeleine knew that after the last bold step the accomplices would remain quiet for a while; she knew resistance could have no worse results than would cowardly submission; and therefore assumed the entire responsibility of managing the affair so as to keep at bay both Raoul and de Clameran.

She knew that Madame Fauvel would be anxious to accept any terms of peace, but she determined to use all her influence to prevent her doing this, and to force upon her the necessity of preserving a dignified silence.

This accounted for the silence of the two women, who were quietly waiting for their adversaries to renew hostilities.

They even succeeded in concealing their anxiety beneath assumed indifference; never asking any questions about the robbery, or those in any way connected with it.

M. Fauvel brought them an account of Prosper's examination, the many charges brought against him, his obstinate denial of having stolen the money; and finally how, after great perplexity and close study of the case by the judge of instruction, the cashier had been discharged for want of sufficient proof against him.

Since de Clameran's offer to restore the notes, Madame Fauvel had not doubted Prosper's guilt. She said nothing, but inwardly accused him of having seduced her son from the path of virtue, and enticed him into crime—her son whom she would never cease to love, no matter how great his faults.

Madeleine had perfect faith in Prosper's innocence.

She was so confident of his being restored to liberty that she ventured to ask her uncle, under pretext of some charitable object, to give her ten thousand *francs*, which she sent to the unfortunate victim of circumstantial evidence; who, from what she had heard of his poverty, must be in need of assistance.

In the letter—cut from her prayer-book to avoid detection by writing—accompanying the money, she advised Prosper to leave France, because she knew that it would be impossible for a man of his proud nature to remain on the scene of his disgrace; the greater his innocence, the more intolerable his suffering.

Besides, Madeleine, at that time feeling that she would be obliged to marry de Clameran, was anxious to have the man she loved far, far away from her.

On the day that this anonymous present was sent, in opposition to the wishes of Madame Fauvel, the two poor women were entangled fearfully in pecuniary difficulties.

The tradesmen whose money had been squandered by Raoul refused to give credit any longer, and insisted upon their bills being paid at once; saying they could not understand how a man of M. Fauvel's wealth and position could keep them waiting for such insignificant sums.

The butcher, grocer, and wine-merchant had bills of one, two, and five hundred *francs* only; but, not having even that small amount, Madame Fauvel had difficulty in prevailing upon them to receive a part on account, and wait a little longer for the residue.

Some of the store-keepers threatened to ask the banker for their money, if everything was not settled before the end of the week.

Alas! Madame Fauvel's indebtedness amounted to fifteen thousand *francs*.

Madeleine and her aunt had declined all invitations during the winter, to avoid purchasing evening dresses; having always been remarkable for their superb toilets, seldom appearing in the same ball-dress twice, they dared not give rise to comment by wearing their old dresses, and knowing that M. Fauvel would be the first to ask the cause of this sudden change, as he liked to see them always the best-dressed women in the room.

But at last they were obliged to appear in public. M. Fauvel's most intimate friends, the Messrs. Jandidier, were about to give a splendid ball, and, as fate would have it, a fancy ball, which would require the purchasing of costumes.

Where would the money come from?

They had been owing a large bill to their dressmaker for over a year. Would she consent to furnish them dresses on credit? They were ashamed to ask her.

Madeleine's new maid, Palmyre Chocareille, extricated them from this difficulty.

This girl, who seemed to have suffered all the minor ills of life—which, after all, are the hardest to bear—seemed to have divined her mistress's anxiety.

At any rate, she voluntarily informed Madeleine that a friend of hers, a first-class dressmaker, had just set up for herself, and would be glad to furnish materials and make the dresses on credit, for the sake of obtaining the patronage of Madame Fauvel and her niece, which would at once bring her plenty of fashionable customers.

But, after this dilemma was settled, a still greater one presented itself.

Madame Fauvel and her niece could not appear at a ball without jewellery; and every jewel they owned had been taken by Raoul, and pawned.

After thinking the matter over, Madeleine decided to ask Raoul to take some of the stolen money, and redeem the last set of jewels he had forced from his mother. She informed her aunt of her intention, and said, in a tone that admitted of no contradiction:

"Appoint an interview with Raoul: he will not dare to refuse you;

and I will go in your stead."

The next day, the courageous girl took a cab, and, regardless of the inclement weather, went to Vesinet.

She would have been filled with consternation had she known that M. Verduret and Prosper were following close behind, and witnessed her interview from the top of a ladder.

Her bold step was fruitless. Raoul swore that he had divided with Prosper; that his own half of the money was spent, and that he had not a *napoleon* wherewith to redeem anything.

He even refused to give up the pledges; and Madeleine had to resort to threats of exposure, before she could induce him to surrender the tickets of four or five trifling articles that were indispensable to their toilet.

De Clameran had ordered him to refuse positively to give up a single ticket, because he hoped that in their distress they would call upon him for relief.

The violent altercation witnessed by de Clameran's new valet, Joseph Dubois, had been caused by the exaction of this promise.

The accomplices were at that time on very bad terms. De Clameran was seeking a safe means of getting rid of Raoul; and the young scamp, having a presentiment of his uncle's intentions, was determined to outwit him.

Nothing but the certainty of impending danger could reconcile them. The danger was revealed to them both at the Jandidier ball.

Who was the mysterious *mountebank* that indulged in such transparent allusions to Madame Fauvel's private troubles, and then said, with threatening significance to Louis: "I was the best friend of your brother Gaston?"

Who he was, where he came from, they could not imagine; but they clearly saw that he was a dangerous enemy, and forthwith attempted to assassinate him upon his leaving the ball.

Having been followed and watched by their would-be victim, they became alarmed—especially when he suddenly disappeared—and wisely decided that the safest thing they then could do was to return quietly to their hotel.

"We cannot be too guarded in our conduct," whispered de Clameran; "we must discover who he is before taking any further steps in this matter."

Once more, Raoul tried to induce him to give up his project of marrying Madeleine.

"Never!" he exclaimed fiercely, "I will marry her or perish in the attempt!"

They thought that, now they were warned, the danger of being caught was lessened. But they did not know the sort of man who was on their track.

Chapter 22

The Catastrophe

Such are the facts that, with an almost incredible talent for investigation, had been collected and prepared by M. Verduret, the stout man with the jovial face, who had taken Prosper under his protection.

Reaching Paris at nine o'clock in the evening, not by the Lyons road as he had said, but by the Orleans train, M. Verduret hurried up to the Archangel, where he found the cashier impatiently expecting him.

"You are about to hear some rich developments," he said to Prosper, "and see how far back into the past one has to seek for the primary cause of a crime. All things are linked together and dependent upon each other in this world of ours. If Gaston de Clameran had not entered a little cafe at Tarascon to play a game of billiards twenty years ago, your money-safe would not have been robbed three weeks ago.

"Valentine de la Verberie is punished in 1866 for the murder committed for her sake in 1840. Nothing is neglected or forgotten, when stern Retribution asserts her sway. Listen."

And he forthwith related all that he had discovered, referring, as he went along, to a voluminous manuscript which he had prepared, with many notes and authenticated proofs attached.

During the last week M. Verduret had not had twenty-four hours' rest, but he bore no traces of fatigue. His iron muscles braved any amount of labour, and his elastic nature was too well tempered to give way beneath such pressure.

While any other man would have sunk exhausted in a chair, he stood up and described, with the enthusiasm and captivating animation peculiar to him, the minutest details and intricacies of the plot that he had devoted his whole energy to unravelling; personating every character he brought upon the scene to take part in the strange drama, so that his listener was bewildered and dazzled by his brilliant acting.

As Prosper listened to this narrative of events happening twenty years back, the secret conversations as minutely related as if overheard the moment they took place, it sounded more like a romance than a statement of plain facts.

All these ingenious explanations might be logical, but what foundation did they possess? Might they not be the dreams of an excited imagination?

M. Verduret did not finish his report until four o'clock in the morning; then he cried, with an accent of triumph:

"And now they are on their guard, and sharp, wary rascals too: but they won't escape me; I have cornered them beautifully. Before a week is over, Prosper, you will be publicly exonerated, and will come out of this scrape with flying colours. I have promised your father you shall."

"Impossible!" said Prosper in a dazed way, "it cannot be!"

"What?"

"All this you have just told me."

M. Verduret opened wide his eyes, as if he could not understand anyone having the audacity to doubt the accuracy of *his* report.

"Impossible, indeed!" he cried. "What! have you not sense enough to see the plain truth written all over every fact, and attested by the best authority? Your thick-headedness exasperates me to the last degree."

"But how can such rascalities take place in Paris, in our very midst, without—"

"*Parbleu*!" interrupted the fat man, "you are young, my friend! Are you innocent enough to suppose that crimes, forty times worse than this, don't occur every day? You think the horrors of the police-court are the only ones. Pooh! You only read in the *Gazette des Tribunaux* of the cruel melodramas of life, where the actors are as cowardly as the knife, and as treacherous as the poison they use. It is at the family fireside, often under shelter of the law itself, that the real tragedies of life are acted; in modern crimes the traitors wear gloves, and cloak themselves with public position; the victims die, smiling to the last, without revealing the torture they have endured to the end. Why, what I have just related to you is an everyday occurrence; and you profess astonishment."

"I can't help wondering how you discovered all this tissue of crime."

"Ah, that is the point!" said the fat man with a self-satisfied smile. "When I undertake a task, I devote my whole attention to it. Now, make a note of this: When a man of ordinary intelligence concentrates his thoughts and energies upon the attainment of an object, he is certain to obtain ultimate success. Besides that, I have my own method of working up a case."

"Still I don't see what grounds you had to go upon."

"To be sure, one needs some light to guide one in a dark affair like this. But the fire in de Clameran's eye at the mention of Gaston's name ignited my lantern. From that moment I walked straight to the solution of the mystery, as I would walk to a beacon-light on a dark night."

The eager, questioning look of Prosper showed that he would like to know the secret of his protector's wonderful penetration, and at the same time be more thoroughly convinced that what he had heard was all true—that his innocence would be more clearly proved.

"Now confess," cried M. Verduret, "you would give anything in the world to find out how I discovered the truth?"

"I certainly would, for it is the darkest of mysteries, marvellous!"

M. Verduret enjoyed Prosper's bewilderment. To be sure, he was neither a good judge nor a distinguished amateur; but he was an astonished admirer, and sincere admiration is always flattering, no matter whence it comes.

"Well," he replied, "I will explain my system. There is nothing marvellous about it as you will soon see. We worked together to find the solution of the problem, so you know my reasons for suspecting de Clameran as the prime mover in the robbery. As soon as I had acquired this certainty, my task was easy. You want to know what I did? I placed trustworthy people to watch the parties in whom I was most interested. Joseph Dubois took charge of de Clameran, and Nina Gypsy never lost sight of Madame Fauvel and her niece."

"I cannot comprehend how Nina ever consented to this service."

"That is my secret," replied M. Verduret. "Having the assistance of good eyes and quick ears on the spot, I went to Beaucaire to inquire into the past, so as to link it with what I knew of the present. The next day I was at Clameran; and the first step I took was to find the son of St. Jean, the old valet. An honest man he was, too; open and simple as nature herself; and he made a good bargain in selling me his madder."

"Madder?" said Prosper with a puzzled look; "what did you—"

"Of course I wanted to buy his madder. Of course I did not appear to him as I do to you now. I was a countryman wanting to buy madder; he had madder for sale; so we began to bargain about the price. The debate lasted almost all day, during which time we drank a dozen bottles of wine. About supper-time, St. Jean was as drunk as a bunghole, and I had purchased nine hundred *francs*' worth of madder which your father will sell tomorrow."

Prosper's astonished countenance made M. Verduret laugh heartily.

"I risked nine hundred *francs*," he continued, "but thread by thread I gathered the whole history of the Clamerans, Gaston's love-affair, his flight, and the stumbling of the horse ridden by Louis. I found also that about a year ago Louis returned, sold the *château* to a man named Fougeroux, whose wife, Mihonne, had a secret interview with Louis the day of the purchase. I went to see Mihonne. Poor woman! her rascally husband has pounded all the sense out of her; she is almost idiotic. I told her I came from the Clameran family, and she at once related to me everything she knew."

The apparent simplicity of this mode of investigation confounded Prosper. He wondered it had not occurred to him before.

"From that time," continued M. Verduret, "the skein began to disentangle; I held the principal thread. I now set about finding out what had become of Gaston. Lafourcade, who is a friend of your father, informed me that he had bought a foundry, and settled in Oloron, where he soon after suddenly died. Thirty-six hours later I was at Oloron."

"You are certainly indefatigable!" said Prosper.

"No, but I always strike while the iron is hot. At Oloron I met Manuel, who had gone there to make a little visit before returning to Spain. From him I obtained a complete history of Gaston's life, and all the particulars of his death. Manuel also told me of Louis's visit; and the inn-keeper described a young workman who was there at the same time, whom I at once recognised as Raoul."

"But how did you know of all the conversations between the villains?" said Prosper. "You seem to be aware of their secret thoughts."

"You evidently think I have been drawing upon my imagination. You will soon see to the contrary," said Verduret good-humouredly. "While I was at work down there, my aids did not sit with their hands tied together. Mutually distrustful, de Clameran and Raoul preserved all the letters received from each other. Joseph Dubois copied them, or the important portions of them, and forwarded them to me. Nina spent her time listening at all doors under her supervision, and sent me a faithful report. Finally, I have at the Fauvels another means of investigation which I will reveal to you later."

"I understand it all now," murmured Prosper.

"And what have you been doing during my absence, my young friend?" asked M. Verduret; "have you heard any news?"

At this question Prosper turned crimson. But he knew that it would never do to keep silent about his imprudent step.

"Alas!" he stammered, "I read in a newspaper that de Clameran was about to marry Madeleine; and I acted like a fool."

"What did you do?" inquired Verduret anxiously.

"I wrote an anonymous letter to M. Fauvel, informing him that his wife was in love with Raoul—"

M. Verduret here brought his clinched fist down upon the little table near by, with such violence that the thin plank was shivered. His cheerful face in an instant clouded over.

"What folly!" he exclaimed, "how could you go and ruin everything?"

He arose from his seat, and strode up and down the room, oblivious of the lodgers below, whose windows shook with every angry stamp of his foot.

"What made you act so like a child, an idiot, a fool?" he said indignantly to Prosper.

"*Monsieur!*"

"Here you are, drowning; an honest man springs into the water to save you, and just as he approaches the shore you entangle his feet to prevent him from swimming! What was my last order to you when I left here?"

"To keep quiet, and not go out of the hotel."

"Well."

The consciousness of having done a foolish thing made Prosper appear like a frightened schoolboy, accused by his teacher of playing truant.

"It was night, *monsieur*," he hesitatingly said, "and, having a violent headache, I took a walk along the quay thinking there was no risk in my entering a cafe; there I picked up a paper, and read the dreadful announcement."

"Did you not promise to trust everything to me?"

"You were absent, *monsieur*; and you yourself might have been surprised by an unexpected—"

"Only fools are ever surprised into committing a piece of folly," cried M. Verduret impatiently. "To write an anonymous letter! Do you know to what you expose me? Breaking a sacred promise made to one of the few persons whom I highly esteem among my fellow-beings. I shall be looked upon as a liar, a cheat—I who—"

He abruptly stopped, as if afraid to trust himself to speak further; after calming down a little, he turned to Prosper, and said:

"The best thing we can do is to try and repair the harm you have done. When and where did you post this idiotic letter?"

"Yesterday evening, at the Rue du Cardinal Lemoine. It hardly reached the bottom of the box before I regretted having written it."

"You had better have regretted it before dropping it in. What time was it?"

"About ten o'clock."

"Then your sweet little letter must have reached M. Fauvel with his early mail; probably he was alone in his study when he read it."

"I know he was: he never goes down to the bank until he has opened his letters."

"Can you recall the exact terms of your letter? Stop and think, for it is very important that I should know."

"Oh, it is unnecessary for me to reflect. I remember the letter as if I had just written it."

And almost *verbatim* he repeated what he had written.

After attentively listening, M. Verduret sat with a perplexed frown upon his face, as if trying to discover some means of repairing the harm done.

"That is an awkward letter," he finally said, "to come from a person who does not deal in such things. It leaves everything to be understood without specifying anything; it is vague, jeering, insidious. Repeat it to me."

Prosper obeyed, and his second version did not vary from the first in a single word.

"Nothing could be more alarming than that allusion to the cashier," said the fat man, repeating the words after Prosper. "The question, 'Was it also he who stole Madame Fauvel's diamonds?' is simply fearful. What could be more exasperating than the sarcastic advice, 'In your place, I would not have any public scandal, but would watch my wife?' The effect of your letter must have been terrible," he added thoughtfully as he stood with folded arms looking at poor Prosper. "M. Fauvel is quick-tempered, is he not?"

"He has a violent temper, when aroused."

"Then the mischief is not irreparable."

"What! do you suppose—"

"I think that an impulsive man is afraid of himself, and seldom carries out his first angry intentions. That is our chance of salvation. If, upon the receipt of your bomb-shell, M. Fauvel, unable to restrain himself, rushed into his wife's room, and cried, 'Where are your diamonds?' Madame Fauvel will confess all; and then goodbye to our hopes."

"Why would this be disastrous?"

"Because, the moment Madame Fauvel opens her lips to her husband, our birds will take flight."

Prosper had never thought of this eventuality.

"Then, again," continued M. Verduret, "it would deeply distress another person."

"Anyone whom I know?"

"Yes, my friend, and very well too. I should certainly be chagrined to the last degree, if these two rascals escape, without having obtained complete satisfaction from them."

"It seems to me that you know how to take care of yourself, and can do anything you please."

M. Verduret shrugged his shoulders, and said:

"Did you not perceive the gaps in my narrative?"

"I did not."

"That is because you don't know how to listen. In the first place, did Louis de Clameran poison his brother, or not?"

"Yes; I am sure of it, from what you tell me."

"There you are! You are much more certain, young man, than I am. Your opinion is mine; but what proof have we? None. I skilfully questioned Dr. C—. He has not the shadow of suspicion; and Dr. C— is no quack; he is a cultivated, observing man of high standing. What poisons produce the effects described? I know of none; and yet I have studied up on poisons from Pomerania *digitalis* to Sauvresy *aconite*."

"The death took place so opportunely—"

"That anybody would be convinced of foul play. That is true; but chance is sometimes a wonderful accomplice in crime. In the second place, I know nothing of Raoul's antecedents."

"Is information on that point necessary?"

"Indispensable, my friend; but we will soon know something. I have sent off one of my men—excuse me, I mean one of my friends—who is very expert and adroit, M. Palot; and he writes that he is on the track. I am interested in the history of this sentimental, sceptical young rascal. I have an idea that he must have been a brave, honest sort of youth before de Clameran ruined him."

Prosper was no longer listening.

M. Verduret's words had inspired him with confidence. Already he saw the guilty men arraigned before the bar of justice; and enjoyed, in anticipation, this assize-court drama, where he would be publicly exonerated and restored to position.

Then he would seek Madeleine; for now he understood her strange conduct at the dressmaker's, and knew that she had never ceased to love him.

This certainty of future happiness restored all the self-possession that had deserted him the day he found the safe robbed. For the first time he was astonished at the peculiarity of his situation.

Prosper had at first only been surprised at the protection of M. Verduret and the extent of his investigations: now he asked himself, what could have been his motives for acting thus?

What price did he expect for this sacrifice of time and labour?

His anxiety made him say nervously:

"It is unjust to us both, *monsieur*, for you to preserve your *incognito* any longer. When you have saved the honour and life of a man, you should at least let him know whom he is to thank for it."

"Oh!" said M. Verduret smilingly, "you are not out of the woods yet. You are not married either: so you must wait a little longer; patience and faith."

The clock struck six.

"Good heavens!" exclaimed M. Verduret. "Can it be six o'clock? I did hope to have a good night's rest, but I must keep on moving. This is no time to be asleep."

He went into the passage, and, leaning over the balusters, called, "Madame Alexandre! I say, Madame Alexandre!"

The hostess of the Archangel, the portly wife of Fanferlot the Squirrel, evidently had not been to bed. This fact struck Prosper.

She appeared, obsequious, smiling, and eager to please.

"What can I do for you, gentlemen?" she inquired.

"You can send your—Joseph Dubois and Palmyre to me as soon as possible. Let me know when they arrive. I will rest a few minutes, and you can awake me when they come."

As soon as Madame Alexandre left the room, the fat man unceremoniously threw himself on the bed.

"You have no objections, I suppose?" he said to Prosper.

In five minutes he was fast asleep; and Prosper sat by the bed watching him with a perplexed gaze, wondering who this strange man could be.

About nine o'clock someone tapped timidly at the door.

Slight as the noise was, it aroused M. Verduret, who sprang up, and called out:

"Who is it?"

Prosper arose and opened the door.

Joseph Dubois, the valet of the Marquis de Clameran, entered.

This important assistant of M. Verduret was breathless from fast running; and his little rat eyes were more restless than ever.

"Well, patron, I am glad to see you once more," he cried. "Now you can tell me what to do; I have been perfectly lost during your absence, and have felt like a jumping monkey with a broken string.

"What! did you get frightened too?"

"Bless me! I think I had cause for alarm when I could not find you anywhere. Yesterday afternoon I sent you three despatches, to the addresses you gave me, Lyons, Beaucaire, and Oloron, but received no answer. I was almost crazy with anxiety when your message reached me just now."

"Things are getting hot, then."

"Hot! They are burning! The place is too warm to hold me any longer; upon my soul, I can't stand it!"

M. Verduret occupied himself in repairing his toilet, become disarranged by lying down.

When he had finished, he threw himself in an easy-chair, and said to Joseph Dubois, who remained respectfully standing, cap in hand, like a soldier awaiting orders:

"Explain yourself, my boy, and quickly, if you please; no circumlocution."

"It is just this, patron. I don't know what your plans are, or what line you are taking now; but I can just tell you this: that you will have to wind up the affair pretty quickly."

"That is your opinion, Master Joseph?"

"Yes, patron, because if you wait any longer, goodbye to our covey: you will certainly find an empty cage, and the birds flown. You smile? Yes, I know you are clever, and can accomplish anything; but they are cunning blades, and as slippery as eels. They know that they are watched, too."

"The devil they do!" cried M. Verduret. "Who has been committing blunders?"

"Oh! nobody has done anything wrong," replied Joseph. "You know, patron, that they suspected something long ago. They gave you a proof of it, the night of the fancy ball; that ugly cut on your arm was the beginning. Ever since, they have had one eye open all the time.

They had begun to feel easier, when all of a sudden, yesterday, *ma foi*, they began to smell a rat!"

"Was that the cause of your telegrams?"

"Of course. Now listen: yesterday morning when my master got up, about ten o'clock, he took it into his head to arrange the papers in his desk; which, by the way, has a disgusting lock which has given me a deal of trouble. Meanwhile, I pretended to be fixing the fire, so as to remain in the room to watch him. Patron, the man has an eye like a Yankee! At the first glance he saw, or rather divined, that his papers had been meddled with, he turned livid, and swore an oath; Lord, what an oath!"

"Never mind the oath; go on."

"Well, how he discovered the little attentions I had devoted to his letters, I can't imagine. You know how careful I am. I had put everything in perfect order; just as I found things I left them, when, lo and behold! my noble *marquis* picks up each paper, one at a time, turns it over, and smells it. I was just thinking I would offer him a magnifying-glass, when all of a sudden he sprang up, and with one kick sent his chair across the room, and flew at me with his eyes flashing like two pistols. 'Somebody has been at my papers,' he shrieked; 'this letter has been photographed!' B-r-r-r! I am not a coward, but I can tell you that my heart stood perfectly still; I saw myself as dead as Caesar, cut into mince-meat; and says I to myself, 'Fanfer—excuse me—Dubois, my friend, you are lost, dead;' and I thought of Madame Alexandre."

M. Verduret was buried in thought, and paid no attention to the worthy Joseph's analysis of his personal sensations.

"What happened next?" said Verduret after a few minutes.

"Why, he was just as frightened as I was, patron. The rascal did not even dare to touch me. To be sure, I had taken the precaution to get out of his reach; we talked with a large table between us. While wondering what could have enabled him to discover the secret, I defended myself with virtuous indignation. I said:

"'It cannot be; M. le Marquis is mistaken. Who would dare touch his papers?'

"*Bast*! Instead of listening to me, he flourished an open letter, and said:

"'This letter has been photographed! here is proof of it!' and he pointed to a little yellow spot on the paper, shrieking out, 'Look! Smell! Smell it, you devil! It is—' I forget the name he called it, but some acid used by photographers."

"I know, I know," said M. Verduret; "go on; what next?"

"Then, patron, we had a scene; what a scene! He ended by seizing me by the throat, and shaking me like a plum-tree, saying he would shake me until I told him who I was, what I knew, and where I came from. As if I knew, myself! I was obliged to account for every minute of my time since I had been in his service. The devil was worse than a judge of instruction, in his questions. Then he sent for the hotel porter, who had charge of the front door, and questioned him closely, but in English, so that I could not understand. After a while, he cooled down, and when the boy was gone, presented me with twenty *francs*, saying, 'I am sorry I was so sharp with you; you are too stupid to have been guilty of the offence.'"

"He said that, did he?"

"He used those very words to my face, patron."

"And you think he meant what he said?"

"Certainly I do."

The fat man smiled, and whistled a little tune expressive of contempt.

"If you think that," he said, "de Clameran was right in his estimate of your brilliancy."

It was easy to see that Joseph Dubois was anxious to hear his patron's grounds for considering him stupid, but dared not ask.

"I suppose I am stupid, if you think so," said poor Fanferlot humbly. "Well, after he had done blustering about the letters, M. le Marquis dressed, and went out. He did not want his carriage, but I saw him hire a cab at the hotel door. I thought he had perhaps disappeared forever; but I was mistaken. About five o'clock he returned as gay as a bullfinch. During his absence, I had telegraphed to you."

What! did you not follow him?"

"I stayed on the spot in case of his return; but one of our friends kept watch on him, and this friend gave me a report of my dandy's movements. First he went to a broker's, then to the bank and discount office: so he must be collecting his money to take a little trip."

"Is that all he did?"

"That is all, patron. But I must tell you how the rascals tried to shut up, 'administratively,' you understand, Mademoiselle Palmyre. Fortunately you had anticipated something of the kind, and given orders to watch over her safety. But for you, she would now be in prison."

Joseph looked up to the ceiling by way of trying to remember something more. Finding nothing there, he said:

"That is all. I rather think M. Patrigent will rub his hands with delight when I carry him my report. He did not expect to see me any more, and has no idea of the facts I have collected to swell the size of his File 113."

There was a long silence. Joseph was right in supposing that the crisis had come. M. Verduret was arranging his plan of battle while waiting for the report of Nina—now Palmyre, upon which depended his point of attack.

But Joseph Dubois began to grow restless and uneasy.

"What must I do now, patron?" he asked.

"Return to the hotel; probably your master had noticed your absence; but he will say nothing about it, so continue—"

Here M.Verduret was interrupted by an exclamation from Prosper, who was standing near a window.

"What is the matter?" he inquired. "There is de Clameran!" cried Prosper, "over there."

M.Verduret and Joseph ran to the window.

"Where is he?" said Joseph, "I don't see him."

"There, at the corner of the bridge, behind that orange-woman's stall."

Prosper was right. It was the noble Marquis de Clameran, who, hid behind the stall, was watching for his servant to come out of the Archangel.

At first the quick-sighted Verduret had some doubts whether it was the *marquis*, who, being skilled in these hazardous expeditions, managed to conceal himself behind a pillar so as to elude detection.

But a moment came, when, elbowed by the pressing crowd, he was obliged to come out on the pavement in full view of the window.

"Now don't you see I was right!" cried the cashier.

"Well," said the amazed Joseph, "I am amazed!"

M.Verduret seemed not in the least surprised, but quietly said:

"The game needs hunting. Well, Joseph, my boy, do you still think that your noble master was duped by your acting injured innocence?"

"You assured me to the contrary, patron," said Joseph in an humble tone; "and your opinion is more convincing than all the proofs in the world."

"This pretended outburst of rage was premeditated on the part of your noble master. Knowing that he is being tracked, he naturally wishes to discover who his adversaries are. You can imagine how uncomfortable he must be at this uncertainty. Perhaps he thinks his pursuers are some of his old accomplices, who, being starved, want a piece of his cake. He will remain there until you come out: then he will come in to find out who you are."

"But, patron, I can go home without his seeing me."

"Yes, I know. You will climb the little wall separating the Archangel from the wine-merchant's yard, and keep along the stationer's area, until you reach the Rue de la Huchette."

Poor Joseph looked as if he had just received a bucket of ice-water upon his head.

"Exactly the way I was going, patron," he gasped out. "I heard that you knew every plank and door of all the houses in Paris, and it certainly must be so."

The fat man made no reply to Joseph's admiring remarks. He was thinking how he could catch de Clameran.

As to the cashier, he listened wonderingly, watching these strangers, who seemed determined to reinstate him in public opinion, and punish his enemies, while he himself stood by powerless and bewildered. What their motives for befriending him could be, he vainly tried to discover.

"I will tell you what I can do," said Joseph after deep thought.

"What is it?"

"I can innocently walk out of the front door, and loaf along the street until I reach the Hotel du Louvre."

"And then?"

"*Dame!* De Clameran will come in and question Madame Alexandre, whom you can instruct beforehand; and she is smart enough to put any sharper off the track."

"Bad plan!" pronounced M. Verduret decidedly; "a scamp so compromised as de Clameran is not easily put off the track; now his eyes are opened, he will be pretty hard to catch."

Suddenly, in a brief tone of authority which admitted of no contradiction, the fat man said:

"I have a way. Has de Clameran, since he found that his papers had been searched, seen Lagors?"

"No, patron."

"Perhaps he has written to him?"

"I'll bet you my head he has not. Having your orders to watch his correspondence, I invented a little system which informs me every time he touches a pen; during the last twenty-four hours the pens have not been touched."

"De Clameran went out yesterday."

"But the man who followed him says he wrote nothing on the way."

"Then we have time yet!" cried Verduret. "Hurry! Hurry! I give you fifteen minutes to make yourself a head; you know the sort; I will watch the rascal until you come up."

The delighted Joseph disappeared in a twinkling; while Prosper and M. Verduret remained at the window observing de Clameran, who, according to the movements of the crowd, was sometimes lost to sight, and sometimes just in front of the window, but was evidently determined not to quit his post until he had obtained the information he sought.

"Why do you devote yourself exclusively to the *marquis*?" asked Prosper.

"Because, my friend," replied M. Verduret, "because—that is my business, and not yours."

Joseph Dubois had been granted a quarter of an hour in which to metamorphose himself; before ten minutes had elapsed he reappeared.

The dandified coachman with Bergami whiskers, red vest, and foppish manners, was replaced by a sinister-looking individual, whose very appearance was enough to scare any rogue.

His black cravat twisted around a paper collar, and ornamented by an imitation diamond pin; his long-tailed black boots and heavy cane, revealed the employee of the Rue de Jerusalem, as plainly as the shoulder-straps mark a soldier.

Joseph Dubois had vanished forever; and from his livery, phoenix-like and triumphant, arose the radiant Fanferlot, surnamed the Squirrel.

When Fanferlot entered the room, Prosper uttered a cry of surprise and almost fright.

He recognised the man who had assisted the commissary of police to examine the bank on the day of the robbery.

M.Verduret examined his aide with a satisfied look, and said:

"Not bad! There is enough of the police-court air about you to alarm even an honest man.You understood me perfectly this time."

Fanferlot was transported with delight at this compliment.

"What must I do now, patron?" he inquired.

"Nothing difficult for an adroit man: but remember, upon the precision of our movements depends the success of my plan. Before arresting Lagors, I wish to dispose of de Clameran. Now that the rascals are separated, the first thing to do is to prevent their coming together."

"I understand," said Fanferlot, snapping his little rat-like eyes; "I am to create a diversion."

"Exactly. Go out by the Rue de la Huchette, and hasten to St. Michel's bridge; loaf along the bank, and finally sit on the steps of the quay, so that de Clameran may know he is being watched. If he doesn't see you, do something to attract his attention."

"*Parbleu*! I will throw a stone into the water," said Fanferlot, rubbing his hands with delight at his own brilliant idea.

"As soon as de Clameran has seen you," continued M. Verduret, "he will be alarmed, and instantly decamp. Knowing there are reasons why the police should be after him, he will hasten to escape you; then comes the time for you to keep wide awake; he is a slippery eel, and cunning as a rat."

"I know all that; I was not born yesterday."

"So much the better. You can convince him of that. Well, knowing you are at his heels, he will not dare to return to the Hotel du Louvre, for fear of being called on by troublesome visitors. Now, it is very important that he should not return to the hotel."

"But suppose he does?" said Fanferlot.

M. Verduret thought for a minute, and then said:

"It is not probable that he will do so; but if he should, you must wait until he comes out again, and continue to follow him. But he won't enter the hotel; very likely he will take the cars: but in that event don't lose sight of him, no matter if you have to follow him to Siberia. Have you money with you?"

"I will get some from Madame Alexandre."

"Very good. Ah! one more word. If the rascal takes the cars, send me word. If he beats about the bush until night, be on your guard, especially in lonely places; the desperado is capable of any enormity."

"If necessary, must I fire?"

"Don't be rash; but, if he attacks you, of course defend yourself. Come, 'tis time you were gone."

Dubois-Fanferlot went out. Verduret and Prosper resumed their post of observation.

"Why all this secrecy?" inquired Prosper. "De Clameran is charged with ten times worse crimes than I was ever accused of, and yet my disgrace was made as public as possible."

"Don't you understand," replied the fat man, "that I wish to separate the cause of Raoul from that of the *marquis*? But, *sh*! look!"

De Clameran had left his place near the orange-woman's stand, and approached the bridge, where he seemed to be trying to make out some unexpected object.

"Ah!" said M. Verduret; "he has just discovered our man."

De Clameran's uneasiness was quite apparent; he walked forward a few steps, as if intending to cross the bridge; then, suddenly turning around, rapidly walked in the direction of the Rue St. Jacques.

"He is caught!" cried M. Verduret with delight.

At that moment the door opened, and Madame Nina Gypsy, *alias* Palmyre Chocareille, entered.

Poor Nina! Each day spent in the service of Madeleine seemed to have aged her a year.

Tears had dimmed the brilliancy of her beautiful black eyes; her rosy cheeks were pale and hollow, and her merry smile was quite gone.

Poor Gypsy, once so gay and spirited, now crushed beneath the burden of her sorrows, was the picture of misery.

Prosper thought that, wild with joy at seeing him, and proud of having so nobly devoted herself to his interest, Nina would throw her arms around his neck, and say how much she loved him. To his surprise, Nina scarcely spoke to him. Although his every thought had been devoted to Madeleine since he discovered the reasons for her cruelty, he was hurt by Nina's cold manner.

The girl stood looking at M. Verduret with a mixture of fear and devotion, like a poor dog that has been cruelly treated by its master.

He, however, was kind and gentle in his manner toward her.

"Well, my dear," he said encouragingly, "what news do you bring me?"

"Something is going on at the house, *monsieur*, and I have been trying to get here to tell you; at last, Mademoiselle Madeleine made an excuse for sending me out."

"You must thank Mademoiselle Madeleine for her confidence in me. I suppose she carried out the plan we decided upon?"

"Yes, *monsieur*."

"She receives the Marquis de Clameran's visits?"

"Since the marriage has been decided upon, he comes every day, and *mademoiselle* receives him with kindness. He seems to be delighted."

These answers filled Prosper with anger and alarm. The poor young man, not comprehending the intricate moves of M. Verduret, felt as if he were being tossed about from pillar to post, and made the tool and laughing-stock of everybody.

"What!" he cried; "this worthless Marquis de Clameran, an assassin and a thief, allowed to visit at M. Fauvel's, and pay his addresses to Madeleine? Where are the promises, *monsieur*, which you have made? Have you merely been amusing yourself by raising my hopes, to dash them—"

"Enough!" interrupted M.Verduret harshly; "you are too green to understand anything, my friend. If you are incapable of helping yourself, at least have sense enough to refrain from importuning those who are working for you. Do you not think you have already done sufficient mischief?"

Having administered this rebuke, he turned to Gypsy, and said in softer tones:

"Go on, my child: what have you discovered?"

"Nothing positive, *monsieur*; but enough to make me nervous, and fearful of impending danger. I am not certain, but suspect from appearances, that some dreadful catastrophe is about to happen. It may only be a presentiment. I cannot get any information from Madame Fauvel; she refuses to answer any hints, and moves about like a ghost, never opening her lips. She seems to be afraid of her niece, and to be trying to conceal something from her."

"What about M. Fauvel?"

"I was just about to tell you, *monsieur*. Some fearful misfortune has happened to him, you may depend upon it. He wanders about as if he had lost his mind. Something certainly occurred yesterday; his voice even is changed. He is so harsh and irritable that *mademoiselle* and M. Lucien were wondering what could be the matter with him. He seems to be on the eve of giving way to a burst of anger; and there is a wild, strange look about his eyes, especially when he looks at *madame*. Yesterday evening, when M. de Clameran was announced, he jumped up, and hurried out of the room, saying that he had some work to do in his study."

A triumphant exclamation from M.Verduret interrupted Madame Gypsy. He was radiant.

"*Hein!*" he said to Prosper, forgetting his bad humour of a few minutes before; "*Hein!* What did I tell you?"

"He has evidently—"

"Been afraid to give way to his first impulse; of course he has. He is now seeking for proofs of your assertions. He must have them by this time. Did the ladies go out yesterday?"

"Yes, a part of the day."

"What became of M. Fauvel?"

"The ladies took me with them; we left M. Fauvel at home."

"Not a doubt of it!" cried the fat man; "he looked for proofs, and found them, too! Your letter told him exactly where to go. Ah, Prosper, that unfortunate letter gives more trouble than everything else together."

These words seemed to throw a sudden light on Madame Gypsy's mind.

"I understand it now!" she exclaimed. "M. Fauvel knows everything."

"That is, he thinks he knows everything; and what he has been led to fear, and thinks he has discovered, is worse than the true state of affairs."

"That accounts for the order which M. Cavaillon overheard him give to his servant-man, Evariste."

"What order?"

"He told Evariste to bring every letter that came to the house, no matter to whom addressed, into his study, and hand them to him; saying that, if this order was disobeyed, he should be instantly discharged."

"At what time was this order given?" asked M. Verduret.

"Yesterday afternoon."

"That is what I was afraid of," cried M. Verduret. "He has clearly made up his mind what course to pursue, and is keeping quiet so as to make his vengeance more sure. The question is, Have we still time to counteract his projects? Have we time to convince him that the anonymous letter was incorrect in some of its assertions?"

He tried to hit upon some plan for repairing the damage done by Prosper's foolish letter.

"Thank you for your information, my dear child," he said after a long silence. "I will decide at once what steps to take, for it will never do to sit quietly and let things go on in this way. Return home without delay, and be careful of everything you say and do; for M. Fauvel suspects you of being in the plot. Send me word of anything that happens, no matter how insignificant it may be."

Nina, thus dismissed, did not move, but said timidly:

"What about Caldas, *monsieur*?"

This was the third time during the last fortnight that Prosper had heard this name, Caldas.

The first time it had been whispered in his ear by a respectable-looking, middle-aged man, who offered his protection one day, when passing through the police-office passage.

The second time, the judge of instruction had mentioned it in connection with Gypsy's history.

Prosper thought over all the men he had ever been connected with, but could recall none named Caldas.

The impassable M.Verduret started and trembled at the mention of this name, but, quickly recovering himself, said:

"I promised to find him for you, and I will keep my promise. Now you must go; good-morning."

It was twelve o'clock, and M.Verduret suddenly remembered that he was hungry. He called Madame Alexandre, and the beaming hostess of the Archangel soon placed a tempting breakfast before Prosper and his friend.

But the savoury broiled oysters and flaky biscuit failed to smooth the perplexed brow of M.Verduret.

To the eager questions and complimentary remarks of Madame Alexandre, he answered:

"*Chut, chut*! let me alone; keep quiet."

For the first time since he had known the fat man, Prosper saw him betray anxiety and hesitation.

He remained silent as long as he could, and then uneasily said:

"I am afraid I have embarrassed you very much, *monsieur*."

"Yes, you have dreadfully embarrassed me," replied M. Verduret. "What on earth to do now, I don't know! Shall I hasten matters, or keep quiet and wait for the next move? And I am bound by a sacred promise. Come, we had better go and consult with the invesigating magistrate. He can perhaps assist me. You had better come too."

Chapter 23

As M.Verduret had anticipated, Prosper's letter had a terrible effect upon M. Fauvel.

It was toward nine o'clock in the morning, and M. Fauvel had just entered his study when his mail was brought in.

After opening a dozen business letters, his eyes fell on the fatal missive sent by Prosper.

Something about the writing struck him as peculiar.

It was evidently a disguised hand, and although, owing to the fact of his being a millionaire, he was in the habit of receiving anonymous communications, sometimes abusive, but generally begging him for money, this particular letter filled him with an indefinite presentiment of evil. A cold chill ran through his heart, and he dreaded to open it.

With absolute certainty that he was about to learn of a new calamity, he broke the seal, and opening the coarse cafe paper, was shocked by the following words:

> Dear Sir—You have handed your cashier over to the law, and you acted properly, convinced as you were of his dishonesty. But if it was he who took three hundred and fifty thousand *francs* from your safe, was it he also who took Madame Fauvel's diamonds?

This was a terrible blow to a man whose life hitherto had been an unbroken chain of prosperity, who could recall the past without one bitter regret, without remembering any sorrow deep enough to bring forth a tear.

What! His wife deceive him! And among all men, to choose one vile enough to rob her of her jewels, and force her to be his accomplice in the ruin of an innocent young man!

For did not the letter before him assert this to be a fact, and tell him how to convince himself of its truth?

M. Fauvel was as bewildered as if he had been knocked on the head with a club. It was impossible for his scattered ideas to take in the enormity of what these dreadful words intimated. He seemed to be mentally and physically paralyzed, as he sat there staring blankly at the letter.

But this stupefaction suddenly changed to indignant rage.

"What a fool I am!" he cried, "to listen to such base lies, such malicious charges against the purest woman whom God ever sent to bless a man!"

And he angrily crumpled up the letter, and threw it into the empty fireplace, saying:

"I will forget having read it. I will not soil my mind by letting it dwell upon such turpitude!"

He said this, and he thought it; but, for all that, he could not open the rest of his letters. The anonymous missive stood before his eyes in letters of fire, and drove every other thought from his mind.

That penetrating, clinging, all-corroding worm, suspicion, had taken possession of his soul; and as he leaned over his desk, with his face buried in his hands, thinking over many things which had lately occurred, insignificant at the time, but fearfully ominous now, this unwillingly admitted germ of suspicion grew and expanded until it became certainty.

But, resolved that he would not think of his wife in connection with so vile a deed, he imagined a thousand wild excuses for the mischief-maker who took this mode of annoying him; of course there was no truth in his assertions, but from curiosity he would like to know who had written it. And yet suppose—

"Merciful God! can it be true?" he wildly cried, as the idea of his wife's guilt would obstinately return to his troubled mind.

Thinking that the writing might throw some light on the mystery, he started up and tremblingly picked the fatal letter out of the ashes. Carefully smoothing it out, he laid it on his desk, and studied the heavy strokes, light strokes, and capitals of every word.

"It must be from some of my clerks," he finally said, "someone who is angry with me for refusing to raise his salary; or perhaps it is the one that I dismissed the other day."

Clinging to this idea, he thought over all the young men in his bank; but not one could he believe capable of resorting to so base a vengeance.

Then he wondered where the letter had been posted, thinking this might throw some light upon the mystery. He looked at the envelope, and read the post-mark:

"Rue du Cardinal Lemoine."

This fact told him nothing.

Once more he read the letter, spelling over each word, and trying to put a different construction on the horrible phrases that stared him in the face.

It is generally agreed that an anonymous letter should be treated with silent contempt, and cast aside as the malicious lies of a coward who dares not say to a man's face what he secretly commits to paper, and forces upon him.

This is all very well in theory, but is difficult to practise when the anonymous letter comes. You throw it in the fire, it burns; but, although the paper is destroyed by the flames, doubt remains. Suspicion arises from its ashes, like a subtle poison penetrates the inmost recesses of the mind, weakens its holiest beliefs, and destroys its faith.

The trail of the serpent is left.

The wife suspected, no matter how unjustly, is no longer the wife in whom her husband trusted as he would trust himself: the pure being who was above suspicion no longer exists. Suspicion, no matter whence the source, has irrevocably tarnished the brightness of his idol.

Unable to struggle any longer against these conflicting doubts, M. Fauvel determined to resolve them by showing the letter to his wife; but a torturing thought, more terrible than any he had yet suffered, made him sink back in his chair in despair.

"Suppose it be true!" he muttered to himself; "suppose I have been miserably duped! By confiding in my wife, I shall put her on her guard, and lose all chance of discovering the truth."

Thus were realised all Verduret's presumptions.

He had said, "If M. Fauvel does not yield to his first impulse, if he stops to reflect, we have time to repair the harm done."

After long and painful meditation, the banker finally decided to wait, and watch his wife.

It was a hard struggle for a man of his frank, upright nature, to play the part of a domestic spy, and jealous husband.

Accustomed to give way to sudden bursts of anger, but quickly mastering them, he would find it difficult to be compelled to preserve his self-restraint, no matter how dreadful the discoveries might be. When he collected the proofs of guilt one by one, he must impose silence upon his resentment, until fully assured of possessing certain evidence.

There was one simple means of ascertaining whether the diamonds had been pawned.

If the letter lied in this instance, he would treat it with the scorn it deserved. If, on the other hand, it should prove to be true!

At this moment, the servant announced breakfast; and M. Fauvel looked in the glass before leaving his study, to see if his face betrayed the emotion he felt. He was shocked at the haggard features which it reflected.

"Have I no nerve?" he said to himself: "oh! I must and shall control my feelings until I find out the truth."

At table he talked incessantly, so as to escape any questions from his wife, who, he saw, was uneasy at the sight of his pale face.

But, all the time he was talking, he was casting over in his mind expedients of getting his wife out of the house long enough for him to search her bureau.

At last he asked Madame Fauvel if she were going out before dinner.

"Yes," said she: "the weather is dreadful, but Madeleine and I must do some shopping."

"At what time shall you go?"

"Immediately after breakfast."

He drew a long breath as if relieved of a great weight.

In a short time he would know the truth.

His uncertainty was so torturing to the unhappy man that he preferred the most dreadful reality to his present agony.

Breakfast over, he lighted a cigar, but did not remain in the dining-room to smoke it, as was his habit. He went into his study to try and compose his nerves.

He took the precaution to send Lucien on a message so as to be alone in the house.

After the lapse of half an hour, he heard the carriage roll away with his wife and niece.

Hurrying into Madame Fauvel's room, he opened the drawer of the *chiffonier*, where she kept her jewels.

The last dozen or more leather and velvet boxes, containing superb sets of jewellery which he had presented to her, were gone!

Twelve boxes remained. He nervously opened them.

They were all empty!

The anonymous letter had told the truth.

"Oh, it cannot be!" he gasped in broken tones. "Oh, no, no!"

He wildly pulled open every drawer in the vain hope of finding them packed away. Perhaps she kept them elsewhere.

He tried to hope that she had sent them to be reset; but no, they were all superbly set in the latest fashion; and, moreover, she never would have sent them all at once. He looked again.

Nothing! not one jewel could he find.

He remembered that he had asked his wife at the Jandidier ball why she did not wear her diamonds; and she had replied with a smile:

"Oh! what is the use? Everybody knows them so well; and, besides, they don't suit my costume."

Yes, she had made the answer without blushing, without showing the slightest sign of agitation or shame.

What hardened impudence! What base hypocrisy concealed beneath an innocent, confiding manner!

And she had been thus deceiving him for twenty years! But suddenly a gleam of hope penetrated his confused mind—slight, barely possible; still a straw to cling to:

"Perhaps Valentine has put her diamonds in Madeleine's room."

Without stopping to consider the indelicacy of what he was about to do, he hurried into the young girl's room, and pulled open one drawer after another. What did he find?

Not Madame Fauvel's diamonds; but Madeleine's seven or eight boxes also empty.

Great heavens! Was this gentle girl, whom he had treated as a daughter, an accomplice in this deed of shame? Had she contributed her jewellery to add to the disgrace of the roof that sheltered her?

This last blow was almost too much for the miserable man. He sank almost lifeless into a chair, and wringing his hands, groaned over the wreck of his happiness. Was this the happy future to which he had looked forward? Was the fabric of his honour, well-being, and domestic bliss, to be dashed to the earth and forever lost in a day? Were his twenty years' labour and high-standing to end thus in shame and sorrow?

Apparently nothing was changed in his existence; he was not materially injured; he could not reach forth his hand, and heal or revenge the smarting wound; the objects around him were unchanged; everything went on in the outside world just as it had gone on during the last twenty years; and yet what a horrible change had taken place in his own heart! While the world envied his prosperity and happiness, here he sat, more heart sore and wearied of life than the worst criminal that ever stood before the inquisition.

What! Valentine, the pure young girl whom he had loved and married in spite of her poverty, in spite of her cold offering of calm affection in return for his passionate devotion; Valentine, the tender, loving wife, who, before a year of married life had rolled by, so often assured him that her affection had grown into a deep, confiding love, that her devotion had grown stronger every day, and that her only prayer was that God would take them both together, since life would be a burden without her noble husband to shield and cherish her—could she have been acting a lie for twenty years?

She, the darling wife, the mother of his sons!

His sons? Good God! Were they his sons?

If she could deceive him now when she was silver-haired, had she not deceived him when she was young?

Not only did he suffer in the present, but the uncertainty of the past tortured his soul.

He was like a man who is told that the exquisite wine he has drank contains poison.

Confidence is never half-way: it is, or it is not. His confidence was gone. His faith was dead.

The wretched banker had rested his every hope and happiness on the love of his wife. Believing that she had proved faithless, that she had played him false, and was unworthy of trust, he admitted no possibility of peaceful joy, and felt tempted to seek consolation from self-destruction. What had he to live for now, save to mourn over the ashes of the past?

But this dejection did not last long. Indignant anger, and thirst for vengeance, made him start up and swear that he would lose no time in vain regrets.

M. Fauvel well knew that the fact of the diamonds being stolen was not sufficient ground upon which to bring an accusation against any of the accomplices.

He must possess overwhelming proofs before taking any active steps. Success depended upon present secrecy.

He began by calling his valet, and ordering him to bring to him every letter that should come to the house.

He then wrote to a notary at St. Remy, for minute and authentic information about the Lagors family, and especially about Raoul.

Finally, following the advice of the anonymous letter, he went to the Prefecture of Police, hoping to obtain a biography of Clameran.

But the police, fortunately for many people, are as discreetly silent as the grave. They guard their secrets as a miser his treasure.

Nothing but an order from the chief judge could open those formidable green boxes, and reveal their secrets.

M. Fauvel was politely asked what motives urged him to inquire into the past life of a French citizen; and, as he declined to state his reasons, the chief of police told him he had better apply to the *procureur* for the desired information.

This advice he could not follow. He had sworn that the secret of his wrongs should be confined to the three persons interested. He chose to avenge his own injuries, to be alone the judge and executioner.

He returned home more angry than ever; there he found the despatch answering the one which he had sent to St. Remy. It was as follows:

"The Lagors are very poor, and there has never been any member of the family named Raoul. Madame Lagors had no son, only two daughters."

This information dashed his last hope.

The banker thought, when he discovered his wife's infamy, that she had sinned as deeply as a woman could sin; but he now saw that she had practised a system more shocking than the crime itself.

"Wretched creature!" he cried with anguish; "in order to see her lover constantly, she dared introduce him to me under the name of a nephew who never existed. She had the shameless courage to bring him beneath her husband's roof, and seat him at my fireside, between my sons; and I, confiding fool that I was, welcomed the villain, and lent him money."

Nothing could equal the pain of wounded pride and mortification which he suffered at the thought that Raoul and Madame Fauvel had amused themselves with his good-natured credulity and obtuseness.

Nothing but death could wipe out an injury of this nature. But the very bitterness of his resentment enabled him to restrain himself until the time for punishment came. With grim satisfaction he promised himself that his acting would be as successful as theirs.

That day he succeeded in concealing his agitation, and kept up a flow of talk at dinner; but at about nine o'clock, when Clameran called on the ladies, he rushed from the house, for fear that he would be unable to control his indignation at the sight of this destroyer of his happiness; and did not return home until late in the night.

The next day he reaped the fruit of his prudence.

Among the letters which his valet brought him at noon, was one bearing the post-mark of Vesinet.

He carefully opened the envelope, and read:

> Dear Aunt—It is imperatively necessary for me to see you to-day; so do not fail to come to Vesinet.
>
> I will explain why I give you this trouble, instead of calling at your house.
>
> Raoul.

"I have them now!" cried M. Fauvel trembling with satisfaction at the near prospect of vengeance.

Eager to lose no time, he opened a drawer, took out a revolver, and examined the hammer to see if it worked easily.

He imagined himself alone, but a vigilant eye was watching his movements. Gypsy, immediately upon her return from the Archangel, stationed herself at the key-hole of the study-door, and saw all that occurred.

M. Fauvel laid the pistol on the mantel-piece, and nervously resealed the letter, which he then took to the box where the letters were usually left, not wishing anyone to know that Raoul's letter had passed through his hands.

He was only absent two minutes, but, inspired by the imminence of the danger, Gypsy darted into the study, and rapidly extracted the balls from the revolver.

"Thank Heaven!" she murmured: "this peril is averted, and M. Verduret will now perhaps have time to prevent a murder. I must send Cavaillon to tell him."

She hurried into the bank, and sent the clerk with a message, telling him to leave it with Madame Alexandre, if M. Verduret had left the hotel.

An hour later, Madame Fauvel ordered her carriage, and went out.

M. Fauvel jumped into a hackney-coach, and followed her.

"God grant that M. Verduret may be in time!" said Nina to herself, "otherwise Madame Fauvel and Raoul are lost."

Chapter 24

The day that the Marquis de Clameran perceived that Raoul de Lagors was the only obstacle between him and Madeleine, he swore that the obstacle should soon be removed.

He at once took steps for the accomplishment of his purpose. As Raoul was walking out to Vesinet about midnight, he was stopped at a lonely spot, by three men, who asked him what o'clock it was; while looking at his watch, the ruffians fell upon him suddenly, and but for Raoul's wonderful strength and agility, would have left him dead on the spot.

As it was, he soon, by his skilfully plied blows (for he had become a proficient in fencing and boxing in England), made his enemies take to their heels.

He quietly continued his walk home, fully determined to be hereafter well armed when he went out at night.

He never for an instant suspected his accomplice of having instigated the assault.

But two days afterward, while sitting in a *café*, a burly, vulgar-looking man, a stranger to him, interrupted him several times while talking, and, after making several rough speeches as if trying to provoke a quarrel, finally threw a card in his face, saying its owner was ready to grant him satisfaction when and where he pleased.

Raoul rushed toward the man to chastise him on the spot; but his friends held him back, telling him that it would be much more gentlemanly to run a sword through his vulgar hide, than have a scuffle in a public place.

"Very well, then: you will hear from me tomorrow," he said scornfully to his assailant. "Wait at your hotel until I send two friends to arrange the matter with you."

As soon as the stranger had left, Raoul recovered from his excitement, and began to wonder what could have been the motive for this evidently premeditated insult.

Picking up the card of the bully, he read:

W. H. B. Jacobson. Formerly Garibaldian volunteer, Ex-officer of the army of the South. (Italy, America.)
30, Rue Leonie.

Raoul had seen enough of the world to know that these heroes who cover their visiting-cards with titles have very little glory elsewhere than in their own conceit.

Still the insult had been offered in the presence of others; and, no matter who the offender was, it must be noticed. Early the next morning Raoul sent two of his friends to make arrangements for a duel. He gave them M. Jacobson's address, and told them to report at the Hotel du Louvre, where he would wait for them.

Having dismissed his friends, Raoul went to find out something about M. Jacobson; and, being an expert at the business of unravelling plots and snares, he determined to discover who was at the bottom of this duel into which he had been decoyed.

The information obtained was not very promising.

M. Jacobson, who lived in a very suspicious-looking little hotel whose inmates were chiefly women of light character, was described to him as an eccentric gentleman, whose mode of life was a problem difficult to solve. No one knew his means of support.

He reigned despotically in the hotel, went out a great deal, never came in until midnight, and seemed to have no capital to live upon, save his military titles, and a talent for carrying out whatever was undertaken for his own benefit.

"That being his character," thought Raoul, "I cannot see what object he can have in picking a quarrel with me. What good will it do him to run a sword through my body? Not the slightest; and, moreover, his pugnacious conduct is apt to draw the attention of the police, who, from what I hear, are the last people this warrior would like to have after him. Therefore he must have some reason for pursuing me; and I must find out what it is."

The result of his meditations was, that Raoul, upon his return to the Hotel du Louvre, did not mention a word of his adventure to de Clameran, whom he found already up.

At half-past eight his seconds arrived.

M. Jacobson had selected the sword, and would fight that very hour, in the woods of Vincennes.

"Well, come along," cried Raoul gaily. "I accept the gentleman's conditions."

They found the Garibaldian waiting; and after an interchange of a few thrusts Raoul was slightly wounded in the right shoulder.

The "Ex-superior officer of the South" wished to continue the combat; but Raoul's seconds—brave young men—declared that honour was satisfied, and that they had no intention of subjecting their friend's life to unnecessary hazards.

The ex-officer was forced to admit that this was but fair, and unwillingly retired from the field. Raoul went home delighted at having escaped with nothing more serious than a little loss of blood, and resolved to keep clear of all so-called Garibaldians in the future.

In fact, a night's reflection had convinced him that de Clameran was the instigator of the two attempts to kill him. Madame Fauvel having told him what conditions Madeleine placed on her consent to marriage, Raoul instantly saw how necessary his removal would be, now that he was an impediment in the way of de Clameran's success. He recalled a thousand little remarks and events of the last few days, and, on skilfully questioning the *marquis*, had his suspicions changed into certainty.

This conviction that the man whom he had so materially assisted in his criminal plans was so basely ungrateful as to turn against him, and hire assassins to murder him in cold blood, inspired in Raoul a resolution to take speedy vengeance upon his treacherous accomplice, and at the same time insure his own safety.

This treason seemed monstrous to Raoul. He was as yet not sufficiently experienced in ruffianism to know that one villain always sacrifices another to advance his own projects; he was credulous enough to believe in the adage, "there's honour among thieves."

His rage was naturally mingled with fright, well knowing that his life hung by a thread, when it was threatened by a daring scoundrel like de Clameran.

He had twice miraculously escaped; a third attempt would more than likely prove fatal.

Knowing his accomplice's nature, Raoul saw himself surrounded by snares; he saw death before him in every form; he was equally afraid of going out, and of remaining at home. He only ventured with the most suspicious caution into the most public places; he feared poison more than the assassin's knife, and imagined that every dish placed before him tasted of strychnine.

As this life of torture was intolerable, he determined to anticipate a struggle which he felt must terminate in the death of either de Clameran or himself; and, if he were doomed to die, to be first revenged. If he went down, de Clameran should go too; better kill the devil than be killed by him.

In his days of poverty, Raoul had often risked his life to obtain a few guineas, and would not have hesitated to make short work of a person like de Clameran.

But with money prudence had come. He wished to enjoy his four hundred thousand *francs* without being compromised by committing a murder which might be discovered; he therefore began to devise some other means of getting rid of his dreaded accomplice. Meanwhile, he devoted his thoughts to some discreet way of thwarting de Clameran's marriage with Madeleine. He was sure that he would thus strike him to the heart, and this was at least a satisfaction.

Raoul was persuaded that, by openly siding with Madeleine and her aims, he could save them from de Clameran's clutches. Having fully resolved upon this course, he wrote a note to Madame Fauvel asking for an interview.

The poor woman hastened to Vesinet convinced that some new misfortune was in store for her.

Her alarm was groundless. She found Raoul more tender and affectionate than he had ever been. He saw the necessity of reassuring her, and winning his old place in her forgiving heart, before making his disclosures.

He succeeded. The poor lady had a smiling and happy air as she sat in an arm-chair, with Raoul kneeling beside her.

"I have distressed you too long, my dear mother," he said in his softest tones, "but I repent sincerely: now listen to my—"

He had not time to say more; the door was violently thrown open, and Raoul, springing to his feet, was confronted by M. Fauvel.

The banker had a revolver in his hand, and was deadly pale.

It was evident that he was making superhuman efforts to remain calm, like a judge whose duty it is to justly punish crime.

"Ah," he said with a horrible laugh, "you look surprised. You did not expect me? You thought that my imbecile credulity insured your safety."

Raoul had the courage to place himself before Madame Fauvel, and to stand prepared to receive the expected bullet.

"I assure you, uncle," he began.

"Enough!" interrupted the banker with an angry gesture, "let me hear no more infamous falsehoods! End this acting, of which I am no longer the dupe."

"I swear to you—"

"Spare yourself the trouble of denying anything. I know all. I know who pawned my wife's diamonds. I know who committed the robbery for which an innocent man was arrested and imprisoned."

Madame Fauvel, white with terror, fell upon her knees.

At last it had come—the dreadful day had come. Vainly had she added falsehood to falsehood; vainly had she sacrificed herself and others: all was discovered.

She saw that all was lost, and wringing her hands she tearfully moaned:

"Pardon, Andre! I beg you, forgive me!"

At these heart-broken tones, the banker shook like a leaf. This voice brought before him the twenty years of happiness which he had owed to this woman, who had always been the mistress of his heart, whose slightest wish had been his law, and who, by a smile or a frown, could make him the happiest or the most miserable of men. Alas! those days were over now.

Could this wretched woman crouching at his feet be his beloved Valentine, the pure, innocent girl whom he had found secluded in the Château of La Verberie, who had never loved any other than himself? Could this be the cherished wife whom he had worshipped for so many years?

The memory of his lost happiness was too much for the stricken man. He forgot the present in the past, and was almost melted to forgiveness.

"Unhappy woman," he murmured, "unhappy woman! What have I done that you should thus betray me? Ah, my only fault was loving you too deeply, and letting you see it. One wearies of everything in this world, even happiness. Did pure domestic joys pall upon you, and weary you, driving you to seek the excitement of a sinful passion? Were you so tired of the atmosphere of respect and affection which surrounded you, that you must needs risk your honour and mine by braving public opinion? Oh, into what an abyss you have fallen, Valentine! and, oh, my God! if you were wearied by my constant devotion, had the thought of your children no power to restrain your evil passions; could you not remain untarnished for their sake?"

M. Fauvel spoke slowly, with painful effort, as if each word choked him.

Raoul, who listened with attention, saw that if the banker knew some things, he certainly did not know all.

He saw that erroneous information had misled the unhappy man, and that he was still a victim of false appearances.

He determined to convince him of the mistake under which he was labouring, and said:

"*Monsieur*, I hope you will listen."

But the sound of Raoul's voice was sufficient to break the charm.

"Silence!" cried the banker with an angry oath, "silence!"

For some moments nothing was heard but the sobs of Madame Fauvel.

"I came here," continued the banker, "with the intention of killing you both. But I cannot kill a woman, and I will not kill an unarmed man."

Raoul once more tried to speak.

"Let me finish!" interrupted M. Fauvel. "Your life is in my hands; the law excuses the vengeance of an injured husband; but I refuse to take advantage of it. I see on your mantel a revolver similar to mine; take it, and defend yourself."

"Never!"

"Defend yourself!" cried the banker raising his arm, "if you do not—"

Feeling the barrel of M. Fauvel's revolver touch his breast, Raoul in self-defence seized his own pistol, and prepared to fire.

"Stand in that corner of the room, and I will stand in this," continued the banker; "and when the clock strikes, which will be in a few seconds, we will both fire."

They took the places designated, and stood perfectly still.

But the horror of the scene was too much for Madame Fauvel to witness any longer without interposing. She understood but one thing: her son and her husband were about to kill each other before her very eyes. Fright and horror gave her strength to start up and rush between the two men.

"For God's sake, have mercy, Andre!" she cried, wringing her hands with anguish, "let me tell you everything; don't kill—"

This burst of maternal love, M. Fauvel thought the pleadings of a criminal woman defending her lover.

He roughly seized his wife by the arm, and thrust her aside, saying with indignant scorn:

"Get out of the way!"

But she would not be repulsed; rushing up to Raoul, she threw her arms around him, and said to her husband:

"Kill me, and me alone; for I am the guilty one."

At these words M. Fauvel glared at the guilty pair, and, deliberately taking aim, fired.

Neither Raoul nor Madame Fauvel moved. The banker fired a second time; then a third.

He cocked the pistol for a fourth shot, when a man rushed into the room, snatched the pistol from the banker's hand, and, throwing him on the sofa, ran toward Madame Fauvel.

This man was M. Verduret, who had been warned by Cavaillon, but did not know that Madame Gypsy had extracted the balls from M. Fauvel's revolver.

"Thank Heaven!" he cried, "she is unhurt."

"How dare you interfere?" cried the banker, who by this time had joined the group. "I have the right to avenge my honour when it has been degraded; the villain shall die!"

M. Verduret seized the banker's wrists in a vice-like grasp, and whispered in his ear:

"Thank God you are saved from committing a terrible crime; the anonymous letter deceived you."

In violent situations like this, all the untoward, strange attending circumstances appear perfectly natural to the participators, whose passions have already carried them beyond the limits of social propriety.

Thus M. Fauvel never once thought of asking this stranger who he was and where he came from.

He heard and understood but one fact: the anonymous letter had lied.

"But my wife confesses she is guilty," he stammered.

"So she is," replied M. Verduret, "but not of the crime you imagine. Do you know who that man is, that you attempted to kill?"

"Her lover!"

"No: her son!"

The words of this stranger, showing his intimate knowledge of the private affairs of all present, seemed to confound and frighten Raoul more than M. Fauvel's threats had done. Yet he had sufficient presence of mind to say:

"It is the truth!"

The banker looked wildly from Raoul to M. Verduret; then, fastening his haggard eyes on his wife, exclaimed:

"It is false! you are all conspiring to deceive me! Proofs!"

"You shall have proofs," replied M. Verduret, "but first listen."

And rapidly, with his wonderful talent for exposition, he related the principal points of the plot he had discovered.

The true state of the case was terribly distressing to M. Fauvel, but nothing compared with what he had suspected.

His throbbing, yearning heart told him that he still loved his wife. Why should he punish a fault committed so many years ago, and atoned for by twenty years of devotion and suffering?

For some moments after M. Verduret had finished his explanation, M. Fauvel remained silent.

So many strange events had happened, rapidly following each other in succession, and culminating in the shocking scene which had just taken place, that M. Fauvel seemed to be too bewildered to think clearly.

If his heart counselled pardon and forgetfulness, wounded pride and self-respect demanded vengeance.

If Raoul, the baleful witness, the living proof of a far-off sin, were not in existence, M. Fauvel would not have hesitated. Gaston de Clameran was dead; he would have held out his arms to his wife, and said:

"Come to my heart! your sacrifices for my honour shall be your absolution; let the sad past be forgotten."

But the sight of Raoul froze the words upon his lips.

"So this is your son," he said to his wife—"this man, who has plundered you and robbed me!"

Madame Fauvel was unable to utter a word in reply to these reproachful words.

"Oh!" said M. Verduret, "*madame* will tell you that this young man is the son of Gaston de Clameran; she has never doubted it. But the truth is—"

"What!"

"That, in order to swindle her, he has perpetrated a gross imposture."

During the last few minutes Raoul had been quietly creeping toward the door, hoping to escape while no one was thinking of him.

But M. Verduret, who anticipated his intentions, was watching him out of the corner of one eye, and stopped him just as he was about leaving the room.

"Not so fast, my pretty youth," he said, dragging him into the middle of the room; "it is not polite to leave us so unceremoniously. Let us have a little conversation before parting; a little explanation will be edifying!"

The jeering words and mocking manner of M. Verduret made Raoul turn deadly pale, and start back as if confronted by a phantom.

"The clown!" he gasped.

"The same, friend," said the fat man. "Ah, now that you recognise me, I confess that the clown and myself are one and the same. Yes, I am the *mountebank* of the Jandidier ball; here is proof of it."

And turning up his sleeve he showed a deep cut on his arm.

"I think that this recent wound will convince you of my identity," he continued. "I imagine you know the villain that gave me this little decoration, that night I was walking along the Rue Bourdaloue. That being the case, you know, I have a slight claim upon you, and shall expect you to relate to us your little story."

But Raoul was so terrified that he could not utter a word.

"Your modesty keeps you silent," said M. Verduret. "Bravo! modesty becomes talent, and for one of your age you certainly have displayed a talent for knavery."

M. Fauvel listened without understanding a word of what was said.

"Into what dark depths of shame have we fallen!" he groaned.

"Reassure yourself, *monsieur*," replied M. Verduret with great respect. "After what I have been constrained to tell you, what remains to be said is a mere trifle. I will finish the story.

"On leaving Mihonne, who had given him a full account of the misfortunes of Mademoiselle Valentine de la Verberie, de Clameran hastened to London.

"He had no difficulty in finding the farmer's wife to whom the old countess had entrusted Gaston's son.

"But here an unexpected disappointment greeted him.

"He learned that the child, whose name was registered on the parish books as Raoul-Valentin Wilson, had died of the croup when eighteen months old."

"Did anyone state such a fact as that?" interrupted Raoul: "it is false."

"It was not only stated, but proved, my pretty youth," replied M. Verduret. "You don't suppose I am a man to trust to verbal testimony; do you?"

He drew from his pocket several officially stamped documents, with red seals attached, and laid them on the table.

"These are declarations of the nurse, her husband, and four witnesses. Here is an extract from the register of births; this is a certificate of registry of his death; and all these are authenticated at the French Embassy. Now are you satisfied, young man?"

"What next?" inquired M. Fauvel.

"The next step was this," replied M. Verduret. "De Clameran, finding that the child was dead, supposed that he could, in spite of this disappointment, obtain money from Madame Fauvel; he was mistaken. His first attempt failed. Having an inventive turn of mind, he determined that the child should come to life. Among his large circle of rascally acquaintances, he selected a young fellow to impersonate Raoul-Valentin Wilson; and the chosen one stands before you."

Madame Fauvel was in a pitiable state. And yet she began to feel a ray of hope; her acute anxiety had so long tortured her, that the truth was a relief; she would thank Heaven if this wicked man was proved to be no son of hers.

"Can this be possible?" she murmured, "can it be?"

"Impossible!" cried the banker: "an infamous plot like this could not be executed in our midst!"

"All this is false!" said Raoul boldly. "It is a lie!"

M. Verduret turned to Raoul, and, bowing with ironical respect, said:

"*Monsieur* desires proofs, does he? *Monsieur* shall certainly have convincing ones. I have just left a friend of mine, M. Palot, who brought me valuable information from London. Now, my young gentleman, I will tell you the little story he told me, and then you can give your opinion of it.

"In 1847 Lord Murray, a wealthy and generous nobleman, had a jockey named Spencer, of whom he was very fond. At the Epsom races, this jockey was thrown from his horse, and killed. Lord Murray grieved over the loss of his favourite, and, having no children of his own, declared his intention of adopting Spencer's son, who was then but four years old.

"Thus James Spencer was brought up in affluence, as heir to the immense wealth of the noble lord. He was a handsome, intelligent boy, and gave satisfaction to his protector until he was sixteen years of age; when he became intimate with a worthless set of people, and turned out badly.

"Lord Murray, who was very indulgent, pardoned many grave faults; but one fine morning he discovered that his adopted son had been imitating his signature upon some checks. He indignantly dismissed him from the house, and told him never to show his face again.

"James Spencer had been living in London about four years, managing to support himself by gambling and swindling, when he met de Clameran, who offered him twenty-five thousand *francs* to play a part in a little comedy which he had arranged to suit the actors."

"You are a detective!" interrupted Raoul.

The fat man smiled grimly.

"At present," he replied, "I am merely a friend of Prosper Bertomy. It depends entirely upon your behaviour which character I appear in while settling up this little affair."

"What do you expect me to do?"

"Restore the three hundred and fifty thousand *francs* which you have stolen."

The young rascal hesitated a moment, and then said:

"The money is in this room."

"Very good. This frankness is creditable, and will benefit you. I know that the money is in this room, and also exactly where it is to be found. Be kind enough to look behind that cupboard, and you will find the three hundred and fifty thousand *francs*." Raoul saw that his game was lost. He tremblingly went to the cupboard, and pulled out several bundles of bank-notes, and an enormous package of pawnbroker's tickets.

"Very well done," said M. Verduret, as he carefully examined the money and papers: "this is the most sensible step you ever took."

Raoul relied on this moment, when everybody's attention would be absorbed by the money, to make his escape. He slid toward the door, gently opened it, slipped out, and locked it on the outside; the key being still in the lock.

"He has escaped!" cried M. Fauvel.

"Naturally," replied M. Verduret, without even looking up: "I thought he would have sense enough to do that."

"But is he to go unpunished?"

"My dear sir, would you have this affair become a public scandal? Do you wish your wife's name to be brought into a case of this nature before the police-court?"

"Oh, *monsieur*!"

"Then the best thing you can do, is to let the rascal go scot free. Here are receipts for all the articles which he has pawned, so that we should consider ourselves fortunate. He has kept fifty thousand *francs*, but that is all the better for you. This sum will enable him to leave France, and we shall never see him again."

Like everyone else, M. Fauvel yielded to the ascendancy of M. Verduret.

Gradually he had awakened to the true state of affairs; prospective happiness no longer seemed impossible, and he felt that he was indebted to the man before him for more than life. But for M.Verduret, where would have been his honour and domestic peace?

With earnest gratitude he seized M.Verduret's hand as if to carry it to his lips, and said, in broken tones:

"Oh, *monsieur*! how can I ever find words to express how deeply I appreciate your kindness? How can I ever repay the great service you have rendered me?"

M.Verduret reflected a moment, and then said:

"If you feel under any significant obligations to me, *monsieur*, you have it in your power to return them. I have a favour to ask of you."

"A favour? you ask of me? Speak, *monsieur*, you have but to name it. My fortune and life are at your disposal."

"I will not hesitate, then, to explain myself. I am Prosper's friend, and deeply interested in his future. You can exonerate him from this infamous charge of robbery; you can restore him to his honourable position. You can do more than this, *monsieur*. He loves Mademoiselle Madeleine."

"Madeleine shall be his wife, *monsieur*," interrupted the banker: "I give you my word of honour. And I will so publicly exonerate him, that not a shadow of suspicion will rest upon his name. I will place him in a position which will prevent slander from reproaching him with the painful remembrance of my fatal error."

The fat man quietly took up his hat and cane, as if he had been paying an ordinary morning call, and turned to leave the room, after saying, "Good-morning." But, seeing the weeping woman raise her clasped hands appealingly toward him, he said hesitatingly:

"*Monsieur*, excuse my intruding any advice; but Madame Fauvel—"

"Andre!" murmured the wretched wife, "Andre!"

The banker hesitated a moment; then, following the impulse of his heart, ran to his wife, and, clasping her in his arms, said tenderly:

"No, I will not be foolish enough to struggle against my deep-rooted love. I do not pardon, Valentine: I forget; I forget all!"

M. Verduret had nothing more to do at Vesinet.

Without taking leave of the banker, he quietly left the room, and, jumping into his cab, ordered the driver to return to Paris, and drive to the Hotel du Louvre as rapidly as possible.

His mind was filled with anxiety about de Clameran. He knew that Raoul would give him no more trouble; the young rogue was probably taking his passage for some foreign land at that very moment. But de Clameran should not escape unpunished; and how this punishment could be brought about without compromising Madame Fauvel, was the problem to be solved.

M. Verduret thought over the various cases similar to this, but not one of his former expedients could be applied to the present circumstances. He could not deliver the villain over to justice without involving Madame Fauvel.

After long thought, he decided that an accusation of poisoning must come from Oloron. He would go there and work upon "public opinion," so that, to satisfy the townspeople, the authorities would order a post-mortem examination of Gaston. But this mode of proceeding required time; and de Clameran would certainly escape before another day passed over his head. He was too experienced a knave to remain on slippery ground, now that his eyes were open to the danger which menaced him. It was almost dark when the carriage stopped in front of the Hotel du Louvre; M. Verduret noticed a crowd of people collected together in groups, eagerly discussing some exciting event which seemed to have just taken place. Although the policeman attempted to disperse the crowd by authoritatively ordering them to "Move on! Move on!" they would merely separate in one spot to join a more clamorous group a few yards off.

"What has happened?" demanded M. Verduret of a lounger near by.

"The strangest thing you ever heard of," replied the man; "yes, I saw him with my own eyes. He first appeared at that seventh-story window; he was only half-dressed. Some men tried to seize him; but, *bast*! with the agility of a squirrel, he jumped out upon the roof, shrieking, 'Murder! murder!' The recklessness of his conduct led me to suppose—"

The gossip stopped short in his narrative, very much surprised and vexed; his questioner had vanished.

"If it should be de Clameran!" thought M. Verduret; "if terror has deranged that brain, so capable of working out great crimes! Fate must have interposed—"

While thus talking to himself, he elbowed his way through the crowded court-yard of the hotel.

At the foot of the staircase he found M. Fanferlot and three peculiar-looking individuals standing together, as if waiting for someone.

"Well," cried M. Verduret, "what is the matter?"

With laudable emulation, the four men rushed forward to report to their superior officer.

"Patron," they all began at once.

"Silence!" said the fat man with an oath; "one at a time. Quick! what is the matter?"

"The matter is this, patron," said Fanferlot dejectedly. "I am doomed to ill luck. You see how it is; this is the only chance I ever had of working out a beautiful case, and, *paf*! my criminal must go and fizzle! A regular case of bankruptcy!"

"Then it is de Clameran who—"

"Of course it is. When the rascal saw me this morning, he scampered off like a hare. You should have seen him run; I thought he would never stop this side of Ivry: but not at all. On reaching the Boulevard des Ecoles, a sudden idea seemed to strike him, and he made a bee-line for his hotel; I suppose, to get his pile of money. Directly he gets here, what does he see? these three friends of mine. The sight of these gentlemen had the effect of a sunstroke upon him; he went raving mad on the spot. The idea of serving me such a low trick at the very moment I was sure of success!"

"Where is he now?"

"At the prefecture, I suppose. Some policemen handcuffed him, and drove off with him in a cab."

"Come with me."

M. Verduret and Fanferlot found de Clameran in one of the private cells reserved for dangerous prisoners.

He had on a strait-jacket, and was struggling violently against three men, who were striving to hold him, while a physician tried to force him to swallow a potion.

"Help!" he shrieked; "help, for God's sake! Do you not see my brother coming after me? Look! he wants to poison me!"

M. Verduret took the physician aside, and questioned him about the maniac.

"The wretched man is in a hopeless state," replied the doctor; "this species of insanity is incurable. He thinks someone is trying to poison him, and nothing will persuade him to eat or drink anything; and, as it is impossible to force anything down his throat, he will die of starvation, after having suffered all the tortures of poison."

M. Verduret, with a shudder, turned to leave the prefecture, saying to Fanferlot:

"Madame Fauvel is saved, and by the interposition of God, who has himself punished de Clameran!"

"That don't help me in the least," grumbled Fanferlot. "The idea of all my trouble and labour ending in this flat, quiet way!"

"True," replied M. Verduret. "the *File No. 113* will never leave its portfolio. But console yourself; before the end of the month I will give you a letter to a friend of mine, and what you have lost in fame you will gain in gold."

Chapter 25

One mornong some days later, M. Lecoq—the official Lecoq, who resembles the head of a department—was walking up and down his private office, and looking at the clock, at every moment.

At last, a bell rang, and the faithful Janouille ushered in Madame Nina and Prosper Bertomy.

"Ah," said M. Lecoq, "you are punctual, my fond lovers; that is well."

"We are not lovers, *monsieur*," replied Madame Gypsy. "M. Verduret gave us express orders to meet here in your office this morning, and we have obeyed."

"Very good," said the celebrated detective: "then be kind enough to wait a few minutes; I will tell him you are here."

During the quarter of an hour that Nina and Prosper remained alone together, they did not exchange a word. Finally a door opened, and M. Verduret appeared.

Nina and Prosper eagerly started toward him; but he checked them by one of those peculiar looks which no one ever dared resist.

"You have come," he said severely, "to hear the secret of my conduct. I have promised, and will keep my word, however painful it may be to my feelings. Listen, then. My best friend is a loyal, honest man, named Caldas. Eighteen months ago this friend was the happiest of men. Infatuated by a woman, he lived for her alone, and, fool that he was, imagined that she felt the same love for him."

"She did!" cried Gypsy, "yes, she always loved him."

"She showed her love in a peculiar way. She loved him so much, that one fine day she left him, and ran off with another man. In his first moments of despair, Caldas wished to kill himself. Then he reflected that it would be wiser to live, and avenge himself."

"And then," faltered Prosper.

"Then Caldas avenged himself in his own way. He made the woman who deserted him recognise his immense superiority over his rival. Weak, timid, and helpless, the rival was disgraced, and falling over the verge of a precipice, when the powerful hand of Caldas reached forth and saved him. You understand all now, do you not? The woman is Nina; the rival is yourself; and Caldas is—"

With a quick, dexterous movement, he threw off his wig and whiskers, and stood before them the real, intelligent, proud Lecoq.

"Caldas!" cried Nina.

"No, not Caldas, not Verduret any longer: but Lecoq, the detective!"

M. Lecoq broke the stupefied silence of his listeners by saying to Prosper:

"It is not to me alone that you owe your salvation. A noble girl confided to me the difficult task of clearing your reputation. I promised her that M. Fauvel should never know the shameful secrets concerning his domestic happiness. Your letter thwarted all my plans, and made it impossible for me to keep my promise. I have nothing more to say."

He turned to leave the room, but Nina barred his exit.

"Caldas," she murmured, "I implore you to have pity on me! I am *so* miserable! Ah, if you only knew! Be forgiving to one who has always loved you, Caldas! Listen."

Prosper departed from M. Lecoq's office alone.

On the 15th of last month, was celebrated, at the church of Notre Dame de Lorette, the marriage of M. Prosper Bertomy and Mademoiselle Madeleine Fauvel.

The banking-house is still on the Rue de Provence; but as M. Fauvel has decided to retire from business, and live in the country, the name of the firm has been changed, and is now—*Prosper Bertomy & Co.*

A Disappearance

(A.k.a. Missing)

1

One Sunday afternoon, not long ago, the whole district of the Marais—that busy quarter of Paris which nowadays is but one vast workshop from the Temple to the Rue Saint Antoine, from the Bastille to the Rue Turbigo—was in a state of most unwonted excitement. Bustling as it may be on weekdays, when all the bronze factories re-echo to the sound of toil, when the heavy vans roll over the pavement from druggist's to toy-dealer's, taking at each halt some fresh consignment for despatch by rail, when work-people and customers crowd the thousand and one establishments where every description of *article de Paris* is produced for a value of many millions of *francs per annum*—on Sundays, at least, the Marais usually relapses into silence. Were it not for the multitudinous inscriptions which cover all the houses from garret to basement chronicling the names of manufacturers, dealers and commission agents, one might fancy oneself in the old times, when the Marais was inhabited solely by the *rentier* class, by worthy old couples retired from business on fairly decent incomes, or by relics of the ancient nobility, scarcely wealthy enough to reside in the Faubourg St. Germain.

Such, indeed, was the Marais fifty years ago—a quiet and secluded district—and thus have Honore de Balzac and Paul de Kock described it in their novels. But, nowadays, it is a vast hive of industry, whence peace and quiet are utterly banished during the six days set apart for toil. It is only on the Sabbath, when workshops and storerooms are closed, when the weekday toilers are making merry in their native Belleville, or chinking glasses in the *bosquets* of Montreuil, that it regains a semblance of its old tranquillity.

And yet, on the particular Sunday we have mentioned, the usual

"Sabbath-hush" was wanting. True enough, no heavily laden vans were rolling through the narrow streets; no din of hammers and anvils came from the closed *ateliers.* The foot-ways were not bestrewn with packing cases, and no crowd of commissionaires and receivers clerks and commercial travellers, hurried hither and thither peripatetically proving the truth of the axiom that "Time is money." But then, there were unusually animated groups of customers in all the wine shops, unwonted knots of people at the street corners, gatherings of housewives in front of the fruiterers' stores, and conclaves of doorkeepers and kindred scandalmongers in every convenient alley.

Something very extraordinary must have happened, as passersby correctly opined. The fact is, that one of the most honourable manufacturers of the Rue du Roi de Sicile had disappeared, and all efforts to find him had so far proved unsuccessful. The grocer at the corner of the Rue St. Louis possessed full information on the subject—information obtained first hand from the cook of the missing gentleman—and his shop was most extensively patronised that afternoon, even by people who pretended that he mixed dust with his pepper, and sweetened his jam with glucose. For once in a way, they put up with his adulterations to enjoy the benefit of his conversation. "It was yesterday evening," repeated the worthy grocer over and over again, as he assisted in weighing pounds of sugar and penn'orths of salt, "yesterday evening just after dinner, our neighbour M. Jandidier went down to his cellar to get up a bottle of old wine, and since then no one has seen him. The cellar door was found wide open, but M. Jandidier had disappeared, vanished, evaporated!"

From time to time it happens that mysterious disappearances are spoken of. Alarm is spread in various directions, and prudent people invest money in sword sticks and revolvers. But as a rule the police shrug their shoulders when these occurrences are mentioned. They are acquainted with the "seamy side" of the cunningly embroidered canvas. They start an investigation and discover the truth, so different to popular exaggeration: in lieu of a romance, they come upon some sad story.

However, to a certain extent the grocer of the Rue Saint Louis spoke the truth. It was a fact that M. Jandidier, who did a most extensive business as a manufacturer of imitation jewellery, had altogether disappeared since the previous night.

M. Theodore Jandidier was some fifty-eight years old. He was very tall and very bald, gifted with fairly good manners and deportment, and according to popular report, possessed of a very considerable fortune. This was not to be wondered at, for in Paris the trade in imitation jewellery is simply enormous, and some manufacturers like the Bourguignons and others, whose creations are exported all over the world, are simply millionaires. One could not say as much concerning M. Jandidier, but he was, nevertheless, a man of means. A pretty little collection of scrip and bonds were said to yield him an income of twenty thousand *francs* a year, and his business brought him an average annual profit of another fifty thousand. He was esteemed and liked in the neighbourhood, for his probity was above all question, and his morals perfectly exemplary. When five-and-thirty, he had married a portionless cousin, who had proved a happy and faithful wife.

This worthy couple possessed an only daughter named Thérèse, who was literally idolised by her father. At one time it had been said that she was to marry M. Gustave Schmidt, the eldest son of the senior partner in the great banking house of Schmidt, Gubenheim, and Worb, but somehow or other—no one knew why—the marriage had been broken off; and this had caused all the more surprise, as the young folks were apparently very much in love with each other.

Some friends of the Jandidier family pretended that old Schmidt, the father, the most avaricious of all our Parisian financiers, and an inveterate "fleecer," had required that Mademoiselle Thérèse should bring her husband a preposterously large dowry, such as her father could not possibly furnish despite his comparative wealth. However, this was only a rumour which nothing had so far authenticated.

On this Sunday afternoon, when the news of M. Jandidier's disappearance spread through the Marais, all the incidents of his past life which the gossips were acquainted with, were duly recorded and submitted to public appreciation. A hundred stories of his honesty and good nature were told. He had been an honour to the district, an excellent worthy man in every respect. Given his rigid morals, it was altogether impossible to imagine that he had "gone off on the loose." His family ties were too strong for him to have abandoned his wife and daughter. No, he must have fallen a victim to some base scoundrel—he must have received a foul blow; and the honour of the Marais required that his remains should be recovered and fittingly interred, and that his murderer should be brought to justice.

So thus, during that Sunday afternoon, the rumours flew through the district, spreading in every ear and growing on every tongue, till, at last, having learned the reports from his agents, the district commissary of police considered it his duty to repair to the missing gentleman's residence with the view of obtaining precise information.

He was ushered into the grand drawing-room which was in a state of semi-obscurity, the shutters being half closed and the curtains drawn. Both Madame Jandidier and her daughter were distracted with grief, and he had considerable difficulty in calming them and inducing them to answer his questions. However, he was at length placed in possession of these particulars.

On the previous evening (Saturday) M. Jandidier had dined as usual with his family. He had made, however, but a poor meal, for he was troubled with a bad headache. After dinner he had gone downstairs—not to the wine cellar as the grocer of the Rue Saint Louis pretended—but to his warehouse, where a couple of employees were still at work. Having given them some orders, he retired for a short time into his private-room, occupied himself, no doubt, with various business matters, and then came upstairs again and told his wife that he was going out for a stroll. From that stroll he had never returned.

The commissary of police carefully noted down these particulars, and then asked Madame Jandidier if he could not speak with her alone for a few minutes. She looked at him with some surprise but finally signified her assent, and Mademoiselle Thérèse discreetly left the room.

"You must excuse the question I am about to ask you, *madame*," exclaimed the commissary, as the young lady closed the door behind her. "But this is a serious affair, and if we, the officials of justice, are to clear up—the mystery, we must know the whole truth. Excuse my indiscretion, I beg you, but can you tell me whether M. Jandidier, your husband, ever had—to your knowledge—what shall I say? Well, any passing fancy, any feminine acquaintance away from home?"

Madame Jandidier sprang to her feet as if impelled by a spring. Anger had dried her tears, and it was in a snappish voice that she answered, "I have been married three-and twenty years, *monsieur*. Never on any one occasion has my husband given cause for such a supposition. If I was not with him of an evening, he never returned home later than ten o'clock."

"Well, *madame*, was your husband in the habit of frequenting any club?" asked the commissary. "Had he any special café where he met his friends?"

"I should not have allowed such habits," curtly replied the lady.

"Do you know if he was accustomed to carry large sums about his person, *madame*?"

"On that point I can give you no information. I have always attended to my household, and not to my husband's business affairs."

The commissary found it impossible to obtain any further information, for the worthy dame's grief was now blended with a strong admixture of anger and resentment. The supposition that her husband might have a mistress revolted her feelings as a wife, and the barely veiled insinuation that he might frequent a club, and no doubt gamble there, incensed her as an attack on his recognised probity and integrity. However, despite Madame Jandidier's stiff air, the commissary thought it only right to try and assuage her affliction by repeating a few hackneyed "compliments of condolence," and then, with a profound bow, he retired.

Before leaving the house, however, he considered it his duty to question the servants, and their statements, which generally corroborated Madame Jandidier's, made him feel somewhat anxious. He began to think that a crime had really been committed.

A few hours later he sent his report to the Prefecture of Police, and the same evening the case was submitted to the consideration of the public prosecutor. The latter, in his turn, delegated an investigating magistrate to examine the affair, and on the Monday morning the famous detective Retiveau, better known in the Rue de Jerusalem by his nickname of "Maitre Magloire," received orders to scour Paris, and if needs be, the provinces, in search of M. Jandidier—or his corpse. A capital photograph of the manufacturer, taken only a short time previously, was handed to the detective, who at once commenced his difficult task.

2

Maitre Magloire was a man of no little energy, and a fervent believer in the value of time. His alacrity was proverbial, so that the investigating magistrate, entrusted with the Jandidier affair, was by no means surprised when, on the Monday afternoon, his usher announced that the detective wished to speak with him, having already obtained some important information.

The magistrate at once gave orders for the police agent to be admitted. "Here already, M. Magloire," said he. "So you have fresh news, eh?"

"I am on the scent, *monsieur*."

"Well, tell me what you have ascertained."

'To begin, *monsieur*, I have learned that M. Jandidier did not leave home at half-past six on Saturday evening, but at seven o'clock precisely."

"Precisely?"

"Well, yes. My information comes from a clockmaker, in the immediate neighbourhood of M. Jandidier's house. This clockmaker knew him well, and noticed that he paused in front of his shop. In fact, M. Jandidier pulled out his watch and compared time with the clock above the door. The circumstance induced the clockmaker to look at the time himself, and he recollects perfectly well that it was then exactly two minutes past seven. Those two minutes would have amply sufficed for M. Jandidier to walk from his house as far as this shop. It is fortunate that he should have paused to compare time, for this apparently trivial circumstance has guided me to all my subsequent discoveries. For instance, the clockmaker noticed that M. Jandidier was munching an unlighted cigar. It occurred to me that he must ultimately have lighted it, and I asked myself where and how? Had he a box of lucifers in his pocket? No; for I learned at his house that a little silver-plated box he usually carried about with him, had been found on the mantelshelf in his room since his disappearance. In this case, I reasoned, he must probably have gone into some tobacconist's shop to get a light."

"Yes, no doubt," opined the magistrate.

"I had considerable difficulty in finding the shop in question," resumed the detective; "but as the course taken by M. Jandidier from his residence to the clockmaker's shop seemed to indicate that he was going towards the *boulevards*, I went in that direction. To my delight, just as I reached the Boulevard du Temple, sure enough I came upon a tobacconist's shop. I went in and made inquiries. The woman behind the counter was well acquainted with M. Jandidier, and she recollected perfectly that he came in on Saturday evening to get a light. She was all the more certain on the point for, at the same time, he purchased a packet of *londres extra,* which greatly surprised her, as he usually smoked very cheap cigars."

"How did he seem?"

"The woman told me that he looked preoccupied. I obtained from her an important piece of information, which shows that Madame Jandidier was altogether wrong when she told the commissary of police that her husband did not go to any particular *café*. However, husbands don't always tell everything to their wives; and according to the tobacconist, M. Jandidier frequently went to the Café Turc, which is hard-by. I went there and questioned the waiters. Two of them remembered having seen him on Saturday evening. He drank two small glasses of brandy neat, and talked with some friends who were there. He seemed sad. The waiter who served at his table told me that he and his friends talked all the while about life insurances. It was half-past eight when he went away, accompanied by one of his friends, M. Blandureau, a merchant of the neighbourhood. I immediately went to M. Blandureau's warehouse and questioned him. He told me that on Saturday evening he walked down the *boulevards* with M. Jandidier, as far as the corner of the Rue de Richelieu, where M. Jandidier left him, saying that he had business to attend to. He was not at all in his usual frame of mind, M. Blandureau tells me; he seemed out of sorts and worried with melancholy presentiments."

"Very good, so far," muttered the magistrate.

"On leaving M. Blandureau," continued Maitre Magloire, "I returned to the Rue du Roi de Sicile to inquire of the people of the house if M. Jandidier had, to their knowledge, any customers or friends, might be even a mistress, in the Rue de Richelieu. I more particularly questioned the manservant who generally did his master's errands, but all he could tell me was that M. Jandidier's tailor lived in that street. I thought it, after all, advisable to go and see this tailor. 'Yes,' said he, 'M. Jandidier came to see me on Saturday. He came to order a pair of trousers. It was past nine o'clock.' It seems that whilst he was being measured a button fell from his waistcoat, and he asked the tailor to sew it on again. For this to be done, he took off his coat, and at the same time removed a packet of papers and a notebook from the breast pocket. Holding these papers in his hand he half sorted them, and the tailor noticed that they comprised several bank notes?"

"Ah! That's a clue. So he had a large sum on his person?"

"Large? Well not so, perhaps, for a man of his position; but still a fair amount. The tailor thinks there must have been twelve or fourteen hundred *francs* in notes."

"Continue," said the investigating magistrate.

"While the button of his waistcoat was being sewn on again, M. Jandidier suddenly left off sorting his papers and complained of indisposition. The tailor had already noticed that he looked far from well; and at his customer's request he dispatched an apprentice to fetch a cab. M. Jandidier said that he had to go as far as the Halle aux Vins to see one of his work people who lived hard-by. Unfortunately the apprentice could not tell me the number of the cab he fetched, but on the other hand he recollected that it had yellow wheels, and was drawn by a big black horse. The yellow wheels proved that the vehicle did not come from the stables of the Cab Company, but that it belonged to some petty job-master. I sent a circular note to all the authorised cab-keepers, and a few hours ago I had the satisfaction of learning that the vehicle in question was No. 6,007. The driver remembered that on Saturday evening he was hailed by a lad in the Rue de Richelieu, and that for ten minutes or so he waited outside the shop of a tailor named Gouin. I asked him if he would be able to recognise the gentleman he drove to the Halle aux Vins, and he told me that he thought he would. Thereupon, I showed him five photographs, and he at once picked out M. Jandidier's portrait. There was a bright moonlight on Saturday evening, he said, and whilst the gentleman was counting out the money to pay his fare he had a good look at him."

Maitre Magloire paused and noted with satisfaction the approbative expression on the magistrate's face.

"Well," said he, "this cabby drove M. Jandidier to the immediate vicinity of the Halle aux Vins, to No. 48, in the Rue d'Arras-Saint-Victor; and in this house there lives a workman, whom M. Jandidier employed, a workman of the name of Jules Tarot."

The significant manner in which Maitre Magloire articulated these words "Jules Tarot" was well calculated to impress the investigating magistrate.

"Have you any suspicions?" asked the latter, giving the detective a keen look.

"Not precisely; but still here are the facts. On reaching the Rue d'Arras, M. Jandidier discharged his cab. He asked the doorkeeper if Tarot was at home, and on receiving an affirmative reply he went upstairs. It was then about ten o'clock. Half an hour afterwards the doorkeeper went to bed, and he was just falling asleep when he heard Tarot come downstairs. Tarot called to him to pull the rope which opens the door, and, thanks to the night light, the doorkeeper perceived that the workman was accompanied by the gentleman who had called. They went out together; and shortly after midnight Tarot returned home alone."

"And M. Jandidier?" asked the magistrate.

"Ah! I have been unable to trace him any further," replied Maitre Magloire.

"That seems significant; suspicious even."

"Yes, *monsieur*. I fancy it's a bad job. Of course I could not question Tarot; it would have put him on his guard."

"Have you found out what kind of man this fellow Tarot is?"

"Oh! On that point I questioned the doorkeeper. Tarot, he told me, is a mother-of-pearl worker. He polishes the shells, and is most skilful in imparting the proper nacreous iridescence. Altogether, he seems to be a clever fellow, and he and his wife together—for he has taught her the work—earn at times as much as a hundred *francs* a week."

"So they are well off, for people of their class."

"Well, no, *monsieur*. They are both of them young, both of them Parisians born and bred, they have no children, and so they amuse themselves. Not content with Sunday relaxation and pleasure, they habitually make Monday a fete day, after the fashion of so many work-people, and the result is, that long before pay day arrives they are desperately hard up."

"*H'm*," said the magistrate, stroking his chin with a pensive air. "All this seems very suspicious—very suspicious indeed. So the Tarots lead rather a loose life? Their purse is often empty; and very likely they are in debt. Those twelve hundred *francs* that M. Jandidier had about him, no doubt, excited their covetousness. He probably called on Tarot to entrust him with some work, and no doubt pulled out his pocketbook to make a memorandum. Tarot must have seen the banknotes. And no trace, you say, can be found of M. Jandidier after he left the house with his workman at eleven o'clock at night?"

"No, *monsieur*, no trace at all," answered the detective. "I have made diligent inquiries in all directions but without result."

"Very strange, very suspicious," muttered the magistrate; and then in a louder key he added: "I must say, M. Magloire, that you have conducted this inquiry admirably. Guided by M. Jandidier's unlighted cigar, you have traced him to—well, to the man who is probably his murderer. Yes, his murderer, I have very strong suspicions on the point."

A brief pause ensued, and then the magistrate asked: "Was Tarot at home when you made these inquiries this afternoon?"

"Oh, no, *monsieur*. He and his wife had gone off. It's Monday, remember."

"Are you certain that they had merely gone off holidaymaking?"

"Why, yes, *monsieur*; the doorkeeper said they had left early in the morning with a couple of friends, two of Tarot's comrades, I believe. They were going to picnic near Chaville."

"Ah! That was a splendid opportunity to make a perquisition in their absence, Maitre Magloire."

"Certainly, *monsieur*, but I had no search warrant, and besides, it was only an hour or so ago that I went to the Rue d'Arras."

"I suppose that doorkeeper is to be depended upon?"

"Oh, yes, *monsieur*. He's affiliated at the Prefecture, No. 920." (It should be remembered that a very large number of Parisian doorkeepers Or *concierges* are secret agents of the Prefecture de Police.)

"Then he's safe. Did you leave him any instructions as to what he ought to do, if the Tarots returned home before you saw him again?"

"I did better than that, *monsieur*, I left a comrade at the house to wait and watch."

"Very good. Well, M. Magloire, we must have a perquisition; and here are a couple of warrants which you can use if occasion requires. Be here at eight o'clock tomorrow morning."

So saying, the magistrate returned to some documents he had been perusing when the detective arrived. The latter pocketed the warrants, made a deep bow, and hastened out of the room.

3

It was already six o'clock, and before repairing to the Rue d'Arras-Saint-Victor it was necessary that Maitre Magloire should call at the office of the district commissary of police, show him his instructions, and request him to preside at the perquisition. As the commissary was away at his dinner, some little time was lost, "We must have a locksmith," the detective reflected, "for the Tarots will hardly have returned, and it will be necessary to force open the door." A locksmith was accordingly procured, a couple of *gardiens de la Paix* were summoned to serve as an escort, and on the commissary's return the party set off.

At the corner of the street the detective asked his companions to wait a moment, and then went ahead. It was necessary that he should reconnoitre the ground, and ascertain from the comrade whom he had left with the doorkeeper if anything noteworthy had occurred during his absence.

As he entered the house he heard heavy steps climbing the stairs, and a man and a woman singing a gay refrain. "Have they returned?" thought Maitre Magloire, and he hurried into the doorkeeper's room.

His comrade was there, and on perceiving him raised his forefinger to his lips: "Hush, they've just come home. They are only halfway upstairs."

"They are singing loud enough," rejoined Maitre Magloire in an undertone. "I must say that they are unusually gay for—for murderers."

"Oh!" replied his comrade. "The wine has got into their heads. As for their gaiety we'll see about that by-and-bye."

Despite this rejoinder Magloire remained for a moment pensive.

"Am I mistaken?" he asked himself. "But, then—" However, his hesitation was of short duration. "At all events we must clear up the mystery," he added, and leaving the house he went in search of the commissary.

Joyful the Tarots had certainly seemed as they climbed the stairs, singing a popular ditty. They were laden with field flowers, which the wife tastefully arranged in two large blue vases as soon as they had entered their lodging.

"Now, Clementina," called the husband, "you must make haste with the supper, or else the concert will be over by the time we get there."

Both Tarot and his wife were very partial to the entertainments given at a little *café concert* in the neighbourhood, and it was with the view of going there that evening, that they had returned so early from their excursion.

"Oh! I've only the stew to warm," answered the wife; "but, Eugene, while I light the fire would you mind running down to fetch a quart of wine?"

The husband took an empty bottle from a corner in the kitchen and went toward the outer door of the apartment, but when only halfway he paused with surprise. *Rat-tat-tat, rat-tat-tat.* Some very noisy visitor indeed demanded admittance.

"Who's there?" cried Tarot.

"Open, in the name of the law," answered a stern voice.

Husband and wife turned pale with terror.

"Open, in the name of the law," repeated the same voice.

Still Tarot did not budge. Fear seemed to root him to the spot.

There was no further parleying, for at that moment Maitre Magloire perceived that the key had been left in the door outside. So he just turned it and walked in, followed by his comrade and the commissary of police.

On perceiving the latter functionary, whose stomach was spanned with his broad tricolour sash of office, Tarot and his wife were seized with a nervous trembling, of which Maitre Magloire took careful note.

"Why didn't you open the door?" sternly asked the commissary of police.

"I was so surprised—*monsieur*—I didn't know—I—" stammered Tarot.

"Ah, you look as if you had something on your conscience," retorted the functionary, "I suppose you know what has brought us here?"

Tarot gave the commissary an anxious look, and stammered an incomprehensible answer.

"We have come to make a perquisition," said Maitre Magloire. "Do you know that your employer, M. Jandidier of the Rue du Roi de Sicile, has disappeared? He was last seen in your company late on Saturday night."

Both Tarot and his wife were too overwhelmed to speak.

"Come give us the keys of all your drawers and cupboards," said the commissary; and as the wife timidly drew them from her pocket he added, turning to the detective: "There you are, Maitre Magloire, you may set about your task."

The search was a protracted and a difficult one, for dusk had now set in, and a careful scrutiny could scarcely be made by lamplight. However, all the drawers were turned out, and all the cupboards carefully explored. Magloire ferreted in every nook and corner, ripped up the mattresses and pillows on the bed, tried the stuffing of the chairs, but all to no avail. Nothing suspicious could be found.

"It's singular," muttered the detective; and he once more asked himself, "Have I been mistaken after all?"

At this moment it occurred to him to look at the Tarots who stood by, watching the proceedings in silence. Perhaps their demeanour might give him a clue; otherwise he and his companions would have no other resource but to apologise and withdraw. At first he observed nothing particular, save an expression of fright in their looks, but as he carefully followed the direction of the wife's glance, he noticed that it was fixed on a birdcage hanging near the window.

"Eureka!" he cried, "I have it!"

Springing towards the cage he unhooked it, and careless of the canary roosting on the perch, he examined it in every sense. As in most cages there was a movable floor which drew out to admit of proper cleansing, and sure enough, between the thin boards, Maitre Magloire found a sum of twelve hundred *francs* in banknotes.

The Tarots exchanged looks of terror. The husband seemed overwhelmed, but the wife broke out into piteous lamentations, repeating again and again that she and her husband were innocent.

However, the commissary and Magloire paid little or no attention to her wailings. "You had much better make a clean breast of it," exclaimed the detective, "instead of kicking up that row."

Whereupon both husband and wife answered in piteous tones: "Oh! we are innocent, sir, we are innocent!"

This time the detective shrugged his shoulders. "In the name of the law, I arrest you," said he. "I charge you with the murder of M. Jandidier." And he called to the two *gardiens de la Paix,* waiting below, to come upstairs.

The Tarots showed no signs of resistance, but as they were charged with a capital offence, the commissary thought it prudent to have them handcuffed. They passively allowed themselves to be removed to a cab which was sent for, and half an hour later they crossed the threshold of the depot, and were duly locked into separate cells.

Magloire was fairly elated, and, forgetful of discipline, hurried off to the private residence of the investigating magistrate, to acquaint him with the capture and the recovery of M. Jandidier's money. The magistrate was pleased to express his approval, and renewed the appointment for the following morning at his office at the Palais de Justice.

The Tarots were interrogated separately. They both looked pale and careworn when they entered the magistrate's office, but, after passing the night under lock and key in a prison cell, this was only natural. However, they had both found their tongues again, and apparently they had preconcerted a system of defence, for their answers were identical.

They admitted that M. Jandidier had called on them on the Saturday evening. He seemed very poorly, and they asked him if he would not like to take a drop of something, but he refused the offer.

"What was the object of his visit?" asked the magistrate.

"He wished us to execute an important order, and proposed that we should take workpeople on our own account."

"That's singular. Had he not numerous workmen of his own?"

"Yes, but he said that his health was failing him, that he could no longer give his usual attention to business, and should prefer to transfer the order to us."

"And what was your answer?"

"We told him that we lacked the capital to execute it."

"Ah!—ah! And what then?"

"Why, he replied, 'Oh, that's of no consequence. I'll advance you enough money; and he pulled out his pocketbook, and laid twelve hundred *francs* in banknotes on the table."

"Had he so much confidence as that in you?"

"Well, he knew we worked fairly well."

"Yes, but you have dissipated habits. You spend your money faster than you earn it. Your story is altogether improbable. M. Jandidier must have known how prodigal you both were. Well, did you at least give him a receipt?"

"Yes, *monsieur*."

"Who signed it?"

"We both did."

"*H'm*, and what then?"

"After that," answered Tarot, "M. Jandidier asked me to see him further on. He said he was going in the direction of the Faubourg St. Antoine."

"And where did you leave him?"

"At the Place de la Bastille. We crossed the Constantine footbridge and followed the canal."

"Ah! you followed the canal?" exclaimed the magistrate, eyeing Tarot attentively. "And you reached the Place de la Bastille safely?"

"Certainly we did, *monsieur*," answered the workman, with a flushed face.

Naturally enough, the magistrate asked both the husband and the wife to explain why they had hidden the money in the birdcage, and they each gave the same answer. On the Sunday night, as they were going home, Tarot met a comrade who, while he was playing cards in a wine shop in the Marais during the afternoon, had heard of M. Jandidier's disappearance. The news greatly frightened them, and Tarot said to his wife:

"If it were known that he came here on Saturday night, it would be a bad job for us. Didn't we cross the bridge together, and walk along the banks of the canal? The police would certainly suspect me, and if those twelve hundred *francs* were found in our possession, we should be altogether lost."

"We didn't sleep all Sunday night," said Tarot's wife; "we lay awake thinking about M. Jandidier. And we certainly shouldn't have gone out on the Monday, if one of my husband's cousins hadn't come to fetch us according to arrangement. However, in the country we almost forgot about the matter, and as the detective says, we were no doubt gay when we came home. Before going out, I wanted to burn the bank notes, but Tarot wouldn't let me. He meant to refund the money to M. Jandidier's family, he said; and besides, as he explained, we might have put ourselves in a bad position by destroying the notes, for, even if M. Jandidier were dead, his body might be found with our receipt in his pocket, and then we should have to refund the money; and how could we do so if the notes were destroyed?"

The magistrate listened attentively to this explanation, which was plausible if not probable, and the prisoners' line of defence struck him as a very artful one.

"How did you know," he asked at length, "how did you know that M. Jandidier's body had not been found when the police searched your place? It might have been recovered, and the detectives might have had your receipt with them. It was your duty to produce that money at once. Why didn't you do so?"

"We didn't know what to do or what to think, *monsieur*; we were too frightened."

"Innocent persons have no reason to feel frightened," sententiously retorted the magistrate. "Justice knows how to distinguish between the innocent and the guilty."

He said this, and yet, at that very moment, he was asking himself in sore perplexity, "Are these people culpable or not? "After all, there was nothing to corroborate the explanation of the Tarots, and it was utterly impossible for him to content himself with their mere word. A further search must be made for M. Jandidier. Perhaps his body might be found, and then it would be possible to form a positive opinion. In the meanwhile, the workman and his wife must be retained in custody.

4

A week elapsed, and the magistrate was still in the same perplexity. The Tarots had each been re-examined three times, but nothing fresh had been elicited from them, and their later statements failed to contradict their earlier version. Were they innocent, then? Or had they merely cleverly preconcerted a plausible system of defence?

M. Jandidier's remains had been searched for far and wide. The Seine and the canal had been dragged. The missing manufacturer's photograph had been sent all over France, but utterly without result. In this situation, the magistrate asked himself what course he ought to pursue. If he sent the prisoners to the assizes they would very likely be acquitted for want of sufficient proofs, especially if they were defended by a skilful advocate. No doubt there was the circumstance of those twelve hundred *francs* found in their possession; but would that suffice to ensure a conviction? The prisoners explained their possession of this money in a most artful fashion, and, besides, the true *corpus delicti* was wanting. What should the magistrate do then?

He was asking himself this question for the hundredth time, when a strange, almost incredible report reached his ears. The well known firm of Jandidier *ainé* had suspended payment, and was going into bankruptcy!

"Who would have expected that!" grumbled the magistrate. "Well, perhaps, we are coming to the truth."

On the morrow a detective who had been duly instructed, brought him a full report of circumstances which none of M. Jandidier's family had ever dreamed of. The revelation was an astounding one, and had caused immense surprise throughout the district of the Marais where M. Jandidier had been so respected and esteemed. In fact, the man whom the denizens of the Rue du Roi de Sicile so delighted to honour, the idol of the trade in imitation jewellery, had fallen from his pedestal with a crash. People had imagined he was wealthy, and yet in reality he was ruined—utterly ruined: and during the last three years he had only kept up his credit by means of expedients. Less than a thousand *francs* had been found in his safe, and on the Saturday after his disappearance, bills for sixty-seven thousand five hundred *francs* were presented for payment by the Bank of France. Yes, Jandidier, the man of severe morality, gambled at the Bourse; the virtuous husband kept a mistress!

The magistrate could scarcely believe his ears, and was giving vent to his astonishment when Maitre Magloire appeared, quite out of breath.

"You know the news, *monsieur*?" asked the detective as he crossed the threshold.

"Yes, I have just been told everything."

"The Tarots are innocent!"

"I think so—and yet that visit Jandidier paid them—how do you explain that visit?"

The detective sighed. "Ah, *monsieur*," said he, "I was a fool, as my colleague, Monsieur Lecoq, has just shown me. You will recollect that at the Café Turc, Jandidier and his friends talked all the time about life assurances?"

"Yes, I remember; but what connection—"

"Ah! *monsieur*, that was the point I ought to have kept in mind! Jandidier's life was assured for 200,000 *francs*."

"Indeed!"

"Yes, and as you are aware, *monsieur*, in France assurance companies don't pay when the holder of a policy commits suicide. Now, Jandidier was no doubt anxious to provide for his family; and so he made it appear as if he had been murdered, in hopes that the companies would pay his wife."

"Do you think he has destroyed himself?"

"I cannot say, *monsieur*, At all events we cannot find his remains. Maybe he has simply taken himself off. And yet I don't know; he can only have had very little money with him, and at his age a man scarcely has the courage to begin life over again. At all events, he certainly laid a trap for poor Tarot, and would have sent him to the guillotine for the sake of his policies being paid."

"What a scamp!" growled the magistrate; and he took up his pen to sign an order for the release of the workman and his wife.

****

Thanks to M. Gustave Schmidt—of the great house of Schmidt, Gubenheim, and Worb—the firm of Jandidier did not go into bankruptcy. Old Schmidt had just died, most opportunely, and M. Gustave was able to dispose of the paternal inheritance as he pleased, and more than that, he means to dispose of himself as well, for the papers announce that he and Mademoiselle Thérèse Jandidier are to be married next month.

Tarot and his wife have set up in business, thanks to the twelve hundred *francs* returned to them at M. Gustave's request; and, mindful of the investigating magistrate's reproaches anent their "prodigality" and "dissipated habits," they have quite given up "merrymaking" on Mondays.

But what has become of M. Jandidier? Is he dead, or has he gone to America? If any of our readers are acquainted with his whereabouts, they may communicate with the authorities, who offer a thousand *francs* reward!

LEONAUR

ALSO FROM LEONAUR

AVAILABLE IN SOFTCOVER OR HARDCOVER WITH DUST JACKET

THE COLLECTED SCIENCE FICTION AND FANTASY OF STANLEY G. WEINBAUM 1—INTERPLANETARY ODYSSEYS *by Stanley G. Weinbaum*—Classic Tales of Interplanetary Adventure Including: A Martian Odyssey, its Sequel Valley of Dreams, the Complete 'Ham' Hammond Stories and Others.

THE COLLECTED SCIENCE FICTION AND FANTASY OF STANLEY G. WEINBAUM 2—OTHER EARTHS *by Stanley G. Weinbaum*—Classic Futuristic Tales Including: *Dawn of Flame* & its Sequel The Black Flame, plus The Revolution of 1960 & Others.

THE COLLECTED SCIENCE FICTION AND FANTASY OF STANLEY G. WEINBAUM 3—STRANGE GENIUS *by Stanley G. Weinbaum*—Classic Tales of the Human Mind at Work Including the Complete Novel The New Adam, the 'van Manderpootz' Stories and Others.

THE COLLECTED SCIENCE FICTION AND FANTASY OF STANLEY G. WEINBAUM 4—THE BLACK HEART *by Stanley G. Weinbaum*—Classic Strange Tales Including: the Complete Novel The Dark Other, Plus Proteus Island and Others.

THE COLLECTED SCIENCE FICTION & FANTASY OF JACK LONDON 1—BEFORE ADAM & OTHER STORIES *by Jack London*—included in this Volume Before Adam The Scarlet Plague A Relic of the Pliocene When the World Was Young The Red One Planchette A Thousand Deaths Goliah A Curious Fragment The Rejuvenation of Major Rathbone.

THE COLLECTED SCIENCE FICTION & FANTASY OF JACK LONDON 2—THE IRON HEEL & OTHER STORIES *by Jack London*—included in this Volume The Iron Heel The Enemy of All the World The Shadow and the Flash The Strength of the Strong The Unparalleled Invasion The Dream of Debs.

THE COLLECTED SCIENCE FICTION & FANTASY OF JACK LONDON 3—THE STAR ROVER & OTHER STORIES *by Jack London*—included in this Volume The Star Rover The Minions of Midas The Eternity of Forms The Man With the Gash.

Milton Keynes UK
Ingram Content Group UK Ltd.
UKHW041146231023
431175UK00001B/130

9 781782 828013